HUMANITY

THE DIARY

BASED ON TRUE EVENTS

DERRICK JOHNS

HUMANITY
THE DIARY
DERRICK JOHNS

VIEW PARK COUNTRY CLUB PUBLISHING

Cover by Michelle Moore graphics
Photo by Liam O'Neal

ISBN: 978-1-09838-399-2

Contents

FOREWORD

I was once told BAD CHOICES make great books and through that canal of trial and error this project was birthed. In this book you will take a roller-coaster ride side by side with Da'Quan through his brutal and at times heaven-sent journey. As the hands on the clock dripped like sand in an hourglass within the last hour of life as he knew it, you, the reader, will witness his search for HUMANITY smeared by the imperfections of his LOS ANGELES inner city surroundings.

Although at times the evil, lust and greed have a stronghold on his spirit, Da'Quan still finds a way to muster up the remaining fragments of his broken HUMANITY. A true conversation piece that will keep you on the edge of your reading chair striking emotions and igniting your senses the whole ride. In short he is like most others who battled internal demons as he navigates through his unique and unparalleled journey. Buckle up!

JITTERS

SEPTEMBER 28TH 2006 • 37 years old

The steam from the hot shower clouded the bathroom as Da'Quan wiped the film from his gold-trimmed vanity mirror with his hands. As he stared deep into his own eyes, looking for the strength to battle another day in LA's concrete jungle, his cell phone began spinning and vibrating aloud on the bathroom sink. When he looked at the Colorado area code, he knew it was the same person who had called the night before. The guy on the other end of the line just kept telling him we have some unfinished business to handle. Since he had no idea who the individual was, he ignored the morning call and went into the bedroom to get dressed.

His girlfriend, Candy, sat nude on the edge of the bed with cotton balls wedged between her toes, painting her nails with the hand precision of a neurosurgeon. She extended her succulent lips for a kiss. He ignored her motion for affection and put on his underwear; she knew something was bothering him. While he continued to get dressed his phone began buzzing and vibrating uncontrollably on the nightstand. When he looked with uneager eyes at his phone, the same Colorado number came flashing through.

Candy, who was very intuitive, asked, "Babe, is that the same number of them dudes from Colorado calling you?"

He nodded his head with a look of concern on his face as he confidently responded, "Yeah, but fuck them niggas. I got other shit to handle, plus I don't know what the fuck he talking 'bout!"

She stared at him with worried, almond-shaped eyes and replied, "Well, why don't you find out what they talking 'bout babe. It might not be all that serious."

He knew she was right but he had done and been exposed to so much in his past that he wanted to make sure he had a cover for any bullshit he may encounter. He just needed time to sort his mental and be prepared. Deep in the bottom of his soul he knew this was a serious situation that he would have to be on point to attack.

As he looked at Candy's cocoa-brown, blemish-free body sitting like a work of art at the edge of the bed, her phone began rumbling. When she grabbed her phone from the dresser, she looked at it with a disgruntled look on her face before asking him, "Babe, what's the area code of that number? 'Cause I got a text just now, look."

When Da'Quan grabbed her phone his heart dropped as he read, "HEY SUNSHINE TELL YOUR MAN IGNORING ME WON'T SOLVE NOTHING. I JUST NEED HIM TO MAN UP AND HANDLE HIS BUSINESS. YOU DESERVE BETTER".

His blood began boiling as he read the disrespectful text to his girlfriend. He hurled her phone across the bed and blurted angrily, "How the fuck this nigga got your number, too? Let me hit this nigga back!" He paused as his chest began pounding to the point where it constricted his breathing. After a moment to calm down, he glanced at Candy, who sat on the bed frozen in terror staring blankly at him through teary eyes as he began to dial. He hit each number gently like they were thorns growing from the keypad. He closed his eyes as the phone rang, praying that it was a hoax and not some backlash from his past shenanigans. After the fourth ring, just as Da'Quan began to hang up, the husky voice on the other end picked up.

"Baby boy, you a hard dude to catch up with." Da'Quan recognized the voice but couldn't put a face to it. He copped an attitude to masquerade his fear, "Man, who the fuck are you homie? What's cracking?"

Candy tried to finish her nails, but her nerves had her hands trembling like a heroin junkie as she splashed red polish over her toes and cotton swabs. There was a moment of silence on the line before the husky voice replied,

"Look here, that's why I've been getting at you. I want you to know who I am. Let's meet at your spot on the block at eleven."

Da'Quan looked at his phone that read 9:59 a.m. before he replied, "Homie, that's only an hour."

The husky voice replied "Yeah, that's all I'm giving you. Don't make us come to your house where your girl is cause it ain't got nothing to do with her and I would hate for something to happen to that cute little tender." The innuendo from the husky voice aimed at his girlfriend made meeting this person more compelling.

Da'Quan took a second to calm down before replying, "Yeah, OK homie we can meet, but what's it about?"

The husky voice chuckled and blurted, "I'm glad you asked. Let me take you back a few years. Remember that Double Whammy you and ya boy Blizz pulled on me?" Da'Quan frowned as he tried to recollect as Candy stared at him with the fear of God on her face. The voice continued, "Do you remember? My boys came, the ones from Ohio, c'mon D don't catch amnesia on me."

Da'Quan's heart began pounding triple time. He knew exactly what situation he was referring too but he couldn't admit just yet. Da'Quan continued to play possum, "Shiiit man, I don't know what you speaking on homie!"

He could hear ice shaking as the guy on the line began sipping on a straw before replying, "Oh, OK, so that wasn't you in the bedroom when they sold my guys twenty fake ones?"

Da'Quan uttered, "Fake ones?"

The guy's voice became increasingly agitated as Da'Quan played stupid. The man on the other end of the call put his mouth close to the receiver and spoke in a heinous tone, "Look, nigga, I worked a nine to five at a shipping company. My wife had twin girls that were born premature. On top of that my grandmother was terminally ill so I had to provide the morphine patches and home care for her, too. So I started doing what I was doing to have extra income to take care of my girls who passed away at six months and my grandmother who passed six weeks later. After you robbed me for that 100k, I couldn't keep up their treatments and God took them home. So now I need to holla at you and yo boys about y'all squaring me up today."

Da'Quan stood silent and numb from his hair follicles to his toenails. He knew this would be a very uneasy situation and rightfully so. After a moment the husky voice continued, "So, yeah, let's not play dumb. I know where you at now. I can see your truck park behind your girl's Honda in the driveway. We could come now but her little fine ass didn't have nothing to do with it. So give her a kiss goodbye and come handle this business. You got forty-five minutes!"

The guy hung up in Da'Quan's face without another word said. Da'Quan blurted, "Aye, aye, homie," as the sound of the dead line buzzed in his ear. He paused for a moment before turning to see Candy sitting on the bed like a helpless orphan. He went and sat next to her, gave her a kiss on her forehead as he told her, "Look, don't trip ima head to the block and handle this business with these niggas. It's a big misunderstanding. If you don't hear from me by eleven thirty, call my aunt. You got her number or if not I'll just call and let you know everything is cool." She nervously nodded her head yes as she wiped the stream of tears that poured from her bloodshot eyes. He also added, "And look, don't answer the door for no fucking body. If you see something strange or suspicious, call me or the motherfucking police, OK?" She nodded her head yes while he grabbed his Glock and stuffed it snug in his waistline.

He put on a huge black pro club hoodie to hide his weapon and walked to the door. He paused and took one last glimpse at Candy's doll face and blemish-free body before walking possibly for his last time out the door. The air outside felt humid and thicker than a wooly afro as he perused his driveway like a detective for any unusual activities. When he sat in his truck a tear fell freely down his cheek as he began to reflect on the day of *The Double Whammy* along with a plethora of other life events that all added up to the predicament he was now faced with.

Chapter 1
BLOOD MONEY

JULY 1997 • 27 years old

The rap game is filled with criminals, goons and con artists who opted for the entertainment industry to monopolize and benefit from the lucrative amounts of money available. Coming from the deadly streets or from behind the wicked walls of steel made the entertainment industry appear to be a playground for villains and crooks. Artists oftentimes find themselves bound to the underworld as a means to have allied muscle for protection against the wolves seeking prey. The lavish, carefree lifestyles painted by the media are fabricated images designed to keep fans and onlookers enamored with their character of choice. These smokescreens are nothing more than a shield to the vile and corrupt acts that take place behind them.

It was an overcast Monday smothered in silver clouds, as Mother Nature shed light spurts of rain over turbulent and gang-infested South Central Los Angeles. Da'Quan had just dropped off a pound of chronic to a client in which he made eleven hundred dollars for one transaction. He drove his ninety-five black Chevy Stepside, riding carefree in the euphoria of attaining fast cash. As he hit a left on Thirty-Ninth headed to *The Den,* he saw his homeboy Gee standing on the corner counting a fistful of cash. Da'Quan pulled up while Gee fumbled with at least a thousand in wrinkled fives, tens and ones.

Gee was a staple in the neighborhood. His mom, Connie, was a known hustler and his dad, Jamaican Bruce, was a reputable Crip from the set. From the time of his conception, he had no other choice than to be bound to the rollercoaster ride of LA's street game filled with a circus of devils. When he was a baby, Connie would push Gee through the neighborhood in his stroller with multiple milk bottles. One or two would actually be filled with milk for Gee while the other bottles would be filled with bags of cocaine powder or heroin. She'd make her rounds throughout the area serving her chemically dependent clientele while using Gee as a shield against police harassment. As shapely and beautiful as Connie was, she was also one of her own best clients. Her secret heroin addiction fueled her daily to get out and grind to keep the monkey on her back tamed. She always wore long sleeve shirts to cover the often infected and pus-filled lesions on her forearms from years of shooting "Brown Sugar". Gee always bragged that before he could read Dr. Seuss, he knew how to weigh bricks on the triple beam.

Da'Quan sat in the driveway where Gee stood in his all-white K Swiss fresh off the rack, blue 501s creased sharp enough to slice apples and a first-time-worn pro club white T. After counting his wad of wrinkled currency, he turned to Da'Quan, smiled, revealing a mouth of yellow separated teeth, and yelled, "What up, Big D?" He began laughing as he always did for no apparent reason. His dark skin glistened with a coat of sweat as the sun began baking through the cluster of clouds.

Da'Quan responded with the same energy, "What up, my nigga? Trying ta get like you cuzzo!"

Gee walked up to Da'Quan's window and reached out to shake his hand while saying in his loud raspy voice, "Big D, cuzz, if I had yo hand, homie, I'd turn mine in on God!"

They both started laughing in unison as Da'Quan, who really took to Gee, asked, "Wassup, my nigga, I ain't seen you in a minute?"

Gee paused and as he walked up to the door of Da'Quan's truck he whispered, "Yea, Big D, I had to give 'em 180 days, cuz, on a punk ass gun possession, but I told my mouthpiece if you want the other half of that payment get my heat back!" Gee burst into uncontrollable laughter as he raised his T-shirt revealing his chrome Desert Eagle glued to his malnourished waistline. After the laughter subsided Gee, who was most definitely an old soul continued, "Whew, yeah, Big D, yo truck smell good, baby boy. I need that thang like you. Ya boy just touch down last night."

Da'Quan reached under his passenger seat and pulled out a quarter pound of some quality hash plant and handed him five or six grams to last him the day. Gee put the product to his nose, closed his eyes and inhaled the potent marijuana fumes through his fist. He then put his fist out to Da'Quan and said, "That's why you my nigga, cuzz, ole Big D!" He continued, "Yea, homie I was down the block earlier I seen that crazy nigga Loud chopping it up wit Terrib or whatever his name is and some other nigga cuz!" Da'Quan shook his head as if to say "Interesting."

After a brief moment, Connie, Gee's mom, came storming by foot from around the corner. Her hair was wild and unkempt and the dingy long sleeve sundress she wore couldn't cover her multiple infected needle marks on her hands and wrist. As she beelined straight to Gee, he shook his head, took a deep breath and told Da'Quan, "Hold on cuz lemme see what this bitch wants cuzz."

Connie motioned to Gee like a savage as she hysterically blurted, "You little piece a shit. How you gon do yo own goddamn momma like that?" She began swinging her flabby arms at Gee before throwing a piece of tinfoil at his head and demanding, "Nigga, if you don't fatten my load imma be yo worst nightmare you son of a bitch!" A flustered look appeared on Gee's face as he tried to calm his mom, who needed an immediate fix for her apparent jones. Da'Quan, without saying a word, cranked up his truck and headed down the block while Gee tended to his troubled mother.

As Da'Quan drove off, he tried, but couldn't imagine keeping his mom hooked on heroin if that was the case. He could clearly see in Gee's eyes the embarrassment of having a mother strung out on dope, but even more so that he was her supplier. The emotional dust was quickly brushed off his shoulder once he heard his group's single "Pistol Packing" getting airplay midday. He turned it up and let his custom Kenwood sound system rattle his speakers, sending Da'Quan to the point of oblivion. The energy from the song created hundreds of thousands of hip hop heads, thugs and yuppies to engage in a movement of gun awareness. Horrib Lee, who sat undisturbed on the wall of Loud's porch, listened to an animated Loud, who stood inhaling a Camel with a teeth-revealing smile from ear to ear. Horrib Lee stared Da'Quan in the eyes as Da'Quan walked up while Loud stood pointing his finger at Horrib, saying, "This nigga Horrib Lee is the man D!"

Da'Quan, with an unenlightened expression on his face, stuck his hand out to Horrib Lee for a fist dap all the while thinking, *why is Horrib's mutha-fucking ass dressed in a filthy mechanics jumpsuit?* Horrib gave him a fist dap as he stood to his feet and motioned for the three of them to head into the house.

Before the rod iron door could close, Loud began ranting, "D, remember that ten g's that punk ass promoter in Palm Springs didn't pay us for that spring break show or whatever?" Da'Quan couldn't focus on Loud due to the extremely pungent odor of ammonia strangling his eyes and nostrils. He looked to the floor and noticed a huge ceramic bowl filled with murky red water and looked at the two of them for an explanation. There was also a string running from wall to wall with twenty, fifty and one hundred dollar bills clipped to it with clothes pins. Da'Quan glanced at Horrib Lee, who stooped down to clean some money at the bowl.

He began explaining to Da'Quan and Loud as he carefully handled the bloody currency, "Yea fool didn't appreciate, you know, a brotha coming business like and professional, know what I mean, Big D"?

Da'Quan stood in awe of the situation and just numbly responded, "Yeah, uh huh."

Horrib Lee continued as he nursed the bloody money clean in the ceramic bowl, "So you know how it goes, Big D, we had to go a different route that made more sense." He looked back at Da'Quan, who stood paralyzed in the moment, and said, "Look, Big D you gotta put a quarter cup of vinegar and ammonia in about this much ice cold water and scrub the money together until the red comes out. Then my nigga hang it up for about twenty-four hours and y'all good to go." He began giggling hysterically as he stood to his feet. Loud stood by quietly observing Horrib Lee and Da'Quan's interaction almost like a fly on a wall. Da'Quan hesitantly stooped down and put his hands in the blood-tainted water and began scrubbing a fifty-dollar bill. As the freezing bloody water splashed on his hands and wrist, he could almost envision the torture and pain the victims of this money were put through for the exchange.

He could clearly hear the agonizing cries of men dying in his subconscious as the bearded face of Grant was washed clean of human blood.

The whole ordeal was eerie. Da'Quan cleansed the money in an out-of-body, trance-like state reminiscing back on the day when his buddy Lamar was beaten to death by numerous baseball bats back in junior high. Lamar had been waiting on the Crip side of Audubon for Bad News, Aaron and Da'Quan to get out of school. Witnesses said a group of boys on two dirt bikes with bats and red hats rode up on him, asked Lamar where he was from, and when he responded forty Crip, they hopped off the bikes and mercilessly beat him to death. Once Da'Quan and his crew made it to the scene, the police had his body covered and the area was taped off. All that could be seen was his left leg with blood to the bottom of his Levi's and smeared stains from his struggle on his white Nikes. Whenever the wind blew the sheet up you could see his open eyes staring blankly at the sheet as flies danced around the open mouth of his fourteen years' young, lifeless body. He could also remember the pain he felt as the two redneck officers stood nonchalantly next to the body debating over who was the greater player between Larry Bird and Magic Johnson. They acted unbothered as if he was nothing more than a dead squirrel or raccoon they ran across.

Loud's barking baritone snapped Da'Quan out of his stupor. "Hey nigga, thirty-five hundred of that is yours. I ain't telling them other niggas so keep this within these walls." Da'Quan just responded with a head nod and an "Aiight," before Horrib Lee interjected.

"Come on, Big D, that's good money my nigga!" He then began laughing hysterically before saying, "Look, that's all you and Loud cause I already got my cut from the deal, trust me." He continued to laugh while Da'Quan kept his hands busy in the blood murky water. With each fifty-dollar bill he pinned to the wire he began to slowly see that he'd be gradually removing himself from this lifestyle just as he did when he backed out of the gang culture after Lamar's murder. The emotional parallel between the two incidents both signaled for a lifestyle change if he was to continue to exist on the planet.

Loud walked to the front door and gazed outside from behind his fortress-style door, took a drag from his Camel and said, " I never thought I'd ever be counting blood money, my niggas."

Chapter 2
HOT MONGOOSE

JUNE 1980 • 10 years old

Bang! Bang! Bang!

"Hey Dee, Dee, cuzz, open yo window!" yelled MC as he banged on Da'Quan's bedroom window. Da'Quan hesitantly responded, as MC had never been bold enough to step on Da'Quan's property without acknowledging his grandparents. Da'Quan slowly moved the curtain and saw MC sitting on a dirt bike with a look of urgency on his face.

Da'Quan raised his window and replied, "Damn, nigga, why the fuck you banging on my house?" in a hostile tone. Since his cousins had been teaching him how to fight Da'Quan's confidence soared, as he knew that if anyone gave him a hard time he had substantial backing to get the situation handled. MC could sense his confidence as he toned down his own demeanor.

He cracked a sheepish smile and calmly said, "Come to the door, cuz, I got something for us."

Da'Quan hesitated as he scanned MC up and down in thought and replied, "Hold up, nigga, I'm eating. Give me a second.. This was all fabricated, as Da'Quan was simply buying a minute to get his mind ready to deal with MC.

After five minutes Da'Quan went to the back door to see what his caper entailed. MC had a look of desperation on his face as Da'Quan opened the door. He aggressively walked up the steps in Da'Quan's face and told him, "Don't get big headed, cuzz, remember I know where you live."

Da'Quan replied, "And me and my family know where you live too, mutherfucka."

MC cracked a diabolic grin and didn't push any harder. He replied, "Look, little homie, I got a bike we can get and split the parts, my nigga." MC was a well-known bike thief and would do his best to get his hands on any new bikes within the local radius. His passion for thievery was comparable to a nympho's for sex or a fat man's to sweets. He kept his eyes and ears open for any upscale bicycles or minibikes in the neighborhood.

Da'Quan sat on the steps and asked, "What bike, cuzz?"

MC pointed towards Da'Quan's neighbor's house and said, "That yellow mongoose at yo punk ass friends' house. I see you with that soft ass nigga all the time."

Da'Quan responded, "Hell naw, that's my homie. I can't fuck with it, MC."

MC's patience grew short as Da'Quan adamantly resisted his offer. The more Da'Quan declined MC's proposition, MC's feral personality began to erupt. He slammed down the stolen bike he was sitting on and stood face to face with Da'Quan. MC's breath reeked of low grade marijuana and his eyes were bloodshot red. He grabbed Da'Quan by his collar with a tight grip and told him, "If you don't do it, cuz, me and you gone have problems every time I see you."

Da'Quan was undoubtedly a bit nervous but stood by his decision by replying, "Damn, MC, I eat and kick it over there. His mom and pops is cool with me and they know you be stealing all the bikes anyway, fool, let me go," as he shoved his dirty hands from around his neck.

MC`s blood began to boil. His beady, bloodshot eyes looked into the soul of Da'Quan, as he blurted, "Nigga, I'll catch yo grandma on her walk and snatch that bitch's purse on my momma." Before he could finish completely, Da'Quan manhandled MC into a wall of bougainvillea complete with thorns that pierced deep into the back and neck of MC. The spiky thorns, which could actually penetrate through a fingertip and fingernail, instantly caused MC to yell frantically, "Aww, cuz, you're tripping," as blood leaked immediately from the back of his dingy T-shirt.

Da'Quan stood bold without regret or fear and mumbled, "I'll kill you if you do something to my grandma, nigga."

MC could clearly see he pushed the wrong button and although he could have probably demolished Da'Quan, he knew that Da'Quans cousin Dray wouldn't hesitate to kick in MC's door and leave bodies stiff. Being the criminal he was, he gave Da'Quan a pass and let him feel a sense of accomplishment by not bashing his head against the back porch. There was a distinct dichotomy between the two boys in overall behavior, but MC knew that Da'Quan wasn't a punk and had the real scoop on how to get the bike he so desired. So, instead of the bully approach, he befriended Da'Quan and used his gangster charm to persuade him to see the benefits of stealing the bike. MC was by now a career criminal and stopped at nothing, not even eating a little crow, to hit a lick, so he opened his right hand out in an apologetic gesture. Da'Quan, who was utterly shocked, hesitantly reached out and shook it with a strong tight grip he learned from uncle Buddy.

MC calmly told him, "Look, cuz, I was just bullshittin' I wouldn't hurt yo granny. I feel like she my grandma," as he shed fake tears to draw sympathy from Da'Quan. He went on to say sobbingly, "Cuzz, I ain't even got no grandparents. You lucky. If anybody ever fucked with yo granny, I'd kill 'em myself. Cuzz, I respect how you would fight me for her, you my homie now foe life! Cuz, let's just get that little buster's bike together cause he's riding around like a little rich boy."

Da'Quan's mind began to embrace the knowledge MC was kicking. MC continued by saying "Me and you riding around on these cheap ass Huffys and that punk got a brand new mongoose on alloys. Does he let you ride that mutherfucka?"

Da'Quan replied, "Naw his dad don't want nobody too fuck it up so I can't ever ride."

MC said, "See what I mean? What kinda home boys won't let you ride his shit, cuzz? He probably wouldn't have yo back in a fight. That's why I rob pooh butts, cuzz. Really, they ain't nothing but weak ass momma boys, cuzz." The more MC spoke, the more Da'Quan began to see his side of the spectrum. Da'Quan stared at the Huffy on the ground and allowed MC's antagonistic speech to sink in. He began to think silently *This fool might be right. Why can't I ride his bike? He always coming up with an excuse why he won't let me ride his.*

Fuck, maybe MC is right and he ain't my true homie. After a brief moment of silence, Da'Quan responded, "OK, cuz, what's in it for me?"

MC cracked a smile from ear to ear and said, "Nigga, we can break that bitch down, split the parts and sell em. I got a Japanese fool that buy all this shit. We could make about sixty or seventy dollars a piece, cuzz. That's on my momma."

Da'Quan's eyes jumped out of his head at the amount MC proposed. Seventy dollars might as well have been a half a million because it prompted Da'Quan to reply, "All right, cuz, I'm in," as they shook hands and shed devilish grins.

MC asked, "I know you know where he keeps it at night."

Da'Quan replied, "Yeah, next to his parents' window in the backyard."

MC hesitated in a moment of thought and asked, "OK, what time they go to sleep?"

"Shit, about ten or eleven," Da'Quan replied.

MC began to rub his hairless chin with his right hand trying to keep his cool, he sighed and said, "All right, cuzz, Ima be at yo window at ten thirty, cuzz. I can't come out that late," MC said, "Nigga, u gone sneak out the back when you granny sleep and we gone handle this business."

Da'Quan's heart began to rattle but seeing as how he agreed he just answered, "All right, cuz, but don't be loud and shit."

MC gave him a sarcastic look and said, "All right then, cuz, I'll be back tonight," as he mounted up on his Huffy and sped off down the driveway. From that moment on Da'Quan was in a bundle of nerves, his stomach felt like a million cocoons and butterflies had been set free in it. He entered back into the house in a dreamy, zombie-like demeanor.

As he sat in his room watching "What's Happening" he couldn't focus on Rog and Rerun's antics thinking about the crime he was to commit that night. After an hour or so of contemplating his evening, Delilah knocked on his door. *Bang, bang.* "C'mon boy grab your plate before it gets cold," Delilah said.

Da'Quan replied, "Naw, Grandma, I don't feel good. I'm not hungry."

Delilah, who rarely got a response of this nature, came abruptly into the room and put her hand on his forehead. She proclaimed, "Hmm, you don't have a fever, boy, what's wrong with you, my love?"

Da'Quan lay on his bed to keep up appearances and said, "Grandma, my stomach been hurting all day."

She said, "Well, lay down and get some rest. I'll come check on you later, and turn the TV off." He obliged and laid across the bed like he had sickle cell or pneumonia. Before she exited the room she placed her hand on his head and prayed, "Dear God, please remove any harmful or serious ailments from this child's body, give him the strength to heal as we know you can do all things in Christ Jesus' name, amen." She gave him a kiss on his forehead, which added more guilt to his spirit because of the upcoming thieving he'd embark on.

Da'Quan lay on his bed wide awake until he heard three soft knocks on his window. The time had arrived. It was 10:29 p.m., and MC was eager as a beaver to get into some deviant activities. Da'Quan peeled himself from his mattress, put on his Chuck Taylors and quietly made his way through the house out the back door. MC, who wore all black, was excited but serious about the heist.

He grinned openheartedly as Da'Quan eased out of the squeaky back door. MC rubbed his palms together like an old gangster from a black and white prison movie and said, "All right, nigga, it's on. Let's get it, cuzz." The two tiptoed down the driveway and made their way across the street. Before they entered Philip's backyard, MC stopped Da'Quan and said, "Look, see all the lights is out? We gone sneak back there, you gone open the gate and imma grab the bike. Once I'm on the bike, cuz, you take off running and imma be right behind you. Oh yea, do they got dogs?".

"Yea, but he is in the house at night."

MC replied, "Cool, let's roll, cuzz. You scared, nigga?" he asked in a relaxed tone. Since this was business as usual for him, Da'Quan replied, "Naw, nigga, let's get this shit over with."

The two made their way to the back in complete darkness. As they approached the back gate, Da'Quan pointed and said, "See where the light from the TV is? That's the bedroom. Look right there, his bike leaning on the house,"

MC shook his head and said, "OK, go open the gate and be quiet, fool, and imma walk in." Da'Quan followed suit and quietly opened the squeaky gate. It squeaked like a cat's meow, but there was no sign of anyone being alarmed. MC made his way to the bike like a seasoned criminal. When he reached the window he peaked in and to Da'Quan's surprise he stood by the window looking with his eyes bulging out of his head. Da'Quan's nerves had him delusional as he wondered what MC was so fascinated with. MC looked at Da'Quan, smiling and waved him over. Da'Quan crept next to MC and as he peeked through the window he saw Phillip's mom getting stroked doggy-style by Phillip's dad. Da'Quan looked in shock as Philip's dad appeared to be a well-endowed porno star banging his wife, Sherry, relentlessly into the headboard. Her 46D breasts swung back and forth as she begged him, "Fuck me harder, fuck me harder, nigga."

MC burst into laughter to the point where we almost forgot why they were there. Da'Quan had never seen the couple in this light and it was disturbing to watch considering he knew them as God-fearing, square adults. Da'Quan nudged MC and whispered, "C'mon, cuzz." MC reluctantly agreed as they eased the expensive bike out of the backyard.

Just as they were exiting the gate, the back porch light popped on. Sherry stood topless screaming, "They got the bike, they got the bike!" MC hopped on and darted down the driveway like a lightning bolt. Da'Quan, who by now was in complete shock, panicked and crawled under the house in an open crawl space. He could hear Sherry yelling, "Oh my god, they stole Phillip's bike. Those mutherfuckers stole his bike." Just then Da'Quan heard click clack. It was Philip's dad, but Philip's dad told Sherry, "Stay here with the kids, babe."

By now Da'Quan was shaking under the house like an epileptic. Sweat ran from his eyebrows to his groin in fear. He knew that if he lived and Uncle Buddy found out it would be his last breath on earth. Da'Quan saw a rat the size of a kitten two feet away but refused to move in fear of the loaded .45 in Philip's dads hands. The moment was tense and he`d either have to deal with a huge wood rat or a loaded .45 in the hands of a military vet. The fear he felt left him paralyzed under the house as he saw Big Philip's army boots quickly pass by the open crawl space. Da'Quan prayed, "God, please let me get home. I promise I won't do this again and please don't let this rat eat me under here, please."

God had a not so mysterious way of working, as an alley cat appeared and distracted the rat enough to make him far less of a threat to Da'Quan. Da'Quan laid in complete silence until he saw the army boots pass the crawl space. The whole ordeal may have been no more than seven minutes, but it felt like a decade of animated confusion. He heard the gate slam in anger as he overheard the couple's conversation. Big Philip said angrily, "Some little punks got li'l Philip's bike, babe. Shit, that bike cost me two hundred and fifty dollars, babe. I woulda kilt those punks if I saw 'em."

Sherry replied with tears in her eyes, "Oh my god, we gotta call the police." That statement sent more chills down Da'Quan's spine; he shook his head and closed his eyes in disbelief at what he had gotten himself into. A part of him wanted to fess up but what would happen kept him planted right where he lay. Big Philip replied, "Naw, babe, the gone police can't do nothing plus by the time they get here them knuckleheads ah be long gone."

Sherry said, "I believe it was that nasty li'l nigga Michael down the street that did it. I can't stand him or his trifling parents."

Big Phillip answered, "OK, well, I'll go down there tomorrow and talk with his dad, see what I come up with." Da'Quan's heart dropped at that moment, but they never mentioned anyone specifically but MC, which gave him a glimmer of hope.

Da'Quan lay under the house until he heard Big Philip start pounding that thick chocolate body of Sherry's again. The moment he heard her moan, he eased from under the house in complete silence and made his way back across the street to his house. When he finally made it to the back door, Delilah was in the kitchen grabbing her midnight cookies and milk. Da'Quan thought, *What the fuck is going on tonight?* He could see her ease back through the house as he quietly made his way through the kitchen to the bedroom. His clothes were dirty like he worked as a gardener, and his heart was still racing at an unhealthy pace. His body was shivering as he undressed; he realized this wasn't the life for him. The seventy dollars didn't compare to the wood rat and .45 caliber handgun he was up against. Da'Quan sweated so profusely he smelled like a batch of collard greens that had sat for days. He had never been petrified to that degree and realized MC may come with a cockamamie story as to why he wouldn't be able to get him half for the bike. The composition of thoughts cradled him into a lifeless coma.

The next day as Da'Quan made his way home from school he saw Big Philip knocking on MC`s door. Mr.. Chambers abruptly answered, "Yea, what can I do for you?" Big Philip said, "Yeah, my son's bike was stolen last night and I was seeing if your son Michael knew anything about it."

Mr.. Chambers, who wasn't a stranger to these types of allegations, yelled, "Michael, Michael, get yo ass in here." Mr.. Chambers asked, "Did you steal a bike?"

MC replied, "Naw, I don't steal bikes."

Big Philip looked at the two and said, "Yeah, well it was a yellow mongoose on alloys, and if I call the police and they find it here, I'm pressing charges. It cost me over two and a half yards, and I intend on getting it back, jack!"

Mr.. Chambers replied, "Naw, naw, no need for that. Come on around back and come take a look."

MC blurted, "Dad, I didn't take no bike."

Big Philip made his way around the back and to his amazement, it looked like a makeshift bike store in the backyard of their home. There were Redline and Huffy frames laying around like carcasses in the desert. From where he stood he could see bike wheels hanging on racks with an array of spray paint cans on the ground next to a bucket. Wrenches and screwdrivers sat openly amongst chrome nuts and bolts . Big Philip's blood began boiling and he began trembling in anger while his eyes searched for his son's bicycle.

Mr.. Chambers came out and asked, "Well, do you see it buddy?" Big Philip glanced meticulously high and low before spotting it tucked between the garage on a side fence already with parts missing.

Big Philip pointed and said, "Yea, that's half of it right there."

Mr.. Chambers in a sincere and humble tone said, "Look, I get paid on Friday. I can pay for the missing parts, but please don't call the police. I'll make sure you get your son's bike back in running condition, man."

Big Philip replied, "Yea, OK, but I don't want him nowhere near my property again or I'm calling the police."

Mr.. Chambers replied, "OK, good deal, my man. I'll give you the money for the parts and labor and you won't never have a problem out of Michael again."

Big Philip grabbed the half pieced bike and rolled it out on one wheel and said, "All right, but if I don't get that on Friday, ima do what I said."

Mr.. Chambers said, "Brother, I got you!"

Big Philip walked out and told him, "I'm Mr.. Green to you, and my brother wouldn't do this. Have a good day. See you Friday at—?" He gestured to his wrist like what time.

"No later than four o'clock, Mr.. Green," replied Mr.. Chambers. Big Philip in a doubtful tone replied, "All right, man" and proceeded out the gate with his pistol visibly tucked as a sign of I'm about that life.

Chapter 3
PRANKSTERS

AUGUST 1985 • 15 years old

It was the summer of 1985, and Mother Nature rattled the city with a blistering hot afternoon. Da'Quan trudged quickly through the heatwave to his homeboy White boy Tone's house. On his way down the block he could see the Baldwin Hills inferno blazing black smoke as high up as the eye could see. Even the birds chirped irritatingly because of the heat. Neighbors' dogs kept their snouts buried in their water bowls while wasps and bees were forced to produce in hives and honeycombs fulfilling their daily ritual. Late model Chevys and Volkswagens lined the curb of the lower middle class South Central block. June in the ghetto was synonymous to the "Hunger Games," as the adults went to work leaving the neighborhood openly accessible for raw antics to eventuate from adolescent delinquents. Tone was the leading light of this rebellious delinquent movement and had every intention to instigate as much scandal and bullshit as the time in the day would allow. His passion for wrongdoing and mischief made him, in all actuality, a blast to be around. Turbulence and controversy were the absolute least fear within the heart of Tone. Being the only Creole in a neighborhood of more shaded complexioned counterparts, Tone was no stranger to problems and confrontation.

Halfway down the block, Da'Quan came up on the mailman, Mr.. Kendricks. He was a brown skin mixed breed with heavy red undertones from the swamps of Louisiana. Mr.. Kendricks was a slick haired, gold-necklace-wearing civil service veteran. He would oftentimes recommend to some of the young teenage boys to go to the military, come home and slave forty years for the US postal service, until they lowered you slowly into a six-foot ditch. Carrying that burdensome mailbag in the blazing sun wasn't particularly enticing enough to the youth he was preaching his ministry to. They'd rather hustle on the block ducking the police, shoot hoop or gangbang before choosing physical labor for a career choice. The protruding hunch in his back from the endless miles of walking seemed to worsen year after year. In his back pocket he kept a fresh US Postal face towel to wipe the huge beads of sweat that drenched his worn and uninspired face. Mr.. Kendricks over decades had garnered numerous scars and lesions on his forearms from vicious dog bites and heroin use. He, for all intents and purposes, made the life of a postal worker look as inviting as a pit of venomous snakes.

As Da'Quan made his way down the block, he crossed paths with the disgruntled postal slave, who sat on the rear of his truck taking a huge squig of Jameson whiskey. After he slid the bottle deep into his mailbag, he let off a thunderous burp and lit up a Camel unfiltered. He noticed Da'Quan from the corner of his eye and in a slurred drawl blurted, "Say, youngsta, what you and yo buddy's gone, do you understand me?"

Da'Quan, out of respect, replied in a chipper and innocent tone, "Hey, Mr.. Kendricks, good morning, umm we gone just hangout, play some video games. You know, stuff like that."

Mr.. Kendricks forced his drunk-heavy chin up and gestured for Da'Quan to come closer. He was sitting on the back bumper of his postal truck preparing for the day's routes. Da'Quan walked over unwillingly to listen to a drunken lecture from the elderly postal worker. Mr. Kendricks looked with his bloodshot eyes into Da'Quan's and said, "Look here, boy, life can be long or short. That's why I tell y'all youngsters to be like me cause I'm like them. I joined the army because I was a knucklehead like you and ya Patna but, but, but, my, my daddy said, 'Boy, look here, either you join the military, wind up with a bullet in your head or end up rotting away in prison.'" Da'Quan had no response as he stood forced to listen to his drunk rhetoric in the summer heat. He could smell the alcohol on his breath from five feet away as the fumes infiltrated his nostrils. Mr.. Kendricks continued, "Boy, you see I was (hiccup, burp) first battalion, twenty-first infantry. I have nooooo problem blowing a muthafucka's head off his goddamn shoulders, understand me?" He then smiled, revealing his gold fang tooth, hacked up a mouth full of snot before spitting up a heap of yellow phlegm. Da'Quan stood unresponsive. He was ready to continue on with his day without being disrespectful. After wiping the spit off his lips with his pocket towel Kendricks continued, "Boy, you different. I see a ton of potential in you, boy, you got the ability to be successful. Them boys you run with gone be your downfall tho. Mark my words, boy, I ain't get this old by being a fool champ." He chuckled as he re-lit his Camel, giving Da'Quan a wink before hoisting his heavy mailbag to his shoulder. Mr.. Kendricks locked up his truck and proceeded on his route down 39th.

Da'Quan responded, "OK, Mr.. Kendricks, see you later." Mr.. Kendricks should have saved those sincere words seeing as how they went in one ear and even faster out of the other. Da'Quan was hell bent on a full day of mischief and mayhem with Tone.

Da'Quan hurriedly separated himself from the old broken spirit of Mr.. Kendricks, finding himself at Tone's doorstep. Before he could ring the doorbell, Tone snatched the door open and yelled, "Muthafucka, it's on fuck a bitch!" The two laughed and gave each other a fist pound before going in the house to form a game plan. The sudden whiffs of russet potatoes and pot roast teased Da'Quan's tastebuds as soon as he entered the compound. Tone had an exceptional talent for cooking and always took advantage of his mom's overstocked fridge for his culinary excursions. Da'Quan jokingly said, "Homie, you cook like a old fat southern bitch, nigga, ima get you a dress and high heels."

The two laughed as Tony responded, "Fuck you, cuz, bitches love a nigga who can burn in the kitchen, so take notes, fatboy." After some quick jeering, Tone pulled out a finger-sized joint with a devilish grin on his face. He lit it off the stove and took a deep pull from it causing him to choke till his face was red, while saliva leaked heavily from his lips.

Tone tried to pass it to Da'Quan, who declined by saying, "Nah, homie, I'm good. I gotta be focused fucking with you."

Tone responded, "Mo fo me then, nigga." They both laughed as Tone hit the joint halfway to his fingertips. Meanwhile Da'Quan stared at the rump roast and potatoes bake and bubble through the window of the oven. Tone asked Da'Quan, "Say, cuz, grab that big trash bag over there in the corner. It got a gang of bottles in it." Tone snatched the bag from Da'Quan's hand and headed out the back door. When they got outside Da'Quan began taking the bottles and began putting them in the trash bin. Tone who was now high had other plans. Tone giggled as he grabbed a huge empty wine bottle and hurled it high over the back gate into the next yard. The sound of the glass shattering on the concrete was a pure adrenaline rush for the animated teen. His mulatto face was now rose-colored with excitement as the bottles he tossed collided with the house, vehicles and concrete driveway. Da'Quan watched in awe as his buddy hurled more than ten bottles over the gate. Once the bottles were all gone, Tone doubled over in laughter from the thrills of his wrongdoings. Da'Quan thought to himself, *This nigga really is crazy!* Just then a huge wine bottle came crashing to the ground within a couple of feet of the two. A .357 bullet twirled freely in the shattered glass on the ground. The twirling bullet seized the undivided attention of the two, leaving them speechless. They stared at the metallic shell as Tone with a startled look on his face said "Cuz, them bullets right there kill horses and rhinos." Tone had been exposed to artillery from hunting trips down in Louisiana with his stepdad, Johnny. After a moment of silence, Tone looked at Da'Quan and out of nowhere deep from within his gut yelled, "Fuck you, niggas" Da'Quan's eyes began to protrude from his skull as he looked at Tone in disbelief. Tone nonchalantly strolled into the house as Da'Quan followed, all the while staring at the gate where the .357 bullet and bottled hailed from.

Tone, who was still extremely high from his joint, immediately got on the phone with Black Liz, who worshiped the ground he walked on. He began to whisper as they conversed about setting up a rendezvous when her parents were gone. Meanwhile Da'Quan's eyes were fixed on the juicy rump roast and broiling potatoes in the oven. He also made it his business to eavesdrop on Tone's conversation, soaking up game like a dry sponge in a puddle. As the heat from the oven began to singe Da'Quan's nose, he backed up, turned his head only to notice through the blinds three men walking down Tone's driveway. He tapped Tone on the shoulder as his back was turned, totally oblivious to the men in his driveway. As Tone turned around Da'Quan placed his index finger to his lips signaling to Tone to shut up. He pointed to the blinds for Tone to see the activity in his driveway. Tone then whispered to Black Liz, "Look, babe, I gotta go. Ima hit you later." Da'Quan could hear her in the background yelling, "Oh you must have yo other bitch there, huh nigga?" Tone whispered frustratingly, "Look, bitch, I gotta go," and quietly hung up the phone before easing over to the blinds to see who the men were.

The two both maneuvered to the window with caution to get a better look at the men. There were three black men, two were shirtless and the third wore a blue Pendleton, which was odd considering it was 100 degrees already. The shirtless thugs had tattoos from the neck down, with portraits, scriptures and blocked gang letters covering their entire torsos. None of the three could have been more than twenty or twenty-one. They looked athletic, like musclebound fullbacks or tight ends. The fullback prototype brandished a glock 9 semi-automatic in his right hand. He clutched it like it was an extension of his own hand, which was a dead giveaway that he was no stranger to toting guns for a living. The taller of the two had a snub nose .357 magnum cradled in the small of his back. It was quite noticeable when he used his six-four frame to peer over the gate looking for the two. The third thug in the blue Pendleton had a huge gash over his left eye bleeding like a faucet. His Pendleton was drenched in blood and his white Converse were now mismatched due to the continuous dripping of blood on them. Each time he glanced downward at his feet, he noticed the contrast in color from his bloody left foot to the right foot, which was still lily white. His grandmother had just brought him the Converse the day before and to see them destroyed like this infuriated the thug enough to kill. As the blood streamed down his face into his mouth, it was hard to determine the root of his injury. He looked like a creature out of a horror movie. His anger and heavy panting boosted the acceleration of blood flow, causing puddles to form around his brand new Converse. He looked down at the mess by his feet and mumbled, "Whoever hit me with this bottle gon die today cuh, that's on my mama, you punk muthafuckas just missed my daughter, cuzz!"

By this time Tone and Da'Quan were paralyzed in fear. The three men roamed the driveway slowly looking for any sign of life through movement.

There was a no-nonsense overtone in their movement as they began looking into the blinds for activity in the house. Da'Quan, while peeking out, made direct eye contact with the fullback, but the sunbeam hit the window perfectly blinding the assailant to the view on the inside. They stared no longer than ten seconds, which felt like an eternity to Da'Quan. His heartbeat thumped like jackrabbits in an orgy, as the sweat from his armpits raced down his side to his underwear. Tone was a nervous wreck as he lay shiftless on the floor not realizing he'd left the sliding door unlocked. The thug in the Pendleton quickly hopped the fence. He resembled Eazy E even though he grimaced his bloody face as the cut from the bottle began to throb more and more. He walked onto the back patio deck, slowly reached into his khakis underneath his Pendleton and pulled out a Maverick .88 pistol. Although the weapon was a complete handful he handled it like a flute or baton. He then barked in a squeaky voice, "Yeah, you punk muthafuckas, come out and throw some shit now, yeah, uh huh, where y'all bitch niggas at now?" He paused and wiped the blood, which was now gushing from his eyelid out of control. He continued to yell, "Yeah, nigga we got kids over there, if you woulda hit my daughter, I woulda blowed this house up on God nigga, on God!" The thug then cocked it aggressively and let off *Kaboom! Kaboom*! The intense kick from the rifle sent him two steps backwards into the unlocked sliding patio door. Tone closed his eyes and held his breath as he reached skillfully to lock the sliding glass door. Da'Quan knew this was the end, as his knees shook each time the rifle went off. Tone's face was blanketed in fear as he reached with every millimeter of his fingertips to lock the latch on the door. The fullback prototype hopped on the deck, aimed at the glass as Tone and Da'Quan lay on the floor with their ears covered, preparing for the worst. However, as he aimed at the glass door, the sounds of sirens and helicopters rang in the air. Suddenly he put his gun back in his waist at which time they both muscled over the gate in an attempt to beat the cops. The thug in the Pendleton had little to no vision due to the amount of blood that was leaking. He began yelling, "Come on, cuz, the feds is coming. Hurry up, cuz, I ain't going to jail. Fuck that. I ain't going back!" The trio fled post-haste down the driveway moving like gazelles in the wild. By the time they were three houses down, they were surrounded by shotguns and 12 gauges as the LAPD wrangled the trio up like cattle. They strapped their ankles to their wrists and tossed them each in separate squad cars never to be seen again.

Chapter 4
PHARMACEUTICAL CEMETERY

JUNE 1998 • 28 years old

"Game is to be sold not told" is a famous and commonly used adage in "the hood". The streets are like a jungle of wild animals whose primary concern is survival of the fittest. Da'Quan at this point was 28 and had grown into a full-fledged hustler. His chief source of income was made through the weed trade while rap and any other quick money hustles added to his flourishing capital. After realizing there was no available weed within miles of his neighborhood, he and his partner in crime Brent invested in a pound of chronic and began what was to become a million-dollar empire.

It was a warm Los Angeles Saturday afternoon as the sky was a cloud-free electric blue, and the palm trees swayed naturally in the California breeze. Da'Quan sat on the couch on the porch of his spot breaking down weed, taking in the gift Mother Nature provided. As the birds chirped blissfully from the branches on the trees and the bees danced atop rose petals, Da'Quan's focus was pigeonholed on the bountiful amounts of THC that caked his fingertips. In the background blasting through the fifteen-inch Cerwin Vega was Dub C's classic "The Shadiest".

The stage was set as he licked his chops, anticipating the taste and smell of the gram of green dope. As he desperately reached under his leg and scanned the entire porch, he realized he didn't have any zags or blunts. He patted his pockets and searched the couch only finding his .357 and Monsters Mike's tech 9. He irritatingly muttered, "Fuck, all a nigga gotta do is reach in the couch and rob me wit my own pistol!" Da'Quan was a stickler about security and remaining focused, simply because he knew *The Wolves* were always watching and all it takes is one slip up to get rubbed out.

While debating various spots in the living room and kitchen to stash the heat, there was a loud series of banging at the front door. *Bang bang bang bang.*

"General, General, hey my boy it's Face, cuzz!"

Da'Quan yelled from the kitchen, "Aight, hold up, Face, be right there!" When he opened the door he still had the .357 in his hand, instantly entertaining Scarface's infatuated eyes.

"Whoa, shit, my boy that's a nice cannon, my boy, who you gotta plug, General?" He began snickering like the diabolical heathen he was, always intrigued with murder and mayhem.

Da'Quan shook his head and replied chuckling, "Nah OG just figuring out where imma stash this big muthufucka." Scarface stood in his wife beater and cutoff khakis watching Da'Quan impatiently try to figure out where he should stash his artillery. Scarface reached into his hip pocket and grabbed his patented face towel he used to wipe the sweat from his forehead and neck. Whenever he got excited or anxious he'd begin sweating bullets profusely. After a brief moment of silent deliberations, he slapped Da'Quan on his shoulder while guiding him through the house as he instructed commandingly, "Look, General, you need a pistol right here in this here drawer, my boy, next to the butter knives, kno what I'm saying, my boy!" Scarface navigated him throughout the house schooling him. "Now in the bedroom here, my boy, you need one under the pillow. Look here, you need one in the closet in the drawer, and a little itty bitty pistol, my boy, in ya bathroom drawer, my boy, right there. Look now, OG only telling you what I know." As Scarface limped through the house wiping the sweat from his neck and his forehead, he was confident like a college professor, outlining the basics in Gangsterism 101. The smell of PCP that fumed through Scarface's pores made for no distraction as Da'Quan knew these lessons could save his life if *The Wolves* were ever to strike.

The two kept navigating out the backdoor into the backyard where Da'Quan's pit-bull Felony roamed like a predator. The two stood by her doghouse while Scarface, who was petrified of Felony, watched her with an eagle eye as he continued, "Now look, my boy, word in the hood you got that water, my boy, so look, you gotta bury ya jugs underground my boy." Da'Quan looked at him bewildered as to how he knew he was selling sherm as well. He played it cool as if he didn't hear his comment, remaining sponge like soaking up game. Scarface continued, "Look, my boy, you wanna bury those jugs like two feet deep or so, my boy, so the feds' doggy can't sniff it, my boy." He then pointed with his face towel at all of the piles of dog shit throughout the yard and proceeded lecturing, "So, look here, General, you wanna also bury 'em near the piles of dog doo doo, my boy." He looked Da'Quan in his eye and asked, "When you see dog doo doo, whatcha do, my boy?"

Da'Quan knew what he was brilliantly alluding to as he replied, "Walk around it."

Scarface smiled and began chuckling as he blurted, "Yea, General, that's why I call you that cause you sharp, my boy, you use that thang on top of ya neck." On the way back into the house, Scarface, after his great symposium, turned and hit him up for some bread. "Say, General, look here, my boy, could you loan OG a little something my boy?" Da'Quan paused and thought, *This muthafucka put me up on a life or death game, informed me that* The Wolves *knew I was hustling pounds, gallons and birds, ultimately preparing me for defense against the evils in the game."*

Da'Quan reached into his pocket pulling out no less than a thousand dollars in disorganized hundreds and spearmint gum. He handed him a five, but OG without moving, stared at Da'Quan with a humorless smile on his face. He was aware of the significance of the information he had shared with him . Da'Quan got the message, like a bullhorn in a closet, as he handed OG a ten-dollar bill and told him, "Here, cuz, but go grab me a swisher sweet and you keep the change." Scarface grinned ear to ear as he now had enough for a bottle of Night Train and half on a sherm stick with one of his comrades. He nervously grabbed the money and said, "Thanks, General, my boy. Imma shoot down to the corner, imma bring that swisha back to you my boy."

Da'Quan yawned and stretched as the two made it to the front. He was impatient, fiending to smoke his weed and put his day in motion. At the front door stood Mad-E smoking on a black and mild. He was dressed in a silk, avocado-green shirt and matching slacks with his gold-framed Versace shades.

When Scarface glimpsed down at Mad-E's shoes, he excitedly shook his hand and began ranting, "Whew hew, my boy, General, General, look at unc's spit-shined Stacy's cuzz. Whew, my boy, now, that's gangster." Scarface began limping with urgency towards the store.

Mad-E took the compliments in stride, but as soon as Scarface was a ways off, he asked jokingly, "OG a little koo koo, cuzz, you know that, right?"

They both laughed as Da'Quan replied, "Face, my niggas cool. Unc, he a real gangster! Yea so why the fuck you dressed like a young pimp this morning?"

Mad-E went in his shirt pocket and pulled out a crisp hundred-dollar big face and asked, "Nigga, you got some good weed or what?" His agitated tone signaled something was bothering him. He looked perturbed as he scrutinized the bag of chronic Da'Quan gave him and blurted, "Goddamn, cuzz, ain't we family? Why this shit so short? C'mon cuzz." Da'Quan snatched it back and stuffed an extra gram in it which made E feel as though he won. The extra gram in the bag eased his nerves as he answered the original question, "Yeah, I'm going to a real gangsta's funeral today. My homeboy Li'l Daryl"

Da'Quan remained silent as he could sense Mad-E was deeply bothered about his friend's death. He continued, "The last time we talked, cuzz, I cussed him out cause the nigga owes me a hundred dollars." He took a pull from his black 'n mild as he put the sack of weed in his socks. He went on to say, "Ole Daryl, my Patna, yeah ima have to tell his wife she owe me that hundred now." Da'Quan looked perplexed at him without saying a word as he started doing inventory on his weed and money while Mad-E kept reminiscing, "Yea, cuz, Daryl was a down nigga. Back in like seventy-one, we was like fifteen, cuzz, it was this nigga named CK Head who was a known Crip killer, right. OK, so one Saturday night two of the homies saw the nigga walking out the liquor store in his hood. They hooked a U-turn and followed him while he walked down the street. This was before cameras and all that high tech shit; they just wanted to kill him on a side street away from traffic. Got me?"

Mad-E's stories were dark and vivid enough for you to feel as if you were right there where the action took place, from the conviction in his voice to the spine-chilling details you felt as if you witnessed a high-powered gangster flick. He kept steady eye contact with Da'Quan as he proceeded. "So they rolled up and parked. Daryl was driving and the other homie Bear hopped out first. Trip this cuzz, Buddah pulled out his pistol and the bullets fell out. So the CK Head nigga looks, turns and starts busting at Bear. Cuzz, the nigga shot a hole in Bear's acey deucy, cuzz . I'll give it to him. He was what we called a precision shooter. He played a lot of baseball from what I heard. But yeah, cuzz, so Daryl ducked and slid behind you know one of those gardener trucks and lit him up with a forty-five, *payow, payow, payow*! So the CK Head nigga fell behind a old Chrysler, now from what Daryl say he couldn't go home not knowing if he killed the great CK Head, so he eased up on the Chrysler, and CK was laying on the ground with his pistol aimed at Daryl's head." Mad-E chuckled as he went on, "Daryl says he likes to shit on himself, but once he saw his shit jam he gave him one to the head *payow* and two to the chest, cuzz. He said then he saw his brains ooze out on the tire and he knew. Man, later that night him and Bear came dancing and drinking, high off that glue, to the set talking 'bout yeah call me Daryl Kemosabe, I ended ole CK Head's Crip-killing career, cuzz, *boom boom boom!*"

Da'Quan stood speechless as he counted his weed money. Mad-E leaned on the kitchen counter and took another pull from his black and mild with a look of nostalgia on his hardened face. He smiled, chuckled and continued, "Yeah, cuz, so I mean we were happy they got him, but I was mad it wasn't me. You know, that was a big kill. So I says aww fuck you nigga, I don't believe you. You know me always talking shit. So he says to me OK nigga, you can finish him off when we know what funeral home his punk ass gone be at. I'm high and drunk so I say yeah OK I'm in. Now this in front of all the homies so I gotta stay true now. So, cuzz, about six days later Daryl come to my momma's house in some old ass Chevy like a fifty-seven and picks me up. We get to driving, he says, 'You ready?' Now I forgot by now what we talked about and asked him wassup? He says, 'To go finish off CK Head.' I'm like fuck it less go! So we riding, downing thunderbird, sniffing glue not giving a fuck. So it's me, Daryl and Bear rolling. He gave me and Bear pistols and stockings caps we wore under our acey deucey, right."

Da'Quan by now was all ears as the story continued to intrigue him. Mad-E was animated in rare form as he went on. "When we roll by the church we see some niggas and bitches standing outside so we parked a block away and walked. All three of us, cuz, had a acey deucey, leather coats and big guns. When we get half a block away, I'm like let's kill anything moving. You know, I'm young, high, outta control. So Daryl say, look we gone pull these stocking caps over our face right before we walk in, OK? Niggas find the casket let off and walk out calmly."

Mad-E was a firm believer in the element of surprise as a means to not get recognized. It was now obvious where he learned it. He began to whisper as Da'Quan listened in awe, "So we strolled up to the door, cuzz, pulled down the stocking caps and walked in real slow and sad like we belonged. Me and Bear walked right up to the coffin, cuzz, and let off *payow, payow, payow!*" He began chuckling as the look on his face grew nefarious. He paused, took a pull from his black and mild and continued. "So, cuz, everybody, the minister, piano man, all his homies and family was yelling, stumbling over each other, cuz. But the trippy thing to me was when we was letting off at his body. It was clear shit jumping out. It wasn't blood. You know years later I realized it was embalming fluid. Damn, cuz, we was crazy." He chuckled with resentment in his tone and said, "Yeah, cuzz, Li'l Daryl, oh and when we got back to the hood, first thing he said was, 'I ain't never kilt a nigga twice.' His folks know we ain't fucking around, cuzz. They know he was hated." Mad-E paused, lifted his shades, looked directly into Da'Quan's shell-shocked eyes, winked and said, "Now that's a gangster. Alright I'm gone cuz. I'll get back." Da'Quan stood paralyzed by his heartless gangster tale as he gave him a fist dap. Between Scarface's lecture and Mad-E's tale from the dark side he knew he needed to tighten his game up if he was going to survive.

Chapter 5
DUMB BITCH

MARCH 1986 • 16 years old

Ditching school is a game played by students who seek adventure in the rebellion against the ills of authority. Falsifying documentation, creating a day filled with deviant behavior, finding tranquility in liquor, weed and unprotected sex made a casual day away from school undoubtedly a no brainer.

Bang, bang, bang, bang. Da'Quan's bedroom window rattled in four quick successions. It was 6:15 a.m., and as Da'Quan slowly moved the window shade he mumbled, "Who the fuck is at my muthafuckin' window this goddamn early?" While wiping the crust from his half opened eyes, he, with blurred vision, saw his homeboy Whiteboy Tone. He stood in his Levi's 501s, all white five stripe K Swiss classics, with his brand new Duke Blue Devils starter jacket. He brandished a fat sack of marijuana to his nose, laughing and smelling it with a look of deceit painted on his high yellow face.

He whispered loudly, "C'mon, D, get dressed, cuzz, look what I got. C'mon nigga!" Da'Quan gestured with one finger as if to say, hold on, nigga, as he hustled out of bed. While taking a leak and brushing his teeth over the toilet, he already had a premonition of a day spent on the wild side. Tone was always an advocate of shiesty and deviant behavior. If it wasn't illegal, ill-advised or unscrupulous, he found no fun or excitement in it at all. Conventional fun without a dastardly twist was humdrum to him in every sense of the word. Smoking some weed and making it to school on time was just not in his genetic makeup. He thrived on risk. Tone was a natural born thrill seeker at any cost. Da'Quan washed up and slid on his pre-ironed khakis and fresh white pro club T-shirt. Once Da'Quan made his way out the backdoor, Tone quickly ordered, "C'mon, cuzz, hurry up," as he began slowly jogging down the driveway towards the street. Da'Quan followed suit, not sure what he was actually in store for. But what he did know was that there was a huge sack of weed and some mischief lined up for the two without a doubt.

After running five or so houses down the block, Tone put his arms around Da'Quan's neck and flashed a set of car keys with a huge devilish grin on his face. He explained to Da'Quan in an animated tone, "Look, cuz, my momma be carpooling. She's tired of making that long ass ride from Orange County to LA every day. Plus, nigga, I found her spare set of keys she was trying to hide from me. Cuzz, we got the muthafuckin Oldsmobile all day nigga!" Da'Quan just looked and thought, *So we gon be smashing illegally in this nigga momma's car.* Tone elaborated, "Yeah, cuzz, you know that big titty bitch Black Liz I be fucking? She wanna get fucked today!"

Da'Quan replied, "OK, cool, so I mean she trying give me some pussy, too, or what?" He was hoping this was a flip mission because he wanted to fuck her big black, deep-dimpled ass bad.

Tone smiled from ear to ear and shook his head before responding "Naw, cuz, we gon hit a lick. Her parents got hella jewels, money and powder in they bedroom! When I be over there, the dumb bitch won't let me out her sight so I can't go through they shit how I want to. I know it's a gang of shit in there cause the bitch be bragging about how much money they got trying to impress a nigga." He burst out laughing saying, "But the bitch don't know she talking to tricky T. She's lucky I don't tie her ass up and wipe umm out. Plus she knows what school I go to and she kinda know where I live so I gotta play it smart, you know." Da'Quan just shook his head taking in the fact that they were actually about to rob Liz's house while she was in it asshole naked. Tone continued enthusiastically, "Look, cuz, we gon drive to her house. When she let me in, ima send her to the kitchen or something and unlock the door. Ima take my shirt off and wave it so you know it's unlocked, OK? You got me, D?" Da'Quan shook his head yeah. Tone continued, "Give it like five minutes, then ease yo fat ass up in there and when I start fucking the bitch and start yelling *Dumb Bitch,* then, cuzz go up the stairs and her parents' room is the first door on the left hand side, cuzz. Just go in there and do yo thang nigga. Get jewelry, dope, guns whatever you can find with value, my nigga, OK? You got me?"

Da'Quan smiled, gave him a fist dap and responded confidently, "Gotchu, nigga. Let's get this bitch!" Although he sounded convincing, in the back of Da'Quan's mind he had the what ifs. What if her dad or mom comes home? What if she sees me ? What if we get pulled over in this nigga's mom's car with stolen merchandise? The thoughts raced through his mind like NASCAR but in the end, the temptation of easy money combined with peer pressure, prompted him to go through with the mission. Without another word spoken, the two hopped in the Buick and headed to the lick.

When the duo sat in the luxurious bucket seats of the eight-four sedan, in the ashtray sat a half smoked finger-size, rolled joint of chocolate Thai bud. The car reeked like a fresh warm batch of double chocolate brownies combined with the sweet aroma of Tone's mom's Chanel No. 5. Tone fired up the Buick like a race car and shoved the half smoked joint between his choppers as he lit the powerful cannabis in pure delight. On the radio, the hit single by the O'Jays "Keep On Loving Me" serenaded the two as they puffed the potent stogie flying down the backstreets. The higher they got, the faster Tone punched it to the staged setup. He ignored all of the rules of the road, accelerating with his led foot up to and beyond 100 miles per hour. Da'Quan at one point closed his eyes and reclined deep into his bucket seat anxiously awaiting to arrive at the heist at hand. Just then Tone yelled frantically, "Aawww shit, D, they on us. Hold tight, my nigga!"

Da'Quan opened his heavy eyes only to notice a chubby white motorcycle cop racing to the rear of their vehicle with the siren on. Tone ran through the lights as if they didn't exist and began yelling, "Fuck the police, cuzz!" Da'Quan's adrenaline began racing as he felt his heart attempt to leap out of his chest. His palms grew clammy, realizing their high joyride had turned into a felony criminal high speed chase at 6:45 a.m. Tone, who was surprisingly skillful behind the wheel, made a sharp left on La Brea at sixty-five miles per hour. Da'Quan looked back and noticed the motorcycle cop got smaller and smaller as Tone accelerated to the max. Then out of nowhere, Tone yelled, "D, hold on, cuzz," and at that moment he hooked a life-threatening left turn onto

Don Lorenzo Drive, pulling directly into a condominium driveway. He parked and as the two peaked over the wall of the parking structure, they saw the chubby cop speed by totally unaware of the slick move Tone had made at the light. Da'Quan's bowels screamed to be released as he fought to keep his insides from spilling freely. Tone began laughing uncontrollably while he began rolling another stogie, excitedly saying, "Fuck that slow ass pig, cuzz, my momma shit get up!" Da'Quan stared blankly at Tone thinking, *This muthafucka's really crazy. He's going to get us killed out here.* After blazing the second stogie to relieve some tension, Tone slowly backed out of the condominium complex and headed in the opposite direction of the chubby cop. He wheeled the Buick down some back streets until parking the car in the corner of a cul de sac. He turned to Da'Quan and in a serious non-joking manner said, "Aight, cuz, the bitch stay round the corner. We gone walk to the bitch crib so nobody gets the license plate on mom's shit, Da'Quan. When we get next door to her house you gon leave yo shoes in the flower bed next door so yo big ass feet don't be making no noise! So look when I go in because I already know she goes to the bathroom and wash her shit cause she knows I don't play when it comes to fresh pussy, cuzz. And when she do, ima take my shirt off and wave it at you out the door. Ima leave the door unlocked and then give it like five minutes and c'mon in Da'Quan. Then, cuzz, when you get in and when you hear me screaming—"

Da'Quan interjected, "'Dumb bitch,'" Tone smiled and continued, "Exactly, that's when you slide upstairs, cuzz, and get to work. Got me?" Da'Quan just nodded as the butterflies in his core began flapping like bats in a cave.

The two got out and headed briskly down the hilly, affluent neighborhood commonly known as the Black Beverly Hills. The houses and yards were well kept along the way. Da'Quan wondered how blacks lived so lavishly only ten minutes away from his and Tone's houses. Beamers, Porsches and Benzes lined the curb as they made their way to the mark. It was apparent that there was a huge economic gap between their neighborhood and the BBH. The USC and UCLA flags that hung from the garages were another indication that there were a very high percentage of well-educated individuals around these parts. Once they reached the destination, Tone stopped abruptly and slowly peaked around the corner behind a huge rosebush to scope the house they were to hit. He looked back at Da'Quan and whispered, "Look, cuzz, it's the two-story white house with the red trim and red front door, my nigga. Take your shoes off and leave 'em here in the bush, cuzz." While Da'Quan stripped his feet, Tone pulled out some Binaca, took two squirts and headed towards Black Liz`s house. Before he reached the porch, the door flung open, and just before he entered he looked back at Da'Quan, winked and gave him a thumbs up gesture.

Unbeknownst to the two teens, Ms. Lee, the only Caucasian on the block, who owned the corner house, was squatting quietly on the other side of the bush pruning her humongous tree. After eavesdropping an earful of information about Tone and Da'Quan's caper, she with all of her heart wanted to inform Mr.. Corning, Liz`s dad, and the police about the crime being planned. She wanted to dash to the house and grab the phone, but she was a quadriplegic, and her wheelchair was parked on the other end of her spacious yard. Ms. Lee would crawl in her garden, pruning as a form of exercise and tranquility. She was stricken with polio and didn't have the balance or endurance to walk with full stability. Ms. Lee, in search of purpose, adamantly began to crawl and scale through her well-groomed patch of vines and shrubs eager to give notice of the crime taking place. She slithered through the dirt like an earthworm, mumbling, "This is what happens when you let niggers move into your neighborhood, God almighty!"

Meanwhile as she squirmed through her garden to squeal, Da'Quan waited nervously on his cue from Tone to get to work. Not more than five minutes had passed when Tone's T-shirt was waving from the front door. Da'Quan saw his cue and made his way to the mark. He entered slowly and walked as if he were on a bed of nails. Tone was in the living room and pulled Da'Quan close as he whispered, "OK, cuzz, she in the shower. I cracked the bedroom door. Just go up there sit in the closet until you hear me say—"

Da'Quan interjected, "'Dumb bitch,' I got it, cuzz, I got it. Go on, hit that shit for me." They both chuckled and gave each other a fist dap before Da'Quan shot upstairs to the bedroom. Along the stairwell were framed degrees from LMU and UCLA. There were plaques on the wall from Alpha Kappa Alpha and Kappa Alpha Psi. In his mind he thought *Yea, OK, these_muthafuckas do got bread.* As he entered the bedroom he began scanning with his thief eye for any valuables before entering the wall-sized closet. He listened closely and after a couple of minutes heard Tone yelling, "Take this dick, you dumb bitch. Take this dick! He could hear Liz moaning in pure bliss and knew it was time. He eased from the closet and got to work. The bedroom was huge, with expensive shirts and dresses laying across their huge wood frame waterbed. There were Fila sweatsuits and leather pants hanging on hangers on the stationary bike. Out of the bedroom window was a clear view of the entire Northern section of Los Angeles, which was mesmerizing. Da'Quan without hesitation opened the jewelry box and began handpicking items he felt were the most expensive. There were gold link chains, diamond earrings, bracelets, pendants, Rolex watches and custom gold cufflinks. His mouth watered at the options he had to choose from. While Tone stood up in Liz keeping her enamored, he knew time was of the essence and began stuffing jewelry in every pocket he had. All of a sudden the sound of the front door opening silenced the sexual escapades in the next room. Da'Quan's heart jumped into his throat as he instinctively hid back in the closet burying himself deep behind Mr.. Corning's expensive collection of business suits.

As Mr.. Corning quickly made his way up the stairs, he began yelling, "Lizzy, Lizzy, you here?" She began coughing uncontrollably as she responded, "Yeah, Dad. I don't feel good so I stayed home from school." Tone slid under her bed as she threw on a USC T-shirt to cover her huge football-size breasts that swayed with every step she took. She quickly came out of her room with the t-shirt and track shorts revealing her toned legs she'd earned through years of ballet and cheerleading. Liz then nervously asked, "Well, umm, wassup Daddy? Why are you here? Mom said you'd be at meetings all day today." She smoothly closed her bedroom door behind her to eliminate the chance of her dad catching a whiff of the heated sex that was taking place in her room.

Mr.. Corning, who was also caught off guard, came up with a quick fib of his own as he nervously replied, "Well, uh, yea, I do, but um my next meeting won't start till noon. I just left the office to change because me and some of my frat brothers are going to hit some balls at the golf course after the next meeting. You OK, baby? You need anything before I go?" He went to kiss her forehead but she coughed and pushed him back so he wouldn't smell Tone's cologne or her sex scent that lingered. He backed away and said, "Well, OK, baby and look don't mention you saw me to your mother. She hates when I hang with the fellas and I don't wanna hear it tonight. You know how she is, 'You always got time fo them niggas and not me blah blah blah.'"

She laughed, saying, "Yea, I know, she be trippin'. I won't say nothing." She kept clearing her throat to keep him backed off as he started heading towards his room. Da'Quan heard the whole dialogue. As Mr.. Corning entered the bedroom he became motion free and breathless, hiding behind thousands of dollars' worth of Italian material. He instantly came to the closet and began searching for an outfit. Luckily he shuffled through the opposite side of the closet not quite revealing Da'Quan's face. Da'Quan stood mannequin like in apprehension, praying mentally that this man didn't catch him in his closet with all of his jewelry stuffed in his pockets. He finally snatched a Fila golf shirt and matching sweats as sweat trickled like a leaking faucet from Da'Quan's armpits. He prayed Mr.. Corning didn't hear his heart beating or feel the vibration from it on the floor. Sweat began oozing from his head and racing down his cheeks as he thought, *If this man catches me, he may shoot me and do away with my body!* All Mr.. Corning had to do was look and down and he'd see Da'Quan's size twelve feet sitting in socks in between his loafers and expensive custom gators.

Corning snatched the clothes quickly from the hanger and tossed them nonchalantly on the bed. Through the vents of the closet door, Da'Quan witnessed Corning open his jewelry box, searching frantically as he could see things were missing. After a brief, intense moment of searching, he slid his wedding ring into the box and shut it while mumbling angrily, "Um huh, that dirty bitch using again, huh." He then went into the top drawer on his dresser and pulled out a hefty bag of powder with a coke vial, placed it to his nose and snorted aggressively. He checked his watch making sure not to be late to meet his secretary who was waiting across town at the Snooty Fox Motor Inn for some afternoon shenanigans. He quickly began changing his outfit to avoid any speculation from Elizabeth. Meanwhile Lizzy snuck Tone out of the front door while her dad quietly changed and went through his daily coke ritual. Da'Quan was now left to *The Wolves* and just had to sit in silence and pray to get out of this predicament with life in his body. As the high kicked in, Mr.. Corning smiled in the dresser mirror and began cha cha cha-ing with an imaginary partner while singing, "I Do Love You," by the infamous group GQ. After a couple of minutes, he put what had to be at least four ounces of coke back in the drawer. He looked in the mirror while gaining his composure, checked his teeth and slicked his eyebrows with the spit on his fingertips before making his way out of the door. Da'Quan's body was filled with relief as the bedroom door shut. He leaned back against the closet wall and wiped his sweat-riddled forehead as he began to breathe again. All of a sudden the bedroom door flung open and Mr.. Corning shot directly to the closet and opened it without warning. Da'Quan shut his eyes while Mr.. Corning reached directly over him for the shelf in the closet. He was so close to Da'Quan he could feel his body heat and smell his underarm deodorant inches away from his nose. He grabbed an attaché case, took it to the bed, opened it and pulled out a chrome Desert Eagle. Da'Quan's eyes bulged from their sockets as he began to ask for forgiveness out of fear of getting shot dead in the closet. Mr.. Corning cocked it, smiled and stuffed it in the small of his back as he mumbled, "I don't know who this bitch fucking wit, but G Corn gon lay his ass down where he stands if he comes my way, huh." He then put the case under the bed and quickly made his way back out the door. Da'Quan's body was exhausted and all he wanted to do was get the hell out of this house and go home. His nerves were like spaghetti noodles in hot water by now. Da'Quan stood limp as he could hear him tell Elizabeth, "OK, sweetheart, lock up. I'm gone." The door slammed and Da'Quan didn't move an inch until he heard his eighty-five black on black Porsche 911 Carrera fire up and reverse out of the driveway. Soon after, Da'Quan could hear Elizabeth's shower start to run and he knew he'd have to make a break for the door soon. He gave it like three minutes before coming out of the closet. When he did he went to the drawer, grabbed the bag of coke plus what he had and quietly eased to the front door. Although he wanted to see Liz's naked ebony body, he played it safe and slid out the front door. Once he was at the curb he began jogging to his shoes with a pocket full of dope and jewels. Ms. Lee sat on her front porch with leaves and shrubbery all over her talking on her cordless phone. She began yelling, "Hey you, hey you," and simultaneously ranting into the phone, "I'm telling you, goddammit, he just ran out. Get yo asses over here, the nigger is getting away. He's a black chubby sonofabitch in a white T-shirt and blue pants, I'm telling you. Oh shit, the hell with you. Let me speak to the captain, goddammit, the nigger is getting away"

Da'Quan, after hearing the quadriplegic squealing, snatched up his shoes and bolted at top speed to Tone's momma's Buick. When he made it to the car, Tone sat with a concerned look on his face and asked, "Damn, cuzz, I thought you was caught up, cuzz, what chu get my nigga?"

Da'Quan, who was out of breath, thought quickly on his feet and said "Let's go! That ole crippled bitch calling the police!" Tone instantly fired up the Buick and took off. After catching his breath Da'Quan pulled out a ring and a pair of earrings and gave them to Tone while saying, "Cuz, that was a weak lick. This all I got, which one you want?"

Tone took the earrings, which were worth more, and said, "My bad, cuz. I thought they had way more shit, Da'Quan." Da'Quan shook his head in disgust to play it off. He couldn't wait to get to his house and sort the other four watches, three rings, two gold chains and quarter pound of coke he acquired from the Dumb Bitch.

Chapter 6
SHERM STICK

OCTOBER 1990 • 21 years old

Longing for home no matter what the distance is a natural emotional connection directly related to the comfort of one's environment. Certain people, odors, monumental landmarks all contribute to the makeup of anybody's individual characteristic behavior. As humans, our belief systems, thought processes, ideologies and response to external stimuli all equate to whom we ultimately become in our growth process. Humans are sponges equipped with the ability to adapt to various conditions for the sake of survival.

Da'Quan by now was a proven chameleon, able to comfortably adapt to the raw and deadly streets of South Central as well as the serene surroundings of his college environment. His inner city upbringing was a valuable tool in identifying the differences between urban practices as opposed to the South Central culture. Although he enjoyed the unflustered college habitat filled with opportunity and beautiful women, he, without a doubt, missed the edgy and unpredictable mystique that was attached to his South Central roots. Every other weekend when his mother, Lillian, and grandmother, Delilah, would go shopping he knew there would be a sideload of groceries waiting on him. On one particular Friday, he found himself on the 405 navigating to LA through the rugged gridiron traffic. The opaque fog that clouded the highway made it even more of a challenge to get to his destination. The stop-and-go rhythm on the freeway had gotten so bad he was able to roll a neatly packed chronic blunt and fire it up with no qualms. To calm his befuddled nerves, he'd rewound Ice Cube's, "The Nigga You Love To Hate". The angry, heartfelt vocals along with the classic Steve Arrington "Weak at the Knees" sample without fail calmed the savage beast on the streets during that era. After half of the blunt was smoked and seven repeats of the anthem, Da'Quan was pulling up on his grandmother's street eager to see the love in his goodie bags. Sirens and multiple patrol cars were a dead giveaway that he was no longer cruising through the composed streets of the valley. At night in the valley, pedestrians walked their dogs with plastic bags in hand for the waste. In South Central, citizens moved hastily often looking over their shoulders to avoid any potential life-threatening danger. To add insult to injury, the dense fog gave his neighborhood an added sense of terror considering in those parts anything goes. As he pulled up in his grandmother's driveway, he noticed his mom's car was gone and the place was completely dark, which was a clear sign no one was home. With no plan B, he decided to kick back and wait on the duo to arrive back with his package. Feeling safe in his childhood surroundings, he decided to lay back and let the angry and hostile message of Ice Cube saturate his spirit. Just as he drifted into a weed-induced coma there was a series of hard knocks on his passenger window.

Bang, Bang, Bang"! The knocks on his window sent his heart into a violent beating frenzy as he had fallen into complete unconsciousness. It took a minute for him to gather his bearings as to who this huge silhouette of a man was standing outside of his truck. The fog combined with his imposing figure was enough for Da'Quan to grab under the seat for his .380 pistol. He now knew he was capable of shooting someone, and if his life depended on it, he'd do it again. Da'Quan slowly turned his radio down and as he did he began to recognize the familiar voice of OG saying, "General, General, it's me, my boy, OG face cuh." The aggressive palpitations in his heart began to subside as he recognized the offbeat batshit voice that could only be OG Scarface.

Scarface, whose birth name was Tony, lived two houses down from Da'Quan's grandmother. If he knew you he'd position himself to you almost as a pet or mascot, full of love and loyalty. If he didn't, you may find him standing over your bedside, sweaty and inebriated off of hallucinogen, with an icepick in his hands trembling nervously. Tony had been raised by his mother's pimp, Chris, who had grown attached to him during their turbulent pimp-hoe relationship. It was rumored that when she overdosed off of heroin, Chris, who was her pimp at the time, took in the young three-year-old, presumably out of guilt. Tony aka OG had grown up on the wrong side of the tracks, quickly earning the reputation as a menace in the neighborhood. By nine years old, he was climbing through windows for the older homies learning how to steal anything from pistols, jewelry, money and any other valuables that would bring street credibility to his name. He said when he first started they'd have him climb through the window and open the door for them to steal the valuables, but after a while he'd cash in on the valuables before opening the door for them. His criminal IQ, minus the drug use, was extremely high. Being a product of the Black Panther era he quickly learned about the disparate treatment that Blacks encountered from their white counterparts. The countless years he spent in juvenile facilities each summer lifting weights and fighting fires matured him into an imposing figure to be reckoned with. His light skin and long hair made him an instant draw to the ladies each time he was released from bondage. He began exercising his hand in pimping after seeing the power he managed to maintain over the women in his life. He rarely spoke about his mother, but when he did he referred to her as, "that dirty bitch." Quite to the contrary, he adored Chris and lovingly referred to him as papa. There was wide speculation that Chris was in fact his biological father, but no one had the balls to question the truth behind the scenario. OG had another moniker around the neighborhood as well; his enemies referred to him as Scarface. After he went upstate for an attempted murder on a peace officer, he came home with a telephone cord. This was a deep slash on his face from his earlobe to the corner of his mouth. It would be a permanent reminder to never to talk too much about prison business under any circumstance.

Now at ease, Da'Quan rolled down his window saying, "Damn, Face, why the fuck you banging on my window like that? What up, cuzzo?" Scarface chuckled sadistically replying, "My boy, my boy, can't be sleeping out here when the goons and goblins be lurking my boy." His laugh was wicked and had an underlying vibe of hate within it. After he gathered himself he continued, "Whew wee, my boy, I know you out there at college in La La land, but the homies out here puttin' in major work on the enemies, General. We filled up the casket man's pockets, ya dig my boy?" Da'Quan nodded his head at the crucial game Scarface was dropping on him. Scarface knew that Da'Quan wasn't a punk, but he also knew he wasn't a heartless gangster such as himself. He would always act as a street mentor's guardian to Da'Quan, who was more than a decade younger than him. Scarface went on to ask him, "What chu doing here anyways, my boy, ya mami and granny out doing they thing?"

Da'Quan glanced at the dark house and responded, "I see, I see, shit big homie I just rolled down to check on them and see what's popping in the hood cuh, ya dig! Shit, after this ima head back out to the valley folks and run my game on 'em."

He responded "As you should, General," along with a fist dap. After chuckling, there was a brief pause before Scarface proposed, "Well look here, my boy, can you give uncle Scarface a ride, my boy, please?"

Da'Quan hesitated, looked at the clock on his radio, took a deep breath and complied, "Yeah, I guess, OG, but where the fuck you gotta go, cuzzo?"

Scarface's face lit up like a kid on Christmas as he excitedly replied, "Not far, General, not far at all, my boy. Just hold up, don't leave me. I gotta go to the house real quick, hold up my boy." He turned and hobbled on his beat up legs down to his dad's spot while Da'Quan sat shaking his head wishing he would have slept through Scarface's knocks on his window. Da'Quan lit the rest of his blunt and turned Ice Cube back on while he waited.

Moments later, Scarface jumped in the truck with real specific instructions. The cab of his truck went instantly from the fresh aroma of chronic weed to a mix of weed, sherm chemicals, jheri curl activator and unwashed armpits. His demeanor went from jovial and meek to assertive and demanding. His breath reeked of Silver Satin almost blinding Da'Quan with the potent vapors from his choppers. He turned the music all the way down and started finger pointing with specific details, "OK, OK, General. Go up King, make a left and get to the 110, my boy, and slow this thang down, we moving too fast, my boy, we moving too fast." Da'Quan could sense he was up to something but played it cool in the meanwhile. As Da'Quan navigated through the foggy streets, OG glanced over at him and repeatedly said, "Yeah, General, I know you love this gangster shit. I see it all on you, yeah General I can tell my boy." Da'Quan remained silent as he focused on the foggy road ahead. Scarface continued, "Yeah, General I know you love this gangster shit, my boy, I can see it in your eyes." He began chuckling loudly in his batshit tone, sending funky breath fumes throughout the cab of Da'Quan's truck, causing him to roll down his window. Scarface went on, "But, my boy, I see you as a cold guerilla pimp, General. You got them hoes I really like, the one with the braids. Where's that one, General? She look like a cold freak." Da'Quan knew he was referring to KeKe, but he just nodded and kept navigating through the dense weather conditions. Once they hooked a right onto the freeway, Scarface became even more demanding. "OK, my boy, look here, when we get there all I want you to do is sit in here and keep the truck running. You got me?"

Out of frustration Da'Quan angrily blurted, "What up, cuz, what kind of mission you got me on?"

Scarface looked and gave him a barbarous smile while speaking calmly, "Look, General, turn this damn rap down. Just relax. Is you nervous my boy?"

Da'Quan took a deep breath and responded, "Cuzz, just do what you gotta do and get the fuck outta here. That's it!" Da'Quan thought to himself, *Why in the fuck is it so many orders and what the fuck is this retarded mutha-fucka trying to pull off?* Just then Scarface began pointing to the off ramp nervously with his index finger. As they made their way down Manchester to the east side, Da'Quan was apprehensive about the whole situation but figured OG couldn't be as dumb as he looked.

By now Scarface's demeanor grew increasingly high strung the closer they got to their destination. He began sweating profusely and mumbling to himself until he finally blurted, "Slow down, General. Make a right on Eighty-fifth and slow down." The block was dark and foggy with a bunch of older model sedans and pickup trucks lining the curb on the block. He began fumbling in his crotch until he pulled out a black .38 revolver. He then began looking through the fog with squinted eyes while continuously giving directions, "OK, my boy, turn left right here and slow all the way down." Da'Quan shook his head while staring at Scarface thinking, *What the fuck is this high lunatic gon do with this gun and pair of bum legs?* He drove nervously with the notion of, *Here we are on the east side. I'm with a career criminal, two loaded pistols and a half ounce of weed all in the cab of my truck. If we get stopped I'm for sure headed to jail.*

Scarface planted his eyes on a rundown house with two old beat up vans in the front yard. There was an old malnourished hound dog chained to one of the vans. He was only visible due to the flickering porch light near the front door. The dog had one eye and jerked the chain as if he were tired of being enslaved in the cold misty weather. Scarface ordered, "OK, my boy, hurry up. Drive down some more and park right there behind that school bus.

Da'Quan eased up to the curb slowly, cut off his lights and demanded, "OK, cuzz, what the fuck kinda mission we on, Face? Be real."

He gave Da'Quan a snag-toothed grin and replied, "You wanna be a gangsta, my boy? You wanna be a gangsta? Then you gotta do what gangstas do, General." Da'Quan's chest heaved in anger as he silently stared into Scarface's dilated pupils with conviction. Scarface then surveyed the block and looked back at the rundown house with the flickering porch light and said, "Look, my boy, imma go down the street and talk to some OGs. When I get back we going straight to the hood my boy. Just don't panic, General." Da'Quan just nodded his head and agreed with the plan. He realized he'd come too far now to turn back. Scarface then checked the barrel of his .38 and in an illiterate, childlike manner counted the bullets in his artillery, "One, umm, two, umm, three, four, five, umm, six." He then placed the weapon in his pocket, opened the door and proceeded to hobble down the dark foggy street. As Scarface disappeared into the dense cloud of fog, Da'Quan's heart began to race, as he had no clue what to expect in the next few moments. He sat thinking, *Damn, I could be chilling at Mom's house, or fucking with a bitch right now. How the fuck did I let this lame get me out on a bullshit ass mission, fuck!* He wanted to peel out but Scarface was an OG and he knew he had to follow the code of the streets at all costs. While these thoughts ran rapidly through his mind he noticed there were some high beam lights coming slowly from the rear in the fog. The closer the car got, the more he could see the siren's silhouette on top of the slow moving vehicle. When the car passed by the desolate house that Scarface went to, the cops flashed a flashlight on the house as if they had a vested interest in the location. By now Da'Quan's heart began beating like two jackrabbits fucking in the wild. The squad car kept rolling at a snail's pace until they were parallel to Da'Quan's running truck.

Da'Quan looked straight ahead as the two crewcut white pigs shone the light into his truck, sending him nearly into a cardiac arrest. They peered through the cab of his truck through the extreme murky conditions of the night. As they opened the squad car door, Da'Quan shut his eyes and raised his hands from the steering wheel. He wanted to avoid getting shot to pieces by the crooked LAPD unit. By the grace of God as the squad door opened they received a call. As soon as the pig took the call the passenger abruptly shut his door and the duo smashed off with no delay. Da'Quan melted like ice cream on a hot grill as he slumped over the steering wheel soaking in body sweat. Just then he heard three gunshots in the distance. *Pop! Pop! Pop!* Through his rearview, in the thick of the fog, he could see Scarface hobbling towards the truck as fast as he could with a plastic shopping bag in hand. When he made it to the car, he nervously demanded, "Come on, my boy, let's go. Come on, General, punch it, cuzz!" Without hesitation Da'Quan gladly took off and began navigating to the freeway with purpose. In his rearview he noticed the malnourished hound dog turning circles harum-scarum, still chained to the bumper of the old parked van. Scarface smelled like a chemistry experiment gone bad while he fumbled through the pungent plastic bag. He then began grinning from ear to ear, revealing his rotted smile in glee, as he pulled out a huge mason jar filled with a clear liquid. The cab of the truck was almost uninhabitable from flagrant chemical odor. Da'Quan rolled down his window gasping for air while Scarface, who reeked like a musty lab rat, began wiping the gun power from his hands and face with a mildewed rag. He began laughing as he said in a worry-free tone, "Well, my boy, hee hee hee, we got about two thousand in the lab, my boy. Now you a gangster, my boy, whew wee!" He looked at Da'Quan for a response who just drove cautiously paying no regard to the antics of OG. He just wanted to get back to his grandmother's house and get rid of the derelict in his passenger seat. Scarface continued, "My boy, my boy, never leave witnesses. Don't ever forget, my boy"! Da'Quan's chest heaved as he became dizzy from the fumes as well as now knowing he was an accomplice to a robbery and possible homicide for two thousand dollars' worth of formaldehyde. Scarface chuckled in his batshit tone while saying, "My boy, use a gangster now, my boy, use a gangsta!"

Chapter 7
APPLE FRITTERS

AUGUST 1980 • 10 years old

Every three to four days Jose the donut man would drive through the neighborhood and sweeten up everybody's day. Jose had the largest selection of candy and tasty pastries in the area. The sound of the handheld Guiro cowbells combined with the Hispanic accent yelling "rosquillas, rosquillas, o rosquillas," meant the warm baked donuts had arrived. Rosquilla, which means donut in Spanish, was more than likely the only untranslated word blacks understood in Da'Quan's neighborhood at the time.

Jose the donut man who couldn't have been more than thirty-three or thirty-four at the time had a very savvy business mindset. In his teens and early twenties, Jose resided in every correctional facility from YA to Los Padrinos, before earning a five-year stretch in Soledad state prison. His hardened face couldn't mask the criminal lifestyle he had once been absorbed in. On his left wrist he had a tattoo of a grandfather clock with no hands, which was symbolic of doing extended amounts of time behind the wall. He learned and mastered the art of making donuts and pastries in culinary classes he took while serving time. Jose had been convicted of attempted murder and was enduring a five-year sentence for the hail of bullets he rained on rival gang members at a picnic. Jose was a well-respected member of the Mexican Mafia known as "La eMe." He decided after his last stint to put his skill set and business savvy to use. Behind the wall he survived financially off of the donuts and pastries he'd smuggle from the kitchen to his cell. Inmates praised his baked goods especially his famous apple fritters. Once he was released his father, Jose Sr., encouraged him to continue to bake and sell his pastries on the outside. Jose's dad explained that if he sold every pastry at sixty-five cents and every donut for fifty cents, he'd be a millionaire in ten years. His logic was that on an average of sixty-seven cents for each of 1492 items he sold was a thousand dollars. That number to Jose set the goal to make 13,428 pieces per month to make 161,136 dollars per fiscal year. He multiplied that by 10 and came up with his 1.6 million dollar plan. Jose figured the 600 thousand should cover the overhead, living expenses and hired help. He was very frugal with his earnings as he also invested heavily into the family marijuana business. His brothers ran a very noteworthy syndicate.

One sunny Wednesday evening Jose was making his route down Thirty-ninth. The cowbells rang as the young entrepreneur screamed passionately through his loudspeakers "rosquillas, rosquillas o rosquillas!" The crooning voice blaring was an instant indicator to scrape up whatever loose change you could to buy an authentic pastry from the legend himself. As the familiar sounds of the cowbells fortissimo came near, Da'Quan raced into the house to ask his grandmother for some loose change to buy a pastry. He raced in the door yelling "grandma eh grandma where you at? I need a dollar for the donut man"! Delilah, who sat intimately on the toilet doing a word search in an annoyed tone replied, "Dammit, boy, you must think I'm made of money."

Da'Quan, in a desperate attempt to finagle some loose change, made the offer she couldn't refuse, "Grandma, you know you want one of those warm apple fritters to go with yo ice cream tonight." There was a brief moment of silence as her sweet tooth sent a passive message to the sympathetic side of her brain. She replied grudgingly, "Oh shoot go look in the Bible on the coffee table and look in the book of Solomon and take three dollars. Now that's it. Just three dollars."

Da'Quan happily replied, "OK, Grandma, only three. We good. I don't steal God's bread," as he chuckled and rummaged through the good book looking for greenbacks. By the time Da'Quan made his way to the truck, there was a line of loyal customers impatiently waiting on their sugar fix. The first person Da'Quan ran across was MC, who stood with his back glued to the side of Jose's 1972 Ford Econoline van. The restored van was well kept with bright yellow paint and colorful doughnut images displaying on the sides. As Da'Quan approached the truck, MC, who looked infuriated through his dark beady eyes, asked Da'Quan, "Eh cuz, I know you got a quarter." Da'Quan could instantly sense the urgency in his tone. To MC this was to be his dinner, dessert and possibly breakfast the next day if it lasted. Da'Quan wanted to lie and deny him but MC s eyes were plastered to the ones that sat in Da'Quan's palm.

In a moment of brilliance Da'Quan replied "Cuzz, I would, but these for my granny."

MC looked as the hunger pains in his stomach impelled him to beg relentlessly, "C'mon, cuz, what if I asked her then?" Da'Quan reached into his pocket and pulled out a shiny new quarter and dropped it into the dirty outstretched hand of MC. MC replied, "Thanks, cuh, you a real ass nigga. This punk ass Mexican don't wanna hook no black peoples up wit his nasty ass penitentiary donuts."

Jose overheard the comment by MC and as he continued to graciously serve the community, roared from the inside of his truck "Alejarse de mi camioneta, hijo de puta," which meant "Get away from my truck, dirty muthafucka!" MC, in an attempt to dent Jose's van, propelled the bottom of his foot with great force to the side of the van. The line of onlookers watched the whole fiasco in fright and disgust. Mr.. Green, who had a strong dislike for MC, yelled from the rear of the line "Never mind him, Jose. He ain't got no home training my friend." Jose, who had a limited English vocabulary, just smiled at Mr.. Green's remark, sending him a gestured wink. As Jose continued to keep his composure, MC antagonistically stared at Jose through his shallow dark beady eyes with hate. Jose avoided eye contact with him and continued on taking care of his loyal patrons. "Que te gustaria mi amigo?" As the money gravitated to Jose's palms, MC became more and more livid with what he was witnessing. In a moment of uncontrollable rage, MC blurted at the top of his lungs "all this wetback do is come take our hard-earned money, sell us this cheap ass overpriced bullshit he made in his mammy's kitchen and take our coins to go live like a king on the eastside. I ain't dumb, Jose, the donut woman. I seen yo lowrider in Compton fool off Piru and Roseccrans, nigga. My cousin stayed over there. This puto got money y'all. Huh, we riding the bus and walking paying for this fool to live like a king while he feeds us this garbage that ain't good for us in any way."

Mr.. Green in utter shock at MC's observation quietly had a newfound respect for Michael's intellect. Jose, out of anger, grabbed his .38 caliber. His older cousin and driver, Manuel, who rarely spoke told him "It ain't the right time S.A., not now. His day will come." Jose trembled with anger as he placed the pistol back in the stash. Manuel held up a huge roll of assorted dollar bills wrapped in rubber bands and smiled saying, "You want this or three hots and cot holmes?" Jose took a deep breath and continued working his crowd. Jose cracked a devilish grin and stared at MC directly in his beady eyes. He then blurted angrily "con quién crees que estás hablando hijo de Puta?" which meant "Who you think you talking to motherfucker?"

As MC started walking away he sarcastically told the onlookers "He just taking y'all money, getting rich and not giving shit to our community but diabetes. I'd rather eat vegetables over a plate of shit than give him my money. We oughtta rob his wetback ass, cuh." Jose gestured a knife slitting his throat as he replied "Corta la Cabeza hijo de Puta," which translated to "I'll cut your head off mutherfucker." MC blessed him with the middle finger gesture as he tracked down the block in search of more mischief to encounter. The further away MC walked the less tense the vibe around the truck became. Jose after a moment regained his composure and continued to service his customers. Once Da'Quan made it to the front of the line Jose told him, "Tu amigo no bueno holmes," translating to "Your friend is no good buddy." He looked Da'Quan into his eyes and in broken English said, "You much better, he no good, he not gone live a long life my friend, no no." Da'Quan nodded his head all the time with his eyes glued to the enormous display of warm donuts and pastries at his disposal. As his mouth drooled over the rich handmade desserts, Jose asked "Que te gustaria?" Da'Quan paused, took a deep breath while staring at the glass display of goodies and while handing over his three dollars, convincingly replied, "One chocolate donut and two apple fritters."

Chapter 8
INCEST

APRIL 1982 • 12 years old

Friday afternoon for most adolescents is a treasured window of time during the school week. Once the final bell rings and students flood the corridors, a sense of euphoria encompasses the institution, faculty included.

It had been a long and tedious week, but Da'Quan managed to nurse a five-dollar bill the whole week with plans to load up on chips and sugary snacks for the weekend. The students as well as the faculty were anxious to leave on this particular Friday. Even the normal kiss asses who ate crow and dropped dimes for brownie points got doors slammed and bags zipped on them that day. Horseplay and an idle conversation were at a minimum while the security guards acted as shepherds to the large flocks of students. In the midst of the shenanigans, teachers yelling, paper throwing and laughter, Da'Quan managed to keep his eyes glued on his schoolyard crush, Amber, who came sashaying down the hall gracefully as if she were the sole daughter of the earth. Her brown freckles which contrasted against her honey-complected skin tone combined with her copper colored eyes made her a treat to admire. He wanted to stop her and invite her to Shabazz, which was a Muslim restaurant that had the best french fries on the west side. He knew he could score major points if she conceded to it but out of fear of rejection he let her pass. He also didn't want to part with his weekend zoom zoom and wham wham money either. He figured the odds of her taking him seriously weren't worth the risk of a treat-free weekend. Amber walked by, leaving whiffs of sweet jasmine as her naturally seductive movements mesmerized the adoring eyes of Da'Quan. He yearned to be close to her, alone from the distractions of everyday life, staring into her enticing eyes while feeling the warmth from her breath on his face. There was a certain mana about her presence that was captivating. Amber then glided on by, appearing to move in slow motion, displaying the beauty of a goddess in pure bliss. Da'Quan, however, had his mind made up that he'd just go to Lucky Liquor and load up on his weekend junk food as planned.

The walk to the store was filled with the sounds of passing cars and screeching bus brakes. As Da'Quan made his way to the liquor store, he saw Max, the Japanese owner and face of Lucky Liquor, standing out front taking hard drags from an unfiltered Camel cigarette. He noticed Da'Quan approaching, took one last hard pull from the Camel before tossing the butt aimlessly into the street. He released a huge cloud of smoke and said, "Mr.. Da'Quan what chu need buddy?"

Da'Quan responded, "Same ole same, Max, hope you got some crumb cakes today." Max pointed to the Hostess rack where there was a full rack of all fresh desserts. Da'Quan began loading up on Doritos, crumb cakes, Twinkies and soda, eager to get his weekend binge started. While trying to cradle all of his sugary items to the register, he heard a sweet familiar voice say, "Oh and I'll pay for his too." To Da'Quan's pleasant surprise it was his cute friend Zeelah at the register handing Max a twenty-dollar bill with a monumental smile on her face. Da'Quan sighed quietly knowing that he had saved five dollars and had more than enough junk food for the weekend. The two united and both made their way out of the store after Max handed her the change and wished them a nice day . Da'Quan and Zeelah were childhood friends that naturally bonded and shared their most intimate issues to one another. There was nothing but pure adoration between the two as they always engaged in quality conversations and laughs.

Zeelah jokingly told him, "Next time snacks are on you, fat boy."

Da'Quan responded, "I got you, skeletor." They both laughed and began opening their assorted snacks as they walked. Da'Quan then asked with a mouth full of Twinkie cream "Where you headed, Z, and how you got so much money to blow on bullshit?" She gave a sheepish smile and continued to suck on her cherry red blow pop. After a brief moment she replied, "I'm going to my aunt's house for the weekend and my sa, sa, sorry ass dad gave me the money."

She then burst flagrantly into tears causing Da'Quan to give her a perplexed look while asking, "What the fuck, Z, what's wrong?" Silence consumed the moment as she attempted to gather herself. Zeelah clutched his arm with a firm grip saying, "If I tell you, you promise not to tell a soul nigga?"

Da'Quan replied compassionately, "Naw I ain't gon say shit, but if you don't wanna say nothing it's cool, Z." She tried to stop sniffling as she wiped the heavy tears from her beautiful grey eyes.

She stopped walking in an attempt to muster up the words to speak. She began by saying, "Well, you know my dad?" Da'Quan nodded yes as he stuffed cinnamon crumb cakes down his throat. She continued, "Well, umm, he be tripping doing stuff to me I can't stand, D ! He, he, well he did it again today." She suddenly released a floodgate of tears and placed her head gently on Da'Quan's shoulder. He stood dumbfounded on how to react, as he could sense there was something terribly wrong going on by her response. She gathered herself enough to say, "Well, well when my momma's not home he makes me get in the shower and I mean he stands there watching me the whole time, D, saying if I don't obey him that God will send me to hell for disrespecting my father." Da'Quan gave a confused look like OK and. She went on, "Well, today he did it again." She burst into another flurry of tears.

"Did what?" Da'Quan responded.

She tried to reply, "He, he, he ummm, he—"

Da'Quan angrily blurted, "What the fuck the nigga do, Z?"

She screamed at the top of her lungs, "He makes me suck his dick until it's hard enough to fuck me, D, that's what the fuck he does and he don't stop until I'm crying and bleeding, D, OK my dad is the devil." Da'Quan instantly stopped chewing and looked at her in disbelief. He had never heard of something so perverted and nasty. The thought of parental incest had never crossed his mind, as he never had a clue that this type of behavior existed.

"Whaaaat the fuck, naw not yo daddy, the nigga wit the black Benz?" She shook her head yes while wiping her pouring tears with the collar of her shirt. The expression on her desolate face gave no indication of falsification.

She was a ruined spirit being sexually molested by her biological father and had nowhere or no one to turn too. Da'Quan tried to formulate something appropriate or consoling to say but couldn't muster up the words leaving him speechless. The two continued to walk in silence slowly until they reached Da'Quan's grandparents' house. Da'Quan looked deep into her hopeless eyes, grabbed her by her arms firmly with both hands, as he finally exclaimed, "Why don't you tell your mom or call the police Z?"

She snatched herself from his grip and frantically blurted, "It ain't that easy, D, it's my fucking dad, for one, and I don't wanna go to hell plus my momma wouldn't take my side anyway, D. He got the money, which means he got the power!" At this point there was nothing Da'Quan's inexperienced mind could logically come up with. He placed his arm gently around her as she melted like burning candle wax in his arms. As her body jerked from her gut-wrenching sob all he could wonder was why was his friend going through so much turmoil. The abuse she was suffering through at home was a dead giveaway to her promiscuous actions with the boys in the neighborhood. This was her way of lashing out and looking for the comfort of love she lacked in her home. Da'Quan's heart began to accelerate beating double time as the story of her home life made him nervous and uncomfortable.

She slowly gathered herself and chuckled since her tear ducts were empty and said nonchalantly, "This nigga been doing this for two years, D, and every time he's done he hands me money and tells me this is a reward from God for satisfying his will." Da'Quan had no idea what that meant or how to respond.

Just then Delilah came to the screen door. "Hey y'all little lovebirds, how was school?"

Da'Quan responded, "Grandma, ain't no love birds here and school was school." His tone was so drab she knew they didn't want to be bothered with her idle gibberish. She smirked and turned around and walked to the kitchen. Before she made it to the kitchen she yelled, "Y'all must not want none of my mustard greens and hot water cornbread then. Oh well more for me." Da'Quan stared at Zeelah as if she was an alien. The story she just revealed made her seem like a call girl to her daddy. He thought to himself, *Damn, bitch, you only fourteen and you've been taking grown man dick for over two years.* He shook his head in disbelief as they both sat silently for the next hour counting the moments until the sun began to set.

Chapter 9
BATTERAM

OCTOBER 1985 • 16 years old

The year was 1985 early in the fall season when school resumed. Toddy Tee and Mixmaster Spades singalong hood anthem "The Batteram" graced the 1580 KDAY airwaves 24-7. The crack cocaine epidemic had exploded and there was disposable income from drug trafficking in every neighborhood from Compton to Bel Air. President Reagan's crooked administration helped fund the Nicaraguan Contras in the infamous Iran Contra scandal. Los Angeles ghettos finally got a taste of the sweet financial fruits never revealed to them in prior decades. The west coast was in a full transitional phase. Natural afros were an obsolete style, as most male and females opted for the new and highly touted Jheri curl. Gang members with business savvy now had a viable source of income to provide for their families and neighborhoods. Whoever had the direct connect to the source of the dope ruled. Power was delegated to the man who could supply the best product charging the most reasonable price consistently. By now doctors, lawyers, teachers, and entertainers who survived the cocaine snow blizzard of the 70s were now the sacrificial lambs for this powerhouse drug. Beautiful women with full figures became thin and zombie-like with lesions and bruises from the dark life of crack use. There were thousands of women and men who attempted to sell their children for a ten-minute high. The addiction had people stealing from their immediate family and closest friends. TVs, stereos, microwaves, pistols and sex all became items and luxuries available for the dope man. In most neighborhoods crack spots opened and closed like general businesses do. With the money came the gun trade and turf wars. Most OGs gave passes if the money was right but there was always a hardhead to disrupt the financial harmony with a relentless gangbanger mentality.

The police were often jealous of the dope dealer who lived or appeared to live the life they desired too. Many envious cops became liaisons to kingpins and sold dope from raids to friends and family members. Trust was uncommon as the astronomical incomes smeared friendships and family ties. Oaths were broken due to the life-changing paydays that accompanied the wicked crack game. The addiction to fast money was actually worse than the addiction to the drug simply because there was no other way for undereducated people to accrue these large sums of money in such a short period of time.

Da'Quan made his way early around 6:45 a.m. headed to his bus stop. While the cold air prompted him to walk briskly, he couldn't help but notice four officers on each end of his block congregated with deadly weaponry and riot gear. They stood in a semi huddle like a ball squad putting a play together. He stared momentarily at the clan with a muddled look on his face. He had never seen so many officers congregated on his block in his lifetime. They were dressed in bulletproof vests complete with LAPD helmets and riot shields. Each officer had huge iron-laced billy clubs and mean mugged every car that passed by that chilly fall morning. By now, neighbors were flocking to their porches to see what the fleet of officers was preparing for. Ma Duke and Ms. Alma stood boldly in the front of their prospective homes keeping an eagle eye on the events taking place. Da'Quan walked over to Ma Duke, "Good morning, Ma," he said humbly as they both kept their eyes glued to the group of action-starved cops.

Ma Duke took a sip from her steamy mug of black coffee and replied, "Good morning, baby, what chu think these old no good bastards up to this morning?"

Da'Quan replied, "I, I, I don't know, I've never seen so many feds in one place before, Ma."

She went on to say, "I hope you and that boy Tone, Tony, or whatever his name is ain't in too deep with that bullshit." She grabbed him sternly by his chin as he attempted to avoid direct eye contact with her.

He confidently replied "Naw, Ma, we ain't doing nothing like that on this level at all I promise."

She smirked with a look of doubt and said, "Yeah baby cause these devils ain't playing and y'all are the ones they love making examples out of, honey. They've been doing it for decades. See, sweetie, they look at y'all like animals and they just make a living off killing and locking y'all up." She took another sip from her mug and squinted as the steam from here muddy coffee fogged up her forever faithful bifocal lenses. She shook her head slowly and mumbled "Goddamn pussyfied pigs."

Ms. Alma stood tight-lipped while being totally engrossed on the activities of the law enforcement. She had disregarded Da'Quan's and Ma Dukes's existence as she stood high on her tippy toes with her arms folded. You would think from the energy she exerted in her spectating that maybe Jesus was passing out 100-dollar bills on the corner. Meanwhile as the action simmered, Ma Duke looked to the ground in deep thought as she began to ramble, "When I was young, my stepdaddy, they called him Shag, and when I say scandalous, let me tell you, that nasty black mutherfucker had demons' blood running through his veins." As she went into detail about her stepdad an enraged frown grew on her silky smooth face. Her chest began to noticeably heave as she continued reminiscing, "That sonofabitch would come home drunk every Saturday night talking about this here is Shag's house, and you, woman, is my property, now go make me something eat, Daddy's home! I wanted to kill his ass. Oh Lord, the way he would just go upside my momma's head, and for nothing, I mean he'd hit her and she'd look unreal like a rag doll flying across the living room. He cheated and gave her something, I'm not sure what, but she was mad, telling him he got her burning and itching when she pee, um hm, sure did. I just never understood why she left my daddy to be with this lowlife. Well, anyway, to make a long story short my older sister Nola swore if this man beat our momma one more time that she'd kill him." She paused momentarily as the story seemed to trigger a deep hidden emotion, "So anyway, Shag came home drunk as usual and he and my mom began arguing back and forth about booze and women and sure enough he reared back and slapped my momma across the kitchen floor. My sister Nola stormed to her dresser drawer, pulled out a Derringer, walked into the kitchen and shot Shag in his chest. His face looked lost and unsure if what had happened was real as he grabbed the cabinet door before he dropped to the floor. His hands and legs trembled while his eyes wandered around the room looking for anybody to lend him a hand for that moment. I could see the blood pump out his chest like a faucet, Da'Quan. We all just stood around him and watch as his eyes began rolling back into his head. We were in shock and didn't know what to do. I was like seven or eight. I wasn't sure if this was even real or fake." She chuckled and shook her head before saying, "My sister told me years later she had snuck his pistol from his leather coat when he was drunk one night. Her boyfriend at the time showed her how to use it and the rest, well, the rest is history."

Da'Quan stood in awe before replying, "Wow, Ma Dukes, yo sister wasn't playing. What the police do?"

"Well my mother lost her mind. She fell out crying over his dead body until they pulled up. They took my sister Nola to a girls home and she stayed a couple of years until she graduated high school. By then my mother's sister sent for me and I haven't been home since." She took another squig from her mug and as the caffeine saturated her veins she became somewhat energetic. Her braless boobs swayed underneath her poncho as she nervously paced the concrete. From both ends of the block two officers approached the huddle of neighbors who stood dumbfounded looking for answers about what was taking place. They stopped a few feet away from the neighbors as a now spry and energetic Ma Duke blurted, "What the hell y'all over here doing bothering us god-fearing working folks? Shit, why don't you go after some real criminals, you pieces of shit." She fought with every bit of willpower she had to suppress her razor sharp tongue. The demons from her past seeped through her Christian exterior unloading a barrage of slurs at the unconcerned officers. "Y'all ain't shit but a bunch of pawns for the powers that be, baby! Huh, y'all need to earn ya money, go after the killers and real gangstas. Guess that's asking too much from a team of vaginas."

With that comment one of the young redneck rookies stormed over to the uneasy mob saying, "If any one of you wants to go to jail keep up the remarks and we will find space for you, I promise you." Ma Duke lost it; she was livid as she slammed her mug on the concrete causing Da'Quan to restrain her as she attempted to confront the officer face to face. The officer kept her in his peripheral vision as he smirked knowing his sarcasm struck a nerve with the elderly neighborhood activist. She began coughing up chunks of phlegm and spitting them in the area where the cops stood. Just as the cops seemed to flirt with the concept of arresting Ma Duke, there was a huge loud tank that appeared at the end of the block causing silence amongst the bickering neighbors. It sat on four huge wheels with a long steel pole out front leading the way. There was a square attachment to the front of the pole with a happy face painted on. No one had ever seen this type of machinery, and it was obvious from each dumbfounded look on the neighbors' faces. As the unfamiliar tank turned towards Mrs. Gardner's house, peoples' nerves had them biting nails, praying silently and grabbing on to one another for comfort.

Mrs. Gardner was the mean old lady who usually kept to herself unless forced to speak about staying the hell off of her lawn. The silence was deafening as the officers mounted around the tanker as it slowly made its way towards the front of Mrs. Gardner's home. Da'Quan looked with a stone face as he thought, *So this is the muthafuckin batteram.* Ma Duke began yelling, "Oh hell naw, nnnnnno I know y'all not gonna burst through Lady Gardner's front. I know you not gon do no bullshit like this!" Without further notice all the neighbors heard was "One, two, three," and without further notice, the tanker accelerated and sent the whole front end of Lady Gardner's house caving inn. Ma Duke screeched at the top of her powerful lungs, "You stupid dumb fucks y'all gots the wrong house, you fucking butt plugs!"

Two cops hurriedly made their way over to the now irate Ma Duke in hopes to calm her down without incident. She insisted, "She is in the house, you stupid assholes. Y'all might have killed an innocent woman, fucking dickheads!"

One of the cops blurted, "OK, ma'am, anymore and ima take you in!" She shamelessly flicked him off and made sure her pistol was tucked in between the folds of fat in her midsection.

As the officers entered the living room with guns cocked and loaded, the broken antique furniture along with the countless religious ornaments tipped them off that they had hit the wrong location. Just then Mrs. Gardner hobbled down the driveway with her laundry basket in hand and a confused expression on her wrinkled face. When Ma Duke realized she was alive and mobile she sighed, "Oh thank God, Lady Gardener is cool." She then went up to Mrs. Gardner and the goofball cop who was trying unsuccessfully to explain what happened and whispered, "Thank God you're OK, love, and if I were you I'd sue the department for every nickel I could get, baby. If you need me, you know where I'm at, love." She gave the cop a smug stare, harked up a chunk of phlegm and spit it within a couple of feet of the officer before turning and making her way back home. The officer looked as if he were one on one with the elderly Ma Duke he'd have her in some sort of lethal choke hold. Meanwhile the sergeant paced on the porch nervously explaining to his superior, "Yessir, the address does say Thirty-ninth street I do see now, it, it, it, well it was a bonehead mistake, yes I do know the difference between street and place sir, I can assure you, captain, we will never make another ill-advised move such as this again." His face was as red as a rose as his superior maliciously tore him a new asshole over the phone. The rookie cop still had Mrs. Gardner to the side trying to explain his obvious faux pas on this early a.m. All that could be heard was intense whimpering as she lay her head in the chest of the moron who put her in danger in the first place.

Chapter 10
DRENCHED

AUGUST 1987 • 17 years old

Balmy summer breezes, purple skies from the light of the moon highlighting energetic stars often creates moods of heightened physical arousal. Da'Quan sat on the couch in his empty dorm room sipping on his Caucasian roommate Jeff's seventeen-year-old Wild Turkey Master's keeper. The smooth warm liquid impersonated a harmless effect from its initial ingest. With each warm shot and every pull from his pinky-sized chronic joint, his testosterone levels combined with his liquid courage had his hands on the receiver of the phone debating which concubine he'd entice for the night. After scarfing down five shots of whiskey and inhaling a full indica joint, Da'Quan boldly exclaimed to himself, *OK, fuck it. Time to get some pussy!* He put the roach which was burning the prints off his fingertips down and began eagerly punching Roz's phone number. Rosalind was a brown-skinned, thick lipped, all too shapely specimen with an uncanny zest for sex. Roz was a very soft spoken spirit who let her Diana Ross-like eyes and fluid body language communicate what her mouth wouldn't. She wore little to no makeup and kept her hair neatly braided in stylish cornrows. Da'Quan met her through his Irish bed buddy, Julie. The three would often drink, smoke weed and listen to Prince in Julie's dorm on Saturday nights. Da'Quan was aware that Roz was attracted to him from her sensuous eye contact, as well as how she made her heart shaped derriere wiggle whenever she walked in his presence. He never saw her in anything but fitted sweats worn without panties. The three would get inebriated and openly discuss school, sex and future life goals amongst each other. One day as Da'Quan made his way to his dorm he heard his name being called, "Da'Quan, hey boy, turnaround," was all he heard in a sensual seductive tone. To his surprise he turned and saw Roz standing under the stairwell at his place dressed in some waist-hugging biker shorts and a wifebeater worn braless. She wore flip flops revealing her perfectly manicured toes at the base of her shapely blemish-free legs. She stood batting her oval shaped eyes staring deep into the core of his soul. Bashfully, Roz eased up to him, pressed her erect nipples against his chest and planted a libidinous kiss on his neck with her full succulent lips. She slid him a little red book that read Kama Sutra on the cover. She looked around to assure no one was listening and whispered, "Read this book and every time you come fuck me I want to do a different position until we've done every one in the book, nigga. I can't wait to feel that big black dick. White ass Julie always bragging about *Hot Boy*."

Da'Quan was flabbergasted by her gesture as he nodded his head yes while staring at the cover of the unfamiliar book on sex she handed him. He now began to see that Julie and her whole crew were freaks with ambition and he was the sexual proxy between their clique. He looked at the book, glanced at her, then looked at the book again before mustering up the nerves to say, "Shit, my punk ass roommate won't be here till tonight. Come on in; let's kick it."

She responded aggressively, "Open the door, then, nigga. Let's do Chapter 4. My little pussy been throbbing since Saturday, D." The two entered the messy frat house style dorm room immediately. As Da'Quan began picking up shirts and clothes off the floor he began feeling extremely nervous, wondering had Julie put her up to this to set him up. He knew he didn't want to fuck off his cash cow, but at the same time he'd been wanting to see how good Rosalind was in bed for quite some time. After tossing a bundle of clothes in the corner of the room he turned around to offer Roz a seat and to his surprise she stood stark naked with her index finger in her mouth staring him seductively in his eyes. He just stared at her blemish-free skin and perky nipples that stood at attention for him. His mouth dropped wide open as he was amazed at the thickness of her shaved camel foot that sat under her sexy flat abs. She took her index finger and put it in her camel foot while admiring his tall physique. Da'Quan stood in a trance-like state aware he had no condoms but was more than willing to dig in her raw if she was down with it. Suddenly a devilish grin appeared on her face as she now knew she had him where she wanted him. As she made her way to him she pulled his sweats down and eased to her knees. She grabbed his manhood, which was throbbing from blood flow, looked up into his eyes and whispered sensually, "I been dreaming about tasting you nigga." When she put the head in she instantly began moaning uncontrollably while keeping eye contact with him. She slid her long tongue up and down the shaft of his manhood causing his toes to curl almost to the point of cramping. He grabbed her head and forced the issue, naturally taking control of the situation. The more dominant he was the more it stimulated her erogenous zones causing her to squirm and moan on her knees. The noisy slurping had Da'Quan pasted against the wall vulnerable to her every command. She stood up and turned her heart shaped derriere at him demanding him, "Stick that mother fucka in me, nigga. Fuck me hard and slap my fat ass cheeks, nigga." Without delay he was pounding her unprotected from the rear following her every command. He felt dominant as she cried and moaned while still demanding he go harder and harder. Through the window, which was cracked, he noticed the Chinese girl next door pause and listen to what sounded like a raunchy porn scene. The longer she stood and listened, the harder he went as the whole situation heightened. She loudly began panting, "Come on, daddy, you feel that you feel that, ooh shit I'm cumming on that big black dick, ooh can you feel it? Omg don't cum in me, I wanna swallow it, daddy, I want you to cum in my mouth, daddy ooh shit!" The more she begged and moaned the closer he came to exploding, he held up well until she turned and looked him in his eyes like a possessed demon causing him to break. She knew exactly what she was doing as she turned around, grabbed his manhood and vacuumed the life from him through her thick full lips. She had no mercy on him as she now was in control taking complete pleasure in watching him succumb to her demands. Once he was empty he fell back on the couch shoving her to the side while he attempted to catch his breath. She tried touching on him but he shoved her hands away until he was able to regain his focus. Roz knew what she was doing as she smiled and curled up naked in the corner of his couch. Da'Quan opened his eyes as he came to only to notice her staring at him as though she was an innocent little girl. He shook his head knowing that he'd be back for more of her enticing ways. While the thoughts of their rendezvous ran through his mind, her phone just continued to ring until he realized it was time to move on to his next available option.

The Wild Turkey shots began to really attack Da'Quan's hormones causing him to aggressively punch in Ariel's phone number. Her phone began ringing and he prayed she'd pick up asap. Ariel was Da'Quan's educated courtesan who always referred to herself as a geisha. Da'Quan would often notice Ariel staring at him in Professor Obina's class but paid her little to no attention. She was a very low key female, dressing conservatively in button downs and skirts that went below her knees. She never exposed skin or her figure whatsoever. Her hair was worn in an unconventional short crop that downplayed her image even more so. One day as the blistering sun tap danced on the neck and back of Da'Quan he noticed a balloon swaying with the breeze tied to the driver side mirror of his Nissan truck. The closer he got to his truck he began to see the balloon was a pair of thick red lips. On the bottom of the balloon, propped under the windshield wiper, was a red envelope with *hello* written in extremely neat manuscript. The envelope was heavily sprayed with the aroma of White Diamonds. The scent triggered a slight hint of familiarity but he couldn't quite pinpoint the source. Before opening the envelope he quickly snatched down the balloon as other coeds walked by smiling and musing at Da'Quan's situation. When he got in the truck he opened the scented envelope and there was an all-white Hallmark card with lipstick prints all over it inside and out. He anxiously opened it and on the inside was a Trojan rubber taped neatly to the fold of the card. Da'Quan's ego soared to the edges of orbit while his eyes devoured the mystery woman's confession of lust that read, "Hey you I've been watching you for a while. Your tall sexy body and broad shoulders make me wanna climb all over you and please you in any way possible. Your breathtaking smile turns my day from ordinary to intoxicating. I love your thuggish street edge, daddy, it makes my kitty cat drool in my panties. I know you have a lot of girls that wanna get with you, I hear them talk. But I don't mind because I know they see you like I do baby. I hope this doesn't scare you but I'm very shy and I hate rejection. If you want to get to know me let the balloon fly away because I'm watching you right now. If you let it fly baby, I will reveal to you who I am I promise.

"P.s. I am not a psycho.

"I am just extremely shy! Xoxo"

Da'Quan rolled down his window and willfully let the balloon float away into the sunny spring sky. He waited for a few minutes but after there was no sign of the mystery girl he cranked up his truck and sped out of the parking lot. A week had passed and as Da'Quan approached his truck there was yet another envelope cradled under his windshield. The card had the exact same sweet aroma as the previous week. Before opening it he looked both ways over his shoulders, as he knew he was being monitored. He hopped in his truck and swiftly opened the envelope. This time it was a heart shaped card with no inscriptions or headings on the face of it. He opened it and read, "Hey you it's time to reveal to you who I am and show you how much I've been craving your sexy ass. I normally don't do this but you're not a normal dude so I don't feel bad, he he. (kisses) If you want to see who I am come by my dorm room in 20 minutes. My roommates are leaving for the weekend and I'll have it all to myself. Come to the Park apartments. I'm in building H room and 209. See ya soon D baby! Xoxoxo"

Da'Quan paused as he took it all in and closed his eyes praying this wasn't a prank or some God awful ugly chick . Thoughts of *Who is this? Why me? Wonder what she looks like?* all ran through his head. After a few moments of self-deliberation and scrutiny he started up his truck and headed towards the destination. Da'Quan pulled up in the half empty dorm parking lot which was rare. In the back of his subconscious he wondered if this was a prank or some sort of setup. The empty and quiet dorm hallways were a reminder that it was the weekend at the popular commuter school. When he finally arrived at room 209 he caught whiffs of that sweet aroma that was attached to his cards. When he arrived at the door and proceeded to knock the door just glided open slowly. When the door was all the way open he looked to the ground and saw a trail of roses similar to how Julie had once done it. He stood at the doorway nervous until he heard a sweet seductive voice say, "Well, you going to come in or not, D?" When he walked in his mouth dropped as he saw Ariel standing with a glass of champagne wearing nothing but a very high cut terry cloth bathrobe. The front of it was open revealing her sexy caramel colored cleavage that seemed to be ten times bigger than he'd imagined. She had a very sexy mole on her right breast that he kept his eyes glued to. Her beautiful brown eyes lured him right into the door into her welcoming arms. Her hair was brown and curly as if she'd just washed it. It looked a lot more inviting than the slick look she normally forced on the public. Without a word being said, he approached her and stuck his tongue down her throat. He grabbed her small derriere with his huge palms squeezing it until she put his hand in the wet of her mound. The two engaged in a heated lip lock until she dropped her robe to the floor revealing her more than developed physique. Up until this point he'd never engaged in any type of conversation with her, and now within five minutes of them being alone he was completely nude indulging salaciously with the most conservative female on campus. The fact that she was a stranger defenseless to his magnetism turned him on even more so. Her body looked pure and untouched as he maneuvered his manhood into her *drenched* womb that was tight like a balled fist. Her tightness inflated his ego as she begged him to slow down saying, "Oh my god, you're too much, baby, please stop. You're killing me but don't stop it feels so good, daddy." The veins in her forehead pierced through her skin as her nails dug deep into his upper back and shoulders. She wiggled and twisted from the discomfort of his endowment but refused to let him stop. Each time she came she announced it through gritted teeth screaming, "Oh fuck nigga did you feel her, did you feel her, oh fuck, she came again, did you feel her?" He fought to maintain his stroke but in the midst of her orgasmic fury she managed to get a vice like grip on his tool sending his DNA flying uncontrollably over her stomach and breast. They both fell to their backs gasping for air in bliss realizing they were in fact still strangers. Da'Quan reminisced on his first experience with Ariel as he sat with the phone receiver pressed tightly against his earlobe as the phone continuously rang. After repeatedly dialing his geisha he realized she was either asleep or preoccupied with another stranger as he hung up partially miffed at the situation.

As the hands of the clock spun apace and his joint dwindled into a mere roach he began desperately punching in Sharla's number. Da'Quan took a deep breath, kicked his feet up on the coffee table, closed his drunken eyes and listened to the phone ring. On the first ring a soft groggy voice Sharla picked up. "Hello?"

Da'Quan abruptly sat up at attention and in his best attempt not to sound overjoyed that she responded said, "Hey, baby, did I wake you? You busy?"

She woozily replied, "No just laying here on my bed, what time is it?" He looked at the wall clock and answered, "Umm umm just a little after eleven, baby. Want some company?"

Sharla yawned and replied, "I guess it's cool but ima hop in the shower real quick. Gimme twenty minutes before you come." Da'Quan just hung up in her face and nervously began pacing his living room floor. He began getting his mind right to take on Sharla, who was actually a beast in the bed. She was the quiet buddy of Julie and Roz who came around every so often to their Saturday night vibe sessions. Her shyness was actually a turn on to Da'Quan as her eyes always communicated lust for him whenever they met. She laughed at all of his comments even if he wasn't joking and always refilled his cup with liquor. Sharla was a mixed breed, as her dad was a white, well-to-do realtor with a thing for sisters. Her mom was from the Caribbean and made her living as a schoolteacher. She was raised in the suburbs of Los Angeles and was sheltered her entire life. College was the first time she'd been able to break the shackles and tight stronghold her parents had over her. Her unworldly innocence made her a prime target for a slick talker from South Central LA to capitalize on her gullible heart. Da'Quan knew she was naive to the street game but he also knew she loved sex and had a thing for bad boys. As far as physical beauty, her body, which was short in stature lacked shape while owning a huge pair of perfectly shaped breasts. The white gene in her graced her with extremely curly hair and a bosom that demanded attention. Her black gene blessed her with the lips of a tribal queen and the innate urge to love black men. She, just like Julie, always concealed her physical goods under baggy sweats and sweatshirts as a means of avoiding unwanted attention. Da'Quan's patience had run out as he quickly made his way out the door in route to Sharla's den.

When he made it to her door he could smell the aroma of her patented White Diamonds fragrance from beyond her door. The whiskey in his system had him forcefully bang on her door. B*ang, bang, bang!* She blurted loudly while giggling, "OK, D, hold on, baby, here I come." The door swung open as she ran directly back into the restroom with nothing but a towel over her wet curly hair. Da'Quan eagerly entered the living room like a barbarian in search of his prey. His endorphins ran high like a soaring eagle. He looked on the floor and noticed a bedspread laid out with pillows bordering it. She had candles lit and jasmine scented incense burning. While she fumbled through cosmetic items and toiletries in the bathroom, he lit up half a joint that sat in her ashtray. Sharla was very big on good weed considering both her parents were advocates and she'd been smoking since she was eleven. As he burned the high quality weed she yelled from the restroom, "I'll be right out babe. Light that dooby up and chill." Instantly he stripped down to his birthday suit and lay across her spread feeling like an empowered godly figure. A minute later Sharla came out still nude with her massive 42dds swaying naturally from side to side. He fixed his eyes on her huge pink nipples that stood erect as she sat directly under his arms. She cuddled lovingly next to him sighed and said, "You know I hate sharing and what makes it worse you're fucking all of my closest friends, D. I don't know how long I can do this, babe." She then looked him in his eyes as he made no comment, grabbed his chin and forced her minty flavored tongue down his throat. She then took the roach from his fingers, put it in the ashtray, pushed him back and put his manhood in her mouth. She began slurping like he had a candy-coated dick which led him to turn her around and return the favor. He put his mouth in her *drenched* camel foot and with his tongue toyed with her clit until she came to tears. She begged, "Oh my god, don't stop I love you, D, please don't stop." Her mound was so wet he had to turn her around to spare her as it appeared she was almost losing consciousness from the excitement. She wrestled him down and began dominating him with mind blowing fellatio while staring into his soul with her brown Bambi-like eyes. He was aware that the freak in her could easily be credited to the white genes on her father's side. Da'Quan, who was drunk and taken by the moment, snatched the towel off of her head, and took a hand full of her hair and controlled her movements just shy of being abusive. He began commanding, "Taste daddy's dick. Is it sweet like candy, bitch? Huh, is it sweet like candy?" Every time he said bitch she squirted and moaned, "Ooh yes baby ooh yes." He grabbed her and violently slammed her on her back before shoving his manhood aggressively into her *drenched* foxhole. She was so wet he couldn't feel her walls to the point it felt like he was plunging in a warm bottle of milk. Her bouncing breast smacked her in her chin with each explosive stroke. He began feeling lightheaded as the intensity of the moment took its toll on him as well. She began throwing her pelvis with extreme force as her eyes rolled back like an exorcism. Soon after she lost all control and it exploded like a fire hydrant all over his thighs and the comforter. This caused him to yell, "Oh you fucking bitch," as he too unloaded like an Uzi of lust. They both gasped for air as his body went limp and collapsed on top of her soft skin. Moments later as they regained their human awareness, she grabbed the comforter and began wringing the juice out in total embarrassment. The comforter felt as if it had been dipped in a puddle of water. She shook her head and bashfully mumbled, "I'm so sorry, D, I've never come that hard. Babe, scoot over so I can wring your side off, too". Da'Quan raised up and gave her a kiss on her forehead to console her before laying back down as she continued to wring out puddles from her *drenched* comforter.

VIA DOLOROSA

SEPTEMBER 28TH 2006 • 37 years old

The drive to the neighborhood felt like Jesus' final march down the Via Dolorosa. Everything appeared to move in slow motion as he drove from the heart of Watts to the West side. He slowly began taking everything in as he could sense his life would no longer be what it had been. The fear and uncertainty of his future kept him subconsciously consumed in prayer as he made his way down the freeway. He kept his hand on his pistol the whole time he was driving in case his foes decided to try and whack him in traffic.

To calm his nerves, he opened a pack of spearmint gum to help battle against the fear inside that was slowly killing him softly. As he drove along the 110 freeway he thought to himself "Fuck this shit. I oughta just keep rolling, maybe go to Vegas and hide out. It's way too beautiful of a day to die." He knew that whoever this was knew way too much about him and that if he decided to avoid this situation that his family could very well be at great risk of danger.

As he approached King Blvd., sweat began to trickle down his side from his armpits. His befuddled nerves were now getting the best of him, the closer he got to his final destination. When he drove off the offramp, he was caught at the light trembling in fear. He noticed an elderly African-American man standing toothless holding up a brown cardboard box top with *Will Work for Food* scribbled in crayon. His plaid shirt was sick dirty. He couldn't tell what the original color of the shirt may have been. He had on filthy torn jeans as he stood barefoot in the midst of broken glass and gravel. There was a huge rat bite on his left ankle that was swollen and red, full of infection. He stood motionless with his sign shamelessly held high in the air. It was apparent that even in his situation he was at complete peace with himself. Deep down in Da'Quan's soul, he was envious of the homeless man's serenity and would've traded places with him in a heartbeat if he could. Realizing that his money was no longer a factor, he reached in his pocket and pulled out five crispy twenty-dollar bills. He held the money out of the window and yelled, "Hey, buddy, this belongs to you!" The homeless man looked at Da'Quan in bewilderment as he examined the money to make sure it was real. When he looked back up at Da'Quan, he grinned, revealing a mouth of missing teeth between his unkempt salt and pepper beard. Da'Quan stared at the homeless man like he was an angel sent from the gods before he drove off .

While driving down King, the aroma of McDonald's piping hot fries lured him into the drive-thru. He sat behind a beat up landscaping truck with shrubs falling from each side of the bed. In the rear window of the old Ford, he could see two Hispanic kids, a boy and a girl, bouncing excitedly in the back seat eagerly grabbing the children's meals and sodas their mother handed back to them. He began thinking more about his childhood and the innocent times before the game. When he finally pulled up to the drive-thru speaker, a very inspired female voice blurted, "Welcome to McDonald's. What would you like to order?" Just as he began to read off his order, the infamous Colorado number appeared on his vibrating phone. His heart began thumping like jack-rabbits fucking as he looked at the number with hateful eyes. He barked at the attendant, "Hold on one second," before he answered the call. "Yeah, wassup man?"

The husky voice cleared his throat before he calmly responded, "Yeah, baby boy, get me a large black coffee and three straws!"

Da'Quan's heart dropped as he clutched his pistol and jerked around in terror to see where this character might be. There was nobody in the line behind him and the landscapers in front of him were pulling out. He held the phone tight to his ear, took a deep breath and asked in a frustrated tone, "Are you for real, homie?"

The husky voice replied in a tranquil tone, "Everything about me is real. I know all about you. Yo family, yo kids, nigga I even know how much you love your aunt Mary's sweet potato pie. Check this out, you got thirty-nine minutes. Have my coffee and straws, sir."

He hung up before Da'Quan could reply. When he came to his senses he could hear the attendant yelling through the intercom, "Sir, please drive through or make your order." Da'Quan just peeled rubber and smashed through the drive-thru, leaving a huge cloud of smoke for the employees to choke on. He was angry, nervous and unsure of his future as he drove down King wondering what the afterlife held in store while simultaneously reminiscing on the good times he had experienced throughout his journey.

Chapter 11
SLAP BOX

JUNE 1980 • 10 years old

Uncle Buddy's intuitiveness or clairvoyance had become keen in his later years. As he leaned against the trunk of his 69 Caprice, he stood focused like a sniper on a wire in search of accuracy. The misty skies and pounding raindrops made no impact on Uncle Buddy's undisclosed moment. His hair was frizzy and unkempt as the raindrops dampened his son's salt and pepper half fro. As he took slow drags from his filterless Camels, he began shaking his head, as he'd come to the conclusion that before he passed on he wanted to know Da'Quan would be able to hold his own in the streets.

Meanwhile Delilah, who while haphazardly cleaning dishes, paid close attention to Uncle Buddy, who appeared to be losing weight. Just then Da'Quan entered the kitchen and as he surveyed the area noticed his grandfather's plate was half full. Without hesitation he blurted, "Dang, Grandma, Grandpa don't like pancakes and bacon no more. You should start making French toast and sausages." Delilah gave an unenthused smirk and continued to gaze at the only man she truly ever loved. Her heart was getting heavier by the moment, as she could see the silhouette of death encompassing her aging husband. His lack of appetite and sluggish demeanor was a sure shot giveaway that he was going through some serious physical changes. Da'Quan looked at Delilah puzzled until she gave her quick witted reply of, "Yeah, sweetie, we have to make him some hash browns to fatten him back up." She smiled as she wiped a tear and stared lovingly at her only grandson. He could sense something was bothering his grandmother but didn't know what to quite make of it. As he walked out of the kitchen, he glanced back and noticed Delilah slumping her broad shoulders and surrendered to an unusual tear jerking whimper. Just then the phone rang—*ring, ring, ring, ring*—he scrambled to the receiver eagerly answering, "Hallo," in an attempt to sound cool.

On the other end was Price. He told Da'Quan, "Hey, Daryl, tell yo grandaddy Uncle Hobart's package made it. Ima be waiting here so he can pick it up. Ya got me?"

"OK, imma tell him now." He quickly slammed the receiver and dashed out the back door to relay the message to his grandfather. With news of the arrival, Uncle Buddy tossed his cigarette butt and told Da'Quan to hop in and go to Price's with him. The two hopped into the car and as they backed down the driveway, Delilah came out waving goodbye at the two like she would never see them again. The smile on her face was a clear cut indication of how pure her love was for the two men in her life.

The ride over to Price's was filled with life questions between the two. Uncle Buddy without regard for Da'Quan's asthmatic condition fired up another camel as he turned up Aretha Franklin's "Natural Woman" on his custom sound system. After taking a drag on his Camel, he asked Da'Quan, "So, Snodgrass, you gotta girlfriend?"

Da'Quan replied, "Naw, Grandpa, them girls only like Freddie and Bad News. They be saying I'm like a brother." Uncle Buddy rolled down the window after noticing Da'Quan wanting the second-hand smoke and coughing uncontrollably. Once he was able to catch his breath, Da'Quan fired back, "Grandpa, what kinda gun you getting this time in the box?"

Uncle Buddy hesitated and in his mind wondered, *How this li'l muthafucka know I'm getting guns?* He thought quickly and responded calmly, "Why do you think I'm getting a gun, Snodgrass?"

Da'Quan said, "When I play in your drawer when you be sleeping I look in the yellow packages and pretend I'm the police with the guns you be having. They are heavy; are they real Grandpa or models? I like popping those plastic bubbles they be wrapped in too."

As Da'Quan babbled, all Uncle Buddy could think was, *Shit, Delilah would kill my black ass if this li'l nigga shot his self with one of those pistols.* He then told Da'Quan in a very stern tone, "Look here, Snodgrass, don't be going in my drawers again. You hear me? I mean it now!" Da'Quan bowed his head and sheepishly replied, "OK, Grandpa, I hear you." From that point, the rest of the ride was tight lipped highlighting the beautiful sultry sounds of Aretha Franklin until they arrived.

The moment they turned onto Price's street, Da'Quan could see his cousin Dray and two of his hooligans standing in front of his parents' house. As Uncle Buddy parked, Dray instantly gravitated towards the car. Da'Quan instinctively felt a sense of uneasiness as he opened the passenger door. Dray greeted Uncle Buddy with a handshake and "Wassup Unc." He was obviously high off of marijuana, as his eyes were bloodshot red and he had a bubbly tone in his voice. Uncle Buddy replied, "Boy, you high off them funny cigarettes again. You better be aware of what's going on, I keep telling you." Dray disregarded Uncle Buddy's comment with a halfhearted nod and instantly began to focus on Da'Quan. Dray made his way to Da'Quan and grabbed him around the neck saying, "Time to man up today, li'l nigga."

Da'Quan at this point was still unaware of the events about to take place and had an ill vibe about the whole scenario. As Uncle Buddy limped towards the house, he purposely left Da'Quan in the sweaty armpits of his nephew. Dray released him from the headlock as they walked up to the other fellas. They continued to take drags from the finger-sized joint they lit up after Uncle Buddy made it to the house. The three choked and laughed about who had the most dominant fighting skills and best aim with a pistol. One of the thugs, Porky, asked nonchalantly, "Who's the soft little boy?" The others began snickering freely to the question.

Dray replied "My li'l cousin, cuz. We gotta see where his heart is tho." Da'Quan began trembling in fear as he knew something was about to take place. He trusted Dray to a certain degree but still feared something violent was about to happen. Porky began smiling as he looked at Da'Quan like a crocodile does a gazelle sipping water at the riverbank. He began cracking his knuckles with a heartless smile on his face and not breaking eye contact with Da'Quan the whole time Dray spoke.

The adrenaline in Porky ran so high he blurted, "C'mon, cuzz, let's put this li'l nigga on, cuzz. I'm pumped!"

Dray told him, "Shut up, cuzz, for I put you on again. Come on, nigga, we going to the back." Porky shut up and began punching his fist to his palm as they walked to the backyard. There were fighting dogs tied to trees and a host of dumbbells, a punching bag hanging from a tree and a shoebox full of weed all present in the area. Dray grabbed Da'Quan by the shoulder, looked him in the eye and asked him "You ready, cuzz?"

Da'Quan replied in a frightened tone, "Ready for what?" Instantly, as Dray walked to Porky, his heart began beating to the point you could see it through his shirt. He became lightheaded with fear as he heard Dray tell Porky, "Cuz, don't kill him, just get his feet wet, homie."

Porky stared at Da'Quan with malevolent eyes the whole time. He was three to four years older than Da'Quan and had a stocky build from the juvenile camps he already spent years in. Porky's fist was huge and hard like mallets at the end of his wrist. His face was scarred from the battles he had already endured in the system as a youth. This was what he lived to do, and Dray was doing this for Da'Quan's future out in the rugged LA streets. Da'Quan by now figured out he was about to have to deal with Porky as he turned his golf hat to the back and walked towards him with a balled fist.

Dray ordered Da'Quan, "Cuzz, square up. Put yo fist up, nigga." Da'Quan followed command and as soon as Porky got within range, he teed off with a vicious slap to Da'Quan's face, *payow*! Da'Quan's feet elevated from the contact, sending him airborne into a lawn chair. The sting of the blow infuriated Da'Quan as he stared on his back at the blue and white contrast between the sky and clouds. Tears gathered in his eye sockets as he heard Dray's angry voice in the background, "Get up, cuz, and get him." Dray studied the activity like a movie director analyzing each move with a meticulous lens. He was a monster builder by nature and this to him was his real calling in life.

Da'Quan rose angrily to his feet and by instinct motioned towards Porky without fear. Porky danced around smiling, which added more fuel to the fire burning inside of Da'Quan. He attacked Porky only to be met with a fierce two-piece combo—*smack smack wop*! That drew blood from his crying mouth. His head was light from the heavy blows, but he was blacked out, and all he wanted to do was put Porky in a grave however he could. He searched for a weapon through watery eyes but couldn't see anything harmful enough in reach. In the midst of the melee, Da'Quan shut down and turned his back to look at Dray. He glanced back around and noticed Porky looking down dusting his pants when he cocked back and caught Porky in the jaw with his tight balled fist. It was the first time he'd ever hit somebody with all his might to the face. Porky stumbled and cursed aloud, "Punk bitch ima kill you!"

Da'Quan bolted out the yard as Dray grabbed Porky to avoid him really killing his cousin. Dray told the other thug, Devil, to hold Porky back while he went to grab a shell-shocked Da'Quan. By the time Dray made it to the front, Da'Quan was halfway down the block running with the fear of God. Dray whistled and yelled, "Come here, nigga." Da'Quan stood trembling as Dray walked up to him giggling and saying, "Cuz, you got him you on now and if you ever need us, cuz, you on the set just let me know." Da'Quan just looked at him as the tears from unleashed fear kept rolling down his face, yet he was glad to know he now had real backing in the streets.

Chapter 12
DINO AND COOKIE

MAY 1998 • 28 years old

Cookie was the beloved pet snake of Dino and Cassie. Cookie was a two-year-old Burmese python. Cassie gifted him the brown and yellow snake for his twenty-eighth birthday as a gesture of her unyielding love for him. Cookie earned his name from the way he captured and devoured his prey in an unceasing way. He swallowed and digested animals as if they were fresh from the oven, warm baked chocolate chip cookies.

Da'Quan's drug connect and homeboy Dino had a fetish for watching his Burmese python eat rabbits, guinea pigs and any other live animal accessible to devour. The bigger his beloved pet grew, the bigger in size and magnitude of prey Dino would feed him. Dino lived in Da'Quan's apartment building in the valley while Da'Quan attended college. He may have been short in stature but he was a very muscular mulatto cat with light green eyes that seemingly stayed bloodshot red. It was obvious from his demeanor and mental standpoint that he was an original native of Compton CA.

Growing up the youngest of six boys in his home, he witnessed everything from murderous gangbanging and dope dealing, to higher education and homosexuality. His father was a civil engineer for the city while his mom was an elementary school teacher in the city of Compton. Between the two, they were able to provide an above average lifestyle for themselves and the boys. Dino was very fond of his eldest brother Kilo Dave who inadvertently introduced him to the world of dope dealing. While growing up his brother needed a stash spot at the house for his product and would pay Dino, who was seven at the time, forty dollars a week to keep his packages hidden in the bottom of his toy box. He was so young that he couldn't spend or show the money to anyone, so for years he let his stash grow. By the time his mother discovered the lump sum of money during spring cleaning, he had accrued well over three thousand dollars stuffed in the bottom of his toy box. His father beat him mercilessly to get the truth out of Dino, but he under no circumstance would give his brother up. He told his parents he found it in a bag on the way home from school and was too afraid to tell anyone. His father, who had a suspicion about his eldest son's activities, took his money and put it in the bank for Dino. By the time he was eighteen his dad gave him access to his account, which had grown to a whopping 35 thousand dollars. This was the jumpstart he used to build his own criminal empire.

Da'Quan had been straddling the fence between a career in music and that of a drug lord. From his experiences with the goons and killers in the music industry, he actually found more solace in the high end aspects of the drug trade. He felt as though it was more of a blue collar hustle where everybody who participated was a candidate for financial gain with each transaction. It was a discreet and lucrative way to keep home afloat along with material perks and kudos from the opposite sex. Music was more of a fulfillment of passion that allowed you the freedom to express the message from your soul. It had its own unexplainable euphoria about it that most will never experience. And although the groupie element is comparable to the drug trade, it required too many hands in between you as an artist and your physical cash.

The first of the month had rolled around and like clockwork Da'Quan needed to recoup a substantial sack of chronic weed since his clientele was expanding. He also wanted to cop a few grams of powder for one of his comrades on the block. It was 6 a.m. and as Mother Nature blew the fog from the Pacific over the city, Da'Quan sluggishly picked up the phone to call Dino. He knew that if he waited past 6:30 a.m. to call that Dino may be out surfing in Malibu with one of his snowbunnies. He wrestled himself from the warmth of his bed, reached under his mattress, and began counting his hefty stack of hundreds and fifties as he waited for Dino to answer.

Just before he hung up frustrated, Dino picked up out of breath, "Hello, who this?"

Da'Quan replied in a gratifying tone, "It's Da'Quan. Wassup, man? I gotta come see you. It's the first this weekend homie." Dino, who sounded alert and full of energy responded, "See, Big D, that's why I fucks with you, my nigga, cause you bout yo business, homie! Wassup? When you trying to roll out? I'm about to hit the beach with my girl right now but I'll be around later today."

Da'Quan while yawning the sleep from his body replied, "OK, imma slide out there after traffic die down this evening 'bout seven."

Dino, who always sounded motivated, simply said, "I got whatever you need, my boy, see you tonight." They hung up in unison as Da'Quan dove right back under his comforter into a fetal position.

As the hands on the clock sat horizontal at 6 p.m., Da'Quan sat in his room counting a sizable stack of cash before heading out to Dino's spot. Before he left, he gave Dino a call. Dino picked up full of energy as NWA's "Fuck The Police" blared full blast in the immediate background. "Wassup, D, you coming?"

Da'Quan yelled back, "Yeah, I'm on my way my nigga. You need something from the store?" Dino replied, "Uh uh, yeah, grab some blunts and a fifth of Jameson. I'll shoot you the bread back when you get here, homie. Hurry up, Big D, imma feed Cookie when you get here, bro." After he hung up in Da'Quan's face, Da'Quan closed his eyes, took a deep breath, grabbed his smuggler's backpack and headed out. After he stopped at the store and headed on to the 10 freeway onramp, he lit up a half stick of Thai bud and drove in silence as his mind began to race.

Although he would never openly admit it, he hated when Dino fed Cookie in front of him. Dino had an obsession with snakes and always compared his controlling and aggressive behavior to the species. He always said he could paralyze or intimidate his foes through intense eye contact before determining how to annihilate them. He named his python Cookie because he ate his prey like a fat man wolfing down a freshly baked chocolate chip cookie.

Parking as always was a bitch but after jamming his truck into a snug spot he only had a block to walk. As he made his way to the door, he could hear Chubb Rock's classic "Treat 'em Right" blasting from Dino's apartment accompanied by the fresh smell of chronic smoke. Before Da'Quan knocked, Dino flung open his door with a burning blunt in his choppers, shirtless, with Cookie wrapped around his neck. At first glance, Da'Quan noticed the spark in Dino's bloodshot eyes as he quickly snatched the brown paper bag from him and welcomed him in. He was in a great mood as he had a certain zeal about watching Cookie eat animals live in his living room.

Da'Quan carefully eased past Dino and his seven-foot brown and yellow house pet. Before they did anything with Cookie, Dino pointed to the kitchen counter and said, "Dee, that's yo two pounds of some new shit they call OG Kush and two eight balls, my nigga. I promise they gon be hitting y'all right back. My white boys keep me with grades shit, my boy. That's why you always gotta have some white boys on the team, homie." As Da'Quan examined the bags of weed and coke he began counting out his money while Dino said, "Big Dee since you gone chill and watch the show, Imma take a hundred off the package. Just leave the bread on the counter, homie, and come on, cuzz, this nigga ain't ate in four months."

Da'Quan stuffed his backpack with his product and picked up the burning blunt in the ashtray and nervously began inhaling. Dino cracked open the Jameson and took a squig like it was water before moving the couches around to set up the feeding spot in his living room. He put a huge sheet on the floor and gently sat the 75-pound reptile down. He then went into the closet and pulled out a beautiful black and white pygmy goat. At first glance, Da'Quan hit the weed and took a huge squig of Jameson to prepare himself for the slaughter of the adorable animal. Dino's green eyes were filled with a glow of wickedness as he pulled the terrified goat to the makeshift death ring. The goat out of natural fear was reluctant to go, as Dino forcibly tossed him within a couple of feet of Cookie, who sat in a coil perfectly still. The poor goat bounced around frantically looking for a way out while avoiding eye contact with the deadly serpent.

Dino grabbed the blunt from Da'Quan and began impatiently pacing the floor as Public Enemy's "Bring Da Noise" vibrated through his enormous Cerwin Vega house speakers. While Da'Quan focused on the petrified goat scramble for his life, Dino's bimbo, Cassie, came from the bedroom asshole naked to the refrigerator. She looked at Da'Quan, smiled and waved as he tried not to stare at her huge 38ds, flat stomach and perfectly round derriere that bounced with each step. She had a gorgeous face like a model with her silky blonde hair tied in a bun. As Da'Quan fought not to gape at his extremely attractive girlfriend, Dino turned back, smiled and said with a mouth full of kush smoke, "Big D, don't trip, my nigga, you can check the bitch out. That's what the titties and ass is for, my nig." He began laughing as he passed the blunt to Da'Quan while Cassie threw a handful of ice cubes at Dino saying, "Shut the fuck up, you disrespectful nigga." She then winked at Da'Quan and sashayed back into the bedroom with her ice water. Da'Quan shook his head in disbelief all the while thinking, *Damn, dope dealers can do no wrong with a bitch. Imma get my sack up immediately.*

As Dino's patience grew short, he began getting antsy about Cookie taking on the petrified goat. It seemed as though the goat was so quick it had Cookie uncertain how to attack it. Dino jumped up, went to the kitchen and came back with a rubber mallet. He hopped in the death ring and without warning cocked back and violently whacked the poor goat over the head throwing off his whole equilibrium. Da'Quan squirmed as the thud sounded like two football helmets colliding at full speed. As the goat fell and tried to regain his balance, Cookie realized it was time and began to slowly uncoil and inch towards its prey. Dino sat back on the couch, took a squig of Jameson and as it burned his throat yelled, "Aiight muthufuckas, it's showtime."

The injured goat made every attempt to escape his doom but the heavy blow it took to the head was too intense for him to avoid the sinister moves of the deadly reptile. By now the goat was only able to stand on his hind legs while the front two legs and his head remained plastered to the sheet. Cookie finally made eye contact with the injured goat paralyzing it in fear. Da'Quan cringed as the reptile began easing his body against the wounded animal and slowly began wrapping it's huge body around the goat. Dino hopped up and turned the music off saying, "Shit, D, we can't hear the bones cracking, my nigga, with this shit on."

Da'Quan stared at Dino thinking, *Aww this niggas crazy for real.* Cookie then began expanding his huge mouth over the head of the goat who now began kicking and squirming for dear life. The further Cookie's mouth spread over the goat's head, the more the goat slowly yielded to his unfortunate death sentence. Soon the head and neck of the goat disappeared into the huge mouth of Cookie only revealing the bottom portion of the defeated prey. Cookie then began wrapping his huge body around the goat as it constricted mercilessly on the defenseless animal. Dino got on his hands and knees and said, "Damn, nigga, I hear the bones cracking on this bitch. My Cookie ain't no bullshitter, bro."

He sat next to the killing as if he wanted to take Cookie's place. His fixation with animal cruelty led Da'Quan to believe Dino had the mental capacity to treat a human in the same manner if the situation presented itself. As the hoofs of the goat disappeared into the mouth of Cookie, Dino stood up and rubbed the hump of the goat in his snake's belly and sadistically began imitating a goat's cry, "Baa, baa, baa." He was so enthralled with the process he almost forgot Da'Quan was in the room until he began gathering up his belongings to leave. He then turned around and in a disappointed tone asked, "Awww, Dee, you bout to cut out homie?"

Da'Quan replied, "Yeah, my nigga, my peoples out in LA waiting on this good ass dope you got, but I should be back in a week or so D." Dino, who was now full of adrenaline, walked him to the door breathing heavy from the excitement of the kill.

He patted Da'Quan aggressively on his shoulder and said, "OK, Big D, yo folks gon love every bit of that shit, I promise. So hit ya boy up, you know I got ya back."

Da'Quan looked him in his demonical eyes, shook his hand and responded, "I know, my nig, that's why I fucks wit you." Da'Quan then looked back at Cookie, who lay on the sheet looking ten months' pregnant and said, "Aaaiight, Cookie, catch you next time muthafucka."

Dino smiled as he stood shirtless in the doorway and said, "Yeah, D, I spent 150 on that goat today, got it from the Mexicans down the street. I had to do it or this bitch might try and do me like the goat in my sleep." He burst out in a sinister laugh and said, "Aight, Big D, holla at ya boy."

Da'Quan replied, "And you know this, my nigga," as Dino slammed the door behind him. The rest of the night all Da'Quan thought about was how the poor goat had no chance in that ordeal. He compared the scenario to the life of a black man being victimized by the snakes within the powers that be in the United States.

Chapter 13
VIVA LAS VEGAS

APRIL 1983 • 13 years old

Many days had grown dark and moons lit the sky since Uncle Buddy transitioned. Da'Quan was in the full stages of puberty. His voice was seeking its baritone, his shoulders were squared and his frame had stretched to almost six feet. Through his family and neighborhood he was exposed to the gang culture, seeing the pitfalls and curveballs attached to that lifestyle. His financial awareness had matured, as he was able to distinguish lower, middle and upper class at glance. He knew that race and culture played a pivotal role in how the authoritative powers that be distributed favor. Based on his experience over the years, he developed a preconceived notion on how women should and should not be treated. Conformity became humdrum while rebellion and salacious behavior quenched his desire for wrongdoing. There was a militant echo in his spirit from the conversations he'd heard between Uncle Buddy and his nephew Mad-E.

Marijuana smoke and liquor had flooded his system and there was no denying the tranquil feeling of inebriation he enjoyed from the two. Life had become bittersweet by now and the tunnel vision education from school to church thus far wasn't enough to encompass his intellectual capability. He wasn't afraid to ask logical questions on any subject the more his thought process matured. Reality has a tendency to plant seeds of future noteworthy behavior in our life journey. His thirst for knowledge was a precursor to his future as a writer.

Da'Quan sat reclined on the sofa pretending to show no regard for Delilah's phone conversation. He kept his eyes glued to the TV while the sing along, "I Think I Love You" rerun of the Partridge Family ran its course. She babbled gleefully about the Vegas trip that weekend and how much she planned on snatching from her Bible to gamble with. On the other end of the receiver was her lifelong friend, Festiva, whom she considered her best friend. The two were closer than butt cheeks for decades. They even made Da'Quan refer to her as Aunt T.

He watched his grandmother as she sat in the dining room stuffed into her favorite blue jean gambling outfit. It was a navy blue classic Gloria Vanderbilt two-piece suit. Her hair was rolled in rollers to perfection in order to produce those infamous silver locks and curls she wore proudly against her ebony dark skin. She blurted loudly, "Yes, lawd, I'm just making sure I got so my quarters and nickels rolled in this trash bag T. I ain't gambling no more than five hundred no matter what, child." Out of nowhere she yelled, "Da'Quan, have you been going in my bag of quarters, boy"?

He instantly took offense, "Naw, Grandma, why would I steal from you if I can just ask?" He had already rehearsed his response to this question a thousand times over. He knew there was a chance she'd discover he'd been dipping heavily into her gambling change. She counted her coins repeatedly with an angry dirty look on her face. She began jotting down something with a pencil, making Da'Quan even more nervous. As she scribbled and calculated, her actions incited him to add more comments of guilt, "Grandma, calm down. You probably miscounted or put those quarters in another spot."

She responded, "Mmm hmmm, I need to find another spot, oh and how'd you know I was missing quarters?" Da'Quan then quietly sank low into the couch as she smirked and gave him a stare with menacing eyes. She eased back into her phone conversation, "So yeah, T, we got all our stuff ready to go girl. Ima get ready and see what I can do with this nappy hair of mine, hahahahahahahaha. So how long before you make here, child?"

Aunt T replied, "As soon as Willie gets his big black butt out the shower, we'll be on our way."

Delilah replied, "OK, then see you in an hour or so." As soon as she hung up the phone, he began asking questions. "Grandma, so how is Vegas? What is it for teenagers to do since we can't gamble?" She responded sarcastically, "Well, nigga, seeing as how you got twenty dollars or so you should be able to keep busy in Sin City." Da'Quan remained silent as she began uncurling her hair in the bedroom mirror. She then blurted, "Stop asking so many questions and get your stuff together. Aunt T and Uncle Willy gon be here soon."

Moments later the black 78 Fleetwood Brougham sedan eased up to the front of Delilah's house. Da'Quan yelled out from the living room, "Hey Grandma, they here. C'mon." Delilah grabbed her bag of quarters, her over-stuffed suitcase and hobbled excitedly to the front door. She was so excited that she could barely lock the door with her key as her hands began trembling uncontrollably. Once her compound was locked securely, she fought through the pain of her crippling arthritis to Willie's pimpmobile. Willy hopped out immediately to assist her and Da'Quan with their belongings. Willy was a huge man whose skin tone was arguably a shade or two darker than the paint on his Cadillac. He had only one good eye and managed to salvage enough teeth in his mouth to chew soft food. What Willy lacked in physical appearance he made up for with his style and bubbling personality. He greeted Da'Quan with a bear hug and firm handshake and as he stepped back to look at Da'Quan's growth he smiled and asked, "Hey boy, how them grades and how are the ladies treating you, son?

Da'Quan replied, "They could be better and as far as the ladies, well you know I'm really kinda focusing on sports right now." Uncle Willy smiled, revealing his half set of brown and yellow teeth while simultaneously reaching into his pocket unveiling a 20-dollar bill. He handed it to Da'Quan and told him, "I've been hearing great things about you, boy. This is for you to have some fun with this weekend, now hop on in the back with ya cousins Lauren and Tommy back there."

Da'Quan replied graciously, "Yea thanks, Uncle Willy, for the money." Delilah reached out and gave Willy a loving hug and kiss before handing him her hefty bags of luggage.

Willy grabbed her belongings and as he hoisted them to the trunk asked, "Well damn, D, how many bags of quarters did you bring us? Shit, can I get a loan?" They all burst into laughter as she climbed into the crowded Cadillac. Before they took off, Willy asked, "Now y'all got everything, cut off the lights, stove and iron cause we are about to hit this highway non-stop now?" They both nodded yes as he cranked up his beloved Brougham, lit up his musty cigar and headed off to Sin city.

Tommy, who was a couple of years older than Da'Quan, leaned over and with his weed-stenched breath whispered in his ear, "Look, nigga, when we get there follow my lead and don't say shit to these old muthafuckas or my sister about what we do. They would never understand, aight?" Da'Quan just nodded and kept looking out the window searching for personalized license plates. Tommy was Uncle Willy's step-grandson who he treated as his own flesh and blood. Tommy and Lauren had known Willy their whole lives and until Tommy questioned Aunt T about his dark complexion as opposed to their Creole features, they thought he was their biological grandfather.

Lauren, who was Tommy's older sister, slapped him over his head, rolled her emerald-green eyes and sternly told Da'Quan, "D, don't listen to this fool. He uh have you in all kinds of shit." She then nudged Tommy to scoot over to create room for her full figure. She then laid her head back, shut her eyes and cringed as they were forced to listen to "Down Home Blues" by ZZ Hill.

"Say ya parties jumping/ Everybodys having a good time/ And you know what's going on through my mind/ Do you mind if I get comfortable/ Kick off these shoes/ While you fixing me a drank/ Play me some of them Down Home Blues." Uncle Willy sang the lyrics verbatim while Delilah and Aunt T crooned the chorus for what seemed like an eternity. From the concrete streets of South Central to highway 15 those three in the front seat downed tequila shots and pulled on Uncle Willy's half lit Cohiba cigar. They laughed and cursed while reminiscing about life in the south in comparison to California living. By the time they made a pit stop in Barstow, Tommy, Lauren and Da'Quan were eager to get out of the smoke-filled vehicle as everybody made their way into McDonald's.

Uncle Willy, whose eyes were bloodshot red, called Lauren with his deep raspy voice, "Hey, Lae Lae, come here baby girl, lemme ask you something." She stood listening like a quarterback getting the play from the coach. Lauren by now was mature and in full bloom. Her heavy chest and naturally round buttocks made her enticing to every kind of man. She was an avid gymnast which also gave her body a unique and well-proportioned look. Passersby both male and female discreetly and indiscreetly took peeks at the young beauty. Lauren's long brown wavy hair and emerald-colored eyes were the finishing touches that set her beauty apart. After he gave her the message, Da'Quan witnessed him slap her on her buttocks in an unbefitting manner, while gazing around to make sure no one saw his ill-advised action. Lauren nonchalantly made her way to the restroom as if nothing took place, while Uncle Willy gazed pervertedly at her physique through his wretched eyes.

The rest of the trip was pretty silent as the Big Macs and fries calmed the stomachs of the traveling group. As they pounded the highway, Uncle Willy turned down the stereo and made an announcement, "Alright y'all wake up, we officially in Lost Wages, city of sin. What happens here, stays here, goddammit!" He then burst into a spirited laugh before almost choking up a lung. By the time they arrived at Circus Circus, the anticipation of being unruly and mischievous nearly drove Tommy and Da'Quan crazy. As they climbed out of the car and began walking off, Uncle Willy yelled, "Tommy, Da'Quan, now y'all come here shit." The two sleepily walked over as he told them, "Now we in rooms 211 and 213 if and only if you need us to come back to one of the rooms, ya dig? Oh and goddammit, please don't get in no trouble fellas." He told 'em both to have a ball and be back by midnight. They took off like bats out of hell and headed towards the circus venue while Delilah, Festiva and Willy unloaded their belongings in the room before going gambling.

Meanwhile as Da'Quan and Tommy walked down the hall he noticed Tommy turning every doorknob to see which, if any, were unlocked. Tommy's actions made Da'Quan nervous, but he vowed not to say shit on the way there, so he quietly observed Tommy's play.

Uncle Willy was without a doubt a very charismatic and generous man. He was aware that he was quite fortunate to have scored Aunt T. She was an educated, high yellow Creole woman with a tall and slender physique. In her heyday she was approached left and right by men of all colors and social status. Festiva had a very subtle beauty about herself, as she never appeared to age. Although she was sixty-seven at the time, she didn't look a day past forty-eight. Their union was truly an example of Beauty and the Beast.

Festiva, Delilah and Willy dropped the bags off at the room and began walking towards the gambling floor. Out of the blue, Willy stopped and exclaimed, "Oh shit! Goddammit, Festiva, I left my high blood pressure medicine down in the trunk of the car." They all stopped on a dime as Festiva nervously replied, "Umm, well, do you need me to go get 'em, baby?" Her unwrinkled face was grimaced and unsettled, as she truly loved this ape of a man.

He hesitated and gazed into her tawny-colored eyes and told her, "Naw, baby doll, I'll tell you what," he then took a deep wheezy breath and continued, "look here, ima go down grab the medicine and the rest of the bags then I'll come and catch up with y'all two high rollers in a little bit." Festiva, who would give her right arm for this man, glanced at Delilah, sighed and said, "Well, OK, baby. Only you know how you feel, so I guess we'll see you in the casino." He gave her a heartfelt kiss, reached deep into the crotch of his snug jeans and pulled out a huge bankroll of 100-dollar bills. Delilah's eyes were glued to the wad as if she'd never seen that much cash at once in her entire life. He peeled off a hundred a piece and sternly told them, "Now y'all get started with this and don't stop until you win a million or it's gone." Right then Festiva became pussy as she reached for the money and gave him a huge wet kiss on his snag tooth mouthpiece. Festiva handed Delilah her 100, who also gave Willy a hug before the two turned and eagerly made their way to the casino. Willy stood and watched the duo until they were out of sight before retreating back to the room where Lauren was relaxing.

Meanwhile Tommy had a prayer answered when one of the doors he checked was unlocked. The turn of the doorknob actually startled him as he slowly peaked into the room for any occupants. On the bed there were double extra large male and female outfits neatly laid out for the day. The couple had Polynesian style clothing throughout the room. Items such as flowered shirts, dresses, sandals, sun visors and a mini red, white and blue flag of Samoa lay across a chair. It seemed odd to Tommy, but at this point it was too late to have compassion as the season of the victim had begun. He eased back out of the door, turned to Da'Quan and whispered, "Look, you stand over there about two doors down. If somebody comes while I'm in there, knock three times on the door then haul yo fat ass down the hall that way."

Da'Quan nervously gave him a thumbs up as Tommy eased back into the room in search of any valuable items. As Tommy quietly navigated through the room he saw nothing of true value. Then suddenly his eyes lit up as he saw a Louis Vuitton purse with at least 2000 dollars' worth of gambling chips stuffed inside. While he pocketed the chips he heard what sounded like two heavy, out-of-breath adults panting heavily amongst a running shower in the steam-filled bathroom. Without hesitation he grabbed the rest of the gambling chips and made his way out the door expeditiously. As he bolted out of the door he blurted to Da'Quan, "C'mon, fat ass, let's go." Unbeknownst to the two, there was an elderly Sicilian maid across the hall witnessing the whole fiasco as she dumped dirty towels into her basket. She centered herself to block Tommy but out of fright he bulldozed the sixty-five-year-old like a fullback at the end zone. All Da'Quan heard was her yell, "Fucking mulignane," as she landed violently on her well-cushioned derriere. Her loud Sicilian rant was silenced as Da'Quan and Tommy swiftly dashed through the corridor to the circus room.

Tommy took the chips and instantly dumped the purse into another maid's basket as he ran. Once they found a soft spot in the hotel they stood and counted 2300 dollars in casino chips. He nervously told Da'Quan, "Look, nigga, you ain't see shit and when I fucking figure out how to cash these muthafuckas, I'll shoot you some loot." Tommy paced the floor for a minute before it hit him. He snapped his finger and said, "OK, yea ima give em to fat ass Willy and tell him I found them on the ground. Fuck it ! That nigga can't resist no money. I know how much he loves to have cash to spoil my grandma."

Tommy knew that Willy was too much of a money hound to tell and his only concern was how much he and Da'Quan would actually touch. He turned to Da'Quan and said, "Look, dude, whatever he gives me I'll split with you but if he questions us, remember we found the chips on the ground by the, umm, ummm soda machine. Nigga, don't get weak and break. Just stick to the script, fool." Da'Quan agreed as they made their way to the circus floor. They floated around admiring the bright lights, high wire daredevils and the huge variety of arcade games along the wall. There were tons of pretty teenage girls who had Tommy's head rotating to the point he almost forgot he'd just stolen over two thousand dollars in chips from an open hotel room.

While enthralled by the scantily clad female acrobats on the high wire, Da'Quan nudged Tommy in his rib pointing out two Polynesian looking girls whose eyes were stamped on them. They freely smiled with all intentions of keeping the boys' attention. Tommy, who was somewhat experienced, confidently strolled over to the two and introduced himself to them. He introduced Da'Quan as his little chubby cousin and ignited laughter from the oldest girl, Laloni. She was nothing shy of eye candy. Her long silky black hair played the backdrop to her beautiful untainted skin along with her unique Pacific Islander features. Her physique was extremely athletic due to the fact she was a national soccer phenom. Her younger sister, Sandy, was a miniature version of her, who stood idly as the older two teens conversed. Whatever Tommy kept whispering in her ear had her laughing and giggling until her guard was completely down.

The two began engaging in hugs and booty rubs ultimately leading up to passionate lip locks in front of hundreds of observing passersby. Da'Quan and Sandy stood without speaking as the two older teens set the stage for adult activities. While engaging publicly in their illicit behavior a huge hand from the dark violently yanked Laloni by her neck away from Tommy's lip lock. To her shocking revelation, it was her 350-pound sumo-wrestler-built dad. He had sweat running down his face and neck with hands the size of baseball gloves. He grunted something aggressively in her ear as he maintained the tight grip around her neck. She had a sheer look of panic engraved on her innocent face. Without hesitation, her dad snatched Laloni's now limp body away from Tommy as if he was plagued with disease.

After the three walked away, Tommy angrily blurted, "Fuck!! That fine bitch wanted to give ya boy some pussy, D, damn I fucking hate parents, I swear!" He almost wanted to cry and for good reason; she was playing right into his hand of deceit. The rest of the evening was spent playing video games, while devising a plan to manipulate Uncle Willy to cash those chips for them. At one point during Pac Man, Da'Quan asked Tommy, "How is it that your grandpa is so dark but all y'all so fucking light skinned with green eyes?"

Tommy responded, He ain't really my grandfather. My granny got with that fat fuck after my real grandpa died. She got with this nigga cause he always digging in his bankroll for her, don't be stupid, D!" He broke down their whole dynamic without taking an eye off of the video game he played. Tommy went on, "I don't like how dude be looking at my sister and mother. I really wanna cut his fat ass up with a machete and skin him like he do those red snappers he be fishing for. D, ima tell you, I know he a no good nasty ass perv but my granny love his fat ass so fuck it." Da'Quan after those remarks shut it down and made no more mention about Willy. Once their pockets ran dry, the two made their way back to the room to make the play on Willy for the chips.

On the way to the room they noticed a huge man in Bermuda shorts on his knees with his head glued to the wall. He was sobbing uncontrollably banging his huge fist against the wall causing other visitors to look in fear. Tommy after staring at him realized it was Laloni's dad who cried on his knees while his obese wife tried to rub his back to console him. The Tongan man kept fretting aloud, "They gonna kill us, they gonna kill us!" While Da'Quan and Tommy stared at the crying giant, the old Sicilian maid waddled out of the Tongan family's room. She noticed Tommy and Da'Quan before stopping decrepitly over to the slumping giant. The maid whispered in his ear while pointing at the two boys causing him to look at them like blood to a shark. His swollen, sobering eyes turned instantly into evil lenses of destruction. He effortlessly hopped to his feet in a catlike manor and began sprinting down the hall towards the two. Not only are Tongans huge, muscular humans, they are morbidly aggressive with speed and athleticism. The Tongan giant gave chase barefoot barreling down the hall in nothing more than colorful Bermuda shorts and an undersized tank top. Towel carts and knee high ashtrays got tossed and kicked violently as the boys tried to use those as obstacles to slow the beast down.

White women clutched the frail arms of their less than alpha male mates out of fear from the activities. Tommy and Da'Quan fled with the fear of life back to the crowded circus room. They knew the room was dimly lit and that there were enough guests for them to be camouflaged. Instinctively they blended in the flow of teens and children as they watched the huge Tongan man huff and puff, standing out like a sore thumb. Wherever the Tongan went they swayed to the opposite side, never losing sight of the aggressor. He hunted for them like lions do wildebeest in the jungle. As the Tongan glanced at the half nude showgirl on the high wire, Tommy and Da'Quan catapulted through the corridor and made their way to their safe haven in room 213.

When they entered their room, Aunt T sat on the edge of the bed consoling Lauren, who tried wiping her tears as the boys entered. Luckily for the two, Aunt T was too preoccupied with Lauren's issues to notice the fright and terror in the faces of the boys. Tommy had seen this a thousand times over as he inconspicuously slid into the adjoining room, with Da'Quan right on his heels. Just then there floor vibrations from barbarous bangs on the door.

Bang, bang, bang!

Tommy and Da'Quan looked at each other with unpleasant emotions. All Da'Quan could imagine was being suffocated in the Tongan's powerful choke hold until his pupils exploded from their eye sockets. His heart raced to the point you could physically see it through his shirt. He wanted to urinate but held it with every bit of fight he had. Tommy's dreadful facial expression only solidified Da'Quan's fear of the huge angry beast they had stolen from. Tommy looked through the peephole, which for some strange reason was scratched to the point you couldn't see who was actually at the door. Da'Quan stood and bit his fist in fear as Tommy disguisedly found some base in his voice and asked, "Uh yeah, who is it?"

"It's Grandpa Willy, goddammit, open up. I gotta pee, shit!" Willy entered the room like a bat out of hell and raced straight to the toilet. He let off a loud, "Oooh shit, Lord have mercy. I liable to pee on myself if I had to wait another second. Good Lawd! Umm ummm ummm whew, yeah they gotta big ole Sasquatch-sized muthafucka cuffed up right here at the end of the hall. Took five cops to wrestle his big ass down, shit! Oh well better him than me!"

He went in his pockets without washing his hands, pulled out fifty cents as he handed Tommy the ice bucket and told him, "Look here, run on down and get me some ice. Paw Paw need a stiff one before I go back out to the crap tables."

After a very long pause Tommy stared at the outreached ice bucket like a loaded gun. Uncle Willy noticed his hesitation and said, "Boy, you OK?"

Tommy began crying and confessed to Willy, "Grandpa, I can't go out there. Me and Da'Quan stole that man's chips from his room and he wanna kill us." Da'Quan looked at Tommy in shock and thought, *Awww, this nigga's a bitch and a snitch damn.* Uncle Willy looked at Da'Quan as he shamefully put his head down in silence. Tommy reached in his pocket and pulled out the twenty-three 100-dollar winning chips he had stolen. Willy's eyes inflated as his breathing became more intense, and he appeared to be lightheaded from what he was seeing.

Sweat began to gather on his bald spot and forehead as he sat on the edge of the bed counting the chips. Uncle Willy counted aloud with a look of intrigue on his chubby black face. He sat for a minute quietly staring at the chips before looking at the two and saying, "OK, look here y'all. Don't say nothing to ya grandma's or Lauren, ya hear me? OK, ima turn these here chips in but y'all stay put till I get that man his money back." They nodded their heads yes in pure fright. The rest of the day Tommy and Da'Quan stayed in the room watching "Family Feud" and reruns of the cop show "Vegas."

Uncle Willy cashed the chips out and went to other casinos gambling for the rest of the night, ultimately winning another fifteen hundred on top of the twenty three hundred he inherited from the boys. The next morning Willy woke up the boys and as they got dressed handed them each a Stetson hat, a piece to disguise them from the lurking Tongan beast. They transferred to the Mirage hotel, where they spent the remainder of the weekend eating steaks, swimming and enjoying the fruits of Las Vegas. Sunday morning as they headed home on the 15 south, there was a van that rolled on the side of them. As the women were asleep and Uncle Willy focused on the highway, Da'Quan nudged Tommy and pointed at the blue van next to them. They saw the Tongan man's flag flapping in the wind as it was attached to the back of his vehicle. Inside the van they could see his daughter Laloni reading a book and the mother looking straight ahead as she massaged her husband's neck. He drove with a nervous unanimated look on his face. Whomever he was to answer to about that money had the man shook and fearful for his life. Tommy eased down into his seat and dozed off like the rest of his dysfunctional Vegas crew.

Chapter 14
KILLERS IN A CYPHER

JUNE 1997 • 27 years old

The journey in the rap game can be like that of an intense roller coaster ride minus the rails and breaks. There are no real rules or answers for anything that may take place on any given day or within any situation. Loud 10 and Flowood had cornered the West Coast market with skillfully delivered flows about South Central living over hardcore gangsta tracks. Show dates had gradually begun to decline, but there was still a need to hear from the infamous hip hop group. Kelsey, who was acting as the group's manager, swore he had a golden opportunity for Loud and Flowood. He had been nagging Loud about hitting the stage to stay relevant and most importantly to keep multiple streams of income available. The group was getting antsy, as the money had slowed down while the bills and debit accumulated unmercifully. The whole squad including himself were playing the rap game with no safety net. Either it was feast or famine with the option to do the unavoidable and return to the pitfall-laced street game. Tensions began to flare like popcorn popping, one minor incident after another. The constant influx of drugs and liquor from bitches and dope dealers, with hopes to get put on, began to slowly dissipate into a thing of the past. Radio play had died down considerably, which meant their show value decreased accordingly. The group was now face to face with the harsh reality of taking a pay cut for their musical expertise to regain momentum, or turn to the unpredictable LA Zoo as their means for survival.

Loud rested his palm against his forehead with his eyes closed as the Newport cigarette between his index and middle finger burned a stream of smoke freely to the ceiling. He sat on the end of his beat up sofa in the studio on the phone in a heated argument with his interim manager Kelsey. Loud gritted his teeth and fought with every inch of his temperament to not blow his lid on Kelsey as the two negotiated an upcoming show.

"Look, Kelsey, I know you say we gotta get back out there and work even harder, yea, I get it my nigga, but I can't do no show for no fucking twenty-five hundred with all my overhead and all these niggas that I gotta feed, homie, come the fuck on."

Kelsey was a pure fan of the group and always gave his 100 percent on seeing that Loud and his squad were taken care of to the best of his square ability. He was a college graduate who became a successful financial advisor at Bel Air Investment advisors and after ten years in the corporate structure decided to go after his dream of being a DJ and music mogul. His scrawny frame and nerdy disposition often got him ridiculed as the black Woody Allen. Between his semi nappy half 'fro, muscle-deficient body type and his black, horn-rimmed glasses, in the rap game, he was like a banana in a cage of starved gorillas. Although he had the credentials to set up goals and measure the financial forecast of most industries or businesses, his appearance and the high pitched octaves of his voice only made the wolves salivate even more so when dealing with him.

Da'Quan sat rolling up a blunt of chronic as he quietly listened to Loud and Kelsey play tug of war over a show he had lined up for the group. Loud's face grew more tense as Kelsey pleaded his case to Loud.

"Look, dude, I fucking know it's not the seventy-five hundred your used to, but damn nigga you ain't did but three or four shows in the last six months, and you're not cranking singles out to keep the name hot, bruh." He took a deep breath to adjust his tone in order to keep Loud calm as he continued, "Dude, look if you want the fucking momentum to sway back to the way shit was, you gotta do some local shit, bang out a couple hot ass singles and get back in good with radio man; that's fucking it. So look, the show I got lined up is for my sister's boyfriend's little homie who just got out. My sister's boyfriend is Big Blacc from the Hoovers, and the party is for Lil Black. Dude just did like eight years on manslaughter and Big Blacc throwing him a welcome home."

Loud responded unenthused, "So basically you saying you booked us a goddamn Hoover jail release party?"

Kelsey, who fought tooth and nail to keep his composure, explained, "C'mon man you gotta look at it like this, the dude Big Blacc is a millionaire. Trust me, I know my sister's with him, secondly they love yo shit and they wanna pay you twenty-five hundred for three songs, nigga, damn! Check this out, it ain't gone be no drama. Hust go in do ya shit, imma get the money and we out."

There was a moment of silence as Da'Quan dried the blunt with his lighter and Loud contemplated his fate as a musician. After a moment of deep thought, Loud took a deep breath and as he gestured for Da'Quan to light the blunt he told Kelsey, "OK, look Kelsey, we gon do the motherfucker, but dude make sure ain't no problems with my money and that it's gon be security."

Kelsey, who was relieved, just responded, "You got it. I'll have y'alls ride there at nine p.m. Thursday night. Y'all just be ready to roll."

Loud, who sounded less than enthused, responded, "Aaiight man, Thursday and if they ain't got at least half the bread in my pocket by show time, we ain't going on." He then abruptly hung up the phone in Kelsey's face. As he turned and took the lit blunt from Da'Quan's fingertips, he smiled and said, "Thursday we gone do a show for the Hoovers."

Thursday night was filled with anxiety and extreme caution as One Shot put his compact .380 in the small of his back while mumbling, "Fuck these niggas. Any muthafucka push my buttons gon lay where they stand tonight on my momma." Milkdud stood beside him with a lit blunt in his choppers wholeheartedly agreeing with One Shot's sentiments. Da'Quan leaned quietly against Loud's front gate as Kelsey and Loud nervously bickered back and forth about the upfront and backend pay until the black Lincoln limousine pulled up for departure.

The ride was tense for a minute until Loud blurted, "OK, niggas here's the deal. We doing three songs and getting the fuck up out of there. I know this nigga. One Shot is heated and I got my thirty-eight right here in my pocket, so really if it gets ugly we got some kinda hope." He burst into a chuckle as he harassed Da'Quan to pass the well-lit blunt. By the time their nerves calmed after a few vodka shots and chronic blunts, Loud pulled out his snorting mirror and a huge line of Peruvian powder and his rolled match book cover for his tooting. After a couple of bumps of coke and blunts they arrived in front of the mason hall. There was an immaculate peanut butter-colored 67 Impala on gold Daytons with a huge mural of some popular gangster on the front hood sitting directly at the entrance. As the crew unloaded from the limo, the evil stares and looks of admiration from the gangsters in line smothered the infamous rap tribe. Kelsey managed to get the group in without them being frisked by the huge black-tatted goons in security shirts.

The inside of the hall looked like an old elementary school auditorium complete with a one mic system on a stage with curtains and two flags. One was the American flag displaying stars and stripes while the other was a ripped California flag with the big brown bear symbol. Kelsey saw Jap and went into a side room with him as Da'Quan and the group stood cautiously watching the influx of thugs and killers who piled in eager for a good time. Most of the males wore orange T-shirts of some sort, blue jeans and a blue rag either in their left back pocket or wrapped around their necks like old slave maids. The females were hardened and unladylike. They wore the same type of outfits as the fellas and appeared to move around like divas in the devil's den. The DJ wore a black security shirt with a blue rag attached to his microphone. He looked fresh out of prison with missing teeth, gigantic biceps and tattooed biblical scriptures plastered to his face and neck. When Kelsey came back, he appeared to hand Loud a small envelope creating a picture perfect smile on the worrisome face of Loud.

Within a minute Kelsey guided the group to the side of the stage and told them, "Ooh you niggas gotcha money now. It's time to do the fucking three songs keep these muthafuckas entertained and get the fuck outta here! Fuck a sound check. I'm about to go introduce y'all then you niggas come do ya thing."

Kelsey stood on stage like a bloody steak in a shark pool as he commanded the attention from the old wooden stage, "Yo yo yo, it's about that fucking time to get this muthafucka cracking." The goons and thugs tood unenthused in the depth of the clouds of marijuana smoke, anxiously awaiting Loud and Flowood to spit that raw and skillful street vernacular.

Kelsey confidently continued, "And put yo muthafucking hands together for the one and only Loud and muthafuckin' Flowood riders. Give it up!" The females jumped on the shoulders of their big homies in awe as the group climbed on stage like the Temptations of gangsta rap. The moment Loud grabbed the mic, the DJ began showing his remarkable skills on the turntables, setting the crowd off instantly. The sound system was completely outdated but the energy from the crowd of villains made the shortcomings of the venue irrelevant. After performing their hot single Pistol Packing the hall had grown musty and the smoke filled the room from wall to wall. The crowd began chanting loudly, "Hoova, hoova, hoova!"

Da'Quan and the group became uneasy as they closed out their set. Suddenly, as the DJ began spinning the instrumental of Pistol Grip, one of the Hoover girls was brought to the stage. She was short, very slim and at first glance very unattractive. Her hair was done in a frizzy basket weave and assortment of tattoos on her flawless chocolate complexion. None of her gangsterisms could blind her voluptuous sex appeal. Her T-shirt was tied in a knot under her perky round breasts that bounced braless with every movement, and her brand new Levi's jeans fit snug around her apple-shaped derriere. As she hopped off of her big homie's shoulders, she boldly snatched the mic from Loud and began rapping like she was possessed by Quetesh, the Egyptian sex goddess. Her body language was confident, filled with feminine mannerisms as she grabbed the mic flaunting her street sex appeal to the crowd of goons, "*Yeah I'm that bitch / make ya jitter in ya nightmare / banging wit Hoover on my neck / the tats right there / layin' niggas down from the barrel of my Glock / da big homie front a bird / now we setting up shop / baby Kee Kee a ruthless gutter minded bitch / strap a chicken to my thigh / go outta town it ain't shit / to a Crip like me a g I got that bomb stank / setting niggas up get ta wrapping 'em in duct tape / I wonder to myself / why my momma even have me / a vandal and a scandal / never ever knew her daddy / yeah I pray at night to find love in my heart / 107's what I'm yelling behind the shots in the dark / selling pussy if I gotta / as a means of survival / trick a nigga say it's his / but the baby look like Rollo / I swear I shoulda been born a real nigga / cuzz a bitch ain't shit to me / snatch her soul and run up in her / ima rebel / taking out devils and cops / plus a bad hoe sitting in a million dollar spot"*

The crowd of thugs went apeshit as Baby Kee Kee Crip walked across the stage like it was second nature. The volatile energy Kee Kee transferred from the stage to the congregation set off a wave of scuffles in the rear of the venue. Security battled through the crowd of onlookers and hecklers that thrived on violence and barbaric behavior. Kelsey began shoving Loud and the crew towards the door to secure the money. As they piled into the Lincoln Loud yelled in a candid tone, "See what the fuck I mean, Kelsey, man, you gon fuck around and get a nigga killed for a funky ass twenty-five hundred dollars, goddamn mason hall one speaker having ass spot, fuck this shit!"

Kelsey humbly pleaded his case, "Look Loud, shit, it was easy money on the table plus you need the fucking exposure. It ain't my fucking fault you fell off your hustle, you fucking hardhead ". Kelsey's voice rang at a high octave as he tried to harness his anger that was a result of Loud's approach.

Loud took a huge deep breath as his eyes bulged in anger before violently responding at the top of his lungs, "Fell off, nigga, ain't nobody fell off. Who the fuck is you talking to, you little scary ass bookworm, wanna be DJ ass nigga. You begged for me to put you on, talking about you, one of my biggest fans and you idolize me and shit. Now you gon say a nigga fell off? Fuck you, find another act to manage."

The cab of the limo was filled with silence until One Shot yelled, "Y'all niggas, duck!" Just then a huge forty ounce bottle of Old English collided violently against the car, sending foamy beer suds across the entire front windshield. The commotion from the inside of the music hall flooded out into the parking lot, causing a major traffic jam as the hooligans proudly blocked the streets to make their presence felt. The driver quickly darted in and out of the melee until they were headed to the 110 freeway. The ride back to the block was filled with silence and uncertainty

Chapter 15
90210

JULY 1974 • 4 years old

It was Saturday morning as the warm July sun baked through the murky sky, the disquieting sounds of roosters crowing echoed repetitively down the South Central block. The click clacking of pots and pans combined with slamming cabinet doors was alarming enough to wake a stiff. As Da'Quan lay under the covers with his eyes closed, he dreaded the thought of starting the day. The six-year-old mumbled to himself "Why the fuck do old people get up right now?"

No sooner had he ended his cadence, he heard the bedroom door squeak "Come on, get up, Stink go use the bathroom my love." It was Da'Quan's grandmother Delilah leaning on the doorway with a head full of rollers, purple house robe, three-stripe tube socks and a mesmerizing smile. She whistled then commanded, "Come on, boy," as she walked unevenly to the kitchen, tightly clutching her greasy meat spatula.

By the time the house was filled with the aroma of fresh cut bacon and warm buttermilk biscuits, Da'Quan had relaxed into a slight siesta. As he dreamed of swimming in a gigantic swimming pool with glasses of water in his hands, he was awoken by three large knuckles to his forehead that felt like doorknobs crushing his skull. "Snodgrass, Snodgrass," growled Uncle Buddy, Da'Quan's grandfather. His phlegm-filled, country-nurtured baritone discontinued Da'Quan's snooze; it also prevented him from peeing on a new set of bedsheets. "Look here, boy, I ain't buying another pack of sheets or another mattress cause you too damn lazy to getcha ass up and piss in the bathroom. Shyt, we had an outhouse back in Texas," he said with conviction. Uncle Buddy adored his one and only grandson and made it a point to raise him like a man.

At this point Da'Quan ascended from the comfort of his haven and dashed into the restroom. No sooner than the door shut, his full bladder flooded the floor with urine. It was so bad he gave up the race for the toilet and just stood and let it go while tears dropped rapidly. In sheer fright, within this timeless moment, he took a pair of his grandmother's pantyhose that hung on the door, and exclaimed, "Shit, I fucked up."

Uncle Buddy yelled incredulously, "What chu say, boy?"

Da'Quan was too preoccupied with the chore of mopping urine with Delilah's pantyhose to reply. The intense pounding heart in his chest left him almost nauseated in fear. After a lackluster mop job Da'Quan placed the damp panty hose neatly on the hanger back on the door. He frantically began searching for a fresh pair of pajamas when—

Bang, bang, bang, bang—the bathroom door vibrated aggressively. "Hurry up, boy, ya biscuits getting cold baby," his grandmother pleaded.

Da'Quan replied quickly, "OK, Grandma. I gotta boo boo."

"Wipe good," she replied lovingly.

Once Da'Quan found some dry pajamas, he neatly folded his drenched pair and placed them in the bottom of his drawer. Feeling accomplished and without washing his hands he raced to the breakfast nook and climbed into his seat. As he rose to the table, the smell of hot biscuits with butter melting and fresh bacon slices sent his senses haywire. He eagerly reached for the syrup when his grandmother's heavy hand slapped him.

"Ouch! Why did you hit me, meanie?" Da'Quan asked.

She ordered him, "Now say yo grace first."

He then mumbled, "God is great, God is good, thank you, God, for this food, amen." Uncle Buddy proclaimed, "Shyt, if God did this why in the hell I'm paying out my check?"

"Shut up, Buddy" Delilah rapidly replied.

In between Uncle Buddy's gnawing and smacking, his male ego wouldn't allow him to stay silent. Frank replied, "Look here, Delilah, I bust my black ass twelve hours a day at the packing house, shyt, five days a week, sometimes six, give you my whole damn check and you got Snodgrass here thanking some mutherfucka we ain't never seen."

"Maybe you ain't looked in the right place, dear," she replied abruptly as she awkwardly fumbled with the pots and silverware. She started humming ridiculously offbeat as her nerves boiled when Frank displayed such blatant disbelief in God in Da'Quan's presence.

Uncle Buddy shunned the conversation and stared at Da'Quan quietly nibble through his syrup-filled plate. He told him, "Snodgrass, you love dem biscuits and molasses, huh boy?"

Da'Quan smiled and lovingly said, "Not more than you, Grandpa." Silence dominated the kitchen as the young guiltless voice of their grandson ripped through Frank and Delilah's emotional infrastructure.

While combating a serious tear jerk, Uncle Buddy grabbed a napkin and hurriedly cleared his throat and wiped his goatee. He told Da'Quan, "Hey, look, I'm about to pick up ya Uncle Hobart from the airport, ya hear me? You're going to the white folks house with Granny now, got me?"

Da'Quan gazed, eyes wide open as the lump of heartache commanded his Adam's apple. Uncle Buddy stood up without hesitation, put on his grey Stetson, checked the creases in his khakis and the shine on his Stacy Adams then stuck his right hand out to Da'Quan. "Snodgrass," he said sternly, "shake my hand. Papa gotta go now." Da'Quan stuck his left hand out limply and the bass in Uncle Buddy's voice escalated as he harshly told Da'Quan, "Shake my hand like a man, goddammit !"

"Ah ha, you need God now," Delilah interjected.

"Not now, Delilah, shyt,", he replied, never taking his eyes off of Da'Quan's melancholy face. Da'Quan adhered to his grandfather's order stubbornly by firmly gripping his hand with a solid right handshake.

As Uncle Buddy limped out the back door, Delilah sarcastically asked him, "You coming home, or ya looking for Jesus tonight?"

Uncle Buddy looked back, smiled enough to reveal his gold molar, winked and tauntingly blurted "Hallelujah!" as he bounced out the door.

"You just pick us up at six, Frank, or else," she hesitantly blurted.

By now Delilah had the kitchen virtually spotless and began getting them ready for work. She first cleaned Da'Quan up and got him dressed in his tough skins with the knee patches,and his favorite Number 32 OJ Simpson jersey. While he sat dazed by cartoons, Delilah could be heard in the bathroom faintly saying, "Now I know I had these dry this morning." Soon after she tossed the pantyhose into the dryer, she sat on the floor side by side with Da'Quan laughing and partaking in the subtle messages of the cartoons in pure bliss.

After the dryer alarm rang and an hour long wait for Delilah to get ready, the duo was headed out the door to Beverly Hills. Delilah was hired help on call and would substitute for other maids when they weren't available for the day. The gig paid swell and it somewhat took the load off of Uncle Buddy, as he was getting up in age.

The walk to the bus stop was enveloped with the scent of morning breakfast that permeated their nostrils. Barking dogs and elderly people tending to their prospective lawns and assorted weekend duties added to the canvas of the South Central neighborhood. Da'Quan noticed two older boys wrestling vigorously as he and Delilah moseyed along the pavement in route to the Number 3 line. One of the boys had an oblong-shaped head and was fiercely destroying the bigger boy with tremendous force. Da'Quan was fascinated and wanted to spectate, but the heavy hand of love dragged him briskly down the block.

While waiting on the bus stop Delilah's keen sense of smell had her sniffing with a horrible scowl on her ebony face. She stated "It's a damn shame people pee on the bus stop and everybody after them got to stand here and smell it." She paused and replied to her own statement, "Just nasty."

Just then Da'Quan shouted while pointing down the street, "Look, Granny, the bust, the bust," as he still had something of a lisp. Public transportation to Da'Quan was definitely an exciting adventure for him. A bus ride with grandma trumped sitting around the house reading, doing word searches and sleeping, any day of the week in his eyes.

As the huge piece of machinery halted with screeching brakes, Da'Quan's anticipation grew increasingly. No sooner had the automatic doors flapped open than Da'Quan leaped with both feet onto the first high step. He marched aboard confidently and with his right hand reached out and shook the bus driver's hand, Mr.. Matthews, with a firm right. Bus driver Matthews eagerly sprung out of his driver's seat to assist Delilah on board his vessel.

"Ggg, ggg, good M-morning," he wrestled with his speech-impediment.

Da'Quan giggled loudly and asked Delilah, "Wh, wh, wh, why he talk like that, Grandma?" While bracing herself not to laugh at the poor man, she placed her index finger over her lips, which meant shut up now.

Mr.. Matthews surveyed the entire bus through his rear view to ensure all was safe before departing. The window seat provided tapestries of African-American gardeners and landscapers, creating visible craftsmanship executed by hard work and talent. There were Black and Latino children running playfully through the sprinklers as the morning sun reminded all it was summer.

"Next stop, V-Venice," Mr.. Matthews proclaimed. On board came an older white gentleman who seemed to be down on his luck, with a flask and very dirty rags on. His face was full of whiskers and he reeked of day old puke and liquor which raced from his pores. He sat catacorner to Da'Quan and Delilah and slumped with his head down sipping from his flask.

Directly behind him boarded a bronze-colored Hispanic woman in her early twenties or so. She wore what seemed to be a nanny or nurse's uniform with fishnet stockings and a long overcoat. Her jet black hair was twisted in frizzy Shirley Temple style bangs. The mole which served as a beauty mark on her left cheek added to the draw of this Latina fox. She listlessly flopped next to Da'Quan and Delilah as she appeared to have been up all night. She clutched her handbag tightly as she shut her swollen eyes.

The silence on the bus was interrupted as Mr.. Matthews turned on his portable radio. Liquidating through the speakers came the funk rock classic, "Play that Funky Music, White Boy." Da'Quan was enthralled by the up-tempo beat as he kicked his dangling feet uncontrollably with no inhibition. As the hook of the song blared throughout the bus, Da'Quan mimicked the lyrics verbatim.

"'Yea they was dancing/ and swanging/ and moving to the groovin'/ and just when it hit me/ somebody turned around shouted/ play that funky music White Boy.'"

Delilah with her huge heavy hand shielded his mouth instantaneously. He instinctively pushed it away and asked, "Grandma why did George call that white man a honky last night?" His inquisitive and demanding tone startled Delilah as she attempted to answer but to no avail.

"Shh, well, ummm, oh Lord have mercy," she uttered frustratingly. By now Mr.. Matthews's bubbled eyes were bulging out of his head as enormous beads of sweat plummeted down his chubby, stubble-filled face.

He quickly intervened in his Uncle Tom coon dialect "You, you, just know not to say it, OK."

"Thank you, you hear dat?" said Delilah in an attempt to bring closure to the conversation. She fixed her hand tightly around Da'Quan's little neck, and while gritting her teeth, in an attempt to be discrete, asked him, "Who the hell is George?"

Da'Quan replied, "The man on TV last night with the money and fat wife." He was referring to the TV show, "The Jeffersons." Delilah released her hold and reclined shaking her head in disbelief.

Meanwhile as Mr.. Matthews's and Delilah's conversated back and forth, Da'Quan's eyes were fixed on the Fox as she arose from her slumber to exit. He got a full glimpse of her massive 42D cup boobs jump out of her undersized halter. She struggled with her balance tremendously as the bus decelerated. Her calves were very shapely, and from the looks of her overly worn platforms, the Fx had had had those calves on the ave' for many moons. Da'Quan stared and mumbled, "Damn, you sexy," as she enticingly stood bowlegged in the door well. Before she departed she glanced at Da'Quan and while smacking her Bubble Yum bubble gum, smiled and winked at him. The acknowledgement from the Fox painted an ear-to-ear smile on his young, irresistible face.

His innocent eyes were still glued on the Fox while the bus waited on the light to go green. She was immediately approached by a tall slim black dude parading an Applejack hat, plaid leisure suit and vintage spit-shined men's platforms. He gravitated to the Fox forcibly while barking profanely at the top of his lungs, "Bitch, what fuck you think this is. I told yo stank ass four a.m., bitch. I been here three muthafucking hours."

He simultaneously snatched her purse and as the light turned green, Da'Quan witnessed the pimp openhandedly smack the living shit out of the Fox. She collapsed where she stood and lay motionless on the pavement.

The chilling sight of the Fox succumbing to the abuse of the pimp silenced Da'Quan briefly. He had been attracted to the busty exotic Latina and was disturbed by the sight of her lying, while pedestrians walked by as if she didn't exist.

" Nneh, nneh next stop B-b-b-Beverly Boulevard," announced Mr. Matthews as the bus departed. Delilah began to gather herself in preparation to exit. All Da'Quan could see was the pimp's hand colliding violently to the jaw of the Fox. The pair stood at the front exit, but before they stepped off, Mr. Matthews handed Da'Quan a single dollar bill and told him, "Hu, hu honky aaannnd neh nigga are words for ignorant folks uunun, understand?"

Da'Quan replied "Yes," sheepishly with a smile. He didn't know what ignorant meant but he definitely understood the value of a dollar. Delilah smiled endearingly at the gesture and lip spoke over Da'Quan's head to Mr. Matthews, "Thank you." He responded with a simple tip of his hat and head nod.

The walk from the bus stop to the O'Neal's was laced by presidential-style homes with more than impressive curb appeal. Each home had a Mercedes-Benz, Porsche or Rolls Royce decoratively parked in the driveway. It was quite obvious Delilah and Da'Quan were part of the Beverly Hills labor force. Japanese gardeners, Jewish nannies, African-American maids and limo drivers were in full motion along the ritzy Beverly Hills block. Delilah stopped Da'Quan two houses before their destination and told Da'Quan, "Look at me. You just say good morning, smile, keep your mouth shut and stay put or ima find a switch, now I mean it, shyt."

Da'Quan knew that a switch meant weps on his ass so he agreed willingly. She tightly gripped his hand and they continued on their trek. Da'Quan stared neck up at the tall beautiful Washingtonia Robusta palm trees that graced the entrance of the enormous Beverly Hills mansion. The colonial style architecture with the custom marble walkway screamed nothing but wealth. Da'Quan was taken by the size of the humongous ten-foot doors. They were extravagant complete with the gold-plated, oversized Baldwin colonial-style door knockers. To the side of the mansion was the poodle's doghouse, which was 900 square feet in its own right. As they walked up, Delilah noticed a note on the door hanging on by a thin piece of scotch tape. It read,

"Dearest Delilah,

"Tatum had a callback for a new teen movie they are considering her for. I hate that we weren't able to reach you beforehand as you are such great help. What I did was put an envelope under Cleopatra's food bowl. If you like, you can relax by the pool. We left some gourmet cookies, freshly squeezed lemonade, crackers and brie. Will be in touch. Keep your fingers crossed for Tatum. So excited sheesh"

"Truly yours, Maggie,

"P.s. Tatum left a Bad News Bears hat on the table for Da'Quan. Toodles"

Maggie was Tatum's "nanny." She was a voluptuous blond coed who, when not being a nanny, entertained Hollywood big wigs with her exceptional oratory skills.

Delilah read the letter and instantly made her way to the elaborate doghouse. As Delilah went to grab the bowl, Cleopatra, the O'Neal's vicious poodle, began to snarl. Delilah quickly took hold of a shovel leaning against the house and oscillated it violently at the now whimpering canine. She reached under the bowl unperturbed by the silly pet and glimpsed into the envelope with one eye winked. To her breathtaking surprise there were five crisp twenty-dollar bills inside. She sighed deeply and whispered, " God is good."

The ride had taken its toll on Delilah so she decided to stay and wait on Uncle Buddy to arrive at his due time. Da'Quan ran playfully around the park-like backyard for hours with Cleopatra. He wore his fitted blue jean cap like a badge of honor. The same stood for Delilah, as she sifted through the snacks and sipped on a glass of freshly squeezed lemonade. By now the hands of the clock had turned and the sun sat west. Da'Quan heard his loud sound of reality: *Bonk, bonk, bonk!*

Uncle Buddy had arrived in his 69 Caprice Classic revving his engine repeatedly. Da'Quan raced to the front, bolted out of the gate and sprinted to the car. He hopped in the car fluidly and before he could catch his breath started announcing, "Grandpa, I saw a girlfriend get slapped, Grandma tried to kill the dog …"

Uncle Buddy looked perplexed and said, "Get in the back seat, Snodgrass, and don't get no chocolate on my goddamn seat, ya hear me?" Right then Delilah climbed in humming gingerly.

Uncle Buddy went in on her immediately saying, "What Snodgrass talking about broads getting slapped and you killing dogs, D?" She pinched her nose, as his breath reeked of whiskey. He asked, "Why you holding your nose, woman? My car been smelling like dogs and piss since y]all got in shyt. These white folks ain't right, I'm telling you, D." As Uncle Buddy voiced his drunken opinion, Da'Quan found himself comfortably in a fetal position drifting blissfully into a well-deserved catnap.

Chapter 16
GOD'S BREAD

FEBRUARY 1983 • 13 years old

Shortly after Uncle Buddy's death Delilah dove headfirst into the church's demanding schedule and political expenditures. Sundays became an all-day affair starting with the 7 a.m. breakfast, followed by Sunday school, 8 a.m. service, 10:45 service and more often than not, the day culminated with a greasy, country fried dinner with all the fixings at a random member's home.

The chore of waking up at sunrise, stuffing himself in a pair of uncomfortable slacks and tie and listening to the same sermon for hours had begun to take its toll on Da'Quan. He no longer had the option of staying at home with his grandfather, watching football and enjoying a leisurely spent Sunday morning. Life had taken a drastic turn from cheering for America's team to listening to a man suited and booted crooning sweet nothings to a room full of blacks in desperate need of hope. What was supposed to be a temple of spiritual nourishment was often plagued with not so wholesome intentions driven by human desire. Da'Quan began to observe how some of the younger and more attractive females would sit in the front row directly under the pastor's pulpit. Pastor Belcher sat confident and seemingly unbothered by the sea of cleavage and low cut dresses that filled the rows of his ever-growing church. The women would sit in a docile state with perfect nails and hairdos as they prayed to find guidance and love from his holy tabernacle. At times it was obvious what the intentions were as they sat looking up to the pulpit with alluring eyes that said, "I'm yours for whatever you need in God's name."

Pastor Belcher at the time was in his mid to late forties with a wife and two children. He was without question commander and chief of his vastly growing congregation. His George Benson octaves provided weekly uplifting to a crowd of loyal individuals. The African-American community, especially during the post-Civil Rights era, still remained attached to the decades of despondency that plagued previous generations. Pastor Belcher was educated, eloquent and very precise in how he delivered his messages of pagan Gods and pipe dreams. He provided light within the dark sullen mindset of a people just one or two generations past the Civil War, less than a decade from Selma marches and a host of political assassinations.

Delilah was in a spiritual metamorphosis as she began treating people even more like children of God were supposed to. She had grown to accept Da'Quan's friend MC as a misguided angel from God's heavenly kingdom. She made a habit of inviting him to church, contributing her part in the rehabilitation of Michael's young, tainted spirit. It was First Sunday, and MC was in his third visit at Philips Temple with Da'Quan and Delilah. Pastor Belcher had been informed of Michael's disposition so he and the stewardess board formulated some extra duties for Da'Quan and MC in an attempt to develop them spiritually as young men of the church.

Normally, Felcie, who was an older teen, would collect the offering, but he was stricken with the measles, so pastor Belcher appointed Da'Quan and MC to collect the offering that week.

Pastor Belcher approached the two young men as they sat quietly in the upper balcony by saying in his smooth baritone, "God has chosen you two to collect his offering of goodwill. C'mon, fellas, so follow me if you will." As the trio walked down the stairs, Pastor Belcher's diamond-riddled cloak carried the stench of twenty different perfumes from all of the hugs he'd received from females following the prior service. The diamond rings on his right hand alone equaled the value of most of the members' cars and outfits combined. His nails were manicured to perfection complementing the Baguettes that decorated his every finger. His Sutor Mantellassi oxfords, which were spit-shined to perfection, had to have run him well over six or seven hundred dollars.

His appearance was that of a pimp clutching a Bible for good fortune. As they approached the entrance door, Pastor Belcher turned around on a dime and looked the two boys square in the eyes saying, "Now fellas, ima give y'all a tray. Da'Quan, you start on the left hand side and just simply hand the tray down the row. Now Michael, you take the tray when it's passed to you and pass it to the aisle in back and keep going until you have collected it from all of my people, OK?" The two both shook their heads in full compliance to the flashy minister.

Pastor Belcher while looking them in their eyes said sternly, "When I'm done with the sermon and sister Simmons comes to wipe my forehead with this white handkerchief, ima point my finger at you, Da'Quan. That's when I want y'all two to rise to your feet like soldiers for God and y'all start collecting God's bread. Now do I make myself clear? Are there any questions?" The two stood at attention and shook their heads no to the animated man dressed like Pimp Dracula. Just then the pastor bowed his head and went into a deep moment of silence with his eyes shut. The organist began playing "Sweet Chariot," and as the doors to the congregation opened he began bouncing on his toes up and down like an athlete preparing for competition.

The light from the church came blaring in, revealing a sea of dedicated followers eagerly awaiting spiritual nourishment from the man second to God. Da'Quan had never seen the congregation from this angle and he was in awe of the women who were made up with adoring smiles across their faces staring with dreamy eyes of hope. The men sat with a look of admiration and valor, complete with the mindset of being a soldier for God. True enough it was God's army but Pastor Belcher to his congregation was the general and whatever the command was his people would wholeheartedly deliver.

Pastor Belcher glided onto the stage like a highly touted rock star. His adoring fans gaped at the minister as he was exalted by more people than he could name in a lifetime. The pastor stood momentarily and gazed at his audience like a newborn baby he was in awe of. He had a knack for bringing people together as one and making each person feel as though he was speaking to you on an individual basis through his sermon. The verbiage and timing within his sharp cadence was impeccable, as he wooed thousands into the love of God and self. His diamond-studded hand then seized the microphone causing the audience to inch up to the edge of their seats eagerly awaiting the word of God from the most admired man in the room. He smirked confidently, winked at a couple of the beautifully dressed women in the front row, cleared his throat and began, "Good morning, God's beautiful people!"

The congregation responded instantaneously, "Good morning!" He then went into his sermon, stating, "God don't want no cowards in his beloved army!" His eyes perused the crowd reassuring himself that all focus was on him. He paused as fan waving and gum chewing were the only activities taking place in the crowd. He continued, "This my loving people is a war we are in. No and it's not a physical war with planes, bombs and machine guns. No, no, my people we are in spiritual warfare." He paused briefly allowing the words to sink in. There were multiple amens and hand gestures of approval to his words. He went on to say, "If you would please open your Bibles and turn to Ephesians six with me. Huh, I see I gotta get y'all going this morning, amen, lights and walls," he uttered into the mic causing laughter.

In a very aggressive and intimidating octave he roared "OK, OK, right here it states the Armor of God! Now read along, 'Finally be strong in the Lord and his mighty power. Put on the full armor of God so that you can take your stand against the devil's schemes.' Ok y'all wit me now?" He asked rhetorically, "Listen to me now, for our struggle is not against flesh and blood, but against the rulers, against the authorities, against the powers of this dark world and against the spiritual forces of evil in the heavenly realms." He paused, took a sip of water from his kings mug and exposed a mouthful of pearly whites to the people . He continued sternly, "See y'all it ain't the people you don't know, it's the people right up under you at work, next door, huh, in yo bedroom," he paused again and continued, "y'all know what I'm saying amen, lights and walls, some of y'all sleeping with the devil and don't even know it, huh or maybe you do and just find it hard to resist, amen lights and walls." He began moving around the stage as he wiped his mouth with his handkerchief. The adults in the crowd laughed in response to his antics. The women in the front row were blushing shamelessly and tickled pink by the pastor's message. He then gripped the mic and in an aggressive tone blurted, "You must come prepared to fight, people. The shield of God is unbreakable. We must keep it revealed and ready because, my people, spiritual warfare is in all of our homes, jobs, schools and even within these walls. Can I get an amen lights and walls?"

The congregation shouted "Amen!" One lady in the crowd stood to her feet yelling, "Amen, pastor, tell it like it is!" Pastor Belcher calmed his demeanor and with his now hoarse voice continued, "God don't want no cowards in his army, no halfway soldiers or fair-weather disciples. Either you're in or out, no in-betweens, amen y'all!"

The crowd rose to its feet clapping as the organ began its prelude to the offering. Just then Ms. Simmons waddled hurriedly over to pastor Belcher and began wiping his forehead with the white handkerchief. Once his brow was dry he pointed his diamond-studded index finger at Da'Quan signaling to him to rise and perform his usher duties. MC began passing the tray with zeal. Da'Quan observed MC's eyes plastered to the large dollar bills and envelopes that instantly filled the tray. The message in the sermon had the congregation tossing money in the tray like hot marbles. There was not a bit of hesitation from anyone who contributed to the account of God's army. Once the two collected what seemed like a fortune, they both exited out through their rear door and made their way down the hall to the cloakroom. They each had a tray and hightailed down the corridor guarding the money with their lives. Da'Quan, who trailed MC, noticed him fumbling awkwardly with envelopes as they made their way down the hall. MC motioned to Da'Quan to hurry up as he held the door open for him. The two entered the room and as Da'Quan went to put his tray down MC snatched it and began stuffing envelopes and twenty-dollar bills in his suit coat pocket. Da'Quan's heart began skipping beats as his eyes bulged at the sight of MC's actions. The psychological impact of MC's deviant behavior left Da'Quan paralyzed and speechless.

MC looked up while stuffing the money and sinisterly mumbled, "You better get yours, cuz. Don't be no fool!" Da'Quan eyed a sharp letter opener on the desk and grabbed it while MC was preoccupied in his thievery. It was at this time Ms. Simmons exited the pulpit and began waddling to the cloakroom to seize the money collected by the boys. Da'Quan stared ruthlessly at MC stealing and clutched his weapon firmly.

With that in mind along with the sword-shaped Geneva letter opener in hand, he shouted, "Fuck that, cuzz, you can't be stealing God's bread, Mike!" The no nonsense aura in Da'Quan's tone combined with his weapon shocked MC as he dropped the envelopes to the floor. His reaction startled Da'Quan, but he wouldn't let go of the weapon for fear MC was playing possum in order to grab the letter opener and stab him with it.

MC fell to his knees and whimpered, "My momma and daddy short on rent again, cuz, and I don't wanna be living in the streets." He sat hopeless as he wiped the tears from his beady eyes in search of compassion from Da'Quan, who stood at a distance not sure of what to do next. The screech of the door alarmed the two as Da'Quan stuffed the letter opener in his suit coat. He turned his head and two huge breasts surrounded by a cast iron bra knocked him forward.

Ms Simmons stood with her flabby arms folded, breathing heavily with a look of suspicion on her clammy face. "Where's the money, you two?" she asked as her eyes searched the room for any fishy activity. She wiped the sweat between the loaves of fat on her neck with the same handkerchief she used on the pastor.

Da'Quan responded, "Here, Ms Simmons," as he passed her his tray. MC handed over his tray which was half as full as Da'Quan's. She looked at it with skepticism. She took a deep breath and told the boys, "Thank you for your services. You can go back to your seats." Da'Quan and MC made their way out of the door silently owning an uneasy vibe.

On the ride home after the service Ms Simmons and Delilah babbled nonchalantly about the sermon, people's outfits and other church business at hand. MC and Da'Quan sat silently in the back of Ms. Simmons canary yellow Seville, tuned in to their surroundings. The first stop was MC's house. He had the door opened and was hopping out before the car was at a complete halt. As he jumped out without a word, Delilah yelled, "Michael, go getcha daddy, please!" MC hesitated not sure what she wanted to tell his dad and uncertain if Da'Quan had ratted him out behind his back. Delilah yelled again from the passenger seat, "Boy, go get him. What's the matter, shit."

MC turned and yelled, "Daddy, Daddy, Mrs. Dunn wantchu."

Mr. Chambers came out the door in his usual wife beater, shower cap and some cutoff khakis nursing a dangling Newport cigarette hanging from his chubby jaws. He made his way to the car with MC by his side, saying, "Good afternoon, ladies. Looking nice. What this boy do this time?"

Delilah reached in her purse and pulled out a church envelope. She smiled and told Mr. Chambers, "Look here, baby, my minister is a great man. He sets up an offering every week to help those in his congregation going through rough times. So here is two hundred dollars to help you out on the rent you're behind on."

Mr. Chambers dropped the cigarette from his lips to the ground and tried to speak but he was clearly at a loss for words in the moment. He looked perplexed and asked, "But, but how did you ladies know? I mean who told you how?"

She told him, "Look, baby, that's not the point. Point is God knows everything, so you take this and maybe come show your face in his house from time to time." He stood with the envelope in his hand flabbergasted by the gesture. Mr. Chambers smiled and agreed, "Shoot, if God is this good, I do need to go one day."

Delilah smiled and said, "Ima hold you to it now!" Ms Simmons leaned her obese body over and added, "Yeah, ima hold you to it, too." The yellow Seville departed as the two women chuckled at their good deed leaving MC and his dad at a loss for words. Da'Quan and MC weren't aware that Ms Simmons overheard their whole altercation and instead of crucifying Michael, gave to his household in an effort to teach him God will make a way when there seems not to be one. God's bread is unlimited.

Chapter 17
BEWITCHES

APRIL 1994 • 24 years old

People often associate witches or witchcraft with evil and deadly forces controlled by higher powers attached to sorcery. Witches in days of past were noted to possess mental powers which allured men into sinful acts in exchange for their damnation. The practice and beliefs of witchcraft from the beginning of recorded history are still being passed down the generational ladder till present day. The image of the white female on a broom represents her ability to fly, along with her other tools of persuasion and deceit. The general population, due to this portrayal of her, has not a sneaking suspicion that she could be a coworker, a neighbor or even a bed companion to the unknowing.

The stage was lit as the feverish energy on the stage transcended directly into the multi cultural hip hop crowd. Weed smoke hovered over the 2000 hip hop thugsters and enthusiasts that packed the ritzy venue from wall to wall. As Da'Quan worked the stage he found himself using the sleeve of his sweatshirt to wipe the burning sweat from his eyes that leaked like a faucet from his forehead. The hypnotic baseline from Pistol Packing had the partygoers in the front row in a trance-like state reaching desperately at the feet of their favorite artist on stage. The huge 300-pound security guards stood side by side to form a human wall in front of the stage and speakers to protect Da'Quan and his hip hop entourage from the screaming fans who yearned for a smidgen of attention from them. From the corner of his burning eyes he noticed two conservatively dressed females standing backstage focused directly on the stage show.

They were both Caucasian with bland features almost appearing like two soft spirits from another planet.

As Loud, Konvick and Da'Quan exited the stage the two ghost-like women gravitated directly to the Vip section. Konvick snickered sinisterly as he took a huge pull from a blunt that was being passed backstage. He kept an eagle eye on the Fugees' camp just in case they wanted to continue with the feud from earlier that evening. Da'Quan stood apart from the crowd of groupies and dick riders, wiping the puddles of sweat from his soaked face with a promo T-shirt he found in the dressing room. He noticed the two odd women penetrate through the onlookers, making their way into Konvick's personal space. Konvick's huge frame towered over the two as he made what appeared to be nothing more than chipper conversation. Moments later while entering into the limo, Konvick escorted the two females into the backseat piling in on his lap for the ride back to the hotel.

Loud, who was the furthest thing from shy, blurted, "So Rick, who the fuck are they?" Da'Quan and Rick both put their hands to their faces and shook their heads at Loud's unorthodox approach.

The girl sitting on Konvick's lap turned, held her hand out to Loud and politely responded, "Hello to you, too. I'm Amanda and that's Cookie." She smiled as if his brashness went directly over her head. While the limo sped through Frisco's metropolitan area Da'Quan noticed Amanda's curvaceous shape underneath her gothic ensemble. Cookie was a lean Caucasian girl about twenty-three or twenty-four years old. She had a very youthful face smeared by excessive partying and frequent drug use. Her black pixie style haircut with her black lipstick was a perfect contrast to her pale complexioned face. She sipped on a vodka and orange juice that Konvick made for her and stared at Loud through her baleful lenses. Her energy was now allocated to Loud as she was intrigued by his pompous attitude.

As the wheels of the limo spun, Da'Quan reclined in his seat as Loud made small talk with Cookie. Meanwhile Konvick began putting his hand up Amanda's skirt while she buried her tongue down his throat. Konvick wasted no time when it came to jump offs or groupies; he truly lived in the moment. While Amanda and Konvick engaged in carnal lust, Cookie whipped out at least fourteen grams of pure blow. She held it up and gestured with her lips and shoulders, "Like is it cool to bump?" Loud's eyes widened and began sparkling as they remained blatantly glued to her bag of dope. She stared deep into his vulnerable face realizing she had now found a weak point in her prey. Amanda was abreast of Cookie's play as she began erotically moaning as Konvick shoved his fingers in and out of her womb, full of force, causing it to squelch unnaturally loud in the back of the limo. She kept one hand gripped to Da'Quan's shoulder as she moaned and squeezed harder from the friction on her clit.

Cookie reached back into her black alligator Sasha purse fumbling around until she found her razor blade and dope tray. Loud's eyes were plastered to her every move as she poured out enough for five graciously proportioned lines for the entire crew. She, out of respect, handed the tray to Loud to bump first. He took it, and as he scrutinized it with experienced eyes asked her, "Shit looks pretty good. Where'd you get it?"

She looked him square in the eye and replied, "Why do you ask so many questions?" She began mimicking him, "Who the fuck are they? Where'd you get the dope? Just relax and enjoy." She rubbed his thigh as she lured him with her feminine prowess. She then answered convincingly, "It's some great stuff I get from my Peruvian friends. Trust me, the shit is A 1."

Loud, without another word said, plunged in with no inhibitions. His nose had almost a full bump in residue as he came up from his round. He appeared unattached to reality, seemingly happy in his euphoric state. She took the tray from Loud and passed it to Da'Quan. He declined by hand gesture as Loud blurted, "That nigga Da'Quan weed and water only. He's a fucking square."

Konvick instantly blurted, "But I'm not." He tossed Amanda like a burdensome whore as he scooted up to take his bump. Konvick grabbed the tray with sticky hands saturated in vaginal juice. His nostrils attacked the Peruvian product like a Hoover wind tunnel vacuum. He gave Cookie a wink as he endorsed her powder offering. Amanda took a bump, closed her doll-like eyes and ran her cocaine-covered pinky between her lips and gums as well. Her chest began heaving as Konvick reached into her blouse and pulled out a massive 38DD with a sexy brown mole and pink nipple. Amanda pushed Konvick back, unzipped his zipper, pulled his manhood out and began performing fellatio as if it were just the two of them. Cookie took the tray from Amanda's limp grip as she groomed herself for the huge line that sat full of crystals. Before she took her bump she made sure Loud stared at her effortless attempt to clear the tray.

Loud smiled and asked, "Where the fuck did y'all come from?" His high was intensifying and it was obvious from his jittery movements and the look of paranoia engraved on his face.

While Amanda continued to enthusiastically suck Konvick's dick, Cookie responded, "We have no origin; we're Wiccan."

Loud's face cringed in disgust as he blurted, "What the fuck you say? Aww hell naw, y'all hoes witches."

Amanda instantly took Konvick's swipe from her lips and angrily screeched, "I'm sick of the disrespect you, you …"

Konvick sighed in a frustrated tone, "Aww naw, not now, Loud. C'mon, nigga, chill homie." He began snickering in disgust while both he and Da'Quan shook their heads at Loud's reaction.

Cookie gave Loud a villainous look and calmly replied, "Naw, Amanda my dear, he's disrespecting himself at this point." She kept her eyes glued on Loud the whole time as she asked him, "Sir, would you be so kind as to have the driver stop and let us out?"

Konvick began whining, "Aww nah, c'mon y'all, just chill. Damn, can't we just get high and enjoy this beautiful night?" He began his sinister snickering hoping he'd break the friction. Amanda by now had him hooked on her delightful mouthpiece.

Just then as Loud stared at Cookie like she was the daughter of Satan, she began chanting in an eerie tone, "*I cast this spell into the night/ to bind my enemies and limit their flight/ by earth, by wind, by water, by fire, / I wish to stop their evil desire,/ the evil actions and words they spread/ shall only cause him to feel great dread/ to lead this fight against their deeds/ as I will/ so mote it be.*"

Loud's eyes grew wide in fear as he yelled to the driver, "Aye yo, aye yo, pull this motherfucker over now!" The driver eased the limo over to the curb as Cookie and Amanda eagerly scooted towards the door. When the driver opened the door Amanda jumped out without a word said.

Cookie looked around at everyone with wicked eyes as she calmly said, "You all have a very malevolent life. See you on the other side." She purposely left the rest of the dope on the seat as she climbed over Konvick's lap and gave him a warm kiss on his lips before getting out.

Chapter 18
SNOWBALLS

JANUARY 1979 • 9 years old

January rolled around as old man winter unveiled his sinister smile on California. The early morning frost on vehicles and the cold steam which appeared as fog from speaking lips was an unequivocal indication of the chilly days to come. Mr. Green stood in his backyard concentrated on a frozen kitten who didn't make it back to the nest before the tundra of nightfall. He began reminiscing about the days of his youth back in Philly romping tirelessly in the snow with his siblings and friends. It suddenly dawned on him that his sons had never experienced the cold nor had they been on a family vacation. His mind was made up; he knew that a weekend getaway with his sons and a select few of their friends would make for an excellent bonding retreat. It was at that moment he yelled "Philip, Philip!"

His eldest son from a distance replied, "Yessir."

Philip commanded authoritatively, "Get out here, boy, come grab this shovel. I need to talk to you about something."

As Philip came and searched for the shovel he noticed the frozen kitten on the grass and asked, "What happened to the kitten, Dad?"

Mr. Green put his hand on Philip's shoulder and pointed closely to the lifeless feline and said, "Well, look closely at the edge of its mouth and tail. See all the frost around in those areas? I would say she froze to death trying to make it back to the nest. Look over by the van and grab that shovel so you can scoop her up and put her in the trash bin." Philip instantly adhered to the chore as Mr. Green went on to say, "Look here, boy, would you like to go to the snow with your brother and a few friends for a day?"

Philip lit up like a Christmas tree full of glee and excitement as he asked, "Well, Dad, how many friends can I invite and when are we going?" Mr. Green, who normally masked an unyielding demeanor, cracked a smile in response to his eldest son's zing for his idea.

He responded, "OK, junior, you can invite two or three of your buddies and oh I would say next Saturday, depending on the weather. We can ride out to Big Bear early that morning."

Philip immediately shoveled the frozen kitten into the trash barrel, hugged his dad and dashed into the house screaming, "We going to the snow; we going to the snow. Ooh wee, my dad is the best, we going to the snow." Mr. Green chuckled as he followed behind his animated firstborn into the house.

Later on in the week Mr. Green contacted Delilah to see if it was OK for Da'Quan to go to the snow that weekend. She approved and jokingly asked, "So you gone take ya best friend Michael on the trip?"

To her surprise he answered, "You know what, Mrs. Dunn, that's not a bad idea." He had a great deal of respect for Michael's intellectual flare-up at Jose the donut man, despite all of the debauchery and controversy MC had been attached to as well. Mr. Green, who was from a not-so-well-to-do upbringing in Philly, felt he should be the bigger man and participate in the rehabilitation of Michael's wretched behavior. Delilah informed him of the church fiasco and shared some sound advice on dealing with delinquent behavior. Mr. Green absorbed Delilah's words of wisdom like a sponge and confirmed he'd bring MC along for the getaway.

The morning of the trip Mr. Green had Da'Quan and Philip help him load the 1975 VW bus for their 4:30 a.m. departure. As they loaded blankets, snacks and chains for the tires, MC slowly walked up like a zombie from the grave and blurted with a hoarse voice, "Cuz, this better be worth me getting up this early for some frozen water from the sky." His drab comment, however, made no impact on the excitement Philip and Da'Quan were feeling about the trip. As Philip ran back into the house to gather more items, MC reached into his coat pocket and pulled out a fat sack of pungent marijuana. He put the bag to his nose while staring at Da'Quan with a mischievous smile and whispered, Cuzz, we gon be higher than the mountain top in Big Bear off this shit, cuzz."

Da'Quan, although not surprised, stood in the morning cold shaking his head at what MC was suggesting. In his mind he thought, H*ere we go again with more of this nigga's bullshit*. Just before they finished packing the van for departure, Robert, who lived down the street, came walking up completely bundled up from head to toe eating piping hot oatmeal from his momma's coffee mug. The mug had "Momma Needs Her Coffee" inscribed on the side.

MC, who was always quick witted, laughed and said, "Oh I get it, you act like a bitch cause you eat from a bitch's cup."

Rob, who was fairly new to the block but could hold his own, replied, Call my momma a bitch again, MC, we gone get 'em up, fool."

MC ignored his comment but kept egging him on by saying, "Man, this nigga roll up eating on bullshit after we loaded this whole cheap ass van up." Rob just stared at MC in his beady eyes, never discontinuing from scarfing down his hot morning oats.

The tense moment was interrupted by Mr. Green's semi-baritone voice yelling, "All right y'all, cut that b.s. out and hop in the van. Time to go, fellas!" Mr. Green slammed his door and attempted to crank up his bondo-covered family van. The first attempt was to no avail as the engine wheezed and clicked. Mr. Green pumped the gas pedal mercilessly again as the bus's engine attempted to turn. He then began cursing at his vehicle, "C'mon, muthafucka, not today," but once again the bus failed to ignite. The boys had doubtful looks on their faces as the used van refused to cooperate and start. Mr. Green paused, took a deep breath and as he turned the key again said to the boys, "Y'all excuse my French, fellas, but c'mon you son of a bitch, let's go." The snow gods were on their side as the hippie mobile cranked up full throttle. The boys all smiled simultaneously with Mr. Green as the rumble of the engine signified a fun-filled adventure ahead.

Mr. Green cranked up his static plagued radio, forcing the boys to stomach the sounds of "Break on Through (To The Other Side)" by the legendary Doors. Da'Quan and the fellas cringed for a second or two as Mr. Green bounced in his seat, drumming his hands on the steering wheeling singing the lyrics verbatim to the energetic, eccentric song. The journey began with high spirits, as the boys were excited to get out of the neighborhood and be exposed to new and uncharted territories. As they sputtered to the freeway, the rich and dynamic vocals of Jim Morrison, crooning over the bossa nova-inspired indie rock classic, didn't sound so bad after all. Traffic was fairly light, allowing Mr. Green to push his trusty VW northbound via the 18 to Big Bear City.

By the second hour of traveling, all of the boys, with the exception of MC, had fallen asleep. He sat in deep thought looking through the frosty windows through his deceitful beady eyes. His youth had been sucked from his soul and life to him at sixteen was equivalent to that of a thirty-year-old street veteran. Deep down he yearned to feel innocence but he'd seen and been a part of too much to even fathom that notion. As he bundled in a wool wrapping, the winding roads through the snow-laden mountains cradled MC into a light siesta as well. The family bus swerved and slid, forcing the boys to maneuver for certain comfort. MC, who was half asleep, jerked aggressively, unbeknownst to him, from his sweatshirt pocket, his bag of marijuana dropped to the floor. While driving the sleeping pack of boys, Mr. Green began catching whiffs of a skunky odor. The smell was either a run over skunk on the road or a hidden bag of weed in his beloved hippie-mobile. He knew he hadn't copped anything before the trip, as he checked his coat pocket praying it was his lucky day. He thought, *Some good pot to the head would put the icing on the cake* for his outing with the boys. In his search, however, he soon realized it to be nugatory and chalked up the smell to roadkill.

Before any vehicles were allowed onto the snowgrounds, the chain stop was a mandatory precaution. While Mr. Green had the chains put on the tires, the boys evacuated the minibus to stretch and take a whiz. Mr. Green sat perplexed as the potent smell of marijuana continued to reek in the bus. He sat for a moment and glanced down and within a couple of feet on the floor sat a five finger lid of Columbian Gold. He almost yelled as he was enraptured by his discovery. He wasn't sure how it got there but he immediately stuffed it into his winter trousers. He looked upward to the sky and mumbled, "Thank the good Lord, umm ummm umm." The thought of it being one of the boys' never crossed his mind, so he figured he may have dropped it, considering he was an avid smoker. Once the tire procedures were done, the hippie bus was off again headed straight to the Big Bear Mountain Ski resort.

The boys' eyes were glued to the beautiful white snow-filled ski slopes, decorated with 100-foot-high pine trees that could be seen for miles on out. Skiers and snowboarders flooded the ski zone enjoying one of nature's gifts for recreation and adventure. Mr. Green pulled up to an empty space, smiling as he saw the awe in the faces of the boys through his rearview mirror. Not far from the crew was a father and his four boys comparable in age to Philip and his entourage. They were a Caucasian family who seemingly appeared familiar with the environment from the looks of their fashionable snow attire and Utah license plates. They had skies attached to the roof of their 1974 Oldsmobile station wagon and very expensive Danner mountain cascade boots with the classic red shoestrings in each. As the two groups unloaded their respective vehicles, the White dad gingerly approached Mr. Green, reached out his hand for a handshake saying, "Good day. They call me Prescott and these little rascals here are my boys, my pride and joy. Looks like we'll be sharing the same slopes for the day."

Mr. Green aggressively shook his hand, looked him in the eyes and said, "Green's the name but just call me Philip; pleasure's all mine." The two gave each other a stern head nod and continued to unload their vehicles. Meanwhile MC patted his pockets desperately in search of the weed he brought along. He began mumbling and cursing under his breath as he realized the weed had been lost or stolen. His blood began to boil and he instantly kicked in to bully mode.

He noticed one of the Caucasian boys unloading his vehicle and whispered to him, "Psst hey, why don't you look like yo daddy or brothers?" MC snickered quietly as the young blond gave him a devilish look. MC, who wasn't shy from confrontation, began tossing snow to the back of the boy's head.

After three or four scoops of snow had been tossed on him, the blond turned and angrily blurted, "Would you fucking quit it, you nappy-headed tar baby." Prescott paused as he overheard the heated dialogue between the two but continued to unload in hopes it would blow over. The rage that filled in the eyes of MC was incomprehensible. He had been called a million derogatory names, but this was the first racial slur he'd been faced with. MC picked up a hand full of rock hard snow and began forming a snowball.

As he shaped it, he mumbled angrily, "You fucking paste white, pink dick, onion smelling, slow running, no jumping, pimply faced piece of shit. I got yo muthafuckin' tar baby, bitch!" The snowball wound up the size of a softball and was as hard as concrete. The Caucasian boy smirked at MC and cunningly flicked him off with his middle finger. Without warning MC cocked back the snowball and hurled it at the blonde boy's head like a fastball pitch. The blonde teen with catlike instincts ducked the snowball, but as Prescott turned to put his ski blades down, the blistering snowball connected violently to his face. The contact was disturbingly loud as the impact sent splattering blood airborne over the windshield and his son's jackets. His face came apart in three separate areas as his knees instantly buckled causing his body to collapse backwards into the frozen snow. The blood poured from his face as Mr. Green turned and attempted to mend his split face together with his bare hands.

He shrieked at the top of his lungs, "Somebody call a goddamn ambulance!" Mr. Green began utilizing all of his paramedic skills to the fallen man while looking to the sky as Mr. Prescott's body engaged in violent convulsions. MC stared remorselessly at the bleeding man as he knew his sons were a mirrored reflection of the racism instilled in them by their father. The eldest teen screamed, "Dirty nigger!" and began chasing after the much faster MC, who moved through the snow like a cheetah. Only the two of them knew he threw the snowball, as everyone else was unloading their vehicles at the time of the incident. The resort paramedics arrived within minutes and began questioning Mr. Green who had no idea where the snowball came from. The eldest of Mr. Prescott's boys singled out MC, who claimed he was excited about his first snow trip and was simply throwing a snowball at a totem pole that was directly behind the Prescott's car. The paramedics had to airlift the traumatized man to the local hospital and Mr. Green was cited a 200-dollar fine for MC throwing snowballs in a public safety zone. This would be Mr. Green's last endeavor with MC and the rest of the fellas who came along.

Chapter 19
FRIDAY FIASCO

MAY 1984 • 14 years old

Tension plus high levels of testosterone can almost guarantee disputes amongst adolescent males. Scenarios can rise from the smallest disagreements escalating to the bloodiest and most violent episodes imaginable. This was the case on a very hostile and rigid Friday afternoon at Serra High School. The dozens was a game played with the objective to demoralize another person's persona with the intent of creating laughter at that individual's expense. Boredom was usually the rationale for engaging in this classic game of wits. But sometimes these games don't always end on the brightest note.

It was a blistering hot Friday, as the Serra underclassmen stood restlessly in the quad, utilizing every inch of shade for refuge from Mother Nature's angry scorching. The students were restricted from their normal physical activities. The temperatures soared well past the 100-degree mark, causing irritability and sweat by the bucketloads. In the middle of a crowd of laughter, Alvin was the sacrificial lamb of the cruel cascade of demoralizing jokes. Alvin, who was in the same class as Da'Quan, was a quiet and mild mannered student. He, for all intent and purposes, was a shy introvert who wouldn't bust a grape in a fruit fight. If Alvin could exist in an invisible state of existence, it would not be farfetched to say that he would. He never brought any unwanted attention to himself, as his self-esteem was lower than the soles on his worn down sneakers. The clothes he owned indicated that there was not much petty cash floating around his household. Although Serra was a private school, Alvin had been granted a full scholarship because of his exceptional math skills. Not only were his clothes on the rundown side he was also plagued with an oblong chin which often made him the butt of evil and tasteless ridicule from his heartless peers.

Marc, who was a senior at the time, was in the middle of an Eddie Murphy moment, stirring up a ton of laughter at the expense of Alvin's fragile ego. He punished him in front of the group by asking, "Damn, nigga, why is it you got on a kindergarten-size shirt with size thirteen canoe-shaped no brands on yo feet?" Laughter filled the air as Marc's timing and delivery were flawless. Alvin began laughing only to avoid the faucet of tears he fought waiting to pour freely down his face. Marc then reached into his pocket and pulled out a twenty-dollar bill. He handed it to Alvin while saying, "Look, blood, go by yourself an outfit so I ain't gotta crumb on you, li'l nigga."

Alvin simply held his hand up and said, "Naw, Marc, thanks, but it's cool. I don't want your money, man." Marc was a budding gangbanger from Athens Park Blood, who came from a well-to-do household in south Los Angeles. He had a dark, witty sense of humor and was always inclined to engage in any form of mayhem if need be. He nonchalantly tossed the folded Jackson to the ground directly at Alvin's feet.

As Alvin reluctantly reached down to pick up the twenty, Marc blurted, "Don't rip them tight ass slacks, blood." Laughter roared as Alvin reluctantly reached down to grab the money.

Before he could grab the money fellow classmate Tyrone quickly snatched up the money saying, "Shit, if you don't want it I'll take it." He stuffed the twenty in his pocket and gave Alvin a browbeating stare. Tyrone was a heavyset bully who often got overlooked in his efforts to be a force to be reckoned with. He, as well as Alvin, came from a household on a fixed income. Tyrone was often arrayed in secondhand clothing from thrift shops and hand-me-downs from relatives and family friends. His chubby face was permeated with puss bumps from acne and unkempt facial hair. He hated not having a lot of the finer things in life and found solace in terrorizing those he felt were inferior to him in some sense. There were no extras for Tyrone, who frequently wore the same outfit two to three times per week. Tyrone went to

Serra strictly on the juice of his aunt, who was a long time custodian for the parochial school.

Alvin, who normally shied away from confrontation, walked up aggressively on Tyrone and demanded he give him his money. Tyrone smirked and acted as though Alvin's existence was AWOL. Alvin relentlessly stayed in Tyrone's face, repeatedly saying, "Aye T, c'mon man, gimme my money, c'mon man, you know Marc threw that to me. Come on, dude."

His aggressive tone in front of their peers tested Tyrone's patience, leading him to say, "Nigga, if you want it take it, cuzz. Alvin, I'm not playing homeboy, you better go on." By this time the group of teens had gotten quiet enough to hear a rabbit piss on cotton a mile away. Tyrone shunned his efforts and promptly removed himself from the sweaty pack of students. Alvin tailed him like flies on fresh shit about the money. Tyrone began walking in a circle saying, "Look, Alvin, I ain't playing, cuh, you keep it up ima rearrange yo face, homie, I keep telling you if you want it, take it, nigga, or leave the shit alone. Money gone, homie."

The scene looked like two starving pigeons competing for the same piece of bread. Both Tyrone and Alvin desperately needed that twenty dollars to escape the spam and biscuit dinners they were faced with at home, or to buy some sensibly priced tennis shoes to boost their self-esteem. The struggle for this money had plenty of underlying meaning for each. Poor Alvin's face was filled with anger, first from the heartless roasting, and secondly from being bullied for a life-changing amount of money publicly. At this point he'd rather be beaten to death than take an L on this opportunity. He felt the least he deserved for his humiliation was the reward of a new pair of shoes or a decent meal other than biscuits and spam. With no regard for Tyrone's fighting ability or size, Alvin desperately shoved his hand into Tyrone's pocket and snatched the twenty-dollar bill out with conviction.

Tyrone's eyes bulged from their sockets in disbelief as he swiftly turned with gritted teeth saying, Cuzz, what I tell you," before slugging Alvin viciously over his head with his meaty fists. Alvin hung on like a gazelle in a lion fight, but Tyrone's ox strength and punching accuracy proved too much for Alvin's amateurish fighting skills. Surprisingly, no one intervened seemingly because the act was so volatile and gruesome. Tyrone's eyes were filled with rage as he pounded Alvin's skull to the asphalt repeatedly. Shortly after the sixth or seventh blow, Alvin's tired body grew limp and it was only a matter of time before he'd be permanently comatosed. Marc, who had removed himself from the area, saw the crowd surrounding the melee. He quickly ran over to the scuffle and interjected by connecting a swift solid right and fierce left to the face of Tyrone. The thud from his powerful blows could be clearly heard from across the quad, alarming more students of the ruckus. Tyrone was dazed on his feet as the punches sounded like watermelons dropping from a helicopter to the concrete.

Mucous and blood rushed from Tyrone's face, leaving Marc's fist covered with yellowish red body fluid. He barked viciously at Tyrone, who stood wobbly kneed, "Blood, that's my little cousin, uhh, nigga take that!" He then connected to Tyrone's jaw again, sending his thick pudgy body colliding backwards to the asphalt next to Alvin. He then ripped Tyrone's pocket and stripped the twenty-dollar bill out and gave it back to Alvin, who was just coming to. Tyrone laid awkwardly in an unorthodox position as his face bled pus and blood profusely. Marc stood over the lifeless body of Tyrone and spit on him with a devilish smirk on his face.

By now the small huddle had ballooned into an assemblage of bloodthirsty teens eagerly observing the mayhem that unfolded in front of them. Marc, who now felt invincible, roundhouse kicked Tyrone's head as if he was trying to send him to the mortuary. The sound of the kick was disturbingly violent, snapping Tyrone's neck and causing him to urinate on himself. Many of the observers cringed at the heartless actions by Marc but were simply afraid to get involved for fear of their own safety.

Ryan B, who was a senior, had had enough and aggressively stepped into the commotion saying, "Naw, blood, that's enough, dog. He my little homeboy; he had enough." Marc, who didn't appreciate being reprimanded, publicly gave Ryan a nefarious look with his cold snake eyes. The crowd stood silent, anxiously awaiting the reaction from Marc who had blacked out in rage at this point. The congregation was fully aware that Ryan was a reputable blood, hailing from the rolling 20's. He was the furthest thing from timid and there were also rumors that he'd already been involved in more than one incident of homicide. OGs in their mid-twenties would pick him up from school and treat him as a total equal in their dealings. He carried himself like a grown man and had very little patience for the immature antics of his peers. He often dressed in slacks and leather jackets while toting a Buccio Tuscany briefcase as an alternative to a backpack. Rumor had it that he concealed his pistols along with his books in the briefcase. Whatever the case was, he never divorced himself from his expensive luggage.

Ryan stood firm over Tyrone's lifeless body with his huge fists balled. He acted as Tyrone's shield, who was now obviously *hors de combat*. Ryan, who's street name was RB, had jet black skin as his nose was spread over half of his face. It had been broken a number of times in battles and was now his trademark in the streets. Gang activity had been his M.O. since fourth grade and he, as well as Marc, was no stranger to the ills of the gang culture. What set him apart was his flair for fashion and his flawless grooming habits. His hair was wavy and always cut in a perfect shadow fade almost resembling a dark-skinned Louis Farrakhan. He tried to keep groomed to take notice away from the cuts and scars that plastered his hardened face. He wore a thick gold rope chain that strangled his neck, giving him the look of an ancient African warrior. To see him stand in red ostrich loafers, cream leather pants and a bright red silk button down in battle mode made the scene that more intriguing. Da'Quan thought to himself while watching, *Who the fuck squabs in leather and silk? Wonder which damu gon get they ass whooped?*

Ryan spoke sternly with authority, "Look, moe-bee," which was Marc's gang moniker, "Blood, we fam on damu, but I fuck with this li'l nigga give him a pass, look the nigga done peed on himself, homie, in front a all these cowards, dog, c'mon." Ryan's tone and smooth delivery calmed Moe-Bee somewhat enough to find peace in his warrior's heart. As Ryan stroked his ego, he took a deep breath, and as he looked at the lifeless body of Tyrone he simply smirked, bent down and wiped the blood and pus from his fist onto Tyrone's dingy Lacoste shirt. Both Ryan and Marc had a great deal of respect for one another and neither really wanted to chance getting knocked out by the other.

At that juncture a loud husky voice rang out from the crowd of onlookers saying, "Yeah, cuh, y'all need to see each other head up instead fucking up them little busters." The crowd looked stunned until they saw who it was speaking so boldly against the two. It was Rum, who was an active Crip from one-eleven Crip. Rum was also the starting middle linebacker from the school.

While a few of his thug associates chuckled at his brazen comment, there was an extremely loud command from the P.A. system yelling, "Everybody get on the goddamn ground!" Instantly, the crowd lay face down, all except for Ryan, MoeBee and Rum. The command came directly from the Gardenas special ops division. The closer the police tactically moved on the crowd with guns pointed, everybody lay face down except for Rum. He stood proudly as the last man standing, dressed in a red, white and blue letterman jacket, complete with a blue rag around his neck, cut off grey khakis, bottomed off with a fresh pair of all-blue Chucks. He forced the police to get within arm's reach of him before he obeyed the orders given. He smiled sinisterly as he slowly went face down to the asphalt like the rest of his classmates. Years later a photo which was taken from a bird's eye of the campus by the police surfaced. It monumentally served as a replica of a prison yard on lockdown.

Chapter 20
DOUBLE UP

NOVEMBER 1986 • 17 years old

The year was 1986. Da'Quan was sixteen and his mentality was maturing into manhood. He yearned for consistent money as his prowess for women was at an all-time high. His hormones were the driving force behind his attitude of having a pocket full of Benjamins. In prior years his attempts at achieving financial freedom via quick schemes and thievery often wound up unsuccessful due to lack of planning and/or poor execution. He now came to the conclusion it was time for a steady income to finance his complex teenage lifestyle. He recently transferred from Serra high, which was an all-male parochial institution, to Crenshaw High, where fashion and fanfare set the standard for respect. Scholastic achievement took a back seat to designer shoes, clothes and gaudy jewelry. Many of the students at Crenshaw had access to, sold or dated certain individuals involved in the dope game. The cars that cruised by the school at the end of the day displayed the ostentatious toys that were purchased by the fast and abundant currency. There were nineteen-year-olds driving candy-painted Cadillacs on Dayton tires with chandeliers in the rear seat. Chevy 64s, Nissan Trucks and El Caminos lined the front of the school every afternoon. Older hustlers, gangbangers and pimps handpicked the cutest and most developed female teens for their disposable pleasures. Quite a few of the prettiest girls would have an at-school husband, usually an athlete or humorous dude, and a neighborhood fling for finances and transportation.

Da'Quan at this point began to really understand that a hefty consistent income was what really attracted women. He came to grips with the fact that the Sears and JC Penney fashion selection his mother provided wasn't enough to keep him relevant in this fast-paced, materialistic environment. A few of Da'Quan's good friends, including Tone, began to peddle pebbles of dope. They had new Nikes like there was a giveaway and never seemed to wear the same pair twice. Tone had numerous sweatsuits along with a vast array of earrings watches and baseball caps. Da'Quan's other buddy Bernard went from a grumpy negative Nancy to a free spirit willing to fork out money for burgers and fries every time they went to Hungry Harold's or McDonald's. His jheri curl went from a lifeless dry mop on his head to a sleek and shiny hairdo full of bounce and curls. The cutest girls at school began to gravitate to them and laugh at every joke that spewed from their lips. They were always counting wads of money publicly and never had an issue with the cost of anything. Bernard went from wearing the same dingy cords and sweat-stained silk shirt three times a week, to having a fresh name brand ensemble every day of the week, weekends included.

Tone, who only a few months before had his hands in his mother's purse more than she did, was now a known and established high end customer at the Slauson swap meet. The profit margin was twice the principle, from Da'Quan's understanding, and at the rate they were going they'd be in cars and doing things way beyond Da'Quan's comprehension. Although he was glad to see his buddies elevated, it also perturbed him that he was at a financial standstill. He felt as if they were sprinting freely in the open pastures of life while he remained stagnant with two cement boots attached. It began to affect his self-esteem, going with them places with five dollars in his pocket and they pulled out fifteen and sixteen hundred, spending as if cash grew on trees. Tone would pout about how he only made 600 dollars in three hours and that he needed to at least be making one k a day since his time was valuable. Da'Quan began feeling like an outsider whenever he hung out with them. He was tired of Bernard and Tone paying for him like he was a child whenever they went somewhere. Da'Quan had an ego the size of Mount Rushmore and knew he had to figure a way to get his hands on some dope.

Later that week, Da'Quan had his mind made up that he too wanted in on the financial freedom that Tone and Bernard discovered. With that in mind he called his older cousin Bryce. He knew Bryce would get him jump started and that he was a safe and reliable source. He was the twin brother of Pryce, who always appeared as though his head was way above water. Bryce's veins were filled with the blood of a hustler. He, his mom and twin brother migrated to Los Angeles from the teeny weeny city of Tyler, Texas, following Uncle Buddy's lead. Their biological dad had abandoned them and since their mom was Uncle Buddy's younger sister, he treated them as his own.

Once they arrived it proved to be nothing more than a full scholarship ride in hustling, guerilla warfare and the art of persuasion. By the age of eleven, Bryce and Pryce were shining shoes on Central Avenue during the golden era of Los Angeles in the 1940s. They'd shine shoes seven days a week at the Dunbar Hotel and Lincoln Theater, making themselves a fixture in the premises. The acquaintances they met through the shine hustle would lead Bryce and Pryce down numerous paths of hustle in the years to come. Bryce's charismatic charm and witty personality took him a long way with the ladies making him a shoo-in for the pimp game. After serving in the Navy, Uncle Buddy landed Bryce a job as a butcher allowing him to use that as a smokescreen for his street shenanigans.

Da'Quan snatched up the phone eager for the opportunity to make some real cash. He called numerous times for a week leaving messages until Bryce returned his call.

Ring, ring the house phone rang at eleven p.m. until Da'Quan picked up. "Hello?"

The raspy voice on the other end replied, "Yeah, who this, Daryl?"

"nah, unc, it's Da'Quan seeing wassup, man, I need a job, man."

Bryce cleared his throat and replied, "Doing what, cuzz?"

Da'Quan hesitated before saying, "I don't know, helping you do something, you know, I could be like your assistant. Man, I need clothes, unc, shoes 'n shit. My homies coming up out here and Moms just can't get me what I need, know what I'm saying?"

Bryce understood exactly where he was coming from and replied, "Yea, yea, I know wassup." He continued, "Look here, I'm a holla at my patna Dave at the store to see if he needs somebody. Wait a minute, hold on nephew. Say bitch what I tell you about hitting my shit, bitch! Look here hoe, you snort up my shit again ima put my foot knee deep in yo stank ass." After a minute of commotion, the phone disconnected. Two minutes later the phone rang. When Da'Quan picked up it was Bryce saying in an irritated tone, "Daryl, man, these hoes be outta pocket, but look just come down to the store tomorrow when you get outta class, nephew. Come talk to Dave."

The grin from Da'Quan's face reached from earlobe to earlobe as he responded, "Aight unc, see you then." There was a sound of broken glass and a shrieking female voice in the background as the phone disconnected.

The next day at school Da'Quan roamed the campus in a jovial mood excited about the job interview later that day. As he passed the quad at lunch he saw Bernard standing alone staring blankly through his 100-dollar Gazelles. When he walked up on him Bernard stood in his brand new corduroys, green silk shirt and snakeskin boots. His arms were folded and in his hands was a huge wad of twenty-dollar bills. Da'Quan could sense something wasn't right but kept it cool and played his role by saying, "Wassup, homie, I'm trying be like you when I grow up."

Bernard gave him a pseudo smirk and began griping about the issues with his dope connect, "Yeah it ain't always what it look like, baby boy."

Da'Quan asked, "Wassup, B? What happened?"

Bernard continued to stare stone faced into the crowd of students, "Damn, cuzz, it's all bad. My boy Seany got cracked by the popo last night. That's me and Tone's connect, now a nigga gotta find another plug, cuzz." Da'Quan just shook his head at the news of Seany getting caught with twenty kilos and 150 thousand in cash.

Da'Quan thought to himself, *Holy shit, cuzz.* The numbers were staggering to Da'Quan but he managed to played it cool. He then skillfully asked Bernard, "So how much can u make of that stash there in you hand?"

Bernard just stood there, shook his head and arrogantly said, "What, this little 300 shit? Maybe 600 or 550 if I wanna be generous. Just depends, cuzz. I get powder and play the three to one game, D. I do three parts powder, one part baking soda, then a little water, whip it till it's pasty, cuzz, you know, then my boy cook the shit till it bubbles up. Then, you know, let cool off and it comes back solid ready for sale, homie. Shit, then I go to the spot on Denker and it take about two to three hours to get off, then my money's made, cuzz, profit and all. Shit, D, I do that like five days a week, so do the math. You smart."

Da'Quan's mind raced and as he did the math his eyes bugged out realizing to himself, *This nigga making six thousand a fucking month selling this shit.* Da'Quan was flabbergasted by his calculations as he looked at Bernard sulk and for good reason. Without another moment to spare he gave Bernard a fist dap and told him, "Cuzz, don't even trip. I think I gotta plug for you. Ima get at him now, my nigga. I'll know in a day or two." Bernard had a baffled look on his face as he said, "OK, OK, let me know, D." Da'Quan without hesitation headed to the grocery store to handle his business.

When he made it to the grocery store parking lot he changed into a white button down that was clearly wrinkled from being in his book bag. He had reservations about even working a minimum wage gig especially after hearing what Bernard and Tone were pulling in from the dope spot. He decided to follow through with it since Bryce had put his name on the line for him. Da'Quan entered the store with the traditional L 7 conformist look. He immediately made his way to the meat department where Bryce was slaying cows and pigs with the meat saw machine. He knocked on the window of the swinging door to get his attention. Bryce came out full of animal blood on his smock and goggles. The sight of this type of work made selling crack even more entrancing. Normally Bryce was a jocose spirit but today he had a rigid disposition about himself. He walked up to Da'Quan, gave him a fist dap and said, "Hope you serious, cuz, I don't wanna put my name behind you and you playing."

Da'Quan hesitated, still thinking about the numbers Bernard ran across him. He replied halfheartedly, "Yeah, unc, but my homeboy makes 300 dollars a night selling yay and all he gotta do is sit at the spot and sell it through the mailbox slot in the door. Man, it's gon take me forever to make money like that banging groceries here, I'm just saying."

Bryce took a deep breath, looked at Da'Quan in his eyes and whispered aggressively, "Look, is you serious or is you playing? Don't be fucking around. Dave about to come out." Da'Quan pondered, not really sure if he wanted to be at a job slaving when he could enjoy tenfold the money for sitting around answering a knock at the door. With a sudden look of interest on his face, Bryce inquisitively asked, "Oh yea so umm you say that's yo homeboy?" Da'Quan nodded yes. Bryce pulled him away from his coworkers into the butcher's room and sternly told him, "Look, nephew, get the job, cuzz. You get paid every Thursday, got me ? 'Bout a c-note." Da'Quan nodded like yea ok. Bryce continued, "Then on Friday gimme yo check and ima shoot ya boy three packs. He gon know what it is. You sell it to cuzz for three hundred and keep yo job ya dig. Now you making three hundred a week and while he starts buying more you make more without the risk, make sense?"

Da'Quan's eyes widened as he knew Bernard would need at least five a week which meant he'd make at minimum four thousand a month himself without sitting in the dope house. He also knew if he pulled Tony in then he'd make more than everybody. Da'Quan replied, "OK, unc, I'll take the job, no problem." Bryce gave him a sinister smile, a fist dap and vowed him to secrecy from the family about their arraignment.

Just then Dave came busting in through the double doors startling the two as they spoke of the dope trade. His voice was loud and commanding as he asked Bryce, "Is this big ole strong nephew you been telling me about, BJ?"

Bryce nodded and said, "Yeah, Dave, this my nephew Daryl."

He shook Da'Quan's hand and said, "Look, ima train you up and get you going. All I ask is you be on time, work hard and keep ya smock on when you are on the floor. Can you do that?"

Da'Quan responded, "Yessir."

Dave told him, "OK, just fill out the application for our records up front and you can start Friday from four to ten for training." Da'Quan smiled, shook his hand firmly and went to fill out the application.

The next day at school Da'Quan eagerly caught up to Bernard and ran the play down to him. Bernard looked at Da'Quan like he was Christ walking on water. For the next six months Da'Quan, Bryce, Tone and Bernard ran the play like clockwork. Da'Quan now was a new man, able to buy whatever he wanted plus stack a few thousand for a car and prom. He now saw how the job was a smokescreen to his criminal behavior from his family. It was at this time a hustler was born and he learned the concept of "The Double Up."

THE GAME

SEPTEMBER 28TH 2006 • 37 years old

As Da'Quan drove down Western he glimpsed at his old elementary school only to see young Black and Hispanic kids running carefree in what appeared to be slow motion to him. He felt as if his life was sand in an hourglass and at this point he wanted to utilize every granule of sand that glass had to offer. When he made a sharp right on 39th, a hot splash of coffee released from the cup and singed his thigh bringing him back to his reality. He jumped from his seat cursing as he drove, "Fuck, why I even buy this mothu-fucka some coffee any fucking way, shit!" After the burn died down, he found himself slowly easing up to his spot. He figured he was being trailed anyway so his mentality became, "Fuck it, I'm here for it!"

When he parked he looked around for any suspicious activities or movements. He looked up and down the block before he realized he had a couple of grams of kush and a blunt stashed in his driver's side door panel. The heat had his shirt drenched in sweat as he peeled his soaked back away from the leather seat to grab his weed and blunts. As he split the blunt with his fingertips he began feeling like, *Fuck it. It is what it is. Only God can judge me now.* He studied the crystals on the lime green bud as he crumbled it down into the cigar paper. Once it was twisted he pulled his pistol from his waistline, put it on his lap, reclined his seat and put the fire to the tip of the blunt.

As the smoke filled the cab of his truck, he closed his eyes while inhaling the weed into his formidable vacuum lungs. His hands were extremely jittery as he fought with the fear of the unknown while repeatedly asking God to forgive him and get him safely through this trying episode. He looked down at the cooling cup of coffee and shook his head in disgust at the predicament he had found himself twisted in. After wallowing in self-pity for a minute he decided that if this was his final blunt he wanted to enjoy it like he was smoking with Snoop Dog or Chong. Moments later the potent kush began numbing his senses as he reclined and began reflecting on some of the brighter and exciting times he had enjoyed in the street game.

Chapter 21
PORSCHE BANDITS

MARCH 1997 • 27 years old

Real hustlers don't limit their hustle and oftentimes they wind up with money coming in hand over fist from multiple sources of income. The Octopus theory on achieving separate cash cows is what catapults the multi-faceted hustler light years ahead of an individual pigeonholed in one specific arena. Da'Quan was well into his weed and cocaine hustle and had no plans on doing anything except upping his ante and having as much fun being a D boy as he possibly could.

The block was hot and not only from the blistering sun but from the constant gunplay between the 30's and the Fruittowns. Bodies were dropping daily from the gang feuding, which always slowed drug trafficking due to the extra manpower needed from LAPD. Da'Quan stood aimlessly in front of his known weed spot with a vexatious look on his face. As the beads of sweat from Mother Nature's hot flash gathered on his forehead, he looked down at his brand new all white Air Force Ones and creased Levi's and thought, *Damn, I wish the fucking feds would go get a life so a nigga can get back to making some real money round this bitch.* His patience was growing thin with the lack of foot traffic due to the constant drug raids and killings in the neighborhood. He was down to his last quarter pound of weed and his connect Dino was consequently out of coke and bud until further notice. This was extremely frustrating, as Dino was always 99.9% of the time available with a quality product. Just then his boy Slim pulled up in his brother's ice cream white 1990 Cadillac DeVille to cop the ounce of weed Da'Quan had stuffed in his waistline. When

Da'Quan walked up to the passenger side window and tossed the weed on the seat, Slim marveled at it like it was a rare artifact. Slim was a very loyal client who came no less than three times a day. He and his brother Tommy ran a pool hall and Jamaican juke joint that required an unending amount of weed to keep their clientele pacified. Slim, who earned his name by being 6' 5" without a percentage of body fat on him was a pure hustler who came from nothing. At night he could camouflage himself in the dark so long as his eyes were shut and his white piano key teeth were undisclosed. He was a free spirit who was trustworthy and could be counted on to spend the correct amount each time he showed up for business. While he fumbled through a fist of bundled up cash, Da'Quan stood on the lookout for any undercover or crash units that could've hit the block at any moment. Rumor had it that a couple of jealous homies were in cahoots with the police and turning state's evidence against the money makers in the neighborhood. Even though the area was on high alert, the bills still had to get paid so the hustle had to continue no matter what. After compiling a seat full of dirty money he finally handed Da'Quan $350 in dead presidents. While Da'Quan counted the money, Slim put the bag to his nose before stuffing it under his seat. He looked up at Da'Quan with a troubled look on his face and in his deep Jamaican baritone asked, "Sooo yeah man you gon have thee same ting for me later? You know, man, it's Friday and dem pussy poppers love to hit the ganja, ya dig?"

Da'Quan replied convincingly, "Awwe hell yeah, Slim, just hit ya boy up. I might come up there fuck with some pussy poppers too, cuzz."

A huge grin appeared on Slim's chocolate face as he replied, "My man come on down anytime I put you with Gladys the dick addict. She take you on long ride in the VIP room."

Da'Quan shook Slim's huge, outreached hand and they both laughed aloud, Da'Quan saying, "OK, hit ya boy, I'm on deck and tell Gladys Big Daddy's coming tonight."

They both continued to laugh as Slim replied, "You know it," before pulling off.

Where can I get some bomb weed and coke? This is why the fuck I need another plug? Dino prolly out tricking on that white bitch not giving a fuck! Fuck that nigga not even returning a nigga pages! All of these thoughts ran rampant through Da'Quan's head as he shuffled and organized a huge ball of dirty money. As he walked up the steps to his spot, he heard a whistle. He paused but continued up the steps until he heard a more distinct blow causing him to turn around. He looked down the block and two houses away it was Babo standing in his walkway waving him in his direction.

Babo was an older dude who carried himself as somewhat of a player or mack. He was a brown skinned baby face cat who prided himself on image and the caliber of woman he kept in his presence. He was an octopus hustler known to have his hands in multiple cookie jars. Over the years the ritzy lifestyle filled with lavish cars, expensive jewelry, women who were handpicked and traveling abroad all began coming to a screeching halt for him. Not only had he begun to age and pack on additional weight in his midsection, but the inconsistent flow of cocaine at the time put the clamps on a lot of frivolous spending. As Da'Quan walked up, Babo had a serious look of urgency hidden underneath his colorful grin. Da'Quan, who had a million thoughts racing through his head, grabbed the outreached hand of Babo and greeted him, "Wassup, Babo, what's cracking?"

He replied disappointedly, "Shit from the looks of things, not much, how's everything on yo end?" Da'Quan shook his head like a relative had died. Babo continued, "That's why I called you down here. I know you could use some extra bread while it's slow right?" Da'Quan's antenna was now on alert as he gestured yes with his head. He realized that in the street game you can't just dive into a nine to five gig when things are slow and that sometimes you have to have the balls to take risk in other crimes or hustle to survive. Before Babo spoke again he checked over his shoulders, got closer to Da'Quan's ear and whispered, "Look I got these white boys that need Porsche parts. I can get um, I just need you to drive and trail me. You make thirty-five hundred for each one we get."

Da'Quan let it soak in before asking, "So all I gotta do is drive and trail you once you get it?"

A huge devilish smile appeared on Babo's face as he responded, "That's it, that's all. I just need somebody who's serious, smart and won't snitch. I've been watching you for years, D, I know you are solid for the job."

Da'Quan paused for a moment and responded, "OK, I'm in. I'll check it out, fuck it."

Babo assured him, "It's a piece of cake, shit's easy money. Meet me here at four this afternoon. We gon go scout for the lick." Da'Quan agreed as the two shook hands and parted ways.

The hands on the clock spun until it was 3:55 p.m. Anxiously Da'Quan sat in front of Babo's spot, ready for action. Babo looked out of his window and gestured to Da'Quan *be out in one minute.* Da'Quan sat on his porch feeling a little uneasy, as this was his first go round in the car hustle. After a couple of minutes Babo came out dressed in jeans, Chuck Taylors and a hooded sweat-shirt, which was way unlike Babo. He motioned him down the driveway to the back where he removed the car cover unveiling his souped-up Toyota Camry. It had an immaculate burgundy factory paint with flawless grey leather interior. Babo was wearing his game face as he hopped in and unlocked the passenger door. When he sat inside he was amazed at the condition of the rarely seen Camry. Meanwhile Babo was doing an inventory in his mechanics satchel filled with wrenches and unfamiliar tools. He stared into the bag mumbling to himself with a flabbergasted his face. After a couple of minutes he stuffed a black handkerchief rag, a pair of brownie gloves and a chrome 38 Smith and Wesson special into his mechanics bag and zipped it tightly.

Da'Quan began wondering, *Damn, I didn't know Babo really got down like this. I gotta be on my p's and q's.* As they drove down the block Babo turned up his crystal clear custom Alpine sound system, filling the vehicle with the timeless music of Najhee. He began rambling as Da'Quan paid close attention, "Yea man, this my work vehicle, is real low key, under the radar. You know when you make moves you gotta be shady and see. That way you can watch who's watching you, ya dig?" Da'Quan just shook his head as he gazed out the window listening carefully to each word that left his mouth. The Camry rode exceptionally fast, as he had gotten some engine enhancement work done on it. As they hopped on the 10 freeway west he kept on rambling, "See, Dee, this is it, I'm like a Porsche repo man. If they late on their payments, I come confiscate the car, turn it in to my guy and he pays me and I pay you. I'm one of the few dudes who knows Porsches inside out. You remember the two Carreras I had, right?" Da'Quan, whose only concern was when would I get my money, smiled and shook his head enthusiastically. Babo continued, "So yeah, you know whenever you know I need some extra money, which really ain't a lot, I help him out and make myself some extra bread, ya dig?" Da'Quan just nodded as he looked at the flawless black Bentley that rode next to them on the freeway. There was a blonde teenage girl driving, bouncing carefree to whatever song had her fancy at the time. It made Da'Quan think to himself, *I want the game that gets me the Porsche and Bentley, not be the lame ass luxury car repo man.*

After he exited, Babo drove lead foot through Santa Monica until reaching Wilshire where he turned west to Ocean Blvd. in route to all of the beach homes. He eventually slowed down tremendously and scoured each carport and parking lot taking avid notes of location and time and license plates with his pen and notepad.

After countless hours of driving through the canyons of Malibu and the congested traffic of Santa Monica, Babo pulled over to a low-key tavern called Bennys. The two walked into the semi-contemporary dive that housed a full bar and multiple TV screens. Babo raced to the bar and without looking at the menu ordered a double Benny burger with extra cheese, grilled onions, mayonnaise, a jumbo fries and Coke. He then ordered the bartender, "Russ, gimme three shots of Hennessy and whatever this guy wants."

The bartender, who looked like a washed up rock star, looked at Da'Quan, who declined, "I'm good, Babo, thanks, just bring me a water." The shots were there within seconds, as Babo slammed two back to back with only a slight grimace as he offered Da'Quan the third shot. Da'Quan declined as Babo slammed the third while signaling for another round. Da'Quan wanted to be completely sober and alert as long as he was with Babo, who revealed a whole other persona that he was unfamiliar with. The dive was fairly empty except for an Asian couple who sat inconspicuously in the corner sharing a jumbo fries and a pitcher of beer, while on the other side of the bar sat an elderly white man in golf attire entertaining a husky, younger Latina woman. The tan line on his ring finger was a giveaway that he was out having extracurricular activities outside of his significant other.

Da'Quan observed as the red headed Latina fixture stroked his ego with subtle hand rubs and her undivided attention. She laughed at everything obnoxious that came out of his uncensored mouth. He continuously yelled, "Hey, Rusty, give us another round, me and my li'l quesadilla. Love ya service, Rusty." She giggled, rubbed his cheek and gave him a peck on his paper thin lips each time Rusty slid shots of Patrón their way. She was clearly a man eater, as she positioned her enormous cleavage towards Da'Quan and Babo, sneaking peaks whenever her trick was self-absorbed in his corny jokes or scarfing down a beer. Babo, who was now feeling the Hennessy shots, called Rusty over, "Hey, Russ, he put his arm on Da'Quan's shoulder, burped and continued as Rusty made his second pour, "this here's my guy, Big D. Cool, cool dude, been knowing him since he was on Big Wheels, and D this my muthafucking man, Rusty. We go way, way back."

He stared at Rusty pouring his shots while Da'Quan and Rusty nodded to each other. Just as he slid the second round of shots to Babo, Rusty went to the kitchen and brought back the hellacious burger and fries to the bar. Instantly Babo dug in on the burger like it was going to run from his plate. He looked at Da'Quan, frowned and asked again, "You sure you don't want something? The shit is good, Big D."

Da'Quan calmly replied, "Nah, big homie, I'm good, but thanks." Da'Quan sat and watched Laker highlights on ESPN while Babo and Rusty whispered over the bar back and forth. He noticed Rusty slip Babo a piece of paper as they engaged in what appeared to be a serious discussion of sorts. Rusty had red stringy hair and matching stubble on his thin worn face. The fact that he was a ginger head the color of rust was how he received his moniker in the streets. He kept a cigarette in his ear and from the tattoos of musical notes and guns on his forearms it appeared as though he had some sort of history as a musician.

He and Babo conversed until the old white man yelled, "Hey, Rusty, you know what me and my li'l quesadilla need, baby."

While Rusty tended to the couple, Babo turned to Da'Quan and began rambling with a mouthful of chewed burger, "So this is it." The sight of the chewed meat onions and mayonnaise was disgusting to look at in his mouth so Da'Quan focused on the TV and listened as Babo talked and chewed his food simultaneously, "We gone slide back up to the condo we checked out earlier in Palisades Canyon, the one with the waterfall in front. I've been watching him for a couple of weeks. Old white man, he gets home at seven thirty every night. He takes a shower at ten fifteen and he's out by ten twenty-five religiously."

Da'Quan listened and thought, *Damn this nigga's a low key stalker, he knows this man's whole daily ritual.*

Babo burped extremely loudly as he continued, "So we got ten minutes max to get in get the whip and get the fuck out. All I need you to do is watch my back while I get the whip and trail me all the way back to my place. If somebody comes or you see anything suspicious just honk twice and I'll know what to do, ya dig?"

Da'Quan shook his head and replied, "Gotcha." After he scarfed down his burger and plate of homemade fries he washed it down with two more shots of Hennessy. He pulled out a hundred plus a twenty-dollar bill, signaled to Rusty as he left it on the counter before walking out. Rusty smiled, knowing he was tipped fifty dollars, and threw up his white fist like a black panther as the two walked out of the exclusive dive.

When they got back in the Camry, Babo's demeanor went from level-headed and easygoing to agitated and worrisome. Before starting the car he fumbled through his mechanics bag again while mumbling under his breath. He checked his watch and began giving Da'Quan specific orders. The smell of raw onions and cognac from his hot breath dominated the inside of the car as he spoke, "OK, D, here it is. We got seven minutes to get up here and handle business. All I need you to do is get behind the wheel and do what I told you." He looked Da'Quan in his eyes and asked, "You cool, got any questions?"

Da'Quan replied, "Nah I'm good, OG, let's get this muthafucka.""

Babo smiled and replied as they drove towards the condo parking lot, "That's why I fucks with you, D. You down and you smart." Minutes later, as they approached the second level, he drove at a snail's pace, bypassing Benzes,

Bentleys, Ferraris and other makes of Porsches along the way. The tension grew enormously the closer they got to the mark. Babo signaled for Da'Quan to slow down as a middle-aged white woman in a skimpy Fila tennis outfit slammed the trunk of her Volvo and crossed their path with rackets in hand. She stared at the two as if she knew that two negroes dressed in black in an economy car was not the norm in this complex. After she passed and hurriedly disappeared, he parked with the car running. Babo tied his black rag around his face and reached for his mechanics bag. He surveilled the whole area through his beady eyes, looked at his watch and said to Da'Quan, "OK, the muthufucka's bout to hit the shower. Watch my back. When I get under this muthafucka' back up a few feet and be on the lookout, ya dig? There ain't no cameras on this side either, so we good."

Da'Quan just nodded his head as he looked into the diabolical eyes of Babo. He looked both ways before sliding out of the passenger door like a boa constrictor. He squirmed effortlessly across the pavement, which was indicative that he was a veteran at his craft. Within seconds he had maneuvered his 5'10', 245-pound chunky physique underneath the metallic blue Carrera. Da'Quan slowly backed up the Camry as the butterflies in his midsection began ricocheting violently like scud missiles. While Babo handled his end, Da'Quan sat with clammy palms and peeled eyes, anxious to get the hell out of dodge. He sat drumming his fingers against the steering wheel as beads of sweat formed around his neck and forehead. He looked down in the cup holder and noticed the piece of paper Rusty handed Babo. It read, "Black Carrera 25k" scribbled in pencil. The hands on the clock became motionless as his nerves seemed to have suspended the act of time. Just then in the rearview window a swift image of a black cape or dress appeared to fly across. Da'Quan took notice, not sure if it was a person or if he was being delusional. He kept his eyes fixed in the mirror and seconds later a white-haired Caucasian man in a black robe and silk pajamas scampered across the rearview mirror within feet of the Camry. Da'Quan's eyes exploded from their sockets causing him to honk his horn as Babo by now had hopped in the Carrera and fired it up full blast. The roar of the engine sent vibrations through the ground as Babo punched it with burning rubber full throttle in reverse. In the rearview mirror

Da'Quan saw half of an elderly white man's face behind a pillar draped in a black house robe aiming an automatic weapon. Before Babo was in drive the white man fired twice—*payow, payow!* Babo rolled down his window and with a villainous expression on his face returned the favor with three shots from his revolver—*boom, boom, boom!*

Da'Quan ducked for cover even though neither shooter was aiming directly at him. Babo abruptly slammed it in drive and darted out of the complex shadowed into the dark. With no signs of the bathrobe, Da'Quan instinctively peeled out right behind Babo's trailblaze. As they sped at top speed down Entrada road, the unfamiliar twists and turns at high speed became nauseating and frightful. When they made a left on Cabrillo Road, there were five squad cars making sharp rights on Entrada with sirens blaring. Babo punched it in overdrive towards the 10 freeway darting in and out of traffic like he was in the Indy 500. Da'Quan, whose driving skills were far behind those of Babo, just kept him in sight while monitoring his rearview for police sirens. The 10 freeway entrance was fairly empty, allowing Babo to gain quick access to his infamous straightaway. Da'Quan followed suit only to watch the taillights of the Carrera disappear into the pitch black of the highway.

The adrenalin rush began to subside, as there were no signs of the police trailing and Da'Quan's heart began beating at a normal pace as he turned up the jazz that was playing in the Camry. The soothing sounds of the saxophone with the mild drum kicks allowed Da'Quan to retract the whole event that had transpired. He realized that Babo was a professional stalker and car thief who would go to any length to finish his mission. Looking back he now knew Rusty was his tip off guy of any hot leads in the area. Da'Quan had no idea until today that beneath the surface of Babo's wholesome and fly image housed a monster with a killer instinct. He now truly understood the dynamic between the Dr. Jekyll and Mr. Hyde theory. When he finally arrived on the block he slowly pulled up into Babo's driveway. When he made it to the backyard he saw the Carrera to the side of the house with a car cover, and Babo's bedroom light was on.

Da'Quan knocked on the back door feeling uneasy about the whole episode. After a couple of moments Babo opened the door in a bathrobe drying his head with a face towel. He smiled, as it had appeared he had returned to his passive and conformed behavior. He had a thick diamond cut gold chain on, with a Mercedes Benz medallion riddled with diamonds. It had to be worth twenty thousand or better. As Da'Quan walked in, Babo jokingly asked, "What took you so long? I was about to turn it in." He began laughing as Da'Quan stood silent and emotionless. Babo walked back into the bathroom while yelling, "Yeah, man, that muthufucka knew I was on him or that white bitch let him know and called the police. My game is usually way smoother than that, so I apologize, D." He came back into the kitchen still drying his head and nonchalantly asked, "Did you notice anybody following you or the police or anything strange?"

Da'Quan shook his head and replied, "Nah man, we good." Babo, who could sense the ill vibes Da'Quan was giving, broke the ice by saying, "Oh yeah, Big D, go grab that on the dining room table. That's all you." Da'Quan walked into the dining room and saw a mound of twenties, hundreds and fifties sitting on the table. A sudden feeling of exoneration towards Babo came over Da'Quan as he counted out four thousand dollars in new money.

Babo smiled like a proud father on Christmas as Da'Quan shuffled through the cash. He arrogantly said, "The extra five hunnid's for the old white fool shooting. I never have that problem, but it is what it is."

Da'Quan replied, "It's cool, big homie. I'm 'bout to turn it in, good looking on the lick, I needed it." He knew from the piece of paper in the car that Babo would make at least 20k for that Carrera but who was he to count the next man's pocket? As he put his cash in his pocket and headed to the door Babo put his hands on Da'Quan's shoulder and said, "Yeah, D, I may need you again. We always need more than one hustle."

Da'Quan replied, "Yup I got you." As he walked down the driveway he knew he'd never do any other business with Babo, who revealed a dark side to him he'd never suspected. He was always warned by his relatives about a wolf in sheep's clothing and now he knew Babo was in fact the wolf of the block.

Chapter 22
FORBIDDEN FRUIT

OCTOBER 1979 • 10 years old

Life at times presents rude and eye-opening experiences to all who are granted the privilege to live.

Delilah hummed church hymns as she prepared Da'Quan for his second year of trick or treating. Innately, Da'Quan was very uncomfortable with the glorification of evil, gory masks and the wicked symbolism that was attached to Halloween. He silently observed the divergent behavior of his peers earlier that day at school. Da'Quan, with all the focus on Delilah, stony-faced asked, "Grandma, does God like Halloween?"

She sighed while her placid face cringed and replied, "God gotta love it if he made it, now quit asking so many questions and have fun." The look on Da'Quan's face was filled with bewilderment as his intellectual appetite needed more logic to feed his questioning. He quietly thought to himself, *That sounds like some bullshit. How in the fuck would God want me afraid of him and demons? I don't get how this shit works.*

Just then he heard the adolescent voice yell, "Da'Quan, Da'Quan!" It was his next door neighbor, Andrew. He was the only son of Mallory and was six years Da'Quan's senior. Andrew had a challenging childhood faced with an undiagnosed bipolar disorder his mom Mallory also possessed. Verbal and oftentimes physical abuse infused the home in which he was raised. He wore a halo of guilt over his head despite his mother's offbeat and sometimes unpredictable behavior. Local neighbors always welcomed him, as they were aware of his arduous situation.

Delilah slapped Da'Quan on his bottom with her heavy hand as she guided him out the door. Andrew stood and marveled at Da'Quan's brand new full body Evel Knievel costume. There was envy in his eyes, as he was guised as the Hulk. Andrew's get-up was undoubtedly homemade, being nothing more than a ripped dingy shirt, dated Levis cut unevenly at the knees, bare feet and fifty-cent green washable face paint. His nappy unkempt afro was by far the pinnacle of his whole masqueraded attempt. Delilah handed each of the boys a shopping size brown paper bag for trick or treating. She sternly told Andrew, "Now y'alls go only from here to Arlington back to Exposition down to Gramercy and back here. I mean it." Her face was filled with conviction as she looked Andrew eye to eye without blinking.

"Yes, Mrs. Dunn," Andrew replied respectfully.

The two began their journey down the block. Andrew out of envy began to ridicule Da'Quan's costume. He facetiously chuckled in his adolescent baritone and said, "You look like a gay Elvis."

Da'Quan scrolled down looking at his costume and thinking, *Why this bitch ass nigga talking 'bout the costume my goddamn mama brought me? I'd fuck this punk ass nigga up if I was bigger.* As Andrew continued to jeer unmercifully at his appearance he stared at Andrew diabolically. He could sense the malice in Andrew's comments causing his temper to rapidly elevate.

The laughter from his own jokes and constant finger pointing provoked Da'Quan's ire as he blurted, "You mad cause Mallory can't afford to buy you a costume, nigga." Four knuckles grazed Da'Quan's chin, sending him airborne backwards. He landed on his back dazed as Andrew quickly grabbed Da'Quan's neck and with his knee planted it forcefully in his chest.

He spoke in a heinous tone saying, "If you talk about my mama again, ima kill you li'l nigga. I ain't playing." He then yanked Da'Quan by his collar to his feet like a rag doll. As Da'Quan asked him, "Would you fight my cousin Dray?"

Andrew's eyes widened instantly as the thought of dealing with Dray over this never crossed his mind. Andrew was aware of Dray's vicious reputation on the streets and he wanted no part of the drama that he and his killer hooligans would bring. Andrew knew that Da'Quan was insinuating if he pulled another stunt like this that he would drop a line to his relatives to come handle the situation accordingly. Andrew instantly befriended Da'Quan promising him dibs on any candy he wanted first on their mission. Trick or treating with Andrew was a rollercoaster ride every year.

Andrew's outfit was sullen and had no life to it. He looked homeless and from how he ate the candy as soon as he got it was an indication of his hunger. He even said, "Nigga, tonight candy and apples is dinner for me." He emptied every bowl they ran across with no discretion. Truth of the matter, Andrew was actually too old to be out engaging in these types of activities. People shied away from him, as he was more imposing than all of the other kids and most of the parents. Andrew began to grow more and more discouraged with the awkward treatment he was receiving that night. He finally had had enough and devised a cockamamie bag snatching plan. He told Da'Quan as they walked, "Halloween ain't just for costumes and trick or treating. Kids also get to play tricks on other kids. Da'Quan's inquisitive mind began to process the comment.

Andrew asked aggressively, "Can you run a whole block fast nigga without stopping? I know yo ass got asthma."

Da'Quan confidently replied, "Hell yea, I can do that."

Andrew continued, "OK, we gone hit up Browning where them rich ass chinkheads be trick or treating. You gone just run fast ahead of me and don't look back or be fucking around li'l nigga, keep going all the way to Saint Andrew's and get to the house."

Da'Quan nodded his head saying, " OK, OK, but what if they chase us or I fall?"

Andrew impatiently replied, "Nigga just run."

The two eased up on the corner just as dusk transformed into dark. Andrew placed his right hand on Da'Quan's shoulder and slowly guided him to the corner. There were multiple families of Asians mindlessly basking in the enjoyment of the pagan holiday. They owned a three-quarters-of-a-mile strip of the predominantly black and Latino neighborhood to themselves. They introvertedly existed in a carefree Shangri-La cultured environment. Andrew bent down to Da'Quan's ear and told him, "Look, nigga, just run on the left side of the grass to Saint Andrew's and turn left. Don't look back, don't stop, don't be bullshitting for real, aaiight?" he said in a more than threatening tone. Andrew took a step back and said "Li'l nigga, take off on go and run like yo life is on the line, OK? Here we go. On ya mark, get set, go!"

Da'Quan sprinted down the block with every bit of speed he could muster. As he ran he began to hear Asian voices screaming, "Hey you a nigger come a back a with that bags!"

He heard kids screaming and crying frantically, "That was mine, that was mine, nigger!"

Da'Quan knew from the haunting cries of children and the blatant racial slurs that he was part of some sort of caper. His adrenaline gave him the speed of a cheetah and although he was running at his very fastest, he could hear Andrew galloping near, breathing heavy from his windpipes. As Andrew surpassed Da'Quan, he could see Andrew with a handful of bags held tightly in his grip. He yelled breathlessly, "C'mon, nigga, go faster. Don't stop." Da'Quan turned his head, and two steps behind him was an overweight Asian dad giving chase with a pocketknife in his right hand.

Da'Quan's asthma began to erupt from the fear and strenuous sprint but he managed to outrun the unconditioned dad, who out of exhaustion gave up in the middle of the block. By the time Da'Quan caught up to Andrew, he had emptied the five bags he snatched into the grocery bag Delilah had given them. Da'Quan's eyes bulged at the large amount of candy and treats Andrew had filled his bag with. He reached open handed for a Snickers bar as Andrew snatched the bag away and said, "Hold up, homie, now it was my plan. I did all the dirt and you reaching for my shit, kick back a minute."

Andrew sifted and rumbled through the bag coming out with five or six black jellybeans, which were the worst tasting candy invented. He handed them over to his disgruntled crimee, who frowned and just threw them in the rose bushes angrily. Andrew then handed him a boiled egg to which Da'Quan responded "Naw, fool, you giving me all the nasty shit. Where's the M&Ms or candy apples homie?" Da'Quan's temper began to boil as he said, "This ain't right, Andrew you wrong. I was right with you all night. I want some chocolate or some good shit fool."

Andrew began snacking away in Da'Quan's face, refusing to break bread with the treats of choice. As disappointed as he was, Da'Quan just gripped his consolation reward for thievery. Andrew was overjoyed as he boasted about his feat, "Now that's bag snatching, li'l nigga. Them chinkheads too slow for the kid, even for yo slow ass," while bursting into a sinister laugh. He continued to stuff his face like a glutton with M&Ms, 3 Musketeers and Snickers. Da'Quan made no effort to eat his sullen black candy treats as they walked back to the home front. The two made it back to the side of the porch and began digging into the bag of treats. Andrew pulled out a shiny green granny apple on a stick covered with caramel and peanuts. Da'Quan's jaw dropped at the site of the candy-covered piece of fruit.

Andrew unwrapped it lickety split and began flaunting it in Da'Quan's face, saying, "Here, take a bite nigga." As Da'Quan closed his eyes to plow in with his chompers, Andrew removed the apple screaming "Psyche!" and bursting into laughter. Da'Quan was furious and just stared at Andrew with malice as he watched him bite a mouthful of the delectable treat. Within seconds a look of trauma was plastered on Andrews face. Blood began gushing from his mouthpiece like a water faucet on full blast. He doubled over spitting out what he bit along with a hefty chunk of his razor sliced tongue. The bleeding was so severe it created a stream of blood that traveled down the sloped driveway. Da'Quan looked on in complete shock not knowing if this was real or one of Andrew's tasteless acts of humor. Delilah rushed to the door after Andrew let off a distressing cry from the pain. By now Andrew had fallen to one knee as blood squirted profusely from his face. Mallory came running barefoot down the driveway and stared speechless as Delilah wrapped Andrew's head in her apron to stabilize the bleeding.

Delilah screamed frantically, "Well don't just stand there, dummy, call the motherfucking ambulance before the child bleeds to death!" Mallory began backing up slowly, wiping her tears as she realized her baby was in a serious, life-threatening circumstance. She made her way to the back as Andrew lay languid in Delilah's loving arms.

Andrew's grandmother Ms. Alma came out from all of the commotion and Da'Quan attempted to explain, "Yea so Andrew bit into an apple he took out of one of his bags and blood jumped out everywhere."

Ms. Alma instantly burst into a holy frenzy saying, "In the name of Jesus, please oh Lord, please take the pain away from this child's body please." After what seemed like an eternity, the paramedics arrived. The two rookie medics hoisted him onto a gurney, wrapped his head and shoved him heartlessly into the back of the ambulance. The chief paramedics asked Da'Quan if he knew who may have given him the fruit but Da'Quan's response was "Iono."

Mallory and Ms. Alma hopped into the back of the ambulance with Andrew and they pulled off with sirens blaring. Delilah grabbed Da'Quan, sighed, and gave him a kiss and bearhug as the ambulance departed. This was Da'Quan's first lesson in the power of karma.

Chapter 23
COMPTON RIDE

MAY 1995 • 25 years old

There's nothing more beautiful than a sunny Sunday in Los Angeles, where Mother Nature has blessed the natives with her uninhibited stamp of approval as far as weather conditions were concerned. The weed and cocaine sales were at an incredible high, and the payoff in the streets was bountiful. Whoever was hustling powder, rocks, weed, promethazine or ecstasy reaped huge rewards during that lucrative era. Curb peddlers who started at the bottom of the ladder, such as Da'Quan, had managed to become a distributor to those who now regulated the curb sales. The market wasn't oversaturated and due to the decline in the economy at the time, a huge percentage of people opted to get high as a mental resort from their financial woes.

As his weight went up so did his savoir faire with the ladies and his mental awareness of the pitfalls and obstacles that accompany drug dealing. He began understanding how having cash to fuck off with women enthralled them and brought out their harlot ways. His transformation from a curb peddler to a distributor also allowed him to see the envy and hate in the eyes of those he supplied. He now had a steady stream of income and the perks to him at this point outweighed the consequences. To a certain degree the game had him convinced he was protected by a false sense of invincibility.

Da'Quan sat smoking a fat kush blunt as he waited on his ex-girlfriend and at times off and on concubine, Honey, to pick up her phone.

"Hello, hello?" she answered out of breath with a sense of urgency.

Da'Quan replied calmly, "Wassup, babe? You busy? It's Dee."

She fumbled with the phone and blurted, "Oh shit, hold on, handsome." Da'Quan sat with a perplexed look on his face as he continued to blaze while she gathered herself. After a discombobulating moment she spoke into the receiver, "I ain't never too busy for you, I just got out the shower, the phone slipped out my hand, then I dropped my damn towel, my boobs went flying everywhere but I'm good now, wassup with you?"

Da'Quan smirked as her sensuous voice soothed his eardrum with a visual of her shapely naked peach-colored body standing with dripping wet titties. Da'Quan got acquainted with her at his mom's job when he would visit her or take her lunch. Honey was a teacher's assistant with a voice that was as provocative as her high yellow complexion and her extremely curvaceous figure. Although she was quiet amongst strangers and colleagues, Honey had a rebellious side in her, buried just beneath the surface of her squeaky clean image. She was alluring to the naked eye with a vixen undertone that made for a deadly combination. Da'Quan was attracted to her wit and her nasty sense of humor. She was honest and open about her promiscuous ways as a teen-ager, never hiding the fact she had been around the block quite a few times. Her parents, who were middle class city workers, always provided above and beyond for her no matter the circumstance. They were extremely protective of her since one of her ex-boyfriends shot her in the shoulder with an AK 47. She claimed it was an act of passion and wore the bullet scar as a badge of honor in the game of love.

Da'Quan replied, "Shiid nothing, just sitting here blazing on sum bomb trying to get some more and see what's popping for the day."

She replied in a sensuous tone, "Hmmmm weed and what's popping sounds like Sunday Funday. How can I be down?"

After a silent moment of picturing slamming her doggystyle drenched in sweat, he responded, "Well, shit, check this out, my connect ain't hit me back but when he does and I cop, I'll hit you up see what's popping for later. We can blaze, get a bottle and ima beat dat up."

His bold approach stirred her hormones as she moaned aloud and eagerly replied, "Shoot, if yo boy ain't hit you back, you can get with my homeboy Zoo Bee, who got the fire, and then we can go get a spot and you can beat this peach up baby."

Da'Quan thought for a second and asked, "Can he beat four thousand for a pound, cuz that's what my dude's ticket is?"

She replied, "He ah beat it if I tell him too. I got his ass wrapped around my pinky finger so don't trip baby just let me know what time you can head to Compton and I'll let him know, we can meet at his spot."

He replied, "Well shit if it's like that I can head out in a few minutes. So what, just meet you over on Stanford at his spot?"

She quickly responded, "Yeah so imma hit him tell him we need a pound of his best shit then ima throw something on and head over there. Then we can take it from there. So look, handsome, meet me over there in about an hour, OK?"

Da'Quan smiled and replied, "OK, babe, sounds like a plan. Work that nigga down on the ticket for me."

She instantly endorsed his comment, "Anything for you, handsome, so lemme off this phone. My nipples hard and I'm getting chilly standing naked by my window. See you in an hour, muah." She slammed the phone in his ear letting him know she was adamant not only about the money but the sex as well.

Da'Quan finished the fat stogie he was burning, went into his stash, counted out four thousand in hundred dollar bills, wrapped them in a red rubber band and stuffed the neatly folded money deep into his Levi's pocket. As he cast about his room for any items he may need, he reached under his pillow and grabbed his 380 pistol and before he put it in his waistline thought, *Nah I probably won't need it, it's honey's people.* He put the pistol back and headed for the back door. Suddenly he stopped on a dime in the kitchen, the high he was on had him rationalizing the situation as he mumbled to himself, *Nah, D, them niggas is bloods from Compton, they know you not a blood and nine times out of ten one or two of them niggas is fucking or trying to fuck that bitch, Honey. Plus you can't trust a bitch.* With that epiphany he went back to the bedroom and grabbed his gun just in case things went left. Now that he was secured and had the money he hopped in his truck and headed southbound to Compton.

The ride was nerve racking not only due to the sticky traffic on the 110 but also due to the thoughts of copping a pound of weed from some cats he barely knew. Not only were they red rags which were opposite his family and neighborhood, but also from conversations he'd had with Honey they could be cutthroat and scandalous at any given moment. He also knew that they had the best weed around and that he'd be able to move it more rapidly than even the weed he got from his connect. He drove in silence, meditating on the move until he exited the 110 on Rosecrans, where he popped in his favorite King T song, "Bass," which gave him the jolt of energy and courage he needed to handle this particular situation. The rest of the ride was filled with the desire and heart of a hustler who was ready to die or kill if need be.

As he pulled up on Stanford, there were three dudes including Zoo Bee standing in front of his weed spot. They all had on burgundy grey and black in some way shape or form. Da'Quan began looking for a parking space until he noticed Zoo Bee flagging him down in their direction. He hesitantly drove down to the trio and rolled down his window. Zoo Bee walked up to the driver's side of the truck cautiously, as he may have had doubts about Da'Quan's intentions. The two had done small transactions before but had never done any business over fifty dollars, so this was a huge step in trust earning. Da'Quan turned his music down, rolled down the window and shook the outreached hand of Zoo Bee as he greeted him, "Wassup, my nigga, did honey tell you I was coming?"

Zoo Bee smiled revealing his mouth of white teeth and replied, "Yessir, she said you wanna grab the whole thing, right?" Da'Quan nodded his head as Zoo Bee continued, "OK, well shit, homie, since you Honey's folks, I can do it for thirty-eight hundred, and it's the real deal blood."

As soon as blood came out of his mouth, Da'Quan's antenna immediately went up. He began to look at Zoo Bee's grey suede Pumas with the fat burgundy laces that matched his USC sweatshirt and Trojan hat. His dark face was plagued with acne that appeared pus-filled ready to burst while his bloodshot eyes revealed the years of dirt he had participated in over the years. Da'Quan paused for a second and replied, "All right, where it's at, homie?"

Zoo Bee smirked and told him, "Come on, dog, just park in the back of my apartment next to that ten speed by the trash can and ima bring it out."

Da'Quan replied, "Aight," before easing back to the trash bin. While he waited he hastily counted out the cash while keeping his eyes peeled for any strange or unusual behavior. Five minutes later Zoo Bee came back and hopped in with a turkey bag full of some of the best weed he'd ever laid his eyes on. It was a bag of heavenly delight, huge dense buds with so much THC on them they looked like they were sugar coated.

As Da'Quan inspected the product Zoo Bee smiled and said, "Yeah, blood, that's straight from Humboldt County. The growers just ran it down last night." The whole cab of Da'Quan's truck smelled like a family of skunks were in the glove compartment as he readily handed the cash over to Zoo Bee.

He looked at Zoo Bee in the eye and asked, "So it's all here, my nigga?"

Zoo Bee smiled as he grabbed the wad of cash and responded, "All there, my blood, plus I slid a couple of extra grams in there for you to smoke." Da'Quan gave him a fist dap as he shoved the funky bag under his seat. Just then the roar of a motorcycle vibrated the pavement. The thunderous sound alarmed the two and through Da'Quan's rearview he saw Honey's cute mulatto face smiling as she sat behind them on her custom red Kawasaki Ninja 750.

Zoo Bee looked back at Da'Quan and asked, "So you good, dog? There go ya girl."

Da'Quan replied instantly, "Good looking, homie, I'm straight. Lemme see what this bitch talking 'bout." They both chuckled as they got out of the truck. Da'Quan's nerves were calming down now that he had what he needed and his mind was now set on seeing honey's little sexy ass run around the motel room naked with a joint in her mouth. Honey had a look of adoration for Da'Quan in her eyes as she puckered her lips for a kiss. When Da'Quan kissed her, Zoo Bee and his two goons, who had by now walked to the back, had a look of jealousy engraved on their faces. She gave Zoo Bee a fist dap and nodded at his two goons like she was a mob boss. Her sexy tight jeans and fitted leather top had all four of them lusting over her at once. The two goons paid Da'Quan no nevermind as they kept their eyes glued disrespectfully to her derriere. She revved the engine again and yelled over the roar of her engine at Da'Quan, "C'mon, baby, hop on let's go to the store real quick." Da'Quan's face had a sudden look of apprehension on it, as he didn't care for motorcycles period. He had learned how to ride but never felt safe enough on them. She began pressuring him while he stood aloof not sure what to do. She slapped herself on her ass and jacked it up while licking her long tongue across her heart shaped lips.

As he hesitated, one of Zoo Bee's thugs blurted, "Shit, I'll ride it if he's too scared." Zoo Bee slapped him on the arm and gestured to him to be cool as they all chuckled. Finally with that comment, Da'Quan's ego inflated like biscuits in the oven as he instantly hopped on the back of her supercharged street toy.

Honey, who was elated, revved up her street toy, backed out of the driveway and as soon as they hit the asphalt she took flight sending them from zero to at least 100 mph in the first ten seconds of the ride. The power and torque of her street toy had Da'Quan's stomach lodged in his throat. When he looked to the side, the houses moved in a blur, the high pressure of the wind crushed against his face as he clutched her tiny waist for dear life. When he gathered the nerve to look ahead he noticed the light at Alondra was yellow and that a big yellow school bus was heading through the intersection at the same time. Suddenly, honey yelled out, "Hold on, baby!" as she instantly shot up to 120 mph and pulled a wheelie. Da'Quan's bowels were at the tip of his asshole as his rear end was inches from the asphalt. He cowardly closed his eyes as she rocketed through the intersection like she had a death wish. By now all Da'Quan could hear was the blow of the wind and the sound of the bus driver pressing his horn desperately. When they came off of the wheelie, Da'Quan struggled against the wind to open his eyes while Honey yelled exuberantly, "Yeah, muthafucka, I love you baby!" The kids on the bus admired her move as if she was a superhero while the chunky male bus driver flicked the two of them off. She quickly pulled up into the liquor store relieving him of a possible cardiac arrest.

When he hopped off of the bike his legs were like noodles and he had to literally fight to keep from immediate defecation. She laughed uncontrollably as she wrapped her arm around his waist in the parking lot. As his heart began to beat at a normal rate and he regained his composure, he noticed a homeless man sitting outside of the store skewing meat on a makeshift grill made from a shopping basket. He was a heavy set, dark-skinned man around fifty-five or sixty, with matted hair, dressed in a torn T-shirt revealing his rotund belly, along with a pair of pants that appeared to be two different trousers sewn together. Half of his pants were jeans while the other half was a torn slack material. He had no shoes on his swollen, battered feet covered with cuts and bloody lesions. He was focused on his grill diligently as though he had a horse blinder on. Before they entered the store, Honey reached into her skintight back pocket and pulled out a wad of cash. She grabbed a twenty-dollar bill and yelled, "Squash!"

The homeless man turned and when he realized it was Honey, a huge toothless smile grew on his desolate face. She then balled up and tossed him a crisp Jackson as he caught it like his life depended on it. He then blurted in his husky worn voice, "Thank you, Honey, God bless you, doll."

Honey replied, "You know I gotcha, Squash." When they entered the store, Da'Quan instantly interrogated her, "Why the fuck would you give him twenty dollars? You rich now?"

She instantly retorted with an attitude, "Well since you have to ask, daddy, he was my seventh grade math teacher who lost his will to live after his wife and daughter were killed in an automobile accident." She gave a deep hurtful sigh and continued, "He started hitting the pipe and eventually lost his job, his car and house, nigga. So now does that answer your question?"

She then went on in a sarcastic tone, "Oh yeah, by the way, we call him Squash because he was also like some kind of gang advisor who squashed beefs with a whole bunch of gangbangers in the area since he taught most of them, Da'Quan. Besides I do what I want with my money, OK? So let's just get some drank, zags and liquor so we can do the nasty, OK big head?"

Da'Quan just nodded as he could see Squash meant a lot to her and her community. After he paid for the items for their rendezvous and they walked out of the store, she smiled and waved at Squash as he responded to her acknowledgement, "OK, sweetie, now you be safe on that bike." Da'Quan, who remained silent, noticed something odd as he turned the meat on the skewer atop his makeshift grill. He focused closer and noticed it was a huge wood rat he was cooking on the skewer over the fire. The grotesque and repulsive expression on Da'Quan's face caught Squash's hopeless eye as he blurted, "Yeah, my man, gotta do what you gotta do in life, but you gotta good woman right there, my man, hold on tight, my brother."

After his comment he turned back and continued with his barbecuing. Da'Quan just nodded as he and Honey hopped back on her street toy. As she revved it up, Da'Quan quickly said, "Look, babe, be nice on the ride back. I wanna make it in one piece so I can wheelie up in that pussy."

She winked, smiled and replied, "OK, since you put it like that I'll be nice on the way back." She kept her word as they drove gingerly back to Zoo Bee's to pick up his truck. When they arrived no one was outside and she hopped in with him leaving her bike in the back. They frequented a sleazy motel in the area where they would go, get loaded and have to go at it like animals in the wild. As soon as he cranked up his truck she cocked her ass up, unzipped his jeans and began gobbling his manhood like it was candy laced. Da'Quan was now grateful for his "Compton Ride."

Chapter 24
DURMITES MADD

SEPTEMBER 1994 • 25 years old

Contrary to popular belief that the rap game is full of luxurious living conditions, stacks of money in the safe and beautiful women adhering to your every need and want is fallacious for up and coming artists. In reality the interviews, time in the studio, rehearsals, stage shows, videos, in between traveling on planes and buses all quantify into a very absorbed lifestyle. Living out your dreams in the public eye comes with a majority of supporters who are the foundation and stabilizers of your platform of success. Aside from the jaundiced eyes of naysayers, most are gracious onlookers who appreciate your artistic and or athletic contribution to the world. These are the souls that protect your crown and want to see you defeat the odds no matter the struggle.

As the single Nuthin Ta Lose received more airplay and the miles stacked up on the tour bus, Dred and Da'Quan began to experience the pros and cons of rap life on the road. The VIP treatment, monetary largesse and beautiful women captured by the magnetism, thus treating them with exalted behavior, became the norm. Traveling from culture to culture is also an undisputed educational advantage artists gain as a reward for their efforts. However, with all of that being stated, there is one considerable constituent that cannot be overlooked. In the rap game *The Nigga Element* will always be an integral part of the job description. These are the people who possess latent envy for what appears to be your success. In most cases these individuals are complete strangers who have no idea of the grueling roads that led you to that point of opulence.

Da'Quan and Dred had been on the road for over a month and the growing pains of touring had matured them tremendously as artists and more importantly as men. The tour bus pulled into the less than posh Holiday Inn express at around 4 p.m. It was a crystal clear Sunday evening in the Bull City of Durham North Carolina. The perfect countryside landscape, overlooking green pastures and sunny hills, had the whole entourage in a tranquil state of mind. Mint Condition had a gig at a local nightclub and managed to get Dred a paid gig as the opening act for them. Stokley, the lead singer for Mint and Dred, departed the tour bus first as they discussed the format of the show that evening. Stokley was a perfectionist when it came to performance and wanted everyone involved on the same page.

While the band and crew unloaded the vessel, Da'Quan remained seated, staring through the tinted windows taking in the moment. It dawned on him that he was on the road performing with a platinum status band on the other side of the country. From state to state he'd observed the different dynamics and cultures that are a part of the American fabric that binds us together. Here in North Carolina the white people acted and dressed in a very conservative, aristocratic fashion. The men wore polo shirts and Dockers pants while the women wore summer dresses and carried umbrellas to block the brutal sun rays from their delicate skin. Texas had a completely different type of aura, as the men wore jeans, Brent hats and plaid shirts while the ladies dressed in the same fashion as the men. They had no qualms about portraying the good ole boy and good ole girl image with all of the country props it entailed.

Just as Da'Quan was coming into awareness one of the black crewmen nudged him on his shoulder. He held a balled up paper towel to Da'Quan's nose and as the pungent chronic stunk up the bus, the crewmember Bobby said, "Here, man, we were on the motherfucking road smoke free. I copped this shit before we left. It should help ease ya nerves, youngblood." When he opened the napkin it was no less than a 100 dollars' worth of chronic. He gave Bobby a fist dap and thanked him graciously for the fix that was long overdue. Bobby even gave him a couple of zig zag papers to roll it with. Da'Quan's main objective now was to get away and get high to deal with the unbearable boredom of North Carolina. As he exited the bus he told Bobby once again,

"Thanks, OG, fa real you saved a nigga." Bobby nodded his head and threw up the black power fist as Da'Quan slid off of the bus.

When he made his way into the lobby the pungent aroma of weed caused the entire lobby to look at him as if he were an extraterrestrial creature. He noticed Akbar engaged in a very serious conversation with the front desk personnel. When he walked up he heard Akbar asking the manager in a very pressing tone, "Well, yo, hey how the fuck did these clowns know Dred was staying here? Obviously somebody on ya staff been talking and y'all should of contacted us to let us know some shit like this was going on, I mean what the fuck?"

Da'Quan, who was oblivious to the situation, stood in silence as the lily white front desk manager with Cathy on her name tag calmly responded in her southern drawl, "Well, sir, we had no way of contacting your party prior to your arrival, but you can rest assured the local law enforcement agencies have been notified and that we have a zero tolerance policy for any criminal activity around our guests here, sir."

Anbar began to sweat from his camouflaged headband as he boiled with fury before asking, "Yo, Cathy what fucking room did you assign me to?" She frantically scrambled through a drawer as she trembled in fear.

She pulled out a key nervously and handed it to Akbar as she whispered, "Room 211, sir, and again we are so sorry for any and all inconveniences."

Akbar snatched the key and gave her a baleful stare as he told Da'Quan, "Aye yo, D, come on grab those two bags. Let's get the fuck up to the room, yo." As the two approached the elevator, Da'Quan, who was completely baffled, asked, "What the fuck is going on, homie, everything cool or what?"

Akbar remained silent until they boarded the elevator before saying, "Yo, here's the deal, Dee, it's these bums out here they go by the fucking *DURMITES* or some corny shit like that. But for whatever reason these bums called and left death threats for you and Dred."

Da'Quan's heart rate began beating double time as he replied, "What the fuck they wanna kill us for, cuzz? Who's these niggas anyway? Dred ain't no fucking thug ass MC; he's on some fucking conscious hippie shit."

Akbar agreed, "Exactly, Dee, we know that, but these country bumpkin ass muthafuckas heard him say the schoolyard Crips and they feel like he's dissing them or some bullshit to that effect. These muthufuckas done called like three or four times asking what room y'all in and saying they gon be at the show to handle this shit with him and his crew. Just a bunch of bullshit. The label gave Dred another room to throw these clowns off. That's where we headed now."

Da'Quan then asked, "What Dred have to say? Shit, where's that nigga at, I just saw him?"

Akbar replied, "Yo, he's shook. I just told him to go to the room and relax. The kid is ready to go back to Cali and hibernate yo," They both chuckled as the elevator door opened. As the two walked down the hallway Akbar began sniffing and looking around for the skunky aroma that tickled his nostrils. He turned to Da'Quan and asked, "Yo, is that you kid?"

Da'Quan smiled and replied, "You know it. A nigga need some drugs with all this shit poppin' fuck." Akbar's face showed nothing but compliance in his statement. Walking up to the door it was evident Akbar was figuring a way to calm Dred, who was absent minded in fear. Da'Quan, who was somewhat of a prankster, put his thumb over the peephole while forcefully banging on the door. Akbar just laughed and shook his head at Da'Quan's antics, who by nature used humor as a coping mechanism for life's situations.

It was obvious Dred was horrified as Life yelled, "Aye yo, kid it's Akbar and Dee, open up, Dee got his fucking finger on the peephole, yo. C'mon, champ, we got business to handle, you good kid, I got chu." Moments later Dred opened the door, his face was painted with beads of sweat from the terror that ruled his body.

Da'Quan barged in yelling uncompassionately, "Get yo scary was ready fuck them niggas, cuh! Sick of worrying 'bout rednecks now niggas, too? And the police? Fuck this shit, you come our way you get dealt with!" He paused as his chest heaved in anger and looked at Akbar who stood in solidarity with his rant while Dred looked like "Who is this nigga?" Da'Quan continued, "Nigga, the meek shall perish, if it's my time, then it's my time, but ain't no white boys, cops or some punk ass DURMITES gone stop me from doing me, fuck that."

Akbar interjected smoothly, "Yo, Dred, ya man Dee gotta point, we got business to handle no matter what yo. Check it, I'm from Queens, kid, and we don't never ever back down when it comes to our doe, at least with me. Now I can't speak for everybody, but ya boy ain't having it." He put his arm around Dred's shoulder and whispered, "Look, you got me, Big D and Brenda." Dred and Da'Quan both looked perplexed like, "Who the fuck is Brenda?" Akbar smiled sinisterly, raised his shirt and revealed his steel frame .50 caliber Desert Eagle.

Da'Quan's eyes leaped out of his head and excitedly said, "Now that's what the fuck I'm talking about, big homie! That there are all them punk ass DURMITES scatter like roaches, cuzz"!

Akbar chuckled at Da'Quan's bravado and calmly continued, "So, yo, kid, now you know we good so let's get cleaned up, get yo mind right." He looked at Da'Quan and winked in reference to his weed. "And we head up to sound check, cool? Y'all good?" They both nodded and began unpacking.

The drive in the Lincoln limo was filled with tension. Although Akbar and Da'Quan remained unwavered, for Dred's sake, they still kept their heads on a swivel for any suspicious activities. When the limo pulled up into the parking lot the only vehicles on the lot were the tour bus and their limo. The three hopped out and treated Dred like he was the POTUS or some other elite figure. Dred had never encountered any form of street violence and this situation had him rattled.

The club was uptown in the city region of Durham. The inside was recently renovated and possessed a swanky contemporary night spot vibe. Ingeniously, the stage was built to make the performers appear to be entertaining in midair. The bar was all top shelf, planted directly in the center of the club, glimmering like a spaceship. Two massive security guards met the entourage at the side door and shuffled them inside with urgency. While Da'Quan and Dred played with the cordless mics and the soundboard, Akbar and Brenda took a full circuit tour of the club in case the DURMITES stayed committed to their threats. As the funky basslines and violent drum kicks filled the speakers, the duo disremembered any thoughts of the DURMITES or any other negative force that lingered in the atmosphere. Music was therapy for the two of them as they marinated in the flavor of their artistry.

Once soundcheck was done, the trio headed to the door, but before they could get there the 6'5 275-pound redneck security guard blocked the door with his huge frame. He guided them to the window making them aware of the pack of twenty hooligans that loitered in the parking lot. They stood boldly passing blunts and Hennessy surrounding a pitch black 1970 Chevy Monte Carlo that was in impeccable condition. Most of the brash thugs wore grey khakis, white T-shirts and royal blue Duke Blue Devils hats. Akbar and Da'Quan simultaneously whispered, "That's them muthafuckas." Dred stared terrified at the pack of wolves in fear of the unknown.

After a moment of analyzing the scenario Akbar turned to the security guard and sternly demanded, "Look take Dred and Domino back to the hotel in one of y'all's cars! Fuck it, me and Brenda gone ride in the limo back."

The guard looked flummoxed and asked in his southern accent, "Who's Brenda?" Akbar opened his camouflage jacket revealing Brenda to the unsuspecting security guard. With that confirmation, the oversized corn fed guard ushered Dred and Da'Quan to another exit and instructed another guard to chauffeur the two in his personal vehicle. Akbar boldly hopped into the Lincoln with Brenda and the limo driver unseen in the black of the tinted windows. Da'Quan and Dred sat in the dummy car watching the limo depart. The hooligans began gravitating towards the Lincoln throwing up gang signs while at the same time proceeding with caution. One of the bolder thugs attempted to open the rear door and when he did, Akbar sat in the rear with Brenda aimed to kill. The thug ducked in fear causing the rest of his gang to scatter like roaches from light. The dummy car with Da'Quan and Dred quickly exited out of the back driveway and raced to the hotel. Later for the show, the Durham Police department escorted Dred's entourage to the venue and the DURMITES did not show up.

Chapter 25
DOUBLE WHAMMY

APRIL 2000 • 30 years old

The street game is filled with sex, monetary rewards, snitches, lies, incarceration and murder. In this *Circus of Devils* there are no written rules and to survive in the concrete jungle of Los Angeles it's best to be familiar with your surroundings and be extremely wise about the company you keep. Since his moms demise Da'Quan had been battling with his inner demons for months. He had been questioning his overall faith in a God and was more than willing to test the power of karma by doing whatever he felt with no regard for the repercussions or consequences. He had now been knee deep in every hustle from auto theft to dope dealing. Da'Quan now saw the world through lenses with smudges of hate and pain thus obstructing the beauty and blessings that life had to offer.

It was a normal California Tuesday afternoon. The warm breeze from the Pacific blew light winds over the faces of the natives of beautiful Los Angeles. Mother Nature was calm as she allowed for everyone from the desert to the sea to enjoy her smile from the sun on a carefree day. Da'Quan sat on the side of his porch in a fresh wife beater showing off his broad shoulders and hefty arms. As he sat in deep thought about life and money, the blunt he was smoking began burning the tip of his fingers causing him to bark in pain, "Muthafucka, shit, ahhh fuck." He attempted to toss the hot roach but it stuck to his fingertips, searing them, causing his skin to peel . The pain from his burnt fingertips caused him to hop to his feet as his fingers became numb with pain. While he battled with the burden of his burns, two associates of his, Corleone and Blizz, drove up parking directly in front of Da'Quan's house. When he looked up he saw Corleone's chubby face smiling from the passenger seat of the burgundy 1996 Buick LeSabre. Corleone was a true hustler mixed with a touch of revolutionary and a hint of gangster.

He was a smooth, charismatic Creole player, who always was concocting up a scheme to make some money. He was well groomed and always had on a fresh pair of jeans and flawless tennis shoes. His motto was *you gotta fake it till you make it!* He believed that self-marketing was the express route to wealth. A huge grin revealing his gold canines opened up on Corleone's face as Da'Quan walked up to the car. Da'Quan kneeled to the window and gave him a fist dap with his left hand as his right hand fingers were agitated from the burn.

Corleone yelled out, "Big D, my nigga, just the man I wanna see."

Da'Quan chuckled as he replied, "What up, Corleone, cuzz. Sound like we bout to hit a lick."

Just then Blizz leaned over from the driver's side with his hand outreached saying, "What up, Big D, cuz, we need that size you got, boy." Blizz was Corleone's right hand man in crime. He was a short black fella with a rotund belly from all of the lavish eating and drinking he enjoyed. Even when he smiled it was nothing but the evil and wrongdoings he was committing that brought him joy. It was once said that he set his older brother Rodney up to get robbed for his dope and afterwards he fronted him the same work back to help him get back on his feet. Rodney never got wind that it was his blood sibling by both parents that set him up. He earned the name Blizz from being consistent in supplying the neighborhood with blizzards of cocaine year around. He wore his oversized Cuban link necklace with a gold Blizz medallion riddled in diamonds every day as his status quo to young impressionable girls in the neighborhood. Da'Quan could feel the malicious energy seeping from the vehicle but had no intention of turning down nothing but his collar.

Corleone began running the play down, "Check this out, Big D, you wanna make fifteen hundred for like a hour of work, my nigga?" A look of dubiety emerged on Da'Quan's face as Corleone and Blizz looked at each other and chuckled at Da'Quan's confusion.

Them jeering at each other made him ask, "OK, yeah, nigga, but what the fuck I gotta do? Don't bullshit me, cuzz."

Corleone snapped back into business mode, "Nah, Big D, no bullshit. We just got some hook ass niggas from the Midwest out here. These niggas wanna spend a hundred k on some blow, you know, and take that shit back to Ohio or wherever the fuck they gone send it. But here's the thing, Big D, I fuck with these niggas and they do good business and all but a hunnid thousand cuzz is a nice piece of change and you really can't trust niggas." Blizz began splitting a blunt as he interjected, " real talk on my mama." Da'Quan just absorbed the information as Corleone continued, "So here's what I need from you, Big D, ima give you a pistol, my snub nose, and all you gotta do, my nigga, is sit quietly in the bedroom until we handle our business and them niggas leave. That simple, cuzz. If you hear anything shady going down or hear some rumbling, just come in busting on them niggas. Just don't pop me tho, nigga." Blizz began laughing as he crumbled a few grams of pungent kush to stuff his blunt with.

Da'Quan nodded his head yes as he asked, "So let me get this shit straight, my nigga, all I gotta do is sit in the bedroom, be quiet, and be ready to bust if some bullshit jump off and I make fifteen hunnid that day?"

Blizz, who by now had the blunt rolled and hanging from his choppers, replied instantly, "That's it, that's all, Big D. You got a lighter, cuz?"

Da'Quan handed him his lighter and responded, "Aaaaiight, cuzzo, I'm in. When we doing it?"

A huge smile appeared on Corleone and Blizz's faces as Corleone replied, "Look, cuzz, them niggas suppose to fall through about eight tonight, so come about six thirty in case they are watching us. We gone meet them niggas at the spot I'm 'bout to move out of in the backhouse, my nigga. All you gotta do is show up, cuz, that's it."!

Da'Quan's face lit up at the thought of easy money as he replied, "See you niggas at six thirty."

Blizz, who was choking up a lung, tried to pass the blunt to Da'Quan but dropped it under the seat and began cursing like a sailor, "Son of a bitch, cuz, I hate when I do that shit, cuzz."

Corleone shook his head sarcastically at Blizz's antics, extended his hand to Da'Quan and as they shook hands, said, "Aight, Big D, see you a little later, cuz." He turned to Blizz and began barking at him like it was his younger brother, "See, cuz, that's why you can't be getting high when we working, cuz, that's God sending you a message. Start this shit up, nigga, we gotta handle business, cuz." The duo slowly pulled off bickering back and forth as Da'Quan walked back to the porch nursing his burnt thumb and index finger.

The day had just become worth living for as he now had the task of playing security to a hunnid thousand dollar dope deal. The thrill of quick cash was always the draw for him. It intrigued him to be able to earn, in one hour, what it would take a square with a nine to five to make in two weeks. South Central is a gumbo pot of hustlers and goons all mixed into a fairly small radius. Crime was at his beckoning and for him to resist would be like a malnourished pit bull not pulverizing a hot slab of ribs in his bowl. The temptation was far too great, for anyone who opted for quick cash, to turn down in an hour of need or greed. In the back of his mind, however, he knew Corleone and Blizz were as crooked as the cops they evaded and he knew there was more to his job description than sitting idly in the bedroom with a pistol. Although his logical side spoke the unforeseen reality of bullshit, his greedy and sinister side spoke clouds over his logic, ultimately drowning out the voice of reason.

Six thirty finally showed his face as Da'Quan pulled up at the end of the block as instructed by Corleone. As he got out of his truck and began walking to the spot he had an eerie notion about the whole situation. He began soul searching to himself, "Damn, a hunnid thousand is a lot of scratch shit, and these niggas I know ain't having this type of bread to be trusted. If it goes down, will they set me up or is it the police these niggas is selling, too?" The thoughts showered his brain to the point he almost turned back around and washed his hands of the lick. But his greed, desire for material objects and lust for pretty bitches kept his feet marching directly towards the spot. As he entered the gate to the back, the house looked completely dark and abandoned. Through a small slit in the shade he could see a dim light and the light from a TV screen changing the lighting patterns inside. He eased up slowly to the door and knocked sensibly not to alarm them. Corleone, who stood at a mere

4'7" swung the door open like he was a 7'0 bouncer with a gun. He had a look of relief as he welcomed Da'Quan.

"Big D, my nigga, I knew you was down, that's why I fucks with you, homie." The backhouse was run down with all of the windows covered with ripped shades. It smelled like Camel cigarettes mixed with the unique odor of freshly cooked crack cocaine. There was only a worn down sofa, two fold up chairs, a tiny color TV, a dining room table with a half empty forty ounce of Mickeys on top of it next to a used triple beam surrounded by cigarette ashes. Corleone, who just missed being a legit midget by an inch or so, hobbled on his gimpy legs to the kitchen. When he came back he handed Da'Quan a chrome snub nose 38 and told him, "Look, Big D, this my little trusty bitch, hopefully you ain't gotta use her but this bitch a put a hole in a nigga and send his ass leaking away, cuzz."

Da'Quan grabbed it confidently and stuffed it in the small of his back. The vibe between Corleone and Blizz was drab and monotone unlike any other day. Blizz sat in the corner with a camel dangling from his lip nervously fumbling around, wrapping and bagging the kilos for the exchange.

As Corleone and Blizz prepared the package, Da'Quan sat to himself and watched Alex Trebek challenge people's intellect on "Jeopardy". While Da'Quan silently tested his wit with the show Blizz blurted, "Big D, cuzz, give me a hand with this shit, my nigga." As he helped Blizz tape up one of the packages he looked at Da'Quan, took a drag from his Camel and said, "Check this out, have you ever heard of the Double Whammy, cuzz?" Da'Quan's facial expression exposed his ignorance to it as Blizz chuckled and yelled for Corleone, "Ayye, cuzz, my nigga D ain't up on game or what, cuzz?"

Corleone limped into the room with a drunken smile on his chubby face, "Nah, cuz, but he about to be."

Da'Quan, who was now apprehensive about the move, interjected, "What the fuck you niggas talking 'bout?" In the back of his mind he knew he had a loaded pistol so it couldn't be a set up but he could smell the fishy aroma of bullshit.

Corleone hobbled over, grabbed two of the bricks and sat them on the sofa. He pointed at each and asked Da'Quan, "Big D, what's the difference in those two bricks?" Da'Quan shook his head reacting totally naive. Corleone and Blizz glanced at one another and began cheesing as Corleone continued with his spill, "Look, D, you see this one? I got a triangle window slit in this one big homie so the niggas can see the coke and take a bump if they want to." Da'Quan just listened to his presentation quietly. Corleone continued, "Now I do that so the nigga a know he got some quality Peruvian, cuzz, but now in this one and all the rest is dummies, cuzz."

Da'Quan looked at Blizz perplexed and asked, "What's dummies?"

They both began laughing as Blizz chuckled and yelled, "These niggas from Ohio is if they go for it." Corleone and Blizz burst into laughter leaving Da'Quan confused. It then dawned on Da'Quan that there was only a hunnit and fifty dollar sample of coke in the cut triangle of one pack while all the rest were filled with cotton and newspapers. Whoever was coming was spending 100 thousand on 150 dollars' worth of powder and twenty dollars' worth of dollar store items. He understood now why he had a loaded gun and that if this deal were to go bad there may be casualties behind their fuckery.

Just then Corleone snapped back into business mode, "Aight, Blizz finish that shit up. These fools on the way. Big D, go post up in the room and be extra quiet, cuzz."

Da'Quan sat in the bed-less bedroom on a milk crate, which felt like pins and needles as the time approached for the lick. He knew that Corleone and Snow were tricky but had no idea that this is how they operated. He also was stewing because they waited until five minutes before the play to fill him in on it. As he sat on the milk crate in the room contemplating backing out Corleone announced, "Aaiight, cuzz, them niggas outside on they way in, it's on."

The butterflies in Da'Quan's stomach began bouncing angrily throughout his stomach almost causing nausea. He began sweating in his palms and breathing heavily. Blizz lit up another cancer stick to calm his befuddled nerves while Corleone appeared calm and composed. Just then there were three hard knocks on the door—*bang, bang, bang!*

Through a keyhole in the bedroom door, Da'Quan had a fly on the wall view of the whole living room at his disposal. Corleone opened the door and greeted the two like Russian royalty at Buckingham Palace. Blizz kept his laidback demeanor as he took another deep drag from the Camel to ease understandably bundled nerves. The first cat to walk in was Swerve. He was an Indian red complexioned dude with a diamond studded front gold tooth. He was clean cut and appeared to be a square trapped in the clutches of the dope game. Swerve's demeanor and body language were docile and meek which served as a predatory point for the wolves in the street hustle. Directly behind him was Rasta Ben. Ben was a true Dred from Jamaica who found his soft spot in Ohio and planted his flag. He wore long brown dreds and his face was that of a hardened criminal. He and Swerve together looked like a cop and criminal duo on the surface, but the truth was they were two major cocaine distributors who had the Midwest sewn up.

Swerve played the liaison between Corleone and Ben, who had never been introduced prior to that day. Ben shook Corleone's hand with a strong look of cynicism written all over his face. He stared Corleone in his eyes without blinking or shedding a bit of jovial emotion. He looked around the room multiple times and it was apparent that Ben had an ill vibe about the whole situation. Corleone, who was visibly uneasy about Ben's presence, went right into the spill for the dope, "Well fellas here's what y'all came for, check this out." He reached into the duffle bag full of dummy birds and pulled out the sample pack with the small window cut in the middle. Swerve took it from Corleone and handed it to Ben, who snatched it with brute force from Swerve's manicured hands. He flipped the triangular cut window back and with his long pinky nail dug in the sample of coke with it and took a huge bump from his own pinky fingernail. Everybody in the spot including Da'Quan could feel the tension between the dealers. After a moment with his eyes closed he shook his head in approval.

The tension in the room subsided until Ben asked Swerve, "Yeah man, tastes pret good man, lemme open another one, make sure it's all the same." Silence filled the room as Da'Quan's heart began beating overtime as he now realized Ben was halfway on to the scheme. Blizz put his hand over his forehead and took a huge drag from his Camel as Corleone thought quick on his feet.

"Look, my nigga, we got all that shit wrapped and sealed tight, my nigga, if you don't want it, we got folks in line for it no big deal, my nigga." Rasta Ben began scratching his dreds with a look of suspicion written all over his face. It was clear as day that he and Swerve had pistols in their waistlines and Corleone was very poised in how he dealt with the apprehensive killer.

Just then Swerve interjected, "Nah, nah, we good Corleone, my man, just got hit over the head a couple of months ago and just don't wanna take no more losses."

Corleone replied, "Yeah I can dig it well, bust whatever one you want, but we can't repack it cause all the tape and plastic wrap is used up, my niggas." Ben looked at Swerve, looked around the room and gave Corleone the look of death as he began rumbling through the duffle bag of fake dope pulling out a random brick. Da'Quan reached in the small of his back and grabbed the pistol. Blizz and Corleone's eyes were glued to Ben's hands as he began trying to undo the tightly sealed package.

Just then Swerve intervened, "Look, my nigga, these my folks. The shit is good plus we gotta hurry up and get these muthafuckas over to the bitch's house so we can start driving back." Ben looked at Swerve's innocent face, smiled and took the backpack full of rubber band wrapped cash out. The site of all of that money being dumped on the table sent chills down Da'Quan's spine. Corleone looked at Swerve and asked, "Hunnid thousand, my nigga?"

Swerve replied, "All there in hunnid dollar bills, my boy. You wanna count it up?"

Corleone smiled and shook his and Ben's hands and said, "Nah, no need to, my nigga, you always come correct." Just then Ben put the duffle bag of dummy dope on his shoulders and motioned towards the door. He moved hesitantly as he surveilled the spot with a look of scrutiny on his face.

Swerve, who was totally sure he had just won, whispered to Corleone, "Yeah man, don't trip, he always paranoid so we good. Ima hit you up later, bro." Corleone just nodded his head as they gave each other a fist dap before the two walked out the door.

Blizz watched the duo from a slit in the shade until they made it out of the front gate. Once the gate shut he yelled, "Aaiight, Big D, them niggas gone. C'mon, cuzz."

Da'Quan hurriedly came out the room while Corleone counted out Da'Quan's money. Meanwhile Blizz was moving his triple beam, his pistol and any identifiable items that could trace back to them out the back door.

As soon as the money touched Da'Quan's palm Corleone began gathering items while clutching the duffle bag full of money for dear life. He spoke with trepidation in his voice as he blurted, "Look, Big D, cuzz, come out the back with us we ah drop you off by your car and you gotta hurry up and get the fuck outta here, cuzz, in case they got niggas watching."

Da'Quan shook his head nervously because he knew that when Rasta Ben became aware he'd been beat, he and Swerve would come back to kill no questions asked. As they hurried out the back, Blizz began laughing as he said, "Cuzz, can you imagine the look on them niggas' face when they bust them dummies open?"

They both giggled out of control as Da'Quan replied, "Y'all niggas stupid. Get me to my car, muthafuckas."

Blizz told Da'Quan in a serious tone, "Nah, you right, Big D, just take yo bread and lay low. Them niggas never saw yo face, cuzz, so you all good, my nigga. I gotta take my shit and lay low in Vegas or Arizona for a year or two till shit die down, cuzz."

They all loaded up in a Camry Corleone borrowed from a bitch he was fucking with as he replied, "Yeah, my nigga, ima shoot down to Louisiana with my folks and eat some crawfish and fuck bad Creole bitches till my loot run out, cuzz."

They all laughed as they drove down the back alley to Da'Quan's truck. When they let him out they all looked at each other as they were sworn to silence to avoid the killing spree that could accompany a move such as this. After they dropped him to his truck he sat and recounted the money. He was uneasy about how he earned it, but thankful his face wasn't attached to it. Just then as he started up his truck he noticed Rasta Ben and Swerve slowly headed back towards the back gate with their guns drawn. Ben's body language was filled with fury as he made Swerve go first, barking at him furiously. Da'Quan started his truck and made a quick U-turn as he drove away from a death wish of *Double Whammy.*

Chapter 26
BACK GATE

MARCH 1983 • 13 years old

Junior High was far advanced compared to the wholesome virginal environment of elementary school. There were separate classes for each subject, the walk to and from school was of greater distance, students were in the beginning stages of puberty and gang affiliation was a more prevalent issue. The maturation of the girls would often attract boys in their late teens and unfortunately even males in their early twenties would lurk for companionship from an underaged lass.

It was a cloudy Friday afternoon as the last bell of the week rang, releasing the students from educational captivity. Da'Quan was in a jovial mood that day, not only because school had culminated for the week but also because he had received compliments all day on his brand new TI sweatsuit his grandmother had bought for him. These File knock off sweatsuits raised plenty of eyebrows in the inner city, and to have one made you the topic of discussion. Delilah loved spoiling her only grandchild and she lived to see him filled with happiness and self-confidence. He felt like he was on cloud nine in his royal blue and white ensemble bottomed off with some brand new all white Nike Meadow Max Supremes. His attire that day was equivalent to a custom luxury Mercedes Maybach. A simple outfit changed the whole complexity of his reputation while adding fuel to his budding mack skills.

Outside in the corridor stood Bad News and Aaron. They engaged in a brief slap boxing match until the man-sized paws of Bad News began sounding like thunderclaps each time they connected to Aaron's cheeks and neck.

Aaron's face went from amber brown to cardinal red as a result of the violent slaps Bad News provided. Bad News only had one gear, which was full throttle. He would give 120 percent in any competitive situation at hand. The watery eyes and discolored face of Aaron drove Da'Quan to ask while chuckling, "What the fuck he doing you so dirty foe, cuzz? Yo whole face look like pizza, nigga!"

It was quite apparent Aaron wanted to take the bout further but he ultimately knew Bad News would end up slapping or socking him into a coma without remorse. The comment from Da'Quan eased the tension as the trio headed out through the back gate. The back gate at Audubon was the entrance and exit for students who lived in Crip neighborhoods, while the front gate served as the entrance and exit for students who lived in Blood neighborhoods. By nature it became this way and it also kept a lot of unnecessary violence from taking place on campus.

As they exited the Crip gate there was an older teen getting frisked by security from head to toe. The thuggish teen appeared to be between seventeen and twenty, with a number of tattoos on his arms and neck. He was tall and slenderly built with visible scars embedded on his young mulatto face. His afro was humongous and it waved back and forth from the light afternoon breeze, while security frisked him thoroughly for weapons. Da'Quan glanced at his wrist, which was bound by steel cuffs, as the guard sarcastically asked, "Look, Tracy, why do you think it's OK for you to come up here to harass our kids, man? you too damn old for this."

Tracy abruptly replied, "I ain't up here harassing no kids. I just came to pick up my cousin, cuz, I mean Mr. Snyder. Damn!"

Snyder, as he was commonly known, had worked with Tracy since his volatile days back in middle school. He knew that Tracy was a cunning and violent kid always looking for some mischief to partake in. Snyder cracked a slight grin saying, "Yeah I get it, but that blue rag in ya left back pocket and these sagging 501s give you a certain look, champ."

During the aggressive shakedown, the shades on Tracy's face got smashed into the concrete. Just as Bad News, Aaron and Da'Quan slid past the melee, Tracy turned his head and caught pupil to pupil eye contact with

Da'Quan. The callous stare in his sinister eyes sent a cold chill down Da'Quan's spine as he gazed at him like prey in the wild. He cracked a smile, revealing several missing teeth that would always be cemented in Da'Quan's memory bank. The three just continued to pass as Bad News rambled loud and confidently about never bowing down to no man even if it meant death. Tracy continued to stare at Da'Quan's sweatsuit, aware of its value and the fact it would fit him to a T. The wolf had spotted his prey and now needed to be freed up to strike his target. Da'Quan began to walk briskly as he felt the predator vibe of Tracy overtaking his innate Spidey senses.

Just then he heard Aaron's squeaky voice blurt, "Look, cuzz, what I just found." The three looked down at a shiny pair of brass knuckles next to a switchblade lying camouflaged under some spring leaves in a flower bed.

Bad News picked up the street tools immediately saying, "No, nigga, I found 'em." He placed the knuckles on his fist, smiling like an infant nursing a warm bottle of milk. He stuffed the blade in the small of his back due to its size and he loved emulating having a gun in his possession. They studied the brass knuckles in awe, totally unaware that Tracy saw them near the flower bed playing with his weapons. He wanted to yell but he was being detained and couldn't blow the whistle on himself. The three began to walk off totally unaware that Tracy was being uncuffed and that those were his weapons.

As they walked down the block there was a faint voice in the far background saying, "Eh cuh, eh cuh, that's my shit li'l niggas, eh cuh, I know y'all niggas hear me, that's my shit, cuh."

Da'Quan turned back and to his surprise Tracy was jogging in their direction gasping for air. Da'Quan's heart began to race triple time as he tapped Bad News saying, "Eh, News, here come that older nigga with the big ass fro!"

Bad News looked back and responded, "So what? It three of us and we got weapons, cuzz." He started giggling and said, "That old nigga tired cuzz he smoke too much cuz." Aaron had picked up his pace clearly afraid of dealing with the likes of Tracy. Bad News put his hand with the brass knuckles on it and facetiously yelled, "Naw, it's ours now homie."

From 100 yards away Da'Quan saw Tracy's face go from mulatto to cardinal red in color. He stopped and ran towards the street and out of nowhere he hopped into a green drop top '67 Impala. He sat high on the passenger side instructing the driver to head in their direction. Da'Quan, Bad News and Aaron bolted without a word said. Aaron and Bad News were clearly faster than Da'Quan as they began separating from him with each step. Bad News yelled, "Dee, Dee, go down King, cuzz, go down King home."

Da'Quan out of fear and instinct followed his command. The other two separated and hopped back gates in their route home. The run down King Blvd. was nerve racking. He ran actually looking back more than he looked ahead. Pedestrians honored the fear of his movements by clearing the sidewalk as he ran for his mortal survival. Halfway down King Da'Quan found refuge behind a parked mail truck, which allowed him to catch his breath while he stood paralyzed in fear. Thoughts of not hanging with Bad News again, changing schools and having a weapon for himself ran through his head. After a moment of regretful thinking he saw the green gangsta mobile sliding down King. The driver was much older in the face than Tracy. He had a penitentiary hardened look about him that intimidated Da'Quan even more in this situation. The car slowly passed as Tracy and his driver searched high and low for the trio.

Da'Quan stuffed his sweatsuit jacket in his backpack to not be such an easy target. As the car moved on Da'Quan began sprinting and thinking, *All I want to do is make it home, God. All I want to do is make it home.* He kept his feet moving and focused on the route home. His body was numb all over, consumed in fear. The juice from his jheri curl sweated into his eyes, racing down his cheeks and neck. His wind was again testing his will, but in the near distance he saw Lucky Liquor. He thought to himself, *If I can just make it to the liquor store, I can take a break then shoot home. All I gotta do is get to the store!* As he ran he saw visions of his mom giving him sound advice. Uncle Buddy's voice rang in his head, "Them boys you runnin wit no good, Snodgrass."

The liquor store was now only a few yards away as he stumbled and gasped for air. He glanced back and to his dismay he saw the green gangsta mobile speeding in the direction of the store. He was defeated and ready to throw in the towel. All he saw was Tracy's afro blowing violently in the wind with a grimace of death on his young face. Da'Quan darted into the store screaming at the top of his lungs, "Max, Max, big Max!"

Max, who was in the rear of the store doing inventory, ran out quick to address the sound of distress in his store. He came out with his .38 revolver glued to his palm saying, "You OK, mister? You OK?"

Da'Quan while gasping for air replied, "Naw, naw, Max, these older dudes chasing," he paused for a second to catch his breath. "These older dudes chased me and my two buddies over a knife we found that they say is theirs."

Max asked, "Well, is it theirs?"

Da'Quan replied, "Well, yeah kinda, but it's like we found it and they say it's theirs but they are trying to get me, Max, and I ain't even got they stuff."

Max could see the fear in Da'Quan's face and although he didn't want drama in his store he told Da'Quan to go to the back and chill. Da'Quan adhered to his command and quickly shot to the back. As he sat trembling he quietly sat on a crate hiding behind a rack of Fritos. Da'Quan could hear voices in the store but didn't pay much attention until he heard Tracy say, "Cuzz, I coulda swore I saw that nigga run in here."

The older dude he was with replied in a deep baritone, "Yeah, me too, cuz, go check back over there by the paper towels and bring me a forty, too, cuh, one a dem Ole E's."

Tracy responded, "Naw, cuz, that lol mark ain't here. Get me one too, Bone."

Bone replied, "C'mon bring em. Hurry up, tho, I got the seven double parked, cuzz." As they handled the transaction, Da'Quan sat with his eyes closed in pure fright. Moments later the storage room door came bursting open.

Da'Quan cringed for his life with his eyes closed tight as he heard Max's angry voice yell, "Sir, whatever you doing don't eva bring it to my store again, sir, you got me?"

Da'Quan replied, "Gotchu."

Max told him they were long gone and that he needed to get home. Max then said, "Them dudes are trouble, especially the one with afro. You need to pick better company, sir. You a smart kid, don't get hurt running with dummies."

Da'Quan shook his head, wiped the tears of fears from his face and headed to the door. Before he left, Max handed him a Coke and a bag of Doritos and told him, "Sir, this one's on me. Now go do homework. sir"

Da'Quan nodded his head and began thinking about what Max was saying. As he headed towards the door, still leery of Tracy and his sidekick, Max shouted, "Stay away from bangers and hoodlums; it's not you."

Da'Quan smiled and looked both ways thoroughly before dashing through the neighborhood to his grandma's house. Once he made it to the block, the sight of his grandmother watering her assorted flowers and shrubs surprisingly filled him with grateful joy. He eased up on her and gave her a heartfelt kiss on her cheek and gently whispered, Love you, Grandma." She had a look of skepticism on her wise face but elected to enjoy the moment and not dig too deep for anything. She was just content with the notion of someone having unconditional love for her. As he walked up the steps she wet him with the water hose and said, "Whatever happened, my love, I'm just glad you're OK. Now go wash ya hands before you go digging in them short ribs."

Chapter 27
LOWRIDER

JANUARY 1999 • 29 years old

Hustling and grinding for all intents and purposes comes with a huge risk, be it time incarcerated or the beneficiary of a murderous bloodbath. But on the flipside there are plenty of perks that make it almost worth the risk. Crip Rell, who was Savage's younger brother, was Da'Quan's hustling partner, who always encouraged enjoying the fun side of hustling and/or gangbanging. He had been an active gangbanger from the Harlems since the fourth grade and had amassed a decent reputation as a shooter and a hustler. The streets were aware that he was the younger brother of Savage and that if you had a problem with Rell, Savage would solve it. Rell was the sensible brother with compassion and humanity in his heart while his brother handled society with Medieval tactics. Although they were like night and day, they both had a great amount of respect for one another. Whenever Crip Rell would overanalyze a situation, Savage would come with the barbaric solution that dissipated all of the bullshit involved. In other instances when finesse was the ingredient necessary for a fixed purpose, Crip Rell would carry the torch to the finish line. It was a complementary sibling relationship that propelled them, as a duo, light years ahead in the street game.

It was an average Friday afternoon as Mother Nature graciously relinquished the burden of bothersome weather conditions. Business was slow on the weed and cocaine side as the first was that upcoming Tuesday. Da'Quan sat on the edge of his porch bored as he rolled a tightly packed blunt of hash plant. This particular batch was extremely sticky and coated heavily with THC all over the nuggets. He licked his chops in anticipation of inhaling the robust smoke from the Canadian-grown strand.

Smoking weed was a daily ritual for Da'Quan, but no matter how much he would smoke nothing was as cherished and anticipated more than the first blaze of the day. As he put the damp blunt between his choppers he could taste the rich flavor dancing on his tongue. When the fire hit the tip of the blunt and set the cherry ablaze he knew the day had begun. While the potent smoke altered his rigid and stressed mindset, he became relaxed and as one with the universe. He glanced down at his 357 that sat next to him and began fondling his weapon. The strand he smoked had him in an inquisitive mindset, examining his gun for the pure hell of it. He unloaded the magazine and popped a bullet out to really look at what had killed millions of people over the course of time. He was fascinated with the power a gun in the hand has and began aiming it as if he were shooting at an enemy. As the cherry on the tip of the blunt burned in the wind, Crip Rell pulled up in his 1989 Crown Victoria looking like a narc. He had on his sunglasses and black polo shirt looking similar to a man of the law.

When he wheeled into the yard, Da'Quan jokingly aimed the pistol towards the car, causing Rell to smile from ear to ear as he parked the police style car. He parked and held his hands up and said, "Don't shoot, the loot and dope is in the trunk in the diaper bags." They both laughed as he unlodged his huge 300-pound frame from the car. Da'Quan stuffed the pistol in the small of his back as they greeted each other with a fist dap. Rell, who was always about the money, asked, "So what it look like in the kitty?"

Da'Quan replied in a frustrated tone, "Hell naw, these muthufuckas must be broke as fuck. Ain't no body rolled through. Shit that's why a nigga out here smoking and playing with guns. What up, tho?"

Rell shook his head, popped a few sunflower seeds in his mouth before replying, "No sweat, D, Tuesday is the first. It's gone crack next week fa show." A sudden look of contentment covered Da'Quan's face as he knew that Toe was almost 100 percent at predicting the financial forecast. Rell started limping to the back unbothered as he began venting about the pain in his left ankle, "Yeah, D, ya boy's ankle swoll up, this shit been acting up lately, cuz. I crashed that motorcycle fifteen years ago, homie, and the rods in my leg still be killing ya boy, cuzz."

Although he was tough on the exterior, Da'Quan could see the wrinkles in his face from his grimace after each step he took. He also figured that having a 300-plus frame only added insult to injury in this situation. Da'Quan relit the blunt he had rolled as he followed Rell to the back. He took a pull and passed it to Rell, who almost finished it with one Herculean drag. He then began talking like he was being strangled by the smoke in his throat, "So yeah, D, don't trip. Let's have some fun, cuzz. Pull out the Coupe, get it washed and hit some corners, baby."

The sound of having some fun had a nice ring to it, so Da'Quan went along with it, "Shit, might as well. Niggas ain't making shit, anyways."

Rell replied as he struggled to pull up the garage door, "C'mon my nigga what's the use in taking all these penitentiary chances if we can't have fun, cuzz. I believe you gotta play damn near as much as or more than you work, cuzz. It's called work life balance."

Da'Quan admired Rell's manipulative choice of words because it was logical and always on point. Rell eased into the garage and slipped into his 83 Coupe. The Cadillac was an immaculate sky blue with a navy blue top. She sat on gold Daytons and housed a state of the art Kenwood sound system. For some reason he named her Betty and when he turned her on, "Tonite is the Night" by Betty Wright came roaring from his custom sound system.

Da'Quan backed out of the garage as the carbon monoxide fumes catapulted through his nostrils and choppers. Rell then slowly backed out the classic, put-together gangster mobile. He wedged himself out, nursing his bum ankle as he grabbed what was left of the blunt from Da'Quan, who stood nodding his head marveling at the lowrider. It sat inches from the ground, keeping the two of them in awe while the engine purred like a pussycat getting her belly rubbed. The sun began to bake through the clouds, revealing the residual shine of the previous detailing.

Rell, who was a stickler about his lowriders, couldn't wait another minute, as he instructed, "Look here, D, imma back the low key under cover out and you take Betty out, cuzz, and we gon get her cleaned up, mah nigga."

Da'Quan hopped in without another word said; he loved driving and tipping in Betty. She was a symbol of hood prestige, an eyecatcher and a bitch magnet. He loved the way the seats reclined and how the music blared effortlessly in concert hall. She glided and bounced, making it feel like a water ride on tarmac. By the time he got down the driveway, Rell had parked the undercover and was standing gimpy waiting to get in. When he fell inside, he slammed his 300-pound frame, crushing Da'Quan between him and the driver's door. He fought his way to comfort and told Da'Quan, "Hand me the pistol, my nigga, so I could tuck her in the stash, but keep her cocked."

The two glided down the block tipping and swerving, as Rell reached under his seat and pulled out an unopened bottle of Crown Royal buried in its signature purple satchel. He had a devious look in his eyes as he asked, "Wassup, li'l homie, we sipping straight without ice or what, cuzzo?"

"Pop that shit open, nigga, fuck it. We getting loaded, nigga." Da'Quan's carefree attitude went right along with Toe's plans. The two made a hard right on King Blvd. as The West Side Connections, "The Gangsta, The Killa and The Dope Dealer" echoed at an ear-piercing volume. Cars stopped and gawked as the two stunt drove down King Blvd. and clouds of weed smoke and angry gangsta hip hop cast loose from the sunroof and windows. LAPD drove two lanes over and found themselves spectating their ill behavior without taking action.

The further down King Da'Quan sped, the drunker Rell became and began hitting the switches at sixty-five miles per hour. He looked at Da'Quan with the lit blunt in his choppers as he hit the switch down—*payow.* The car pancaked instantly causing it to swerve around two or three civilian cars sending sparks everywhere. The Cadillac kept all eyes on her as the two approached Crenshaw. While waiting at the light on Crenshaw and King, a teen crossing the street in a red and black striped polo, sagging Levi 501s, original Air Jordans and a greasy bag of fries stared heinously at the two. He moved at a snail's pace as Rell went into the stash spot, cocked the heat and sat it on his lap. Da'Quan sat watching the baby face teen stare at them before he hit 'em up with the P-Stone sign and kept walking. Rell smiled with the gun in his lap and nodded with a smirk on his face. Little did the teen know he was one false move away from being used as target practice on a Friday afternoon. After what felt like forever, the light turned green and the duo sped off giving others in traffic some entertainment as they bounced down the shaw.

Rell leaned back with the pistol comfortably on his lap as he looked at Da'Quan and said, "Let's stop at the Liquor Bank, li'l homie, and grab some blunts and cups before we go get this bitch detailed." Da'Quan nodded his head to the sounds of the Westside Connection as he followed orders without a word said. When they pulled up to the Liquor Bank there was a parking lot full of vendors selling anything from DVDs to sacks of weed.

As Da'Quan eased into the driveway, careful not to scrape the bottom of Betty too tough, the duo noticed a pack of Jungle Bloods sitting in the rear of the parking lot. The loud music coming from the street classic instantly got their attention as two of them rose to their feet. Rell noticed the two in the white wife beaters and khakis stand to attention as soon as they entered the parking lot. He tapped Da'Quan on his arm with the 357 and brought the observers to Da'Quan's attention. The Bloods quickly maneuvered into a circular position as if they were waiting for the duo to drive by. One of the Bloods could be seen reaching behind the milk crate he was sitting on, as Rell instructed Da'Quan to stop in his tracks and see what kind of moves the Bloods would make. In that instance it became a showdown. Rell and Da'Quan sat Betty low to the asphalt in a pancake position staring at the opponent. The Bloods stood staring not sure what to expect as they kept an eagle eye on Betty and the duo.

Rell, who by now was drunk and feeling froggish, turned up the music and told Da'Quan, "Put this bitch in reverse, cuzz, them niggas shady, I can smell it, homie."

The Bloods began slowly inching towards Betty and the duo before Rell commanded, "Aight, cuz, back out now, homie." Da'Quan's nerves were bound like a hostage as he eased the Cadillac back. As they backed out the Bloods began coming towards them with a sense of urgency. When the rear wheels hit Crenshaw, Rell pulled out the 357 and let it ring off in the air—*boom, boom, boom!* The Bloods along with all of the customers and vendors scattered like roaches to light as the duo sped off down Crenshaw in gut-wrenching laughter. Rell had a vigilante look on his face as he kept looking in the rear for cops or any goons that may be trailing for the kill. Da'Quan drove the Cadillac at top speed, unsure if he was driving in fear or was this the feeling of an emotional gangster charge. The trees and light poles moved in a blur as they sped up Crenshaw in search of refuge from the grimy ills of South Central. Rell looked at Da'Quan as he took a squig from the Crown Royal bag and said, "OK, homie, let's get Betty back to the spot cause she hot now, cuz. The police and the jungle niggas is on our heads so let's put this bitch up, cuzz." Da'Quan without a word said hooked a U-turn and immediately headed back to the spot. The duo both looked over their shoulders for anything suspicious as they tipped back to the spot in the *Lowrider*

Chapter 28
STEPPIN ON IT

FEBRUARY 1999 • 29 years old

Black Dan grew increasingly fond of Da'Quan's desire to become a well-respected drug lord. He appreciated his relentless hustle and honesty within his business practices, ultimately granting him the green light on an unlimited supply of cocaine. When he got the call from Da'Quan about the ounces and kilos he would need, he instantly drove around to Da'Quan's spot to discuss the details of his new venture. Da'Quan sat in his living room watching Ice Cube's Players Club, laughing without restraint at Bernie Mac's character Dolla Bill. He could see a lot of parallels between him and the shrewd business tactics of the fictitious strip club owner. It was now, after persevering through turbulence, that he was finally in a good place with a trustworthy squad and unlimited resources. The previous months had been a roller coaster ride, resulting in the brutal murder of Les by the hands of his evil assailants. Even though Da'Quan and BD continued to hustle full throttle, the mental scars of Belizean Les's murder were like fresh knife wounds packed with salt.

The roaring engine of Black Dan's truck was enough to set off three to four car alarms on Da'Quan's block as he pulled up. He jumped out of his truck with a sense of purpose, as he was prepared to mentor Da'Quan and show him the ropes on how to avoid a lot of the pitfalls he had encountered in the game. He wore his Versace shades to disguise his face as he walked up to the house to go further in detail about the play they were putting together. As he walked inconspicuously up the steps, he kept his right hand concealed in the front pocket of his Nike hoodie. Da'Quan noticed his odd movement but knew even if it were a gun, he had no reason to use it on him so he didn't think much of it. Before they entered the black iron screen door, BD turned and yelled to his dog, who sat shotgun in his truck, "Magoo, pass auf." The vicious canine immediately turned his head and sat upright in a guarded position.

When they entered the living room Da'Quan asked, "What the fuck you just say, nigga?"

BD laughed as he responded, "Oh, you mean what I said to Magoo? It means pay attention, watch out. I had him trained by this German fool, D, but he's good . He teaches the dogs in German, you know, so they'll react only to you, D. Dude cost like 150 a session but he gets the job done, tho. But um anyway is anybody here?" Da'Quan shook his head no and instantly Black Dan pulled out nine ounces of the best Peruvian powder coke west of the Mississippi River.

Da'Quan's eyes bulged as he was enthralled by the ruthless and powerful energy the bag of dope possessed. It was equivalent to meeting that rock star that the world loves to hate. The white powder commanded attention and respect for the way it had changed lives for centuries. When he took the bag from Dan's outreached hands he felt like an emperor who held the key to life in his palms. It was powerful like the ocean, forbidden like the passion fruit in a sacred garden and worshipped like some sort of divine entity. The powder had to be the devil's sugar for all of the fallen lives and blood baths that had taken place as a result of the unique substance. He marveled at it and tried to comprehend why and how this particular drug was Public Enemy number one. It had been the star of tons of movies, the subject of brutal homicides and the pleasure principle to thousands in its loyal fanbase. The white horse was a sought-after creature who had the seller equally as addicted to the profits as the user was to the high. She was a double-edged sword with a draw even above sex. She could have you in the heavens atop the clouds, numb to life's irritants or shackled in the devil's basement without an inkling of hope.

Dan just stood observing Da'Quan scrutinize the bag without saying a word. When Da'Quan snapped out of his euphoria he was ready to go after the bird salesman of the year award. He was honored to be in the graces of such a powerful and sought after commodity such as cocaine.

Black Dan cracked a smile and jokingly asked, "Big D, you know how to rock this shit up, right?"

Da'Quan shook his head as he responded with his eyes fixed on the bag, "Nah, bro, I never been taught that part."

Black Dan responded as he took his sweatshirt off, "Oh well, shit, I gotta show you how to rock it up. It ain't hard tho, D, you a smart dude. Shit, D, you got a umm small pot and some baking soda?" He pulled out a small blue bottle with a black squeeze top from his sweats and as he put it up to the light said, "This is my own little ingredient I add to the pot to make it sweet." Black Dan headed to the kitchen to give a crack cooking tutorial as Da'Quan's dope dealing pedagogue. Da'Quan was excited as he was now about to be hands-on with the queen of narcotics.

Black Dan surveyed the kitchen with an eagle eye while Da'Quan grabbed the glass jar, cast iron pot and baking soda. He began instructing with an overabundance of confidence, "Dee, look. Close all these blinds and put the pot on the stove." Da'Quan followed suit knowing that BD was a twenty-year veteran in the life and that he'd endured just about every test the game had to offer. Black Dan poured the bag of magic on the counter and began shuffling and mixing it with his Costco card, separating it as he commented, "OK, Dee, here, take the card and mix this pile up like I did that pile and separate it." Da'Quan enjoyed playing with the devil's sugar, catching a light buzz from inhaling the flying cocaine particles. Black Dan then pushed the glass jar over to him and continued, "OK, Dee, now put those two piles in the jar and put about three to one ratio of coke to baking soda then add a little water in it just to cover it." He followed directions with complete obedience to the game he was learning.

Da'Quan knew that knowing how to cook and blow up dope was a valuable trade to have when dealing in the underworld. He'd heard of plenty of cooks who live a very good life without selling a crumb of dope. After he followed step one, Black Dan turned the fire on high on the stove. He grabbed the jar from Da'Quan, looking at it with scrutiny for a minute before adding a bit more water. He began shaking it gently before sitting it in the semi boiling water that bubbled in the cast iron pot. Black Dan stood over the pot stirring clockwise slowly like a cordon bleu cook serving the royal family.

As the kitchen began owning the distinct sharp aroma of crack he explained in detail each step of the process, "OK, so look here, D, you cook it till it's semi hard and now you add my little secret ingredient right here." He took his little bottle and squeezed the unknown solution into the pot as he continued, "This right here, D, is called *Stepping On It.* This how we stretch it and really see some fucking profit. So look, see how it's thick and semi hard? Now go grab me some ice cubes, D, and put 'em in the jar." Da'Quan did as instructed while BD kept a sturdy smooth stir going the entire time. Within moments the white substance became hardened and as Black Dan took the glass out to check its density, he just put the whole glass jar into the freezer as he explained the what and why to Da'Quan. "So now, Big D, leave this chunk in the freezer for a few until you see the holes appear in the chunk; that's when you know it's ready." Da'Quan was enthralled as he now knew just how easy it was to turn a double-up profit with coke, water and baking soda. After a few minutes Black Dan opened the freezer and pulled the chunk of dope out. It looked like a thick cookie chunk sitting unbothered ready to destroy homes, families and lives with its addictive draw.

Black Dan, who by now had accumulated a head full of beads of sweat, examined the hefty piece of contraband in his hand. He was extremely serious and worked diligently paying very close attention to each move he made. His hands were steady from all of the years of cooking experience he'd accomplished over the last two decades. The substance was now solid and had turned a bit off white throughout the process. Dan then asked, "Aye yo, D, hand me a plate and a sharp cutting knife, my brother." Da'Quan without hesitation grabbed a plate from the dish rack and a huge cutting knife. BD, with the help of the knife, dumped out the cookie-shaped sheet of dope onto the plate. It sat with energy like it had a life of its own. Black Dan wasted no time as he continued to lecture, "OK, D, here it is. Rock cocaine, baby, from the master chef himself." They both burst into a sinister laugh as Dan began to carefully cut the cookie into four separate chunks. He cut with the precision of a surgeon as he continued, "See now, D, try and cut without being messy, my brother, but these crumbs you can sell, too. OK so now get the scale, Big D."

His demeanor reverted back to a relaxed state as it was time to weigh the separate chunks and put a price on them. The thrill of being a dope dealer for Da'Quan was indescribable; it was like a dream come true. He felt as though he had a certain zeal that a nine to fiver would never be able to embrace. His head was above the clouds with visions of exotic tempestuous women, foreign cars and finger pointing power. As Black Dan weighed the hefty chunks on the scale he smiled as if he had witnessed the birth of his namesake. The thrill of stretching money gave the two of them an inner feeling of accomplishment only dope dealers can relate to. After he bagged up the freshly cooked ounces he instructed Da'Quan, "Shit, that's it, D. You got nine hundred sacked up off of four hundred dollars in coke, D. So look, imma just give that to you. Don't worry about paying me, just fetch money, my brother. You know, D, you, my boy, you a good dude. I'm trying to show you the ropes, homie, so you can make some real money out here, D. Quit fucking around."

As he began bagging up the chunks of dope and crumbs he envisioned himself as a tycoon with gaudy jewelry draped around his neck, wrist and fingers sitting atop a platform overlooking the movement and rotation of the city. He knew that cocaine, without a doubt, could bring about financial freedom along with an abundance of alluring females. In his eyes, you were just a dead man walking if you didn't have the balls and ambition to go for the gusto. Black Dan had always addressed the old cliche, "Have heart, Have money" in his pro dope dealing campaign speeches. Taking a risk for huge profits warrants a huge amount of respect from those who take the safe route and help build someone else's empire. After learning how to stretch money, Da'Quan was now just as hooked on the money making side as the user was to the product. He had just been swayed all the way into the devil's sweet bag of sugar after *Stepping On It!*

Chapter 29
WEEPING THUGS

AUGUST 1985 • 15 years old

Football practice, especially during "Hell Week," is designed to be back breaking and brutal as an illustration of the tough scenarios that will take place in the weeks to come. The painstaking drills underneath the sweltering summer sun will ultimately be the deciding factor if this is in fact for you. Football players on all levels are simply wired differently than the average Joe making rounds in his daily routine. The mental and physical toughness of the sport cannot be overlooked or denied. No matter how they try and modify the rules or techniques, there is absolutely no safe way to engage in this barbaric sport.

The day had been long, starting with the 8 a.m. weight room session battling with the squat rack, leg press and sled work. The 6 p.m. practice was filled with hitting drills, bear crawls and endless 100-yard wind sprints. As Coach Washburn blew the triple blow of the whistle Da'Quan along with his depleted teammates ran it in for the culmination of the day. Coach Washburn stood in the middle of his fatigued players, who took a knee as he began one of his post-practice, Lombardi style motivational speeches. He started as always by passionately saying, "Gentleman, we've come a long ways but ima be honest, we are nowhere close to playing to our worst potential. Meaning we are not as good as our worst day yet, so let's kick into gear gentleman. In two weeks we go to war against those warriors at Morningside. And ima be honest, them little niggas over there got speed, aggression and desire. See they thugs we play football so my point is that we have to get our minds set on kicking those little tar babies' ass up and down that 100-yard gridiron. We have to execute like there's no tomorrow. We have to fight like it's the last time we are playing because it may be, who knows? Gentleman, take a look in the mirror and ask yourself, What can I do today that will make me better than yesterday?"

The team stared him in his eyes, as they respected him as a coach and a leader. He yelled like a maniac, "Now do I make myself clear?"

The team yelled back in unison, "Yeah, yeah, yeah!" The energy was electric as they began chanting like a violent tribe of Hausa soldiers ready to engage in battle. After practice all that could be heard was grunting from the fatigued players and cleats scraping the ground. Da'Quan began getting dressed at an accelerated pace, as he didn't want to miss the bus that arrived at 8:20 p.m. He felt a weird sense of unease and anxiety for some strange reason. He just chalked it up to a long day at the office. As he shoved the doors open from the musty locker room he was surprisingly greeted by his mom, who sat in her car with tissues patting her tear-filled eyes. He eased up on the car hesitantly as he could sense there was something terribly wrong going on. Lillian rarely succumbed to tears as an emotional outlet. She'd rather laugh, pray or talk her way through adversity rather than cry. Da'Quan hopped in, gave his mom a heartfelt kiss on the cheek and rested his exhausted body to have energy for the uncomfortable news he was afraid to inquire about at the moment.

As he closed his eyes all he heard was his mom sniffling along with the breaking news on the static plagued KFWB. The faster she smashed her Chevy Nova down Rosecrans, the more he slipped into a deep sleep from reality. When she made the right onto 106 and Vermont, Da'Quan opened his eyes and through his blurred vision saw a pack of villains in his aunt's yard. Afros, braids, acey deuceys, golf hats, Pendletons and khakis on criminals filled his aunt's yard talking while some paced intensely. The sheriff had two cars parked a few yards down the block monitoring the set of gangbangers and gangsters unified at his aunt's house.

As he and his mother made their way towards his aunt's house, she quickly turned around and stopped and stared spot on Da'Quan's eyes. She put her hands on his shoulders and sighed and sadly asked, "You know God is good right?"

Da'Quan looked around and answered, "Yea, sometimes."

She put her head down to fight the tears that must have formulated in the pit of her soul as she managed to blurt, "They murdered Dray. They killed ya cousin Dray." Her body went limp as she fought to hold her tears for the sake of keeping Mary and her family in decent spirits. The words "killed and murdered" felt like daggers and shanks tearing through his spirit, shredding him to pieces as he struggled to maintain at least a small fraction of his composure.

After a moment to let the earth-shattering news absorb into his DNA, he began walking towards his aunt's house. Everything seemed to move in slow motion, the pain was surreal, causing his Adam's apple to bounce violently up and down. As he looked into the huddle of gangsters, he saw Mad-E in the middle of the congregation with the callous look of death engraved on his face. Da'Quan stopped near the group as he listened to Porky, who was overwhelmed with hurt calmly describe what happened.

He sat relaxed on the steps as he took a drag from the joint saying, "So yeah Ers it was a punk in tight jeans and makeup in shit coming round the corner talking 'bout y'all niggas too loud turn yo music down! Then, cuzz, outta nowhere Dray came from under the hood of his car. He was fucking with his battery or something, walked up on the punk and slapped the shit outta cuzz in the mouth so hard his earrings went flying. So," he took another long drag from the joint.

Him being so preoccupied with the weed started to annoy Mad-E to the point he snatched the joint threw it down and said, "Nigga, finish the story."

Porky continued nervously, "So the punk left. We turned the music back up and Dray kept fucking with his motor. About ah hour later the punk came back with makeup on and earrings and shit talking bout I thought I told y'all that shit was too loud! So Dray came back from the hood of his car again and started walking up on cuzz and that's when he pulled out his strap, but Dray kept walking up on cuzz."

Mad-E, irritated, asked, "Where was the homies at when he pulled his shit out?"

The youngsta nervously replied, "Nnnah, we pulled out heat."

Mad-E angrily interjected, "Fuck pulling out heat, kill the motherfucka. What y'all punks good for?"

Porky continued, "What happened, the punk aimed his heat at the ground while Dray walked up and, and well he started busting on the ground like four times and ..." He paused, put his head down and took a deep breath before continuing. "That's when Big Dray fell, cuzz, like the way he fell you knew he wasn't gon ever move again." He started bawling uncontrollably, sitting in his blue-hooded sweatshirt covered in Dray's blood. One of the older homegirls embraced him like a mother, kissing his head to calm him from the shock he was experiencing.

Mad E had heard enough as he shoved his way through the yard full of thugs and hopped in his 79 Riviera slamming the door. He sat drowning in tears behind his tinted windows trying to maintain his gangster poise. The hurt combined with the deadly retaliation motives was written on everybody's face including the female gangsters and family members. The vibe was totally about violence and revenge, with the exception of a few God-fearing loved ones who wholeheartedly believed God would handle the karma on his own accord.

Da'Quan, who still was in disbelief about the situation, made his way into the house where his aunt and cousins sat and told stories about Dray and his brothers in his brief twenty-five-year span. He quietly found solace in the corner of the couch and slightly started snoozing to the tittle tattle stories that chimed in the background. This by far was the saddest and most heartfelt death he had ever dealt with.

Days passed and the morning of the home going service had arrived. The grey skies and cool weather only added more sorrow to the unfortunate situation. As Da'Quan ironed his black church slacks he realized what grief had to offer and how the loss of a loved one can alter one's perception of this existence as a whole. His hand trembled immensely each time he ran the hot Black and Decker over his trousers. By the time everyone arrived at the church with honor and beauty the sun began baking the mournful clouds away. Although over the past few days the reality of the situation had settled in for most, there were still vibes of hate and retaliation existing undeniably in the church's atmosphere. Da'Quan sat sadly in the back of the limo trying to calculate exactly how long forever really is. He couldn't comprehend the notion of being gone forever. There was a line of Chevy lowriders and Cadillacs detailed to perfection with blue rags tied around the antennas all the way up to the church's entrance.

Diablo, who was one of Dray's soldiers, stood directly in front of the church's double doors. He was dressed in a black and white gangster bold pin-stripe suit. In the small of his back there was a bulge in the form of a 357 Magnum. His Stacy Adams were so on point the sun reflected an almost mirror image off of them with each movement of his feet. The locs or criminal shades he wore sat on his face as a shield to hide the pain and rage that had been fermenting within his altered spirit. Anybody was a potential candidate to get merked by the Hoovers during this time of crisis.

Da'Quan, after admiring the flashy gangster attire worn by Diablo and the fleet of beautiful lowriders, decided right then and there he would be a hustler and enjoy the finer things in life. He looked down at his JC Penney slacks, argyle sweater and worn loafers and felt like he had to acquire riches one day by any means necessary.

Just then one of Diablos goons came out of the church and began whispering in Diablos ear. The heavy set goon was a hefty 300 plus pounds of half muscle, half fat. He stood about 6'5" with a bullet wound in his neck surrounded by a tattoo of a fallen angel. The jewelry on his hot link-sized fingers only brought attention to his battered guerilla hands. He was gasping for air as he bent down to whisper in Diablo's ear. At one point, Diablo yanked him down forcibly by his collar and addressed the goon with a face of stone. The two stood both with black Fedoras on in a moment of deliberation until the goon hustled briskly to his lowrider fumbling under the seat for his handgun. Diablo began walking to the curb with his hand reaching for that 357 that he cradled effortlessly. As he passed Da'Quan he aggressively blurted to him, "Get in the church, li'l homie, get in the church." The tone in which he spoke signified trouble on the horizon.

Across the street there was a four-door brown Cutlass with two shady characters sitting inside paying the church, cars or abundance of pretty women no never mind. This was odd considering the flash and glitz of the gangster ceremony. As the car sat, Diablo's goon slowly inched his way to get a good sniping angle on the conspicuous vehicle. Diablo had simultaneously moved to the edge of the curb and by now was brandishing his weapon. He loudly addressed the two men in the car by saying, "Naw naw not today bro, we gon set yo souls free if y'all even think about it." The tenacity in his tone along with the big goon in a sniper's stance was convincing enough for the rival gangsters to proceed cautiously down Vermont.

Da'Quan nervously entered the church and to his surprise the guitar player and drummer were in the middle of harmonizing the Run DMC classic "Rock Box," which was Dray's favorite song. The groove, which was definitely unconventional for the occasion, had the old heads in disbelief. Delilah sat with her hands plastered to her forehead looking like, What the hell are these negroes playing? The more youthful and optimistic service goers stood up and danced freely in their moment of sorrow. After the more than unique prelude the minister, who was draped in gold and diamonds, proceeded to speak. He stood confidently in front of the mic and observed the rebel-filled crowd. He took a sip of water and before he could speak there was a piercing cry from the rear of the church. Da'Quan's immediate thought was, "Who is that old lady crying? By now she should be used to funeral services."

The cries and moans became louder and more intense as it had a domino effect on the church. As the thugs became watery eyed the mood in the church was swaying between hate and hurt. The old lady's cries seemed to intensify with every moment. After minutes of this uncontrollable bawling Da'Quan looked back to see who she was. To his disbelief it was Diablo weeping unapologetically, wiping his tears with a blue rag as his goon stood next to him with his heavy arm wrapped around his heartbroken leader.

Chapter 30
AMTRAK AMY

NOVEMBER 1986 • 17 years old

Friday night in the high school world represented bright colorful uniforms attached to the most athletic and aggressive young men on campus. The pounds of armor attached to the teen's body is comparable to that of Roman gladiators or Medieval knights who skillfully battled on horseback for the Lords of that era. The gridiron sport is by far the most popular and openly admired form of athletics in American educational institutions. Crowds travel from great distances to be entertained by the speed, intellectual play calling and violent collisions that take place on the 53 ⅓ by 120 yard patch of grass or turf. The aroma of popcorn and pizza permeates the air within the crowded bench-filled stadiums. Scantily clad dressed females dance and lead cheers for the onlookers as the band collectively plays tunes with a variety of percussion instruments.

The bass of drums roared across the beach city of Playa del Rey on a cold Friday night as the fog billowed over the brightly lit stadium at St. Bernard's High School. The crowd was thoroughly entertained by the intense battle between The St. Bernard's Vikings and the Verbum Dei Eagles. The cross-town rivals drew inn a huge crowd of teenagers and parents from multiple schools and neighborhoods. Homecoming was typically a sellout event, but on this brisk fall night, people lined the gates from the street to witness the two powerhouses of the league engage in war. Due to the overwhelming amount of Blacks in attendance, the Playa Del Rey sheriff's department showed up armed in multiple wolfpacks. Although this was two parochial schools, the event often attracted riff raff from public schools. The Posers, Sex Jerks and KOds were all in full attendance that night. These groups of teens, which began as trendy dance groups, had begun to evolve into pseudo gangs. They habitually found ways to turn their competitive dance moves into public acts of violence. Wreaking havoc was now a common event whenever the groups congregated in one common location. The cliques would remain segregated in their own areas, fraternizing with liquor under massive clouds of marijuana smoke. They dressed in Pendletons and khakis bottomed out in either Romeos or Chuck Taylors. Most of the trendy thugs wore processed flattops instead of jheri curls and braids which characteristically distinguished them from the original Crip and Blood gangsters.

Da'Quan, who came to see his homeboy Crow play, sat back and chuckled as the priests and nuns frantically attempted to dismember the groups of troublesome teens. Meanwhile, from the oohs and aahs on the gridiron, it was quite obvious the game was hard hitting and entertaining. The first half was coming to an end and Verbum Dei was down to St. Bernard's 7–6. Emotions ran high as the intensity of the game began to overflow into the crowd. Verbal assaults rang out against the opposition, causing friction between the friends and family of the rival institutions. One Black parent who had been turning her flask up to her lips the whole first half stood and yelled, "Number eight is a bitch. Fuck him up, Bo Bo!"

From the other end of her row the white mother of number eight stood and yelled back, "Take all that niggativity back to Watts, sweetie, we don't tolerate that foolishness round these parts!" The Black mother started making her way towards the white mother when security and the archdiocese faculty motioned towards them to diffuse the altercation. Suddenly boos and racial slurs rang randomly from the dark in the sardine-packed stadium. Coincidentally on that same night, neighboring school Westchester was playing their rival University High. They each had playoff spots on the line along with bragging rights as motivational tools to win. The entire neighborhood of Playa Del Rey was patrolled heavily by Marina sheriffs and a host of mounted police who roamed by horseback all night. The dynamic in the Westchester game was slightly different as the 60s, 8 Treys and Inglewood family gangs flooded that arena and its surrounding areas, waiting for the moment to ignite violent activities.

Da'Quan could foresee the lines being long and hectic by halftime so he made his way to the snack bar early. As he stood in line he began to notice the young white girls kept their eyes glued to him in very seductive and alluring ways. He had never experienced intimacy with a white girl or other as his family and friends referred to them as. The stories he had heard sparked a great sense of curiosity as to the freaky stigma attached to them. While he stood in line he lost focus on the chili cheese dog and fries he was going to order. He was preoccupied gawking at the flocks of white girls who passed by exposing skin and smiles to the brothers in the area. The game was chock full of young blondes eager to escape reality with a Zulu of her choice.

As Da'Quan stood oblivious in a trance, Ed who played for St. Bernard's, slid up to him and whispered, "Yeah, nigga, I see you gotta thing for snow bunnies, too."

Da'Quan, who was caught off guard, responded in a self-assured tone, "They OK, my nigga. I've seen better." He kept a pimp demeanor about himself although Edward was 100 percent correct with his observation. He asked Ed, "Why you ain't on the field, homie?"

Ed looked down disappointingly and blurted, "Grades, my nigga, my teachers can't stand a nigga. Shits fucking me up right now."

Da'Quan just nodded not really sure how to respond. The whole time he kept his eyes glued on the array of young girls who passed by giggling and laughing. Ed pulled out a fat wad of twenty-dollar bills, handed him one asking him to grab some soda and gum for him and his little friend. As Da'Quan grabbed the wrinkled currency, Ed nudged him and whispered, "Look, Dee, you see that thick one over there holding the clipboard? She's ready to keep a set of balls in her throat."

They both laughed as Ed's humor was raw and uncut. It was Amy Dunigan, the St. Bernard's baseball coach's daughter. She was a plain-faced Caucasian girl with flaxen-colored hair that lay halfway down her back. Her hazel eyes and rose-colored cheeks gave her the likeness of pure innocence. She was the team statistician and while standing patiently with the clipboard in hand, it was quite obvious that underneath that team polo shirt and khaki shorts was a voluptuous figure in full bloom. Da'Quan could clearly see the silhouette of her round derriere and plump breast protruding through her fitted staff uniform.

Ed slid closer to Da'Quan's ear and whispered, "Yeah, homie, Amy's a stone cold freak. My uncle went to Vegas and he left me the key to his spot for the weekend. What he didn't know is a nigga got the keys to his pickup truck, too. A nigga got some weed and Cisco and after the game she coming with ya boy to get dug out all night."

Da'Quan just nodded his head as the line moved forward. By the time Da'Quan got to the front of the line and ordered, Ed continued to disclose unrequested information. He began to wonder why Ed had even opened up to him. He thought maybe the nigga was excited or was simply a loudmouth who couldn't hold water. Soon after he placed his order the smell of horse droppings surrounded the food barn. Da'Quan wasn't sure if it was the mounted police pets or the hot air that escaped between the bubble lips of Ed. Whatever the case was, Ed just wouldn't stop speaking about Amy as he went on to say, "Yeah, homie, after the game everybody headed to the Ladera Center, and after that ima take this cavebitch straight to Gardena and do her dirty all night my nigga."

Da'Quan became aggravated by Ed's constant boasting about fucking paleface, and the harsh smell of the feces began to make his stomach queasy. Just then the nun yelled out, "Chili cheese dog, fries, three sodas and gum." His prayers had been answered as he could finally shake this weirdo and his little whore for the night. After handing Ed his items, they exchanged a fist dap and both parted ways.

The more the game progressed and as an opaque fog began to cover the field of play, it was clear the Verbum Dei was the dominant force leading by thirteen in the last two minutes of the fourth quarter. The crowd soon began to dissipate from both games, giving the police plenty of overtime to exercise their tactics against the crowd. Da'Quan made his way to Crow's VW, rolled up a fat stress joint and waited on him as hundreds of spectators passed by in the foggy parking lot. By the time Crow made it out, the parking lot was barren and the temperature had dropped to an unwelcome fifty degrees.

Crow was battered and bruised and didn't say much as he opened the door. Once inside he revved his vessel up, reached in the ashtray and pulled out a finger-sized half burnt Tai joint to ease his pain. Da'Quan looked over and as he grabbed the joint he asked Crow, "How y'all lose that shit, cuh?" and started chuckling.

Crow was unamused and snatched the joint back before saying, "Wassup? We going to Ladera and fuck with some bitches or what? Fuck that game."

Da'Quan replied, "Fuck it, let's go."

The two smashed out of the parking lot at top speed blowing Tai smoke out the window with no regard for the law. On the radio "It's Tricky," by Run DMC blared as the two sped from the beach city to the Ladera Center. While they drove and smoked Da'Quan mentioned Ed by saying, "Yea, nigga, ya boy Ed gotta white bitch on his line he dying to hit. He say it's the baseball coach's daughter 'n shit. The nigga act like he ain't never got no pussy, cuzz." The two chuckled wholeheartedly as they became buzzed laughing at virtually nothing.

Crow shook his head and responded, "Yeah, man, that nigga kinda weird, homie. I don't fuck wit cats like that."

Da'Quan just hit the weed, French curled the smoke and said, "Yea man, the nigga kept talking 'bout fucking her plain Jane ass and his breath smelled like one of them horses shitted on his face cuz."

They both burst into an inebriated laugh. As they pulled up into the overly crowded parking lot, VWs, Jettas, El Caminos and lowriders flooded the parking lot. Blazers and Jeeps competed for whose system was the loudest, creating mini concerts from every inch of the parking lot. Hip hop legends LL Cool J, Whodini, Toddy Tee, Run DMC and the new LA group NWA could be heard vibrating the asphalt as teens smoked and drank like it was second nature.

Crow and Da'Quan rolled up into the parking lot half-baked off of Tai bud with slanted eyes and an appetite for adventure. No sooner had they pulled in a parking space, a friend of Crow staggered up to the car with two red cups.

He handed them both one and as Da'Quan sniffed the rim of the cup it almost cut his breath off. He cringed and asked, "What the fuck is this?"

Steve smiled and slurred, "Mah nigga, it's 151, vodka, silver satin and orange crush. Proceed with caution, my boys." He then staggered off to go ruin somebody else's night. Da'Quan boldly took a squig, poured the rest out and told Crow, "Nigga, I'm hungry. I'm a hit Fatburger. A nigga want something munch on, cuz?" Crow shook his head no, laid it back against his headrest and told him he's waiting on his girl to get there to rub his back. Without another word being said, Da'Quan headed across the chaotic parking lot in route to Fatburgers.

Once he made it to Fatburgers it was way too crowded so he made his way across the street to patronize Burger King . While crossing the street he noticed the Burger King had shut it down. He muttered angrily to himself, "Fuck, what ima do now?" He thought, *Shit I gotta take a piss before I do anything tho.* The liquor and soda had his bladder ready to burst as he sought refuge to let loose. Out of desperation he scampered to the back of the burger spot where he encountered a Nissan pickup truck parked isolated with a group of males surrounding it, laughing quietly in a semi huddle.

After taking a wiz on the Burger King drive through menu, he began making his way back to the party in the parking lot across the street. Before he made it back to the front he heard a deep voice yell, "Hey, D, wassup? Wanna get some of this? Da'Quan paused and tried to make out who was yelling at him from the dark foggy parking lot. He squinted to see if he could recognize who it was. The dude motioned his hand to come over but Da'Quan stood still not sure if it was a setup or even if they had a mistaken identity.

The voice rang out again, "Nigga, it's Ed. Come on, homie, I got something foe you."

Hesitantly he checked over his shoulder before walking towards the group of dudes surrounding the truck. The closer he got to the truck the better he could see through the fog. He walked up and thought, *I'll be goddamn cuzz.*

Ed was laying on the ground face down behind the truck while the other dudes surrounded him in a semi-circle. He thought it was odd how they were positioned but he heard a sexy female shrieking sex slurs enthusiastically from the fog. Her vulgarity thus led him over by the horns of his hormones. When he finally made it to the truck, Ed raised up to his knees revealing a huge white ass underneath him lying face down on the cold asphalt. He then turned the white girl over and raised her head as he stuck his manhood in her mouth. The thick thoroughbred grabbed his meat and quaffed a mouthful of semen causing his head to roll back as he screamed, "Yeah bitch, swallow the whole thang." She willingly did so as she looked him dead in his eyes under his full command. He then gently laid her head on the asphalt, stood to his feet, pulled up his shorts and asked, "Who's next? Step up."

Da'Quan stood motionless as he couldn't believe what he was witnessing. There was an empty bottle of Cisco lying next to her half-naked body as the other teens looked at each other to see who was next. There were at least six dudes surrounding Amy who began yelling, "Well come on, you scary muthafuckas. Who wants some of this good white cunt, quit pussyfooting around, nigga."

Da'Quan thought to himself, *If the fucking police rolled up on us now we'd all do life for raping this fucking cavebitch.* Even with those thoughts he just stared at her plump breast with pink nipples laying there looking very inviting to his eyes. She went from a plain Jane to a seductive slut under the soft light of the moon. She continued to drunkenly rant, "Would one of you scary muthafuckas stick a black dick in me? What the fuck y'all staring at shit? For God's sake would somebody fuck this hot pussy"!

Ed began to regulate the orgy. "OK, hold up, hold up. Tee, come on, nigga, I promised you was next." Tee was his teammate who had never had any parts of pussy. He looked as fearful as a first time grenade inspector while attempting to unbuckle his pants. Then he did the unthinkable. He got on his knees and put his face right between her legs and began savagely devouring her with no shame in his game. Ed put his arm around Da'Quan's shoulders and began laughing uncontrollably saying, "This nigga, Tee, is a beast."

Da'Quan just watched and shook his head in disgust. Amy pushed him away forcefully and yelled, "Get yo fat ass off me. I don't wanna be ate; I want some big black dick in me, what the fuck?"

Her words were beyond slurred as she had obviously drunk way past her tolerance level. Ed pulled Tee back and pointed to another one of his teammates who instantly jumped on her and began fucking her full throttle unprotected. Ed laughed and yelled, "OK, niggas, y'all each get three minutes wit my bitch and then it's next man up." He then began mimicking the sound of a train, "Choo, chooo, chooo!"

The crew of teens burst into laughter while passing a sixty-four-ounce of Ole E and joint around. Amy became animated while screaming, "Oh my god, you weak nigga, come on nigga, fuck me harder, nigga, fuck me like you mean it, little bitch!"

Da'Quan couldn't believe what he was seeing as she continued to yell, "Fuck this little dick nigga. Who got a horsedick? I wanna get fucked hard, goddammit." By the fourth contender blood began to drip from her blonde vagina to the cold asphalt. Although he was tempted Da'Quan thought, *How could I explain to my mom I was doing life in jail behind fucking of all things a white girl in the back of a Burger King parking lot.*

It was time for round five and as Ed wiped her bloody cunt with a team towel, he looked at D and said, "Come on, D, she clean and ready to go, my nigga, come hit this rib." Da'Quan slowly backed away saying, "Naw, homie, I'm cool. Y'all have fun. Ima bounce." Ed without another word said climbed back on top of her and started pounding her relentlessly against the asphalt as she screamed, "Yeah, daddy, beat this nasty white pussy. Beat it, daddy!"

Da'Quan hurriedly made his way back across the street praying he wouldn't be seen by the sheriffs or LAPD leaving the scene of the train. He knew that if the authorities rolled up she'd instantly go from porno queen to damsel in distress and have all of their black asses locked up till the new millennium or beyond. White women have historically been America's irrefutable pride and joy and any violation of her well being spawns grave consequences.

Chapter 31
MIDNIGHT PLANE TO GEORGIA

SEPTEMBER 1999 • 29 years old

All successful business ventures thrive on the structure they have created for profitable gain. There is always a risk, which is why every single detail of the maneuver must be addressed in order to succeed.

The clouds sat white in the sky, floating against the blue atmosphere provided by Mother Nature. The warm September sun complemented the ocean breeze that gusted throughout the hostile city that day. L.A., which is noted for its Mediterranean climate and vast entertainment industry, is also a breeding ground for crime. For most, the only way to survive in the circus of L.A. is to do dirt. It's a pimp's den, a drug ring and a war zone all encompassed in a thirty-plus-square-mile radius. Bodies had been dropping locally and the rumors of different known killers who may have had their hands in them were milling around the city. The police and investigators now had to get out of their office seats and doughnut shop sanctuaries to earn the checks they were receiving.

Thursday morning had finally arrived. Da'Quan was up early feeding his pit bull, Felony, and cleaning her living quarters. He was excited about the play he set up but at the same time a little nervous about taking the show on the road. His job was to meet at Black Dan's, package up the three kilos and get them to FedEx asap. He was just buying time until BD paged him with the green light. The whole time he toiled in the dog's pen shoveling shit and filling her feeding bowl his mind drifted on the what if's of the trip. What if the package gets intercepted? What if the dudes in Georgia are wolves out to rob? He could clearly feel the unrest in his spirit about the whole charade. He was tense and on edge for no apparent reason. His dog was extremely affectionate, licking on his hands and rubbing against his leg more than usual. She looked him in his eyes as if she was trying to convey a message. Today was special because this was a test to see if he could manage California and Georgia effectively. The amount of money he'd be making with dual states under his belt would send him well past 300k a year. This was the goal on paper, and he had all intentions of running the play successfully.

At 10 o'clock a.m. sharp Black Dan's number lit up Da'Quan's pager. Instantly Da'Quan's nerves went haywire. Part of him was excited to get the ball rolling while a hint of his enthusiasm was tainted with doubt and apprehension. He took a deep breath, closed his eyes and meditated. His yang intuition spoke, *You are bright enough to legally generate tenfold the amount of this move with careful planning.* His yang intuition barked a different tune, *Nigga, fuck that. The money's on the table, all the pieces are in place and you wanna back out? That's some bitch ass shit. These niggas got families, you got the plug and now you wanna back out like a hoe! What other excuse do you have muthafucka? Look, the money is waiting for you. It's a piece of cake, just get on the plane, have a drink, relax and get to the package. After that, shoot it to the hookup, count ya bread and come back home with pockets full of dough nigga.* His yang once again convinced him that you absolutely gotta have heart to have money. He immediately finished up filling up his dog bowls, enough for three days, and headed to the phone.

He nervously pressed the numbers. He didn't understand why his nerves were jittery, but he fought through it as the phone rang.

"Hello?" Black Dan picked up on the first ring with zeal and enthusiasm.

Da'Quan replied confidently, "Yeah, wassup? Ready to make this happen, O.G.?"

"Hell yeah, I'm waiting on you, Big D." He hung up, went to the bathroom and washed his hands and face before staring into his doubtful eyes in the mirror above the sink basin. After a moment of soul searching he headed to his truck to get the ball rolling. Black Dan's block was low key and under the radar. That day it was quiet enough to hear a rabbit pissing on cotton a mile away. He looked over his shoulders and up and down the block before he walked up to BD's secured fortress. Magoo, his bowling ball head canine bully, came running full speed to the gate with a ton of water or spit oozing from his choppers. He lunged at the gate causing Da'Quan to jump back a few feet from his flare up. In the back of his mind he wondered, *Why are all of the dogs acting different towards me today what the fuck?*

Black Dan came out yelling authoritatively, "Get yo ass back here Magoo!" He came hustling to the gate in the black hoodie and sweats he wore on packaging days. Da'Quan must have looked off as BD asked, "You good, Big D, don't mind Magoo. He just been grumpy. He's getting old. So yeah, we gon package this shit up get to FedEx, Big D, and y'all gotta go handle yo business cause really, you know, it's all on you now."

Da'Quan took a deep breath and replied, "Yeah I know but I got this shit, my nigga." The two walked into the living room where another ice cooler and fisherman paraphernalia sat to be shipped off to their favorite uncle in the south.

Da'Quan was aware of the setup as Dan reached behind the couch and pulled out a black duffle bag. He unzipped it and revealed thirty kilos of uncut Peruvian cocaine as he boasted, "Yeah, Big D, I got y'all's three to get ready and a few more of my folks need work this week too. Shit, I been busy." Da'Quan just stared at the white packs in the bag dumbfounded as they appeared to be staring back. This was the first time he really became cognizant of his status as a dope dealer. He realized he was sitting in a room with over a million dollars in cocaine in street value, he was heading out to Georgia with a known killer with kilos and he had three pounds of chronic weed stashed under his bed at the house. His money was stacking by the minute and he had a plethora of bitches in the shadows waiting patiently to be tended to. Guns were as accessible as oxygen, and he knew his squad was prepared to make use of them if needed.

Black Dan began busting the ice chest apart, separating the inner plastic from the outer shell. He then put a kilo against three sides of the cooler on the inside before putting the inner lining back in, keeping the kilos safely jammed and concealed. Da'Quan lit up a half a joint. Da'Quan sat on the TV while Dan worked meticulously at gluing the lining of the cooler back. Beads of sweat gathered at the top of Dan's bald head as he battled for the perfect innocent look of a fisherman's ice chest. Once the base and the dope were sealed tightly he began putting the coffee beans, fishing magazines, hooks, hats and canned tobacco in the cooler.

After the cooler was complete he grabbed the joint from Da'Quan and began schooling him. "OK, D, this bitch is ready to fly. So look, I got my homegirl. Imma pay her 150 to run this to FedEx. Once she does I'll give you the tracking number and time it should make it." He pulled out a little piece of paper with the address Savage had them sending the package to and asked, "So D, this the address you gave. You sure it's the right one?"

"Yup," he replied as he French inhaled the potent chronic smoke. Black Dan's calm demeanor always had a way of easing Da'Quan's bundled nerves. After he sealed the package he grabbed his D boy phone, which was presumably untapped and called his homegirl, Tiffany. Tiffany was his special friend who was lean and curvy with lips women get surgery for. Her breasts were perfectly proportioned and perky sitting alert over her slender waist. Her diamond shaped eyes were pure and innocent. She spoke in a very soft soprano tone with a dimple ending smile revealing her well-kept ivory white teeth. Her easy on the eye exterior played a pivotal role in her success as a hoe and a mule.

Black Dan wiped his forehead and took a deep breath as Tiffany picked up the line, "Hey baby girl, I'm ready with those groceries." He paused and listened briefly before firmly interjecting on her reply, "I know. I understand, but I told you to be ready by eleven and its ten forty, so I need you to get ya ass here, babe. It ain't the time for that." He closed his eyes, put his hands over his sweaty face, took a deep breath and continued to listen to her grievances. Finally in a frustrated tone he barked, "OK, OK, just get here. I'll sweeten it up for you. C'mon babe, we wasting time." He paused, "Uh huh, OK, see you when you get here, love you too, bye."

He slammed his flip phone shut and began bitching, "Man, D, these broads be tripping. Now she been, you know, running for me like a year, D . She got her own spot, cool car, hair done and cable, D. She keeps her waitress job money for herself and goes to school. Look, she ain't got no kids with all that ass and talking 'bout she need more cause she risking her job and education doing this. So I'm getting charged for helping the broad, D? It doesn't make sense. The only thing about her is she don't get high, she is square and she's smart. It ain't a lotta good mules out here like it used to be, D . You gotta choose wisely."

The two began cleaning up the rubbish throughout the living room until BD's phone vibrated. "Aight, D, she outside so here's the play. Ima take the package out and talk to her then when I give you the signal you go to your truck and trail her. Make sure nobody gets behind her, D, OK?" He grabbed the package and headed outside. Da'Quan sat on the edge of the couch by the curtains for what seemed like centuries before BD motioned for him to come out.

As he walked out, everything appeared to be moving in slow motion. Black Dan stood to the driver's side of her Altima bedazzled by her innocent beauty. His body language gave off a simpish defeated vibe which was unlike BD's personality. Her eyes were noticeably glued to Da'Quan as he strolled low key up the block to his truck. When he revved up his Chevy and headed out after her, BD flagged him down, walked up to his window and whispered, "Look when she goes in and comes out, she will call me and I'll hit you." Da'Quan nodded his head and mashed out after the mule.

Traffic was light and as he drove he listened to Prince's "Adore" on the radio. He noticed her eyes attached to his through her rearview mirror all the way from Jefferson Park to outer El Segundo. When they pulled into the FedEx, Da'Quan eased his truck into the first spot he saw while she drove closer to the entrance. When she got out Da'Quan watched her walk sensually with the package into the building. Her perky breasts swayed in her tank top with each step she took and her round derrière couldn't be disguised in her overly fitted sweats. The light breeze blowing her wavy brown hair back revealed her flawless, blemish-free skin tone and succulent lips. Although Da'Quan was completely engulfed in the mission he could partially see why BD couldn't resist her tempestuous ways.

Ten minutes later she came sashaying out seemingly without a care in the world. She bypassed her car and walked straight up to Da'Quan's driver's side window unapologetically. She looked him in the eyes the whole time she approached his truck. The closer she got the more her beauty was revealed to him. She came within inches of his face and seductively said, "That's done and since you following me, don't stop now, I'll lead you to paradise, D." The spearmint on her breath was warm and inviting; she was even more attractive up close. He never noticed her dark freckles and neutral grey eyes from a distance. Now it made sense as to why BD kept her somewhat sheltered from everybody. She was actually a dime piece with street savvy. Da'Quan sat speechless as his mind raced, *Awwe, shit, is this a setup to see if I'm loyal? Damn, as much as I wanna fuck, ima just play it cool and be politically correct.*

He jokingly replied, "Paradise, where's that? BD ain't said nothing 'bout that." She smiled as she smacked her gum and replied, "You're cute but you know what I'm saying, D. Look, imma keep it real. I only kept driving for him because I love looking at you and I wanna see you with it, Daddy." That was the first time he'd been called daddy. It gave him an erection as hard as Chinese arithmetic. He still remained speechless as he looked into her seductive grey eyes. "Look, D, imma call him tell him everything's cool. Then we can drop your truck off and chill until tonight. I'll take you to the airport. I know what time you gotta be there; he told me already."

Da'Quan quietly listened as she rubbed his hand and continued, "Why you think I made him give me that 250 extra that he was probably bitching about? I want to spend it with you, baby. Have some fun before you go. I ain't stupid. I know ya boy married and got a family; our relationship is business. Besides he forty years old, D; he too old for me anyway. I wanna finish school and be a nurse one day. This shit is playing out, D. So you coming ? I got weed, vodka, OJ and me."

The alpha male in Da'Quan blurted, "Fuck it, OK, I do need a ride to the airport, aight follow me to the house and imma hop in with you." Her racy smile told the story as she immediately bounced in her voluptuous skin back to her Altima to follow.

The whole drive to his house he was aroused but at the same time leery about if this was a setup or not. He knew bitches were the downfall of every empire and he didn't want to lose out on his anticipated earnings behind a bitch. No matter what rationale he tried to muster up not to do it, his weakness for the flesh reminded him that this was way too great an opportunity to squander. When he pulled into his driveway and got out of the truck he grabbed his overnight bag and looked in every direction for BD before he eased into her car. She smiled from ear to ear as if she'd captured her prey as a big game hunter. The pheromones in the car ricocheted like bullets in a lunch-box as they drove off to the sounds of Sade's "Sweetest Taboo."

Her car smelled like a combination of spearmint flowers and honey. She could barely keep her eyes on the road as she twirled her hair and smacked her gum. Da'Quan just sat back, closed his eyes and played it cool letting the game come to him. A few seconds later he felt her hand squeeze his thigh just inches under his groin. He placed his hands on top of hers as assurance that they were on the same page. Moments later he felt the car turning into a driveway. When he opened his eyes he read Airport Park Hotel on the sign facing Manchester. He felt uneasy and excited at the same time. She pulled into the first available slot and hopped out with her Louis Vuitton's handbag full of cash to the lobby. Her innocent hoe-ish swag intrigued him as she maneuvered confidently for what she wanted. Da'Quan sat still, a bit uneasy, but anxious to see just how bad she wanted him. He looked in the back seat and saw nursing guides and healthy eating brochures along with an assortment of shoe boxes and shopping bags. When she came back to the Altima she smiled, showed him the key as she grabbed her overnight bag. They both silently walked up the stairs to the room anxious to cross the lines of friendship, loyalty and trust for a few rounds of animalistic, carnal lust.

When they entered the room the smell of the motel instantly had them ready for foreplay. She hadn't taken three steps in the room before she turned around and forced her tongue down Da'Quan's throat. She took off every inch of clothing revealing her perfectly shaped bosom with big brown nipples and a fat flawless shaved monkey. She turned to her purse and pulled out at least a half ounce of chronic, threw it on the bed and said, "Ima hop in the shower. Roll up, D, and chill. I already called you know who so we good. Just chill, D."

Da'Quan just began splitting a swisher sweet to roll and kept letting the game come to him. When he lit the blunt he took it into the bathroom to let her hit it from the shower. BD swore she didn't smoke and was a good girl but she had him bamboozled to the third power as she was revealing her hand to

Da'Quan on every level. When she got out of the shower she approached him with the blunt still lit and began unbuckling his jeans. Without a word said she pulled out his manhood and shoved it in her choppers, slurping it like a big stick from the ice cream truck on a blistering summer day. She made constant contact with him and rubbed on her huge, beautiful tits while doing so. He put his finger in her soaking wet womb and began aggressively massaging her clit sending her into a sexual erogenous climax. He reached into his pockets and slid a condom on before turning her around and punishing her from the rear. She moved like a pro, and her moans were almost enough to make him explode. After a few minutes of killing it doggy style she crawled around and made her way on top of him. As he stroked her he was amazed at the size of her breasts, which bounced with every stroke, and the beauty of her blemish-free skin.

While riding him she burst out in a sexual rant, "Damn, baby, I'm sick of this rubber. It's burning my coochie, D."! She rose up, took off the rubber, tossed it nonchalantly to the floor and sat back on him unprotected. Da'Quan just let her do what she pleased as he was enthralled by the whole experience. The wetness of her walls made their connection even more intense. He thought about the money she pimped BD for to make this happen and the risk she took being down with the squad causing him to fuck her relentlessly on that Thursday afternoon. He couldn't believe how wet the sheets had become and how much better she began to look with each stroke. He had to remind himself over and over again, *This bitch ain't shit but a conniving scandalous hoe with good wet pussy.* He also reminded himself that this was one of the perks of selling dope as well and a huge reason why he did it. She looked at him with sheepish eyes as he manhandled her for at least an hour. The only drawback to this was BD was head over heels for her and if he ever got wind of him fucking her, the plug may be done and he might have a hit put out on him. He was aware that men would kill over a bitch even before money. But even with all of the risk involved combined with the disloyalty he wouldn't have turned her down no matter what. She was a fine ass dope dealer's girl who knew how to get what she wanted and that turned Da'Quan on.

The time on the clock motioned effortlessly as the two indulged in three to four rounds of gut-busting sex before taking a well-needed power nap. Da'Quan was awakened by her kissing him on his forehead saying, "D, D, it's time for me to take you to the airport, babe. It's ten thirty." He woke up completely unaware of his surroundings as she lay fully dressed next to him with a sensuous smile on her face. She gazed at him in his eyes and said, "Baby, c'mon get on that plane so you can handle your business and hurry back to me so I can take care of you like you deserve, baby." The sincerity in her tone motivated him to get going so he could come back and enjoy her. She was the icing on the cake, his saving grace and a helluva sex partner. She held his hand down the stairs to the car as if they had been dating for years. She couldn't keep her eyes off of him as they drove down the street to LAX. When they got to TWA, she looked him in his eyes, grabbed him by the back of his head and shoved her soft wet tongue down his throat. Deep down he now wanted to stay and be with her, but his hustling pimpish ways was obviously the reason she was drawn to him in the first place. She looked a little sad as she said, "OK, baby, be safe. I'll see you next week and we can run it back and fuck all night. Be safe, daddy."

When he got out of the car they gave each other a last look of lust, blew each other a kiss before she sped off expeditiously. When he walked into the waiting room to check in he heard a deep voice blurt, "That's, that's a fine little broad, homie." He turned around to see Savage already waiting with an excited look on his face. He looked at Da'Quan's three quarter length leather jacket and fresh white Air force ones and said, "They gone think you a millionaire in Georgia, D, you watch." They both laughed as he sat down to wait to board the plane.

After twenty minutes the intercom announced, "Flight 549 to Atlanta, Georgia, now boarding." The two hopped up eager about their mission at hand. When he sat in his window seat, he gazed out into thick night fog deep in thought. He thought about the money he was about to make and what he'd invest in next. He also couldn't get Tiffany off of his mind. He kept picturing their rendezvous and couldn't wait to be next to her again. His only fear was BD or Savage finding out he was fucking the mule and risking the whole operation behind a piece of pussy. With his mind racing at the speed of light he laid his head back, closed his eyes and began his *Midnight Flight to Georgia!*

Chapter 32
SNITCHED ON

SEPTEMBER 1999 • 29 years old

The perks of being a dope dealer far outweigh the simplistic narrative of a basic nine to five with guaranteed pay and no risk. Most opt for the nine to five simply because they don't have the gusto or heart that it takes to be an illegal entrepreneurial force in their prospective communities. We are conditioned as a society to believe that if you go to school and excel through college that there will be a well-paying career with lifelong benefits waiting at the end of the "rainbow."

The sound of brakes screeching against the runway and a host of coughing from phlegm-filled throats woke Da'Quan up from his well-needed comatose. He noticed a multitude of crispy green trees in the distance shining blissfully under the radiant Georgia sun. As they exited the plane, Savage muscled his way through the stagnant crowd of southerners in route to the luggage claim. He wanted to get there before the crowd so he could get his stuff and get to the car where his cousin Country was waiting to take them to the package. Da'Quan could tell from the way people dressed and moved that they were in another state. The whole time they maneuvered through the airport he couldn't get his mind off of Tiffany. He repeatedly had flashbacks of the heightened moments of sex he shared with BD's sidepiece.

As they rode on the autowalk, Savage turned around with a huge smile on his face and said, "My nigga, she must a put that thang on you good, cuzz." His comment jolted him back into reality and focused on the business at hand.

He just shook his head and denied it, "Nah, Big homie, I'm just feeling that jet lag. She my homegirl."

Savage replied confidently, "Well, homie, the way she got out the car for you she wanna be more than the homegirl. Shiid, she got any friends?"

Da'Quan answered quick, "All them bitches on pussy."

Savage laughed and blurted, "So what? Them be the best freaks, cuzz, but anyway we 'bout to head to the car. My cousin Country outside waiting on us. Then cuz we gone go out to the sticks where I had it delivered and pick the shit up. Then we drop it off at our hideout and go to the hotel. Remember this, too, cuzz, you never keep the work where you sleep, man, nigga." While walking out of the airport his gut intuition told him to run around and hop back on the first thing smoking. But the stage was set and there was absolutely no turning back from this point on.

Savage led the two into the airport parking lot into an area that appeared to be their normal meeting place. There was a frail brown skin dude leaning against a 94 four-door Volvo rental. He wore a mid-sized nappy afro with a bushy beard underneath it. His clothes looked worn and defeated. The white T-shirt he had on was loose around the neck and extremely dingy. He reminded Da'Quan of a rebellious sharecropper from the mid-1800s. He knew he was in the south, as the dude was standing against the car barefoot with a straw piece in his mouth.

As they walked up, the dude smiled at Savage and gave him a huge hug and blurted in his country tone, "Wassup, cuzzo, you walking up with a big ass bodyguard now, boy, ha ha whew, we gotta grab my shit now."

They both laughed as Savage broke the ice, "Nah, nah, this, this m-my nigga, Big D. Good dude I was telling you about from my hood. He solid tho."

He reached out with a huge smile on his face and gave Da'Quan a fist dap, "What up, bro? I'm his big OG cousin Country, mayne. We run this here part of the south, Big D, what you no good playa?" It took a minute for Da'Quan to absorb his offbeat southern flavor as he looked and sounded as if he were from another stratosphere. No matter how frail or bizarre he may have appeared, Savage warned him that Country was a stone cold killer, the furthest thing from a milquetoast individual.

Da'Quan played it cool and replied, "What up, Country, I already know cuzzo. Let's get this doe." Country's face lit up like ten Christmas trees as he cackled from the excitement and energy he felt from Da'Quan's aggression.

His gangster animation was comical as he continued, "Well hop in this bitch, boy. This li'l nigga starving. C'mon Savage, let's go cuzzn. I got the munchies, mayne." Savage looked at Da'Quan and laughed fully aware that Da'Quan had to adjust to the overall Southern environment. Country sped out of the terminal parking eager to get some fried anything in his body. As frail as he was, he made it apparent he was a gourmand for heavy greasy southern cuisine.

The highways were virtually empty, as opposed to the overcrowded freeways in Los Angeles, lined with green shrubbery rooted in bright red clay dirt. From the looks of the environment he had a false sense of being alleviated from the miasma of the L.A. streets. He learned quick, however, that he was in the same circus of devils only disguised differently as Country spit game, "Now look here, we gon stop by my getaway, boy, then got up ta Mama Lou's kitchen get something on my belly, boy. Damn, a nigga hungry."

He scratched his arms and hair habitually as he drove full speed through a twisted road he was obviously familiar with. He looked at Da'Quan through the rearview with sinister eyes as he continued, "Yeah, Big D, Savage and me got it locked up down here. We run this whole Southwest, boy, the whole entire Southwest. I mean it now, no bullshit. And with this shit here, boy, you got, we gon take over Georgia and Alabama boy."

He began nudging Savage, who sat quietly agreeing by nodding his head to his cousin's testimony. After twenty minutes of enduring the twists and turns of the inconspicuous road, they arrived at the crest of the elevated hill to a huge brick and stone home with a four-car garage. Country hopped out barefoot and began heading towards the front door confidently in his stroll. Savage and Da'Quan followed suit behind the frail thug. The inside was huge with only a leather sofa, designer glass coffee table and a mahogany Steinway grand piano. Country went straight to the piano and sat therapeutically before his fingers danced across the black and white ivory keys harmonizing the Lenny Williams classic "Cause I Love You," bringing a sense of ease to the whole situation. Da'Quan looked out of the huge glass patio door and was flabbergasted by the view.

There were acres of land in the rear of the house with an Olympic-sized pool, basketball court, tennis court and three to four huge barbeque grills. To the side of the mansion sat multiple four wheelers and jet-skis lined up in a partitioned area next to an extravagant dog kennel. In the distance he saw two huge and well-kept quarter horses standing soaking up the coolness of the morning air. Country began laughing hysterically as he blurted to Savage, "Look at ole Big D cuzzin thankin' how in the fuck did this dirty crazy country muthafucka get the keys to a spread like this here." Savage ignored his banter while he fumbled around with his pager. Country, who was in a jovial mood, continued, "Shiid, look here, Big D, down round these parts you gotta blend in and make ya money. Half of Atlanta Georgia think I'm on dope but they don't know fam this my million dollar spot. I dress like them but live like a king boy."

Da'Quan was shocked at the news of Country's wealth. It was going to take a minute for Da'Quan to wrap his brain around the idea that this country bumpkin was living a better life financially than most people could even dream about living. Country began laughing as he went into a side room and came out in a brand new all white pair of Air Force Ones. He went into the kitchen and pulled out a Heineken from the refrigerator while asking, "Eh y'all want a brew or something to drink?" Savage and Da'Quan both declined as they started heading towards the front door. Before getting back into the car Da'Quan glanced at Country's mansion and vowed to live as good or better than his southern counterpart.

The three drove through the Georgia country setting for twenty minutes before pulling into a strip mall with a variety of stores and Mama Lou's southern diner. The diner was packed with a mix of black and white southern patrons chowing down heartily on Flintstone-portioned plates. The waitress was an older black lady in her mid to late sixties. Her salt and pepper hair was wrapped in a tight bun underneath her Mama Lou's work hat. She was a hefty woman who was quick on her feet with a smile that glowed to the moon and back. Country spoke in complete deference as he asked, "Good morning, Mrs. Betty." She blushed at his almost flirtatious tone. It was obvious they were acquainted as he continued to woo her, "Look here, these two men standing right here my relatives from the west coast, sweet Mrs." He spoke with zeal as if they were rock stars or astronauts.

She smiled graciously and responded, "Welcome, handsome men. If you're a friend of Buke, then you're a friend of me. Come on let me sit you fine men down right on down over here, baby, in the biggest booth we got. Ima go get some menus for you men." Da'Quan sat and looked at the huge steaks, homemade potatoes and pancakes that filled a lot of the patrons' plates. It was a different more friendly vibe than L.A., almost to the point he didn't trust it. His gut instinct was to remain focused and stealth.

Savage, who had gone to the phone, came back excited, "Wassup, y'all th-the package made it to Jo Jo's so we good and my boy wanna meet up at four in Columbus, cuzz, so it's on. He say he got the bread and everything. So let's hurry up, finish this shit up and handle business, cuz. I can't really eat till I make some bread, ya feel me, D? This nigga, Country, cuzz, eat like a goddamn 300-pound lumberjack or something, cuzz, and never gain a pound."

Country just smiled as Mrs. Betty walked up with Country's three plates of pancakes, porterhouse steak and a mound of southern fried potatoes and onions. The plates were steaming hot with melted butter and grease everywhere. By the time Da'Quan's and Savage's steak and eggs arrived, Country had mowed viciously through his porterhouse. Savage's beeper began buzzing halfway through the feast, "Oh shit, let's go, cuz, my guy hitting me, so let's pick that shit up and swing to the spot. Country, grab the pack with D, ima sit with him and the money and y'all bring the shit to us."

Country responded with a mouth full of pancakes, "Let's do it, fam"! Da'Quan finished his water and as the butterflies began stomping in his stomach replied, "Get money, muthafucka."

Country drove relaxed and carefree his cousin Jo Jo's, who had a trailer in the sticks. They pulled up and a malnourished woman with a dingy nightgown worn over a pair of Chuck Taylor All Stars walked out nonchalantly with the package in her hand. She flaunted it like a purse as she strutted with what little dignity remained in her to the car. Country slid her a hundred-dollar bill as she handed him the package through the window.

She looked in the car with desperate eyes as she spoke to Savage with erotic energy, "Wassup, boo, you back in town sugar? Um hmm you know where I'm at sugar."

Savage just laughed as Country scolded her, "Look, shut yo fucking trap and make sure yo kids eat tonight. Ima come check one ya heard me."

She eased away from the car and replied humbly, "Yes, Country, ima head to the market now but a hundred ain't shit, Country." He sighed and reluctantly pulled out another hundred-dollar bill, balled it up and threw it violently at her hitting her in the head.

He pulled off yelling, "And it better be groceries, gal, when I come back."

Savage was excited like a kid as they drove off, "OK, cuz, let's, let's a drop this shit off at the spot and take me to dude." They drove another ten minutes on the highway and pulled off into a residential area full of townhomes. Da'Quan's stomach was in knots as he didn't want to get pulled over with three kilos of cocaine. They pulled up into one of the units and they hopped out as Savage grabbed the package. Once again Country led the way, confidently opening the door to another one of his places.

The spot was virtually empty with nothing more than a sofa and a black and white TV. There was a triple beam on the dinette table and a ton of baggies and other random drug paraphernalia. Country went into the bedroom and came out with two Glocks. He cocked 'em both, kept one and handed Da'Quan one. Savage smiled and calmly told Country, "Nah, cuz, no need for them. This my homie, he good people. I trust him, cuz, we did a lot business."

Country looked at Da'Quan with doubt as he handed him the gun back. He sighed disappointedly and blurted, "You heard what the mayne said, Big D."

Savage got on the phone and called his buyer, "Hey wassup, homeboy, you ready? Uh huh, I'm ready for you, where you at?" Savage listened as Country and Da'Quan sat in silence. In Da'Quan's mind he felt anxiety and uneasiness about the move. He wanted to call it off but it was too late. Just then Savage yelled from the phone, "D, so it's three of 'em, right homie?"

Da'Quan answered, "Yup, three birds."

Savage continued, "Yup, yup, I know where that is, right over there by the Burger King off the freeway, yup. OK meet me there then in twenty minutes. I got on the Denver Broncos jersey."

In the forefront of Da'Quan's mind he wondered, *What the fuck? If you did business with him why wouldn't he just recognize you?* It didn't add up logically, but it was too late.

When they walked out of the townhouse, Savage sniffed and asked Country, "Cuzz, do it smell like dogs out here?" Country remained silent as they got in the rental. Savage began reiterating the play, "OK, cuz, just pull in. He said he's in a white Honda Accord. He kept pressing me to bring the shit but ima just count his money and sit with him. It's gone take that much time to count it up anyway." By now as they circled the parking lot there was no sign of a white Honda Accord. There was a squad car rolling slow on the next aisle and one pulling in.

Da'Quan noticed the squad cars but tried to control the butterflies in his stomach which now felt like elephant dancing as sweat began trickling profusely from his armpits. Two seconds later, Savage shrieked, "Awwe fuck! They on us, take the battery out yo pagers, cuzz." No sooner had Da'Quan's nervous fingers released the battery, there were narc cars and a fleet of DEA cars flooded in the parking lot.

There was a huge 6'7" redneck sheriff with a fat gold chain wrapped around his rose-colored neck. He had to weigh 350 pounds or better and wore a thick Fu Manchu mustache. He had fixed hate in his eyes as he knocked aggressively on the glass with his huge black pistol. When Da'Quan gently unlocked the door, he reached in, grabbed Da'Quan by his shirt collar and flung him like a rag doll to the asphalt. His face connected with a thud to the asphalt knocking him unconscious. He could hear confusion, cursing, along with the baritone voices of men being tortured in the distance. He was struck in the head by a boot thus waking him out of unconsciousness back into the reality of his situation. All he could feel was a knee in his neck smashing his head forcefully against the scorching hot asphalt.

The redneck officer kept saying, "Where's the fucking dope, Cali nigger? Where's the fucking dope, nigger?" The blood from his busted lip began running into his swollen eye which was jammed to the asphalt by the officer's knee. He could barely breathe let alone answer any questions logically. The whole time Da'Quan kept thinking, *They ain't got shit. We ain't bring the dope so fuck 'em, keep your mouth shut.* After an hour of them disassembling the rental all they found was beepers, batteries, two Tylenol and a box of half-eaten pancakes.

As the cops stood around like a disgruntled football team in a huddle they came back to the three and lifted them from the ground. The smallest white officer with blonde hair and blue eyes said, "OK, slick guys, we're taking you in on conspiracy to distribute cocaine. We got you niggers on tape." They bunched the three of them in a squad car like caged dogs in a Yulin festival before transporting them to the station. In the squad car Savage and Country began complaining about how tight the cuffs were and making threats to fuck them up once free. When they arrived at the station and got out the car, Savage spit a loogie directly in the face of the assaulting officer. They immediately took him away for disciplinarian action. Meanwhile they took Country and Da'Quan to separate cells until the next morning.

The next morning the judge stated that they were under arrest for conspiring to sell over a million dollars street value in cocaine. He posted each of their bails at 100k and sent them to Muscogee County Jail. Country was fortunate enough to post bail and get out to make moves for them. He had enough property and cash to hurry out before they found something else under his name. The ride on the jail bus was quiet and depressing. Most of the convicts' heads were turning, gazing regretfully at the scenery they soon would be isolated from.

Ironically, the deputies stopped at the same Burger King where they were to have done the transaction and brought the ten convicts in the bus their "last meal," so to say. When they arrived at the six-level, all-brick facility in the deep brush of the woods, Da'Quan began to feel nauseated. The jail had a huge automatic gate, which was a grim reminder of your incarceration, that slammed loud when it closed. The inmates were shackled like slaves into the intake. They lined everybody up, made them strip nude, bend over and cough before they were issued their county blues. The walls were a dull grey, and the place had a very depressing vibe about it. The guard released Da'Quan to the third floor and buzzed the heavy steel door open. Loud baritone laughs and screams could be heard echoing from the belly of the beast as he walked in. When the guard walked him in, the dorm of 200 became silent as they instantly began sizing him up as new bait. He could see the broken souls of men through their hopeless eyes as he maneuvered aggressively to a spot to be alone and cry his eyes out. He began thinking about home, his dog and the plethora of women he had left behind. Tiffany's smile and thoughts of her nude body ran through his mind as he sat alone in a corner and wept about his misfortune. The placed smelled of Pine Sol and Irish spring as the anger, pain and sadness could be felt in the air. Da'Quan just sat to himself and watched everybody's moves without saying a word in his first day in Muscogee County Jail.

Chapter 33
MUSCOGEE COUNTY JAIL

NOVEMBER 1999 • 30 years old

The smell of Pine Sol shot directly through the nostrils choking Da'Quan awake from his first wink of sleep in Muscogee County Jail. His eyes were black and blue from the assault dished out by officer Traino and his notorious goon squad. When the five a.m. light began flickering on, it made his head feel as if he had slept on a pillow of bricks. It took a minute for him to remember exactly what happened and where he was. Normally nightmares end when you awake but today being awake started the nightmare. Since there were no available bunks, he had the pleasure of sleeping on a portable floater that felt like a cold cement hammock. His mouth was extremely parched, like he had eaten a box of sand cookies, while his nose still had dried blood under it from the ass whipping he took the day before. In the far distance he could faintly hear an offbeat southern voice crooning "Send Me" by the late Sam Cook. He slowly rolled over pulling the pillow too tight to his head. There was still a smidgen of hope that this was still part of a surreal dream and that he could close his eyes and wake up in his own bed.

After ten minutes of trying to sleep this away, he was disturbed by harsh coughs, loud yawns and toilet flushing. Moments later the crooner from the shower stood on the tier next to Da'Quan's floater drying his hair. In his distinct country accent, he blurted, "So there he is, fresh from Cali."

Da'Quan fought to open his sore eyes to make sure he was talking to him. He hadn't said a word the day before and nobody spoke to him. Between his battered eyes he saw a heavy set shirtless mulatto dude standing in the door of his cell. His left front tooth was missing and he had huge dark rings under his eye sockets. His eyes were seedy and told the story of a man who had journeyed millions of miles in search of a high only to remain mentally stagnated. He was a victim of his own circumstances . His approach was harmless but bold. He was also giving Da'Quan a heads up that the dorm knew who he was and why he was there. Da'Quan would soon learn that jail is the streets and that your reputation combined with how you carried yourself is all that you could depend on at the end of the day.

Da'Quan sat up to gather his bearings as he replied, "Yeah, homie straight from South Central."

The mulatto dude wiped his hand against his leg before reaching out and saying, "Yessuh they call me Screws. My momma named me Lamar but to the rest these muthufuckas I'm Screws. So yeah I hear you went down with Country and Savage?"

Da'Quan declined to answer but shook Screws's outreached hand. After the way he'd been snitched on and put in this predicament he didn't trust his own shadow. Screws kept rambling as he chewed aggressively on a piece of gum between his missing teeth, "Eeeewwww wee boy ,they shoulda told ya this here is snitch city. Sorry. Nigga. I'm Trying to Come. Home."

His delivery and slick wit using the acronym forced laughter from Da'Quan's defeated body. When he smiled his nose and jaw ached but nonetheless he enjoyed his first laugh in days. He shook his head and responded, Yeah, a muthafucking snitch got me beat up and stuck in here."

Screws stood in his cell mirror battling with a huge pus bump on his acne-infested skin as he replied, "Well nah. not exactly. You got yourself in here, boy. Can't be trusting folks, especially not here, no sir. Everybody and I mean everybody even the guards looking for a way out, boy, either through that gate or through the cemetery across the road. But we all want out, don't forget it."

Da'Quan just sat quietly as his words of accountability uneasily sunk in. He hated hearing it but Screws was spot on and it burned him up to admit it to himself. As he woke up, his reality began to set in; he became infuriated with himself for not speaking up when he saw the writing on the wall. He should've called Savage out on who this dude he was on the phone with, and why wouldn't he recognize him if they'd done business. Screws continued to battle with his pimples while saying, "Now look here,, I'm Country's folks that's my folks, and he done looked out for ya boy a whole lotta days when I was out there on that shit, boy. So ima tell ya don't trust nobody in here, Cali, not even me, understand? Goddammit, whew that monster right here boy been waiting to pop that sonofabitch a month, whew we! Look here, hand me a paper towel, Cali, would ya?"

Da'Quan handed him a paper towel to wipe the huge thick yellow pus mixed with blood that ran down his face. Da'Quan leaned against the door when all of a sudden down the tier they heard, "Well-come muthafucka, I ain't never scared boy."

It was the smallest dude in the dorm standing shirtless yelling at the top of his lungs at a much huskier and hardened-faced convict who stood silently staring at the young thug through nefarious lenses. The husky convict took the pick out of his afro, pulled off his tank top revealing his huge muscular frame to the dorm. He smiled, revealing a mouth with missing teeth, as he began stretching his neck and shoulders to engage with the young loudmouth in the terror dome. By now most of the convicts in the all-black dorm began to eagerly gather around the dispute to get an up close look at the fight about to take place.

Screws wiped his face as he looked down at the commotion saying, "Goddammit, here we go again. Li'l Tommy at it again. Now see this li'l muthufucka right here ain't got a lick of sense. I think some of these ignorant muthafuckas actually like it here." He went back to tending to his facial while Da'Quan watched to see how li'l Tommy fared against the muscular con. The muscular con just stared unbothered as li'l Tommy moved to the center of the dorm yelling and ranting, "C'mon, muthufucka, talk that shit now, boy, I ain't no punk in here." The muscular con eased out into the middle of the dorm with li'l Tommy as the onlookers gathered around to block the commotion from any potential guards who may try and break it up.

Within seconds the muscular con swiftly attacked Tommy. He tackled him to the hard paved floor in a wicked gladiatorial fashion. Li'l Tommy's head split open like an eggshell as blood seeped from his forehead between the toes and sandals of the sadistic inmates who watched in awe. Although Tommy squirmed and fought in the puddle of his own blood he managed to connect some solid blows to the head and face of the muscular con. The more blows li'l Tommy managed to connect only infuriated the muscular con into pounding Tommy's head even harder against the bloody paved floor. The barbaric expressions on the convict's face was a clear cut indicator that Da'Quan was in a realm of hell. Tommy's slender body amazingly slid away from the now-winded muscular con's vice grip, as he began violently tagging him with sharp blows to the face filled with rage. His mental toughness and stamina allowed him the opportunity to punish the muscular con, who now seemed to be having an asthma attack, with swift sharp blows to his face. After the fifth blow you could hear his fist connecting to the con's face disturbingly loudly, as the muscular con lay helpless struggling for oxygen.

Li'l Tommy's split head continued to bleed like a faucet in the face of the muscular con, who lay unconscious, continually taking blows to his lifeless body. From Da'Quan's view all he could see was Tommy punishing what appeared to be a lifeless stuffed animal or pillow sprawled out at the mercy of his rage. He sat on top of the lifeless con beating his head against the pavement until it had swollen disproportionately to his body. Both convicts' blood covered the floor, as no one intervened in the altercation. Just then, while Tommy attempted to bury a hole in the paved floor with the con's head, the deputies came running in forcing the whole dorm to lay face down. As Da'Quan lay face down he attempted to look up to see what was going on when he was struck instantly to the back of his head with a billy club. The pain from the blow shot straight from the crown of his head to the bottom of his feet. He remained face down paralyzed in excruciating pain as the tears from his frustrating disposition ran freely down his face. The sounds of the melee grew louder and louder as the deputies made examples out of several inmates with the butts of their billy clubs.

The seconds felt like hours and the hours like days as Da'Quan tried to find a way to cope with being confined like an animal. He was still unsettled and had no clue on how to adjust to the truculent environment of the southern county jail. California may as well have been on Mars, as he had no friends or relatives in Georgia he could rely on for assistance. When the guards finally eased up and let them back on their feet, he saw Screws in his mirror nursing a fresh black eye he earned with his slick tongue by the eager-to-whip-ass guards. He could see that this type of behavior was the norm and that the police had a normal system of tactical violence to resolve the bullshit in the dorms. There was a painful throbbing at the crown of his head that felt like it had its own heartbeat. His face wasn't healed and he had already made it through his second ass whipping in forty-eight hours.

Tommy and the muscular con both remained in the dorm separated as a couple of cons began the arduous task of mopping human blood. Da'Quan sat nursing his head as the trustee wrung out the bloody water, unbothered, with his bare hands into the bucket. Screws in the meanwhile continued to bitch aloud, "Ya see this why muthafucking cops get they ass lit up boy. Look a here, Cali, now these muthafuckas can't be doing this shit. Fuck that, ima get a lawyer. I just need my sister to get one for me, but she won't take my calls, bitch, ain't took one in a year."

Da'Quan just sat silently trying to make sense out of his situation while he tended to the lumps and bruises he had acquired from the Columbus County goon squad. He began thinking about how he could get out and start all over. The reality of him being in hell began to set in as he sat helplessly on the floater he was assigned in complete disarray with his life. His biggest concern now was to get out of Muscogee County Jail alive.

Chapter 34
DONALD GOINES

NOVEMBER 1999 • 30 years old

Time cannot be stopped and is rarely appreciated until we are forced into a situation that limits our use of it for our own regard. Da'Quan had been incarcerated a couple of months or so and the monotonous rituals of jail living had begun taking a mental toll on him. He found solace in his workouts but aside from that and sleep, he had no real structure or daily routine. Sitting around talking about who they were and what they had on the streets had become annoying. He had dissected everybody's stories enough to understand that more than ninety percent of the gibberish he'd been hearing was fabricated material.

The heat from summer had begun to taper off and the cool fall winds kept the housing facility chilly. Every morning he would get up at 4:45 a.m. before the lights came on and do his 100 pushups, 100 squats and extensive core work before hopping in the shower before the rest of the cons opened their eyes. It was a Saturday morning and after Da'Quan finished up his morning ritual he sat alone culminating his routine by sipping on a hot black cup of coffee. As he sat deep in thought about his misfortune in the dope game he noticed the trustee who they called Dog sweeping within a couple of feet from him. Dog was the only identity he was formerly known as in the joint. He was a short semi-fit con who hobbled around the jail dorm shirtless even on the coldest nights. His hair was matted with a few wild braids that lay lifeless to the side with silky greys highlighting them. His teeth were rotten, and he never looked anyone directly in their eyes. He stared downward in conversations as if he were speaking to a religious authoritarian or iconic pop star. His sturdy physical build was meaningless since his mind was unable to overcome his powerful and cunning addiction to cocaine. The white horse had taken him on a wild and painful ride from Louisiana to Georgia over half of his existence. He was a known addict whose life was led by the lure of the infamous pipe. Dog only replied to the guards and other cons with his yessuh, yes ma'am antics. Da'Quan was taken aback by his dated pre-Civil War slave dialect. His back was slightly hunched from all of the years of walking with his head down, existing passively in the valley of rock bottom self-esteem. Dog voluntarily carried out all of the tedious chores in the dorm like sweeping up hair, cleaning the shower floors, trash detail and keeping score of dominoes tournaments between the convicts. When he wasn't playing custodian or doing pushups he was on his bunk reading classics like, "Make Me Wanna Holla," by Nathan McCall, "Experience," by Donald Goines and "Whoreson," just to name a few. His intelligence level was buried deep in his inferiority complex. At eighteen, he was released from his foster home and began his uphill crack journey through the southern belt of America.

The look on Da'Quan's face must have been a dead giveaway to the distress he was feeling deep in his soul as Dog stopped pushing the broom and pulled a book out of his rear pocket. He handed it to him with his head down while humbly saying, "This might help you pass the time." Da'Quan gave him a befuddled look as he thought to himself, *Muthafucka I ain't read a book in years I wanna get out not entertained.* Dog stood patiently with the book in his extended hand waiting on Da'Quan to take it. He grabbed it from his outreached hand and found the cover with a dope fiend sprawled out intriguing. The cover photo was a definite prelude to the picaresque characters that would eventually come to life from the pages of the novel.

On the streets he had seen and dealt drugs to junkies but never had an inkling as to what they went through behind closed doors. Dog stood hat in hand with a slight smirk on his rotted grill as he could see just how fascinated Da'Quan was with his token of friendship. While Da'Quan studied both covers, Dog whispered, "Now that's something that'll help you pass the time away sir and I got a whole stack of books whenever you need one."

Da'Quan replied enthusiastically, "Awwe OK, bro, it's cool if I take it and read it?"

Dog eagerly responded, "Oh, oh yeah you can have it. I read it five times, sir, go ahead. My sister send me books every month, sir."

Da'Quan shook his head and irritated said, "Quit calling me sir just call me D, homie, I ain't yo boss or daddy." Dog shook his head humbly and without saying a word continued back pushing his broom throughout the module. Da'Quan stood glancing at a few pages before tucking away into the corner of the module preparing to dive into the novel like a dick in a wet womb. From the first sentence the very descriptive details he gave about the scenarios and characters snatched him into the story, cementing him to his seat on the floor with his eyes glued to the "ghetto realism." The characters were alive and had flaws that made them relatable to the reader. Goines had a way of painting the picture around the reader making them a fly on the wall in each scene. He created visuals of the dark side of drug use with graphic details that would turn the stomach of the reader. Da'Quan was taken by the simplicity of the story that took the reader on a roller coaster ride without any guarantee to end on track. From the details of sores with pus and open abscesses, he knew that this literature was based on hard facts that only a junkie could explain. The world he put the reader in was disheartening and left a mental scar about the realities of hardcore drug abuse.

As he sat on the floor reading with his legs extended out, Tata Bug walked by and kicked his feet as if it were an accident. The blatant disrespect prompted Da'Quan to his feet angrily barking, "Muthafucka watch yo step." His chest was heaving as he was ready to unleash his frustrations on any candidate for his wrath. Tata Bug had a sarcastic grin on his worn face as he just kept walking towards the chow line. Da'Quan knew that he was being tested and was willing to stick some taped metal in his gut if it came down to it. The rest of the cons began hovering around just in case Tata Bug decided to engage. As he walked off, Da'Quan's anger blanketed the dorm. He sat back down, opened the book and fought to regain his focus in the Goines novel that freed him from his gruesome reality.

The more he read the deeper he fell into Goines's scenarios. Characters became living entities in his head almost like old friends or relatives. He developed a sincere connection with them, taking on the emotional freefall that each of them was on. After a few chapters he began feeling the pain, embarrassment, plus the highs and lows of each character. The hands on the clock befriended him by moving steadily through the day as he was engulfed in Goines's literary genius.

"Dopefiend" was an eye opener to the grim and dirty side of heroin. It gave in-depth descriptions of the smell, look and wretchedness that existed in the shady junkie apartments on the east coast. He took Da'Quan's mind thousands of miles away, entertaining him like it was a motion picture of words and pages. At that point he had never read anything but books related to history classes or some whitewashed religious readings designed to manipulate the minds of the masses. This was a different type of literature that was easy to read and almost impossible to put down. He had found his solace in the cage of animals and ruptured spirits.

Weeks had passed and Da'Quan had read three Goines novels and was at the tail end of Nathan McCall's, "Make Me Wanna Holla." He was still without a lawyer and used the reading as a tool to escape his reality. Screws walked by his floater one night before the lights shut out and stood smiling over Da'Quan with a sarcastic grin on his face. Da'Quan put his book down and asked, "What the fuck you smiling at, nigga?"

Screws began chuckling as he called li'l Tommy over from a dice game, "Say Tommy, Tommy, come here, boy."

Tommy responded, "Hold on, Screws, I'm 'bout to break this nigga, boy." His next roll he crapped out and yelled, "Awwe shit, Screws, you fucking with a nigga when he on Tee Lee, now I lost my goddamn store, boy, ima be in yo shit this week."

Screws laughed and jokingly replied, "Aaiight, nigga, but check this out. Should we let Cali in on the Dog shit?"

Li'l Tommy burst into laughter as he said, "Go on, boy, why not? Cali cool wit me. He should know hahahahah." Li'l Tommy pulled out a pinhead joint and lit it up.

He passed it to Screws, who took a hard pull and exhaled a huge cloud of smoke before sarcastically saying, "OK, Cali, so yeah you good wit Dog, I see. Gotcha reading his books and being his buddy." Li'l Tommy took the joint back from Screws and offered Da'Quan a hit. As Da'Quan took a strong pull off of it Screws continued in a serious tone, "Well look here, Cali, the boy Dog, who's a good guy and all, got a rep on the streets, boy." Li'l Tommy began laughing as he took the weed from the fingertips of Da'Quan. The laughter and vibe of the conversation had Da'Quan extremely curious about what Screws was trying to convey. He sat perplexed about the whole situation as Screws continued, "I gotta let you know, Cali, cause you a solid dude. Ya boy Dog got his name the hard way."

He and Lil Tommy burst into uncontrollable laughter as Da'Quan sat with a blank clueless look on his face. Da'Quan began feeling irritated as his high set in, angrily blurting, "OK muthafuckas, what's the joke?"

Screws erased his smile, looked Da'Quan in the eye and replied, "Look here, on the streets ya boy Dog got his name from ..."

He paused as Li'l Tommy put his face in his hands and continued, "Ya boy Dog got his name man from sucking stray dogs' dicks for yayo on the streets, man. That's why nobody messes with that cat, man, ain't you noticed?" Da'Quan sat speechless with a disgruntled look on his face. He looked at Li'l Tommy for confirmation as Tommy shook his head yes.

Screws took the small pinhead and turned it into a roach and jokingly said, "Boy, Dog is man's best friend but that nigga is a dog's best friend." Li'l Tommy and another con walking by doubled over in laughter at Screw's dark humor. Da'Quan just sat quiet realizing he was in the depths of hell and needed to get out. After a few moments of silence he got up, went to his floater, picked up all of the books Dog had loaned him and angrily made his way to Dog's cell.

Dog's cell was immaculate and smelled of Pine Sol and Irish Spring soap. Against the wall neatly stacked, he had a huge assortment of books ranging from the Bible to violent urban street novels. He was laying on his bunk shirtless reading "Invisible Man" by Ralph Ellison when Da'Quan angrily encroached his place of solace with a stack of books in his hands. He wanted to throw the books in his face out of anger and frustration but opted to place them down neatly out of the smidgen of respect he had for Dog. Dog looked up from his novel with a look of embarrassment over his tired face. He didn't say a word as Da'Quan put all of his books down on the floor. As he walked out of his cell, Dog attempted to speak but the anger in Da'Quan's eyes held him silent. Da'Quan was still in shock, as he had never seen or heard anything as disgusting and gutter as Dog's resume. On his way back to his floater he made a mental note to hire an attorney to get the hell out of hell.

Chapter 35
COCAINE ANGEL

DECEMBER 1999 • 30 years old

Da'Quan had increasingly grown tired of his struggle with time vs. money. He knew that if he was on the streets he could hustle and make things happen for himself as opposed to being dependent on the urgency or lack thereof of another individual. Waiting on a response from Mike was as nerve wrenching as waiting on HIV results. Each night he slept with one eye open in case Tata Bug shot some deadly missiles at him. He missed his dog, family and friends. The food was horrible; he would've killed for a thick grilled porterhouse steak. He yearned to be locked at the waist with a woman feeling her warm breath moaning sexual jargon in his ear. The daily stench of Irish Spring and male body odor made him nauseated with frustration. Yella wired five thousand to his office a week prior and he still hadn't received word if Mike had picked up his case or not. His faith in God was being tested on every level in this situation. Screws had given him a run-down pocket Bible that he almost completed after a week of waiting on counsel. He admired how no matter what was going on, Screws would put his knees on the cold hard concrete floor of the cell and prayed wholeheartedly to God thankfully for that moment and better days ahead.

Da'Quan sat on his floater on a Thursday morning monitoring the fluid movement of the cons in the dorm. His mind was preoccupied with the bills at home backing up along with lack of income coming in due to his incarceration. He silently observed a con they called Cosa, who was dealing cards with superior legerdemain as he kept all the players' eyes glued to him while he effortlessly worked the deck. Across his chest he had Cosa Nostra Our Thing tattooed in huge Old English letters.

Cosa was a brother obsessed with the Italian mafia to the point where he used terms like "busting my balls," "he's a good kid" or "capeesh" in his daily conversations. Although he had no physical traits to back the story of his grandfather being a notorious Sicilian mobster, Cosa had shrewd hustling skills and a murderous rep on the streets. While Da'Quan watched the cons engage in a tense game of poker, he realized that the rules on these games were written in blood. They often played for store items or drugs depending on the vice of the con. Some cons were gluttonous and gambled for food to keep a shitload of snacks and perishables for when the store was out. While other cons played strictly for narcotics that would frequently make their way through the dorm. The smack heads played and gambled for keeps with their eyes fixed on the elusive hands from their crafty dealer. Cosa had earned a substantial living over the years performing his patented jailhouse pastime.

During a heated hand one of the gluttonous cons had and issue with the cards he was dealt and rose from his seat roaring, "Nah, you son of bitch, I been pulling teeth a long time, boy, I calls bullshit when I see it, boy, gimme all my stuff back. Boy, you's a cheater, I mean it." The fat con stood with a back as wide as a doorway with huge loaves of sweaty fat that overlapped each other down to the split of his buttocks. He had a back full of tattoos that were unreadable against his sooty complexion. His huge male boobs heaved in anger over his protruding belly that sat like he was seven months expecting. Sweat dripped profusely from the back of his head and down from his armpits. Cosa sat back calm with a rotten smirk on his face staring at the huge black con eye to eye without a blink. He fidgeted with the toothpick that sat between his gold grill fronts without saying a word.

Two of Cosa's associates eased up quietly behind the fat con and acted as if they were watching TV. The huge black con had been transferred from Alabama and had to stop in Georgia for outstanding warrants before catching the chain gain near Florida. He didn't have any affiliates but was adamant about his case against Cosa. The dorm grew silent as Cosa calmly responded,

"You know what, big man, you're right. You seem like a good kid, I mean why would you have to lie? I get it. I apologize for my mistake, no hard feelings."

He put his hands out for a handshake only for the huge con to slap it away. He then attempted to reach over Cosa to take his store back when Cosa's goons attacked the con with broom sticks and open fists. Cosa eased away from the ruckus with a huge grin on his face as his goons swatted the fat con mercilessly from his head to his toes with the cut broomstick pieces. He tried retaliating but he was morbidly out of shape and fell to his knees gasping for oxygen.

They beat him like a wild boar as he whined and begged for mercy. Snot and blood raced from his nose and ears as they continuously whacked away at his forearms, which he used to block the sharp blows. After two minutes of brutal discipline the fat con lay lifeless on his shirtless back choking on his own blood as he gasped for air. The other cons had the window blocked so the guards couldn't see the brutal chastising taking place. Da'Quan had never seen so much concentrated violence, and the animalistic behavior had begun to rub off on him. He was already mentally prepared to murder Tata or one of his goons if he had to. He desperately wanted out before he landed some extra time on some bullshit.

Shortly after the fat con regained consciousness and eased to his cell, the steel door opened. Deputy Patterson, the stoic guard, walked in with a vexed look on his face as if he knew something had taken place. He observed the dorm with eagle eyes before yelling, "Taylor, c'mon!"

Da'Quan eased from his seat and hesitantly made his way to Patterson. He hoped they didn't think he caused the melee but was preparing mentally for anything they could possibly be coming with. The deputy cuffed him and quickly led him out of the dorm. In the chilly hallway on the way to the elevator the deputy calmly said, "Looks like you may be getting out soon. Word is Mike Garner picked up your case. He's here to meet you, sir." He led Da'Quan down to the first floor and sat him in a private room facing a thick glass with a phone next to him. Before he left he muttered, "Good luck, Mr. Taylor, this really isn't a place for you."

Da'Quan sighed and nodded his head as the huge steel door slammed shut. He sat and stared blankly through the glass window wondering what the outcome would be. His stomach churned with anxiety as he prayed to God, "Dear God if you get me out of here I promise to never touch a gram of dope again in my life. I will do my best to hustle without cocaine. I know you don't mind me selling weed so I'll stick to that, God, if you just get me out of this jam I'm in, I promise."

Just then the door on the other side of the window open slowly. In came a white-haired Caucasian man wearing a smoke grey Ermenegildo Zegna bespoke custom fitted suit. From the looks of his twenty thousand dollar get up it was apparent he meant business. His hair was milky white and he wore a come-try-me stare, with a smirk on his oval shaped face. He resembled Santa Claus in the off season of Christmas. Da'Quan was filled with uneasy nerves going haywire as he needed this man as much or if not more so than Jesus at this time. He sat down with a stern look on his face and stared Da'Quan in the eyes before saying a word. It felt as if he were trying to read Da'Quan and get a vibe from him before he started.

Da'Quan nervously asked, "So you're attorney Garner?"

The man began grabbing papers from his leather briefcase before sarcastically replying, "Last I checked on my office door that's what it said. How are you, Mr. Taylor?"

Da'Quan took a deep breath before saying, "I'm OK, just wanna get the fuck outta here."

His raw honesty brought a smile to Mike's face as his response, "Well, that's what I'm here to do, Mr. Taylor, is get you out of here and back to your family and friends." He put his glasses on the tip of his nose and began reviewing Da'Quan's paperwork before saying, "Hmmm OK now, first thing we gotta do is separate you from your two crime buddies. They have very extensive criminal histories and we don't want you connected to that. You, on the other hand, have never been in trouble, which puts you in a great situation. Now let me ask you, Mr. Taylor, why did you come out here?"

Da'Quan hesitantly replied, "To look for real estate."

Attorney Garner excitedly replied, "Goddamn it then, that's it. You came down with a friend to find some property and had no idea about any type of drug activity, make sense?" Da'Quan nodded his head yes. Garner reached in his suit pocket and pulled out a silk black handkerchief and began wiping the sweat from the tip of his nose and the back of his neck as he examined the paperwork. He cleared his phlegm-filled throat and continued, "And Mr. Taylor, please forgive me for being late. I've been running all over hell's half acre trying to get to you so again please forgive me."

He kept his eyes glued to the paperwork as Da'Quan replied, "No worries, attorney, I understand." The looks on Mike's face as he examined the paperwork had Da'Quan's nerves going haywire. After a couple of minutes, Mike continued, "OK, Mr. Taylor, how do you feel? Because I know we can fight these motherfuckers all the way to trial. We're not taking a goddamn deal. From what I see they don't have any admissible evidence, Mr. Taylor."

Da'Quan sat quietly as his conscience barked, *That's easy for you to say motherfucker! They holding fifteen calendars over my goddamn head not yours! Shit you beat your case as a white man of the law, I'm just a nigga from L.A. trying to flip some dope!* After he battled with his inner self, he replied, "OK, attorney, fuck it. I just came to Georgia to look for some property."

Mike instantly looked away from the paperwork at Da'Quan from the top of his reading glasses and responded, "Now that's the attitude we gotta go and fight these cocksuckers with, Mr. Taylor." He went back to examining the paperwork as he mumbled, "Hmm OK. The balance has been paid. We will request bail reduction. I need to call Connie and ummm." Da'Quan sat on pins and needles. He kept having thoughts of a white hand at the end of a judge's walnut wood gavel slamming it violently as a deep southern voice screamed, "Guilty, nigger!"

Mike's aggressive southern accent snapped Da'Quan back into reality, "Mr. Taylor, now hear this, we are gonna fight the prosecution. I know who we're up against and trust me, Mr. Taylor, he's all over the place. He's more confused than a fart in a fan factory, so I'm not too worried. Makes sense?"

Da'Quan shook his head and replied, "I'm with you, attorney Garner, whatever you say as long as you can get me out of here."

Attorney Garner began gathering his paperwork and stuffing it in his briefcase as he huffed and puffed, "OK, so Mr. Taylor we will motion for a bail reduction hearing and get you out of here. Then what we will do is fight these son of a bitches until they run out of ammo and call it a day. And let me add, please, do not let this period in your life define you. From what I see, you're a great gentleman with a lot to offer so with that being said just take this stumbling block as a huge lesson, make sense?" Da'Quan nodded his head as his Cocaine Angel rose to his feet and looked Da'Quan in the eye.

To Da'Quan, Mike represented his ticket to freedom. He was his small glimmer of hope, the liaison between him and the free world. In essence he was Da'Quan's general manager. As Mike finished packing Da'Quan tried to think of some questions, but his mind went blank. Before he left he turned back to Da'Quan and calmly said with his heavy voice,"Mr. Taylor, when you are done with court this week, we need you to come down to the office again to fill out some more paperwork." Da'Quan nodded his head yeah as his Cocaine Angel yelled, "Have an excellent day, Mr. Taylor," before squeezing out of the wooden door into the wonderful land of the free.

Chapter 36
GRANDMA'S COMING HOME

JUNE 1997 • 27 years old

Life is an existence that holds memories from the time we exit the womb until the day we blink our last blink and breathe the last breath of air given. There are no guarantees for anything except what's promised, which is the color of the skin you exist in, debt and the inevitable escape via death we have awaiting. Everything in between the cradle and grave is a daily gift granted for us to work and live out our dreams and goals as humans, no matter how big or small they may be.

Da'Quan had been hustling and enjoying his youthful years so much he hadn't taken the time to observe his grandmother Delilah's slow physical decline. His world changed one day after he pulled up to his grandmother's house and she stood outside with the water hose in hand rinsing her hands, neck and feet as though she didn't have a bathtub or shower inside of her home. From a distance he thought, *Hmm that's strange. Maybe she was sitting in ants and was washing the insects off of her, or maybe something stung her but whatever the case may be she was adamant about using that hose to rinse her body.*

While parking his truck she continued to rinse her neck until he walked up behind her and said, "Hey Grandma, what's wrong?"

She jerked her head up as if she was startled and replied, "Hey boy, you scared me. Ain't nothing wrong, I'm just washing my dirty neck. What's wrong with you?" He remained silent as he looked around for any neighbors who may have been watching them in this awkward moment. He then snatched the hose from her and grabbed her firmly by her arm as he walked her to the steps of her porch.

As he went to turn the hose off she stood dripping wet while scolding him with an attitude, "Boy, don't you come here taking me out my shower. I pay the damn bill here, shit." He looked up at her standing in a robe covering a nightgown with no shoes on her feet dripping wet like a puppy in the rain. It was at this moment he first took notice of her sudden drop in weight. He went and turned the water off and instantly took his grandmother out of the chilly wind in order to avoid her catching a cold. When they made it in the house she quickly snatched her arm from the firm clutch he had on her. Da'Quan stood befuddled as he for the first time realized that she was no longer the strong robust woman she once was. In an instant he now saw that he had now switched roles from the meek and unguided to the protector and guardian of his favorite human on earth.

Delilah, who in the past was the domineering force of the family, was clearly reverting back to her childhood ways as she plopped her wet body down in the corner of her antique sofa. He thought to himself, *Growing up, nobody was allowed to sit in her living room; she kept this shit like a* Better Homes *magazine cover.* He knew from this notion alone that something was terribly wrong with his beloved grandmother. Instinctively. he told her, "OK Grandma, go dry off and change clothes and imma call my mom to see when she's coming home, ok?" She looked at him with a petrified look on her face like a five-year-old who'd been scolded. The whole ordeal, which was surreal to him, had his mind racing with a whirlwind of questions, *What the fuck is going on, is this shit really happening, why in the fuck would God do this to her, who's gone watch her?* All of his emotions ran through his body wild like a bundle of yarn until he felt tangled in an emotional web made of barbed wire.

He went to help her off of the couch, as it appeared that the wet robe combined with her arthritic knees made it almost impossible for her to stand on her own. She violently snatched away from his grip once she was on her feet and hobbled gingerly into her bedroom to change. Da'Quan shut the door behind her and instantly began dialing his mother's work number on the phone.

She picked up after the second ring. "Hello, library, Lillian speaking. How may I help you?"

Da'Quan replied in an angry, volatile tone, "Yeah, Mom, what the fuck is wrong with my grandma?"

Lillian separated her ear from the receiver and stared at it like it was a live rattlesnake in her hand. She had never heard her son so enraged with a venomous tongue, especially directed at her. After a brief moment she gritted her teeth and calmly responded, "First of all, son, how are you? Second of all, I'm at work with people all around me, so why don't we do this when I get home. We will take this up then, and I'll explain everything to you, OK?"

Da'Quan, who wrestled to contain his fiery tongue, responded, Yeah, OK. She was outside taking a shower with the water hose earlier when I came by."

Lillian calmly responded, "OK, well, did you tend to her?"

He instantly replied sarcastically, "Yeah, who else was gone do it?" He began to speak again before she abruptly hung up in his face. He knew she was angry and that he had never spoken to her in that manner before, but the love for his grandmother combined with the frustrating sight of her physical decline enraged him into an irate state. He sat on the couch directly in the damp spot where Delilah sat and put his sorrowful face in his grass-covered hands trying to make sense of the whole ordeal.

Just then Delilah came from the bedroom with a church blazer on top of her drenched robe and gown. She smiled at Da'Quan, who sat taken aback by her behavior, and said confidently, "Well, come on, boy, you taking me to church?" Tears instantly discharged from his eyes as he knew this wasn't a game and that he now had to monitor his lifelong overseer and nurturer with the utmost attention.

He forced himself through his tear jerk enough to take her in the room to find something suitable to wear until his mom came home. He felt uneasy about totally undressing her so he rummaged through her closet until he found a dry robe he could wrap her in temporarily. As he undressed her he closed his eyes and struggled not to look at her frame which was deteriorating seemingly right before his eyes. Her ribcage protruded in a skeletal form seemingly only covered by a very thin layer of brown skin. He fought the tears that eagerly awaited to jump from his face as he made sure her body would be dry and warm. She still knew how to put her arms in the sleeves and maneuvered now like a two-year-old.

Once the robe was on, she snuggled, smiled and said, "Why thank you sir, and let me ask you, what's your name again, boy?"

Da'Quan's eyes bulged as his heart dropped to the floor like a metal anchor. He looked perplexed, as he couldn't believe his own grandmother forgot his name. He shook his head, put his hand on her shoulder, looked her square in her grey eyes and whispered, "Da'Quan, Grandma. My name is Da'Quan, OK?" She pulled him close, gave him a hug and said OK, good night, as she slowly sat on the edge of her bed. By now he was in a sunken place and couldn't muster up the energy to dispute her actions, so he just responded, "Good night, Grandma". Before he shut the door he looked at the alarm clock on her dresser that read 3:15 p.m. and wondered if she was actually tired or believed it was night fall.

He went to the living room and sat back on the couch disgruntled about the whole situation. After a few moments of deep critical thinking he managed to slip off into a light day coma, disconnecting him from his new reality.

Moments later he was awakened by his ear being twisted as though it was in the steel clamps of pliers. He instantly woke up to his mother, Lillian, who towered over him with a heinous look in her teary eyes. She looked over her shoulders not to wake her mother, gritted her teeth and told him, Get yo sorry ass up, come here so I can talk to you." He slowly arose from the couch grabbing his ear, giving her the look of death, as they made their way to the kitchen.

She slammed her keyring that held over twenty keys on it, on the kitchen counter before blurting, "Goddammit, what in the hell is wrong with you, calling my fucking job like some kinda goddamn fool?"

Da'Quan looked her in her eyes and retaliated full of anger, "Because my grandmother out in the front yard taking a shower looking like a fucking fool."

Her eyes squinted with anger as she got within inches of his face. He could smell the minty spearmint gum on her breath as she rambled angrily, "Look at you how you acting? How could I tell yo soft ass anything? Look how you handle stuff. Ain't nobody no goddamn fool, yo grandmother is suffering from dementia and stomach cancer." She instantly began crying as Da'Quan handed her a paper towel to wipe her face as he remained silent. After she gathered herself she continued, "Yeah you wanna cuss people out and act all big and bad huh, I'm the one picking up shitty toilet paper around the house and picking her up off of the ground when she falls. Shit, where are you when she needs to go to the doctor or pick up her prescriptions? Yeah talk that shit now!" She took a deep breath and yelled, "This is real life! Welcome to adulthood. Uh huh, when you out there selling God knows what or messing with one of them nappy head heffas, I'm the one here making sure she's fed and tended to do, so don't be raising your voice at me and talking to me like you ain't got no goddamn sense, shit."

She paused as her chest was heaving uncontrollably and looked away as she said, "Now as much as I don't want to, ima put her in a convalescent home on Wednesday." She leaned her exhausted body against the counter with her palms facing the ceiling as if she needed strength from a higher source as she blurted, "My mama only got six months to live, oh my God, why now father God?"

At this point Da'Quan realized that manhood was not only predicated on fighting, sleeping with a plethora of women and making money, but that it also entailed securing the family and making sure the home was stable. Without another word said, Da'Quan kissed his mom on the forehead as she fought her faucet of tears with a Kleenex box, walked to his grandmother's bedroom door, peaked in and smirked in pain as she lay peacefully asleep like a toddler. He left the house feeling like an emotional casualty. As he cranked up his truck, the color of day was in black in white to him. He instinctively felt the anger to kill, but there was no antagonist to his pain other than God. The thought of losing his number one fan and protector sent sharp pains like a million metal blades discharging like missiles through his body.

Wednesday morning showed its face and while Mother Nature smiled with a beautiful sunny smile that a.m., Da'Quan's mood was crippled with melancholy, as this was Delilah's last day at home as she knew it. He rode in the back seat of his mom's car as they drove her across town to the home she was to reside in. The facility was run by Mrs. Moore, who was a friend of theirs from the church. She ran multiple convalescent homes and knew the church was the perfect breeding ground to prospect for new clients to fill her beds.

When they arrived to the convalescent home Da'Quan and Lillian were greeted at the front door by Mrs. Moore, who invited the three of them in with open arms and a hefty invoice for Delilah's stay. As Lillian and Mrs. Moore placed Delilah in her room and discussed the fine print of her contractual agreement, Da'Quan observed the new home for his grandmother. He saw death and depression in the faces of the seniors who sat around staring blankly into the small color TV set at an episode of Oprah Winfrey. The walls were a dingy off-white with old framed pictures of green pastures and colorful flowers throughout the facility. The convalescents sat slumped in wheelchairs or lifeless on the edges of their twin beds attached to their walkers. Even the enticing aroma of pot roast and garlic potatoes couldn't mask the stench of urine and Ben-Gay that consumed the home.

Delilah's new roommate was an elderly black woman who looked like nothing more than a thin layer of skin over a skeleton fighting with all of her might to hold her drooping head up. Her face was covered in white stubble and the full head of hair on her head was terribly matted. She drooled uncontrollably as Mrs. Moore wiped her lips pretending in front of Lillian to provide the utmost service and care to her dying residents. Mrs. Moore, who had to be at least seventy herself, still maintained a youthful glow and held on to her lifelong Creole beauty. Her expensive rings and $700 dollar pink and white leather Prada sneakers were a dead giveaway to the extremely well-to-do lifestyle she lived because of her family-owned business.

Da'Quan was aware that this was all an act and that when the doors shut behind the family members, that their loved ones left behind would be treated as cattle with no real tender love and care. He had his mind made up that he would be making daily visits to assure his grandmother was receiving the best of care. After an hour or so of getting her situated, the dreaded time to depart had fallen upon them. As they kissed her and said their goodbyes, Delilah rose from her seat on the bed as if she were leaving with them. She began saying goodbye to her new roommate, unaware that she was now part of the death troupe as well. As Lillian sat her back down and began to explain to her mother that she was staying and that this was her new home, she burst into tears as Mrs. Moore consoled her with tissue and a loving pat on her back.

Da'Quan, who by now couldn't stomach anymore sadness, made his way to the front door. Before they left, Lillian signed a waiver for her mother to receive morphine patches to control the pain from the cancer and got the schedule of the weekly pastor visits. The ride on the way home was silent enough to hear a rabbit piss on cotton a mile away as they both rode knowing Delilah would never sleep in her own bed again. A stream of tears lined the cheeks of both Da'Quan and Lillian as they tried to make sense of their new life without Delilah in the daily scheme of operations.

The sadness of the day forced Da'Quan into an early nap filled with constant tossing and turning. He woke up at 9 p.m. fully alert in need of some entertainment. He dialed Co Co's number and was taken by surprise as she answered on the first ring, "Hello? Is this who I think it is? Mr. I don't call Coco until I need my dick sucked Da'Quan? She then began chuckling in a sensuous tone as Da'Quan sat quietly on the line. She could sense he wasn't his normal self as she asked, "What's wrong, daddy, you don't sound like you tonight?"

His response was upbeat to disguise the pain his heart was burdened with, "Nah, I'm good, just chilling, seeing if you were coming out tonight."

She replied instantly, "Yeah I can, but you know who parked outside spying on ya girl, so ima leave out the back and cut through my neighbor's yard and walk around there if he doesn't leave soon, okay boo?"

Da'Quan replied, "Yeah, all right. Don't have that nigga follow you to my place. I'm ready to kill if any nigga start tripping today."

His deadly words aroused her as she said in a tantalizing tone, "Ooh, talking like that made my kitty wet. I'm gone hop in the shower and head right to you bae, this psycho can sit out there all night with his miserable ass for all I care."

Her ex or on and off boyfriend "Slicc" was a childhood buddy of Da'Quan who turned killer and extreme gangbanger after junior high. He and Coco were a hood item and it was common knowledge that he was head over heels for her and would die or kill for her in a heartbeat. She really wasn't attractive in the face whatsoever but she had a nice round derriere and a set of D cups that made up for her buck tooth grill and lack of education. When it came to sex she was a total pleaser and allowed Da'Quan to talk and treat her like the bottom of his shoes. She had a very low self-esteem and knew her holding power existed within the sexually degrading acts she'd allow Da'Quan to pull on occasions.

Twenty minutes later as Da'Quan inhaled a chronic blunt there was a knock at the back door. When he opened it Coco stood with a smile on her ugly mulatto face in a white T-shirt, braless, with a tight pair of ripped daisy duke blue jean shorts. She smelled like soap and two dollar perfume chewing on a piece of gum like a street walker. Her demeanor and huge nipples instantly aroused him as he let her in. She walked in and instantly began complaining about Slicc as he passed her the blunt.

"Yeah that stupid motherfucka can sit outside my house all night. I keep telling his dumbass I'm done, but he won't let go. I think his dumbass is retarded or something."

Da'Quan remained silent as all he wanted to do was stick his dick in her mouth explode some kids down her throat and send her on her way. He let her puff the weed a couple of times before taking her huge, tattooed titties out and fondling her round ass. Within five minutes she was nude on her knees massaging his manhood aggressively between her pink inner-tube-sized lips. After a half hour of deep wet head he turned her over and began plowing in her drenched mound of lust, now oblivious to her face that resembled a sea monster.

She began screaming and panting, "Damn, I love you, D, please don't leave me, D, fuck me harder bae, ooh you make me cum so hard, oh my god, nigga." Her raspy voice along with her soaked womb had Da'Quan at the peak of his climax as he turned her around and positioned her on her knees to swallow his load. She eagerly got on her knees and began jerking and tugging on his manhood with her huge soft lips and tongue. After five minutes his eyes rolled back in his head as every worry or concern was out of the window at this point. As he felt the ton of semen begin to erupt, his toes curled, his eyes closed tight while he gripped her basket weave for dear life and exploded a daycare's worth of kids down her guzzling throat. She played with herself until she came simultaneously with him jerking freely in the moment. After she finished drinking his offspring and he gained his composure, he looked at Coco's ugly face smiling at him and was instantly turned off. She went from making him feel on top of the world to a lowly piece of trash off the streets in less than three minutes.

He became evil and irritated as she spoke, "So bae if I can get rid of Slicc's fat ass will you finally be mine?"

Da'Quan cringed at her pathetic comment and forcefully said, "Hell nah, bitch, we ain't never gone be like that. In fact get yo punk ass up outta here. I don't feel like thinking 'bout no dumb shit like that." His brutal words and harsh tone actually turned her on as she put on her shorts minus her panties and put her T-shirt back on. He impatiently grabbed her arm and marched her to the back door. He shoved her out but before she walked off the porch she turned her fish face around, smiled and said," I love you bae"! He cringed and slammed the door in her face as she smiled and made her way home by foot.

It was now approaching midnight and the pain of not having his grandmother home was eating him alive. Without a second thought he hopped in his truck and made his way to the convalescent home. When he arrived at the door the overnight staffer answered as he gave her a cockamamie excuse about Delilah needing her knee rub for her late night arthritis. The elderly Hispanic worker who lacked English skills allowed him in to tend to his grandmother. He instantly went into her room and woke her from her sleep. He put on her house shoes and robe and quietly snuck her out the front door while the night staff tended to wet beds and washed sheets with liquid waste in them.

When he loaded her in his truck and cranked it up, Dru Hill's "Somebody's Sleeping in my Bed" blasted through his speakers causing Delilah to smile and dance freely in the presence of her only grandson. He turned it up full blast as they rolled down Western smiling and enjoying their last ride in a car together. By the time they pulled up to the house, the police and Lillian were standing out front with the red and blue lights of the squad car blinking. As he helped Delilah out, he could hear his mother say to the officer, "Oh thank God, he's my son and her grandson. She's OK."

One of the cops, who was a young Hispanic with Martinez on his badge, pulled Da'Quan aside and shared a few words with him, "Hey, Mr. Taylor, I'm officer Martinez, LAPD, nice to meet you. Now it's been brought to my attention by your mom over there that you are in fact Delilah's grandson and that you care a great deal about her, which is beyond commendable, but here's the thing. You can't just go and take her from the convalescent home. That's considered kidnapping and can hold up to eight years in the state penitentiary. Now from the looks of things you're a good guy who loves his grandmother and hey I might have done the same thing, but you can't keep doing this, all right Mr. Taylor?"

He shook his head disappointingly as he stared at Lillian, keeping her mother snug in the freezing midnight air. Officer Martinez continued, "So here's what we have agreed on with your mom. We will let her stay the rest of the night here with you guys and first thing in the morning you guys are gonna take her back, OK? Now I have to warn you, if you do this again and we get called we're gonna be forced to book you on kidnapping, a 208. Now we don't wanna do it but I have to give you fair warning, Mr. Taylor, OK?"

Da'Quan shook his head and shook the outreached hand of Officer Martinez. The officer went over to Lillian and explained to her what he just told Da'Quan as they walked Delilah in doors from the freezing night air. The rest of the night Da'Quan slept in the chair in his grandmother's bedroom knowing this would be their last night together in the house she raised him in. Lillian found comfort on the sofa as she too wanted that last night in the house with her mother as well. They both cried themselves to sleep, as Delilah, who was unaware of the commotion, fell asleep like a baby with a bottle. Da'Quan tossed and turned all night knowing that this was the last night Grandma's Coming Home.

Chapter 37
MOMMA'S GONE

June 1997 • 27 years old

We are all born subjoined to our maternal parent at the core by the umbilical cord. This navel attachment connects the baby in the womb to its mother, which is a bond that lasts a lifetime. She is the vessel that transports life from the moment of conception up until the day of childbirth. By nature her motive is to love and nurture her child until he or she can maintain a sustainable lifestyle as an adult. Unlike other species, humans normally only have one child at a time, creating a stronger bond between the two, in contrast to dogs and cats who give birth to litters. There is never a replacement or substitute for a mother and everybody only gets one.

Delilah had been gone for two days and the house without her loud cackling and fumbling around felt awkward to Da'Quan and Lillian. The reality that she was never coming back home put a certain amount of stress on Da'Quan, while weighing very heavy on Lillian's heart. The pots and pans that were once used as tools to create mouth-watering meals from scratch were now only mere cabinet fillers collecting dust. Her bedroom, which still owned the faint scent of Ben-Gay reminded Da'Quan of the many days he sat on the side of his grandmother's bed holding her hand, talking about life until she drifted asleep.

As he rummaged through her belongings looking at old wrinkled black and white photographs of dead friends and relatives, he could hear his mom in the living room sniffling and weeping as she cleaned out Delilah's wall unit filled with memorable artifacts. The pain and hurt was evident between the two as they both sat quietly in separate adjoining rooms battling with the tears that crawled from their swollen eye sockets. Da'Quan made his way into the living room where his mom sat on the sofa patting her teary eyes searching for a soft spot in these hard times.

He put his arm around her and gathered some words of encouragement for his distraught mother by saying, "Hey Mom, I'm sorry about the way I've been acting, it's just," he paused, took a deep breath and continued. "It's just that I hate seeing my grandma like this and I already miss her being around the house you know?" And at that moment his watery eyes discharged buckets full of tears as his mother stood to her feet and embraced his limp body.

She rocked him like a 6'2" baby, patting his back and as she looked to the sky for a sign of hope she began whispering repeatedly, "God is good, my God is good, he gone see us through this, my God is good." After a few woe-is-me moments he unattached himself from his mom's grasp and began to gather his composure. She grabbed his chin sternly, looked him in the eye and said, "You know God is good and he's always right and we have to trust in his decision making, OK? So don't worry. Your grandmother is in good professional care and you can visit her anytime you like."

Da'Quan propped his shoulders back, nodded his head yes as he wiped his eyes and cleared his throat. He then gave his mom a hug along with a huge kiss on her forehead. She sighed, looked around the living room and said, "Well, ya momma's tired. I'm 'bout to go back to my house and lay it down. I got a long day at work tomorrow So get it together, pray and everything's gonna be OK. Just trust in God."

Da'Quan responded, "OK, Mom, love you!" She looked at him through her glassy eyes and said in a dreamy voice, "I love you and always will." She moved at a snail's pace to the kitchen, grabbed her keys and made her way out of the back door leaving Da'Quan standing alone in the living room. He watched her low-spirited body trudge out the back door without another word said. Her lethargic movements put even more of a damper on his fractured spirit as he melted into the living room sofa.

Between the stress of his grandmother's absence, the street hustle and the concern for his mother, his body was exhausted and remained folded like a fetus on the sofa until the crack of dawn. He woke up groggy with saliva stains blatant on his chin. He looked around not exactly sure where he was and how he had gotten there. His stomach was tied in what felt like boy scout knots from his navel to his throat. He felt as though he'd drank a gallon of gin, as saliva began to gather in his mouth due to his chronic nausea.

After trying to avoid the inevitable for a few minutes he pried himself away from the sofa and made chase to the toilet seat where he threw up everything in the lining of his intestines. He prayed for God to lift him from his knees and alleviate the pain from the brutal heaving his body was going through. He humbly whispered, "Oh God please get what the fuck is in me out, oh my god this is some bullshit."

The more he sat at the base of the toilet, the faster his head spun. He tried gaining his composure but the sudden outpouring of sweat burning his eyes shut, combined with the chills that summoned his teeth to chatter something fierce, nullified any normal behavior. He scratched his head trying to recollect what he had eaten the day before that would have made him sick. The strong smell of urine at the base of the toilet triggered another round of gut-wrenching vomit only producing clear stomach acid. With all of the strength he had he shoved himself away from the toilet and lay face down in the middle of the bathroom floor. As he lay there with his face to the cold tile on the floor he thought to himself, *What the fuck did I eat, goddamn? God, first my grandma now you fucking with me. This some bullshit.*

After a few moments of silent meditation, stillness and controlled breathing the ill feeling disappeared just as fast as it had made its presence known. He eased up slowly from his fetal position, careful not to agitate whatever had knocked him to the floor. He stood to his feet, went to the face bowl to wash his face and stared himself eye to eye in the cabinet mirror wondering, *I don't know what the fuck is going on but shit feel a whole lot different than it did a month ago.*

He proceeded to clean his saddened and sleepy face and brushed the awful taste of vomit from his choppers. He was instantly hungry beyond control and decided to make some oatmeal that was left in his grandmother's kitchen. As he searched for the ingredients he needed he realized there was no sugar or butter. He thought to go to the store but realized his mom was still home and that she would have his fix. He knew she would normally be gone by 8:15 but he figured she was running late or something.

He rang the doorbell but there was no response. He then began banging on the side of her house with his fist in case she was in the shower. After he stood on her porch a few minutes that sick feeling instantly began to set back in. Before it got too bad he thought to himself, "OK, imma kick her door in. If she's not here I'll have to pay for it so fuck it." He gave a halfhearted kick but the door was reinforced with thick two by fours. He then reared back and with all of his human power kicked the door in like the DEA sending wood nails and shattered glass in every direction.

He stepped into the living room out of breath but knew there were good intentions behind his behavior. He looked around for any subtle differences but saw none as he yelled, "Mom, mom, you here? It's me!" The silence in the house was nerve jerking as he slowly pushed on her bedroom door that sat half open. He knocked and slowly eased his head in saying, "Momma, it's me." He looked at her bed and saw her laying on her side, lifeless, at peace with the world. As he reluctantly went to touch her arm, the stiffness of rigor mortis had already set in. She felt like hard plastic as he pleaded desperately for her to wake up, "Momma, no. Momma, no, wake up, please, no, how the fuck you gone leave me now? That's some fucked up shit! I hate you! I hate you, God! Momma, no. You know I love you so much. I'm so sorry, please, please come back. Noo, Momma, noo!"

He lay slumped over her body in shock; he kept pinching himself to the point of bruising to see if this was real or some twisted dream he couldn't awaken himself from. Hope was all he had to grasp on to as he fled from his mother's house down to Babo's in a state of shock. He ran, thinking *Maybe if we get an ambulance they can bring her back, maybe Babo got a smooth trick up his sleeve, am I really going through this or is this some bullshit ass game going on?*

His heartbeat was in overdrive as he ran up Babo's steps and began banging on his door in an out-of-body state of panic, "Babo! Babo!" His voice was filled with trauma as Babo opened the door. "Wassup, Babo, checked this out. My mom not breathing. We gotta call 911 but if we hurry they can bring her back, cuz, come see what I'm talking 'bout." Babo had a look of compassion on his face as he grabbed his phone and keys and followed Da'Quan back to his mother's house.

As they walked up to the corpse in the bedroom, Babo shook his head slowly in knowing he was looking at a lifeless shell. With respect for Da'Quan he still called 911 and requested help in a panicked tone, "Hey um yeah we have a woman, it's my buddy's mother who's not breathing, so we need an ambulance as soon as possible."

Da'Quan sat hopeful over his mother's lifeless body, whispering "They on their way, Momma, just hold on, just hold on.: Babo stood quietly as Da'Quan caressed his mother with a small glimmer of hope that the paramedics could perform a miracle on his beloved mother. Within minutes the paramedics arrived full of energy enthusiastic about saving a life. When they made it inside, Babo walked them quietly to the bedroom where Da'Quan sat next to his mom.

The first paramedic looked at Babo like, "You know she's dead," as he checked for her vital signs. He shined a flashlight in her open eyes to see if there was any form of life before gently closing them shut with his hands. He turned to Da'Quan and looked him square in the eyes and asked, "So you're her son that found her here?"

Da'Quan responded, "Umm yeah, I came to get some sugar for my oatmeal and when she didn't respond to my knock I kicked in the door and she was laying here sleeping like this! So can you guys help bring her back or do we go to the hospital?"

The stocky paramedic looked at Da'Quan with total sympathy as he tried to muster up the best way to inform him of his mother's demise. He put his hands on Da'Quan's shoulder and walked him out of the bedroom into the living room. The blue eyed Caucasian paramedic rubbed his hand across his thick goatee, cleared his throat, looked Da'Quan in his eyes and said, "Ummm, Mr. Taylor, look we did all that we could possibly do to save your mom, but at this point there's nothing more we can do. I'm afraid it's too late. She has already transitioned."

Although deep in his heart he knew, it still took the confirmation from another human's voice to solidify his worst nightmare. The words from the paramedic's mouth felt like steel tip arrows piercing his flesh causing him to feel lightheaded and nauseated. He wanted to run away and jump off of the edge of the earth, as his number one fan, mentor, advisor and nurturer had been permanently taken away. He felt anger, confusion, sadness and hurt all encompassed as he exploded into a gut-wrenching session of bawling on the living room floor. He yelled at the top of his lungs, "I hate you, I fucking hate you, what kind of fucking God are you?"

Babo walked the paramedics out to give Da'Quan a moment to himself before they took his mother. He forced himself back into the bedroom to say his last goodbyes while trying to make sense of the whole ordeal. He realized that the sickness through the night was the biological disconnect of the umbilical cord from his mother. As he sat next to his mother's corpse he became numb to life and realized that now he would have to man up since *Momma's Gone.*

THE FINALE

SEPTEMBER 28th 2006 • 37 years old

In his rearview a big black Denali came driving slow from around the corner. The sun reflected off of the polished paint like the president was being chauffeured around. Da'Quan's heart began pounding as he looked down simultaneously at the Colorado number appearing as his phone buzzed violently in the cup holder. He closed his eyes and took a deep breath before answering in a defeated tone, "Yeah, wassup? That you?"

The deep husky voice replied, "Yeah, baby boy, it's me and that chrome Glock on yo hip won't be needed." Da'Quan rubbed his pistol gently not sure if he should fire at them first or take his medicine in the game like a G. As his heart began thumping like jackrabbits fucking he turned to his left to see the truck's shiny rims at his eye level.

The truck sat directly next to him. He didn't know whether to get out or let them make the first move. Sweat began trickling profusely from his armpits as his nerves made the hair on his arms stand erect. He was jittery to the point where he was numb and began losing interest in going another day further. He was now prepared to meet his destiny. When the window of the truck rolled down a hand with a huge gold Cuban link appeared waving him to the vehicle. He swallowed a load of spit as he said to God, "Lord, please forgive me for all of my sins. I'm trusting you with my life."

He paused before taking his pistol and putting it under his seat. As he stood out of the car he hesitantly looked into the Denali for fear he'd get his head blown to smithereens. But to his surprise he saw a mirrored image of himself full of pain, grief and rage highlighted in his face. His heart skipped a beat as he grabbed the door and hopped in. As he gazed into the eyes of his soul, he realized his demons had finally caught up to him as the truck's windows rolled up and pulled off down the street. Da'Quan was now at peace with himself.

Posted wit my cannon on the block / Put candy on the block / Ice cream on top /Rims don't stop / beat don't stop / Car alarms setting off / Knock knocking up the block / Knock knocking up the block / Knock knocking up the block / Y'all know the real / Hood shit don't stop

GLOSSARY

ACEY-DEUCY, brim style hats typically worn by Crips

AMTRAK, trainline; term for multiple men having sex with a single female

BANGING, actively shooting and killing oppositions when in a gang

BEAT, loud music in a car

BIG FACES, money

BIRDS, kilos of cocaine

BITCH, female

BLOOD, rival gang to Crips

BREAD, money

BRENDA, gun

BRICKS, kilos of cocaine, heroin, pounds of weed

BROWN SUGAR, heroin

BUMP, a snort of coke

BUSTING, shooting a gun

CANDY, drugs

CANNON, gun

CAMELS, cigarette

CAVE BITCH, white woman

CHOPPERS, mouth

CHRONIC, potent marijuana

CIRCUS OF DEVILS, a community of crime and wrong doings

COMRADE, companion; teammate

CONCRETE JUNGLE, nickname for SOUTH CENTRAL LOS ANGELES

C.P.T., acronym for COMPTON

CRIP, rival gang of the BLOODS

DEVIL'S SUGAR, cocaine

DOUBLE WHAMMY, when two acts of bad luck happen together; deceit

DRENCHED, dripping wet

DROUGHT, lack of drugs or sex

DUTTY BITCH, underhanded woman

FAKE ONES, imitation kilos of dope

FIST DAP, form of acknowledgment with two fist bumping instead of handshake

GOON SQUAD, group of people who use violence for purpose

HARUM SCARUM, reckless, out of control

HASH PLANT, strand of weed

HOMEGIRL, platonic female friend

HOMIE, friend; accomplice

HOT, hydraulics on a lowrider

HUMANITY, the human race

HUMPS, Camel cigarettes

ICE CREAM, cocaine

JITTERS, nervous

KAMA SUTRA, ancient book on human sexuality and positions

KITTY, stash of cash

KNOCKING, extremely loud music

LICK, heist

MONEY GONE, all bets off

MONGOOSE, dirt bike

MOUTHPIECE, lawyer

MUNCHIES, extreme hunger from smoking weed

NIGGA, term of endearment amongst black people; derogatory term of racism

N.O.T.S., acronym for nigga off the street

ON YO HEAD, pressure

PERUVIAN POWDER, high end cocaine

POPPING, what's going on

POSTED, staying in same location

PUNK, to bully someone; soft person; victim

QP, quarter pound

REPUTABLE, known in the neighborhood for putting in work; undisputed gang representative

RUN IT BACK, do it again

SCRATCH, money

SHERM STICK, cigarette dipped in embalming fluid

SPREAD, assortment of snacks in jail

STEPPING ON IT, process of stretching powder cocaine into crack for profit

TAR BABY, derogatory term for black people

TRICK, a person who pays for sex

VIA DOLOROSA, Jesus' walk to the cross

WHATS CRACCIN, what's going on

WHITE GIRL, cocaine

WOO, sweet talk; persuade

YAYO, rock cocaine

YO, buddy

ABOUT THE AUTHOR

After years of ghostwriting spitfire bars for signed and unsigned rap acts in the concrete jungle of South Central Los Angeles, DERRICK JOHNS, a reformed street hustler turned fitness enthusiast, composed a plethora of colorful and at times menacing short stories based on personal life experiences, with the question, "What would race through your mind with an hour to live?" In the thick of his search for HUMANITY, he creates a world filled with every human emotion and vows to leave his readers mouthwatering for more of his swagger-filled eccentric street tales.

APPRECIATION

First off I gotta give thanks to God, my mother, father, grandparents, my kids and family, South Central Los Angeles, to all my homies and friends who supported me on this journey. Also I have to give a HUGE thanks to Sir Robert Townsend for guiding me to the forefront of my destiny, I will forever be grateful sir.

COMING SOON

THE HYENAS